HOLMES COMING

HOLMES COMING

Kenneth Johnson

BLACK STONE PUBLISHING

Copyright © 2021 Kenneth Johnson Productions, Inc.
Published in 2022 by Blackstone Publishing
Cover and book design by Alenka Vdovič Linaschke

The characters and events in this book are fictitious.
Any similarity to real persons, living or dead, is coincidental
and not intended by the author.

Printed in the United States of America

First edition: 2022
ISBN 979-8-200-70688-4
Fiction / Mystery & Detective / General

Version 1

CIP data for this book is available
from the Library of Congress

Blackstone Publishing
31 Mistletoe Rd.
Ashland, OR 97520

www.BlackstonePublishing.com

For David, Juliet, Michael, and Katie
with love . . .

AUTHOR'S APOLOGY

You would likely think the story I'm about to tell is outrageously unbelievable—that is, if you hadn't by now almost certainly seen mention of it in the media. Numerous outlets have carried reports regarding the apparent reemergence of an extraordinary individual.

It's understandable that many accounts have not treated the matter seriously. Several sources openly satirized it with the cynicism typical of our overhyped, overspun social media age. And some, of course, have declared this remarkable occurrence to be an outright hoax.

It's been suggested that to put the matter in proper perspective an eyewitness should come forward who could recount the entire adventure—a reputable eyewitness who was present from the beginning and also party to it throughout. Such a person should put forth, as concisely as possible, in clinical detail, the full story, complete with all its surprising twists and turns, as well as its intriguing mystery—and seeming magic.

Unfortunately, the person in the best position to accomplish that difficult task is me. So let me confess to you right here that my previous literary efforts have been confined to master's theses and articles in obscure medical journals. What follows constitutes my first attempt as an actual author.

With that caveat, I hope you will enjoy—or at the very least, believe—the story I am about to tell. I expect you will be as astounded as I was while living through the six days and nights during which it took place.

Amy Elizabeth Winslow, MD
San Francisco, California

1

I am certain that when Donald Keating went out for his usual jog in the foggy San Francisco predawn darkness he had no idea what was lying in wait for him.

Keating was a healthy, athletic man of sixty-six, of Anglo heritage but proud that his great-grandmother had been a member of the Paiute Shoshone Nation. His favorite sweatshirt and pants were stenciled with the letters SFPD. He was five-foot-ten with gray hair well-trimmed and still in the tradition of regulation police cuts. It had become his accustomed hairstyle when he was a rookie beat cop some forty-five years earlier, and he still liked it. Sandy-brown highlights amid the gray hinted at the color it used to be. His carefully groomed mustache was thick. His brown eyes were clear and sharp.

For years he had taken the same jog at the same hour through the streets of his sleeping city. This early morning was particularly dark with dense fog, its dampening blanket contributing a serene quietness. Keating left from his apartment on Lombard, heading east through the lovely old North Beach section beneath Telegraph Hill. He turned south along Stockton, following his accustomed route. He saw the fog lights of an approaching squad car glowing through the thick mist. As the vehicle passed, he could just barely see inside the car the faces of Officers Craft and Viramontes, who smiled, nodding respectfully to him. He grinned back, recognizing them as his former students at the police academy.

Detective Keating had often told them and others how much he enjoyed being up and outside running in the darkness while most other citizens in his city were still in their last hours of sleep. It reminded him of his years as a beat cop, striving vigilantly to make the city a safer, more humane place. He had many decorations and honors to show for his years of service, but none gave him more pleasure than the feeling of the city's people slumbering in safety just before dawn.

At the corner of Filbert, beefy, middle-aged Alfonso Nunez had opened his panel van and was dropping off the fresh bundles of the *San Francisco Chronicle* to a still-shuttered newsstand. He and Keating waved and smiled at each other as they always did on that same dark sidewalk. Both were punctual and consistent, and each enjoyed the comradeship of their greetings.

When Mr. Nunez later learned of the tragic horror that befell Detective Keating just minutes after their routine encounter, he was distressed and saddened. He contacted the police to report this earlier sighting and related how Keating had continued past him, running diagonally into shadowy Washington Square Park.

At 5:35 a.m., Keating reached the southwest corner of the park and crossed Union Street toward the new plaza mall recently built at Powell Street. It was a modernist building with a long set of wide steps ascending past a series of five terraces.

Detective Keating was in excellent physical condition. He prided himself on that. Even running up the long flights barely left him out of breath. But this time, as he reached the top of the steps at the fourth terrace, Keating slowed to a stop.

We know this because a stockbroker, Gabriel Farfan, working early, as always, at a building opposite on Powell, happened to glance out his nearby sixth-story window. Through drifting fog, Farfan spotted Keating below. He didn't know Keating personally but recognized him from sightings as the man who often ran up those steps at that hour. Farfan later related to the police the disturbing details of what happened next.

Keating paused on the fourth terrace, which was about forty feet square. Its perimeter was planted with shrubbery about three feet tall, as well as flowers and a few small trees. That terrace, like the others below and above it, contained a shallow pool of water some thirty feet square.

The pool was unique in that it had a glass bottom, allowing daylight to filter pleasantly through it into a large marble atrium lobby built just beneath. It was essentially a skylight with water on top. But in the early-morning dark, the light from the lobby came the other way: up through the water. It cast quavering, unsettling shadows and reflections upon the angular marble walls of the terrace and its surrounding greenery.

Keating evidently sensed something was wrong—perhaps he even scented something. Younger officers were awed by the keen instincts Keating had honed to perfection during thousands of days and nights of policing. But he was about to face something he never would have imagined.

First came an unnerving sound. Two stories above the quiet plaza, Farfan heard it too and thought it was some kind of engine—a hefty motorcycle perhaps, low-pitched and rumbling. Maybe Keating thought that as well as he curiously glanced around. He zeroed in on the direction where the sound apparently came from: damp greenery on the opposite side of the low reflecting pool. Within those bushes, Keating might have seen a large shadow moving toward him.

When the ominous sound came again, Farfan realized—and Keating must've also—that it was the low-throated growl of a large predatory animal. Two luminous eyes would have gleamed in the darkness amid the junglelike greenery across the water from Keating. Farfan saw him draw a breath, then step back unsteadily. Both men gasped at what they saw emerging.

It was a huge Bengal tiger.

Easily weighing four hundred pounds, the creature glided slowly out of the shadows. Its magnificent head was menacingly low, eyes laser-focused across the water on its prey.

Farfan saw Keating turn to run just as the tiger charged.

The massive animal leapt into the pool's shallow water and galloped across it, the light streaming up from beneath the water adding a terrifying hellish aspect to the oncoming beast. Keating ran desperately across the plaza, his shouts for help echoing off the nearby buildings. But no help was to be had.

From his vantage point two stories above, Farfan was frantically dialing 911 while watching in horror as Keating fled back down the steps. But with its eight-foot strides, the tiger closed the distance between them in an instant. Keating looked back just as the giant beast leapt at him, smashing him down onto the concrete steps. He screamed in agony as the tiger's claws clutched him, digging into his flesh as the beast's fearsome mouth ferociously gaped open.

The tiger sunk its sharp teeth into the detective's throat. Blood fountained out.

Q

The arrival alarm sounded as duty nurse Lateesha James shouted, "Incoming!"

The ER doors from Saint Francis Memorial's Pine Street ambulance entrance zipped open. A blood-spattered gurney bearing an unconscious Donald Keating sped in. He was on oxygen and had an IV in his right arm. One paramedic kept pressure on a blood-soaked neck-wound dressing while another pushed the gurney at full speed toward the waiting ER staff.

And me: Amy Winslow, MD.

I was in scrubs, pulling on my blue nitrile gloves but still shaking off sleep. Though I spent most of my time performing pediatric surgery, I worked extra shifts in the trauma center some nights to help out, particularly when there was a surge in patients.

"Take it into 4, Dr. Winslow," Lateesha said as she started entering Keaton's arrival information into our computer system.

In my time at Saint Fran, from a residency starting five years earlier, I'd seen all manner of injury, from gang violence to terrible car crashes to major industrial accidents. But I'd never seen anything like this.

Even Megan, a tall auburn-haired paramedic who was usually unflappable, looked grim as she delivered her rapid-fire brief while pushing the gurney: "Donald Keating. White, male, sixty-six. Attacked and mauled in midtown by a tiger—at least that's what an eyewitness said."

"A tiger?" I was stunned. "In the middle of the city?"

"Multiple lacerations, near amputation of right arm," Megan continued. "Both carotids punctured."

When a fellow human being is as ravaged as Donald Keating was, I can't always remain as coolly professional as I'd like. I strive to remember my training, to hold back feeling too much empathy, which might cloud my professional usefulness, but I confess that I'm not always successful.

Nonetheless, I took charge as I walked beside the rapidly moving gurney, surveying the awful damage. Keating's clothes had been shredded; large flaps of skin had been clawed open and folded back. I lifted the dressing from his face and could see his teeth, white gums, and jawbone through a three-inch hole in his left cheek.

I spread his left eyelids, shining my Maglite into his eye, calling out, "Patient unresponsive, ready an OR, notify neurosurgeon."

A nurse peeled away to carry out my directions as we headed into unit 4, stopping the gurney beside the bed, under the white glare of an operating light. Everyone knew their positions on either side of the gurney and bed as I called, "Transfer on my count: one, two—three."

Together as one, we shifted Keating's limp body onto the bed.

"Get him intubated, Ysie," I directed, "Seven-point-five tube."

Ysabel, the respiratory therapist, went to work. Ysie was barely five feet tall and sturdy. We'd had many smiles together when she shared stories about her quirky family in Peru. But that night she was all business, working like lightning above Keating's head to get a tube down his throat, then calling it: "I'm in."

Megan caught my eye as she glided the gurney out and away. She didn't look hopeful but offered, "Good luck, Doctor."

My team bustled around the bleeding victim. A new nurse I didn't know with frizzy blue hair had uncovered his chest and was attaching cardio sensor patches. I saw how several sets of four parallel lacerations had been clawed deep into Keating's flesh, exposing the ribs and sternum beneath. I called out to the resuscitation nurse: "What's hanging, Curt?"

"Large bore in right and left antecubital," he answered. "Lactated ringers up. IV one has four hundred cc count. Two has six hundred."

The blue-haired nurse, checking the monitor screens, chimed in, "Blood pressure ninety over sixty-four. Falling fast. Pulse one thirty-two."

"I'm ventilating patient," Ysabel said, "One hundred percent O_2."

"Type and cross for six units of RBCs," I said urgently to the nurse who'd just returned from making the neurosurgeon call. "Curt, keep the pressure on that carotid."

A tall thirtyish Latino man in jeans and a leather windbreaker rushed up just outside the unit, breathing hard. After flashing his SFPD badge at Lateesha, he hovered near the unit's door, his face etched with concern.

A steady tone began, and the blue-haired nurse called out, "He's coding."

I waved everybody back as I said, "Paddles."

Curt handed me the cream-colored defibrillation paddles with the stainless-steel bottoms. I grabbed them and rubbed them together to spread out the contact gel.

Curt checked the console and nodded to me. "Charged."

I placed them atop Keating's bloody chest at the apex and sternum, then shouted, "Clear!" The team stepped back. I pressed the button.

Ka-thunk! Two hundred joules of electricity coursed through Keating. His dying body briefly arched up off the table before slumping back down.

The flatline tone continued.

Ysie pressed a stethoscope to his bloody chest and shook her head. "Nothing, Doctor." Nonetheless, I tried again.

"Give me three hundred, Curt. *Clear!*" Another jolt. Another convulsion of his body. But nothing else. I shouted to the patient, "Come on, Mr. Keating! *Clear!*" Another jolt.

No response. And it was apparent to all that there wouldn't be. I paused a long moment. Finally, I glanced at the clock, breathed a regretful sigh, and said quietly, "6:13 a.m."

It was always so hard to call it.

Donald Keating was only the third trauma patient who had died under my direct care since I had begun practicing. I heaved a long sigh and told the nurse to determine whether Mr. Keating was a registered donor and contact his next of kin. Then I looked over at the plainclothes officer in the doorway and saw tears welling in his brown eyes as he stared at the deceased man I'd been unable to save. I was upset, disappointed with myself, but he looked much worse: completely bereaved. He slowly turned away.

A short time later, after I'd cleaned up and collected myself, I went out into the ER corridor, rubbing my eyes. I felt drained.

The ER had quieted by then. I spotted the officer sitting nearby, still visibly overcome with emotion.

Lateesha had told me his name was Luis Ortega. In his early thirties, his face—indeed, his whole persona—seemed to emanate an earnest dignity. He had thick black hair above a high forehead and dark brown eyes, which were downcast with grief. He wore a simple gold wedding ring. He'd been joined by another detective wearing a tan, cord carcoat: Lieutenant Bernie Civita, thinning dark hair, olive skin, a guy who liked his pasta a tad too much. He was completely empathetic and clearly there to lend moral support to his comrade.

I stopped beside them. "Lieutenant Ortega? I'm so sorry." He glanced up briefly, then nodded. I sat on the edge of a chair next to him. "Detective Keating was a close friend?"

Ortega's deep-chested voice was barely a whisper. "One of my closest. A mentor." He thought further about that, adding, "More like a father, really." He looked around the room at Civita and a uniformed cop nearby, who was also wiping her eyes. "For a lot of us."

"I'm sorry for your loss."

"Thanks for trying, Doctor," Ortega barely managed to whisper. "We all appreciate what you and your team did."

I paused for a long moment. Maybe this wasn't the best time to ask, but it was such an unusual circumstance I couldn't help myself. "The wounds were unlike any I've ever seen. I heard it might have been a tiger that attacked him. Is that true? Did the police capture it?"

He glanced up at me and shook his head. "No. The only one who even saw it was the eyewitness who called it in to 911.

And by the time he got down to the street and the paramedics arrived, there was no sign of any animal."

"What about security cameras?"

"The closest two had been tampered with, deactivated," Civita said. "But another one on a building opposite caught the whole thing and showed the tiger running back into the bushes."

"Has the zoo or anyone reported any—?"

"No," Ortega said. "Nothing."

"Then where could it have come from? Where did it go?"

Ortega shook his head again. Civita looked equally baffled. The three of us were likely pondering the same thing. I found myself whispering, "But how does a huge Bengal tiger kill a man in downtown San Francisco and then disappear?"

Ortega raised his red-rimmed brown eyes up to meet mine. To him, as to me, it was a complete mystery.

This question proved to be a life-and-death mystery that would entwine both of us.

But it was also only the first mystery I encountered during that life-changing week.

The very next day, I was on an unexpected mission of my own, driving up into Marin County, north of San Francisco. I'd gotten a troubling voice message from an elderly woman named Estelle Hudson, the widow of a former patient. I heard anxiety and distress in her voice. She insisted it wasn't a medical issue, but she urgently needed to talk to me and hoped I might come up to her house as soon as possible. I tried to call for more details, but her voice mailbox was frustratingly full.

Normally, I enjoyed the drive north into Marin. Though I like the hectic heartbeat of San Francisco, it's often counterbalanced for me by the calm placidity to be found in the old-growth forests north of the city. Unfortunately, placidity had taken the day off. My brow was knit with concentration. I blew out a tense puff, wondering what exactly I was headed for. It had already been a tumultuous few days. First, I'd had an ugly, painful breakup with He Who Shall Not Be Named. Now, in addition to worrying why Mrs. Hudson needed me, I couldn't stop thinking about the horrible last moments of Detective Keating and the unanswered riddle of the deadly tiger.

After turning my red Accord off Highway 1, I left behind the billboards and gas-food-lodging spots. I'd fed the directions on Mrs. Hudson's message into Siri and was making my way along a less well-preserved county road. The houses were spaced farther and farther apart until at last there weren't any at all. The surrounding forest threatened to swallow up even the road I was on.

I thought I might've taken a wrong turn and was about to retrace my path, when I saw the old wooden mailbox Mrs. Hudson had described in her message just as Siri announced, "You have arrived at your destination." Beside the mailbox, a gravel drive led deeper into the coastal pine forest.

Six-tenths of a mile from the road, I was rewarded by the sight of a beautiful old Tudor-style estate. Its main house was large but not grandiose and gave every appearance of having been built in the late Victorian era. It was constructed in a half-timber style mimicking dwellings in seventeenth-century Elizabethan England and was surrounded by large old-growth oaks. Several well-tended gardens blossomed with marigolds, pansies, and wildflowers.

It was the kind of place that always makes me smile, impossible not to be drawn to. What a wonderful retreat from the intensity of the city it would make. I imagined myself inside, wearing cozy clothes, enjoying a cup of English breakfast tea, while curled up in a comfy chair by the fireplace with one of my favorite historical novels. Or maybe even trying again to write something myself. I could get used to a place like this.

I smiled even more when Mrs. Hudson emerged from the house to greet me as I got out of my car. She looked just as she had when I first met her the year before. She was in her early eighties, just over five feet, and quite spry. She had curly snowy-white hair above her sunny face. Hazel eyes shone out from behind white, large-framed glasses.

"Dr. Winslow! *Ooo*, I'm so pleased you could come, lass." The energy of her Dunfermline Scottish ancestors coursed within her, and she retained their lilting Highland dialect. She exuberantly waved me toward her with both hands and gave me a wonderful hug. She smelled like the pink roses on the modest housedress beneath her cream-colored cardigan. She pulled away from our embrace, leaned back slightly, and grasped my shoulders firmly, gazing into my eyes for a moment with an expression of great fondness as I asked, "Are you really alright? Your voice on the phone had me worried and—"

"Oh no. I'm sorry. I'm fine—really," she said insistently. But I didn't completely believe her. There was something curious bubbling underneath. It seemed like some odd combination of stress and yet enthusiasm that I couldn't quite put my finger on. She took my arm as she continued, "I'm so glad you could come up and see the place. Here now, take a little walk with me."

I wanted to ask why she had sounded so urgent in her

message, but it seemed like it might be a subject she had to work her way up to, so I elected to be patient. She guided me around the grounds of the small estate while telling me how she and her late husband, Douglas, had been the caretakers for decades. I'd met the couple when they were on a visit to San Francisco last year. They were dining at Scoma's on Fisherman's Wharf when Mr. Hudson had a severe stroke. I happened to be at a nearby table and had jumped in to help.

"If you hadn't come to his aid, he would've died on the spot," she said to me now. I started to protest, but she anticipated me. "No, don't you deny it—it's true. And the way you went with us to your hospital and took him under your wing, even when we couldn't pay properly because the insurance was bollixed up. Your kindness was a blessing to him, young lady. And it gave me another whole year with Dougy."

"I was sad when I got your note about his passing."

Mrs. Hudson sighed. "And the donation you made in his honor was very dear." She gave my arm a little squeeze of appreciation. We continued walking along a curving path through the flower gardens. I was finally about to ask why she'd called me, when she took a deep breath of the coastal country air. "Ah, how Dougy loved this place. Lived here all his life. It was built about 1890 and bought by an Englishman, a Captain Basil, in 1899. Shortly after he engaged Dougy's grandfather as caretaker, Basil disappeared. But he left a trust fund for the Hudson family and their descendants to continue caring for the place. His only stipulation was peculiar: that electricity must constantly be supplied. At first it was by these steam generators."

She pointed them out to me, the old machines chugging along in a shed beside the house. It seemed very curious.

KENNETH JOHNSON

Mrs. Hudson went on, "Even when electrical service became available out here about 1915, the Hudson family kept those old gennies cooking. Captain Basil had issued specific instructions that there must never be any interruption in the estate's electrical service."

"Why not?"

"No one knew," Mrs. Hudson said. "He was apparently quite an eccentric, a collector as well. There are many curiosities in the cellar, as well as some very fine wines. Basil insisted that a constant temperature be maintained there by means of a special cooling unit he built himself. The original agreement mandated that the electricity was to remain on until January first, 2025. If ever it was turned off, the Hudson family's contract would be immediately terminated."

"How completely odd. Has there ever been any—"

A low, deep rumbling startled us into silence. Frightened birds flew out of the nearby trees. Then we were hit by a sudden and severe jolt.

Mrs. Hudson and I clutched each other in alarm as we both said, "Earthquake!"

The surrounding trees shook and swayed. Two stone birdbaths in the garden toppled over.

We clung to one another as a seismic wave rolled beneath our feet. Once it passed, Mrs. Hudson said, "*Ohh!* That was a sharp one! Don't remember one that strong since '89."

We each drew a long breath, but she doubtless saw by my colorless face and the way I still clutched her arm that I was anything but calm. She frowned with concern. "What is it, dearie?"

I inhaled again. "I lost my parents in a quake."

16

"Oh, dear God." She rested her hand on my arm sympathetically. "I am so sorry. How did it happen? Where?"

"It was in Sumatra—2009. My mom was one of the 'Doctors Without Borders' who rushed over there right after it hit. Dad went along to help. They got caught in a massive aftershock and . . ." I just shook my head. Each earthquake I've felt since has reopened the emotional wound.

"It's terrible that you had to go through that, Amy."

I nodded appreciation and tried to force myself back into the moment of the warm friendly afternoon, but it wasn't easy. I managed a wan smile. "Must have been difficult for you too, losing Douglas. Have you been lonely out here?"

"At first, of course. Though I have so many fond memories here that I truly adore this place." Then it was Mrs. Hudson's turn to draw a hesitant breath, as though about to get into a difficult subject. "But I'm afraid old Captain Basil hadn't counted on all the taxes starting up. There was the '29 crash, the bank failures, and finally the big S&L collapse in '88. Yesterday I learned that this house and property is about to be auctioned off for a fraction of what it's worth."

"Oh, no." I was grieved on her behalf.

"Unfortunately, yes." She shook her head. "I feared it was coming and I've tried to find my son, but he's a gadabout who likely wouldn't have the means anyway, and the sale is in less than a month." She looked at me again with that curious, enthusiastic glint in her eye that I'd noticed earlier. "I wanted you to have the chance to buy the place, Amy."

My jaw dropped. Wow. I was thoroughly astonished.

She went on quickly, "In return for your kindness to my

husband. And I'd be happy to stay on and manage it for you, if you'd consider that."

"Oh, Mrs. Hudson." I was overwhelmed. Conflicting sentiments coursed within me. "I am so very touched. What a lovely, generous gesture."

"More than a gesture, lass, it'd make me greatly happy too. You'll do it, then?" Her eyes positively sparkled.

I would've gladly. My heart raced with enthusiasm at the idea, but my much more pragmatic mind quickly examined even the remotest possibilities and kept running into harsh realities. "Oh, Mrs. Hudson, how I would love to, but I'm barely surviving now. I've still got serious student loans to repay and—" Her disappointed expression inspired me to make one last mental pass at considering the possibilities, but there simply were no straws to grasp. I sighed. "I'm afraid it'd be just impossible for me to buy the house, much as I love it."

"Are you certain, dear? Isn't there any way you could—"

"Believe me, I wish there were." I cast my eyes around the gardens to the quaint house with flowerboxes under the leaded-glass windows and an aging redbrick chimney at one end. What a splendid, secluded, inspiring place to live, and maybe to write—something I'd actually been toying with lately in my less practical moments. "You have no idea how much I'd have loved it."

She was visibly let down, but she touched my arm as the courage of her bravehearted Scottish ancestors kicked in and she drew a breath. "Well. I'm sorry, lass. But I do understand." She squeezed my arm again. "At least let me offer you a wee bit of lunch."

As we walked back up toward the house, I felt a weight in

my stomach. It was frustration at having to miss out on the golden opportunity to own such an enchanting old house. As if sensing my mood, the sky was darkening slightly and an uneasy wind arose, carrying wisps of coastal fog through the pines. I experienced an oddly ominous feeling, like someone had walked over my grave.

Inside the house, my inability to take up Mrs. Hudson's offer felt even more disappointing. Though its exterior was decidedly Tudor, the interior was quintessentially Victorian. In the foyer, mahogany paneling abounded, all finely crafted and polished to a deep, rich luster. Looking ahead into the main sitting room I saw dark blue and burgundy Persian carpets atop polished parquet floors. The tasteful furnishings were in the Morris & Company style from the final years of Queen Victoria's reign, an era of elegant lace and gracefully sculpted wood. On a small table beside the entryway was an antique cylinder phonograph with its distinctive large hornlike speaker. "I've never seen a real one. Is that an original?"

"Indeed it is, lass," Mrs. Hudson said proudly. "Mr. Edison's first 1899 model."

The entire sitting room was inviting. Several chairs and two settees had matching floral prints done in velvet. Three ceramic vases displayed freshly cut flowers from Mrs. Hudson's garden. A large, healthy potted palm nestled between an imposing grandfather clock and a rolltop desk. Tall leaded-glass windows provided elegant frames for the green vistas outside, now with the fingers of fog combing through the trees and creeping across the lawn.

An inside wall had a floor-to-ceiling mahogany bookcase with an attached rolling ladder to reach the topmost shelves. I helped the sweet lady pick up several books and other items that had fallen during the quake. A number of photos on one shelf caught my eye. They were of the younger Mrs. Hudson and her husband. I smiled. "Oh, look at you two!"

With a wistful expression she said, "Aye, we were quite a pair."

In a few pictures they were wearing different sets of theatrical costumes. "And what's going on here?"

She blushed slightly, downplaying it as if a bit embarrassed. "Oh, we appeared together in some local theater productions. I'd done a little acting before we met, and I dragged Dougy into it. A couple of times we performed as a duo doing some bawdy old English music hall songs and sketches."

"I wish I could've seen that!"

She touched the picture frame lovingly. "What fun times we had. My favorite was when he'd play his old pennywhistle." She touched the tiny flute nearby. "He got the knack as a wee lad—played it with a lilt. And I'd clomp through a little jig." She glanced over the photos, then gave a long sigh of satisfaction. "I miss it all. Nothing quite like being on the stage." Then she glanced at me with a twinkle in her eye. "Now, how about that lunch?"

As we entered her cheery white kitchen, with its window boxes and lace café curtains, she pointed toward a door to one side, saying, "There's a rack of Captain Basil's many vintage wines down there in the cellar. We've never ever touched the bottles before, mind you, but now that it's all to be sold, I don't suppose opening one matters." I was about to politely decline, when she pressed on: "And there's nary a one I'd rather share a taste with than you, Amy."

I'm not one to drink much, particularly at lunch, but

Mrs. Hudson had been so kind I didn't want to further disappoint her. I opened the door and carefully made my way down rickety wooden stairs. The chilly cellar made me shiver. Lit by a single hanging bulb, it was more than a little foreboding. Outside, the fog was coming in more thickly, and the meager light came through the tiny cellar window. Indeed, it seemed as though the fog had crept into the cellar. The air felt heavy.

I righted a coatrack that had fallen across the steps and moved on down among dusty remnants of furniture from before the turn of the twentieth century. There were old candelabras and various bric-a-brac. The wine rack along the wall was large—about seven feet tall and just as wide. The many bottles were laden with dust and my personal least favorite: cobwebs.

As I looked for a bottle with the lowest possibility of creepy crawlers, I noticed some recent damage to the wall at the far edge of the wine rack. Several bricks had been recently dislodged—perhaps from the trembler that had just shaken us up outside. I also saw that one section of the wine rack had slipped slightly forward, probably due to the same cause. I reached out and shoved it back into place.

To my great surprise, the section of shelves moved back several inches farther than I'd expected, as though it had actually slipped beyond the brick wall. I was confused and concerned that it not fall over and break any of the bottles. I pushed it a little more in an effort to secure it against the wall, which I now assumed must be slightly farther behind the rack than I'd first thought.

Imagine my escalating confusion when the wine rack kept going back deeper still. My heart leapt as I realized this section of the wine rack was actually a carefully concealed door. My pulse rate galloped with a delightful, excited rush I hadn't felt since I was a kid reading Nancy Drew. Curiosity impelled me to find out what was on the other side. I pushed the wall a bit farther, unmindful of the creepy cobwebs tearing away and drifting around me.

It was then that I made the incredible discovery.

At first, when I peered through the narrow crack I had made, I saw only gloom. Resolved to shed more light on the subject, I shoved the wine-rack door open a few more inches. There was a creaking of wood, and I nearly jumped out of my skin as loud crackling came directly over my head, sending a flurry of sparks sprinkling down upon me. The pivoting wall had gotten bound up with a pair of bare, hundred-year-old wires overhead that the quake had evidently displaced. They were arcing together, with brief electrical flashes. They snapped and popped into the dark distance around what I now perceived was a secret room behind the wine rack's wall.

Visualize the scene: intense darkness punctuated by bright flashes in a sort of chain reaction of electrical arcs and shorts—like lightning illuminating a dark landscape in fits and starts.

I was looking into a dark, windowless cellar chamber with a low rough-hewn wooden ceiling. It appeared roughly thirty feet square, with the dust and cobwebs everywhere I would have expected. But what stunned me were its other contents: before me was a disheveled, but fully equipped, Victorian chemistry laboratory.

Two broad, slate-topped lab tables held racks of test tubes, numerous glass-stoppered bottles of all manner and shapes, from thin and small to large and globular. Over a Bunsen burner was a retort with its long, downward-pointing neck used for distillation, as well as other paraphernalia a master chemist might employ for the separation or mixing and testing of various chemicals. Two of the larger bottles held strange black fish preserved in some liquid. Shelves on the wall above the tables and cabinets nearby held more such equipment, including peculiar items that appeared to date from the earliest days of electricity. There was also a fifty-gallon-drum-sized cast-iron cauldron with heavy iron screw handles tightly securing its lid. Atop this was a vintage hand-crank mechanism, perhaps for creating a vacuum within the cauldron.

In med school I had seen photos of such places, with scientists like Marie Curie or Joseph Lister standing frozen forever in grainy black and white, caught amid valiant historic labors, surrounded by the cutting-edge equipment of their day. But of course it was completely unexpected to find such a laboratory hidden in the bowels of this unprepossessing country house.

I found myself barely breathing. It was as though I had dropped back in time—or disturbed the dead. I imagined Dr. Victor Frankenstein stepping from the shadowy darkness amid these electrical flashes and shouting, "It's alive! It's *alive!*"

There was an unsettling air within this hidden laboratory, primarily inspired by the predominant object lying across the room. Easily three times the size of a traditional coffin, it looked like nothing less than a fantastic sarcophagus. It was not made of wood or stone but was an intricately fashioned copper chest with straps of a darker metal riveted around it. It was festooned with all manner of valves and gauges on its sides and top, with tubes and pipes connecting it to other Victorian scientific equipment nearby. It looked for all the world as if it had been designed by the wildly elaborate imagination of Jules Verne.

Bear in mind that I absorbed all this in perhaps only four or five seconds. The impression was nonetheless riveting—accentuated by the electrical flashes, which abruptly ceased.

The electricity went off, and I was plunged into darkness. Stumbling backward across the cellar and clambering up toward the top of the stairs, I experienced the irrational but visceral childhood terror of being certain that a horrifying nightmarish phantasm was right behind me and about to attack. Could I make it in time up to the dim light at the top of the stairs? Every fiber of my body strained toward it.

I did, of course, arrive there. The lights were also out in the kitchen. I was breathless as I encountered a distressed Mrs. Hudson, who blurted out, "What happened?"

"Some wires shorted out," I gasped, trying to regain my composure, "But listen, Mrs.—"

She was scurrying away, frightened and in a frenzy. "We must get the electricity back on!"

I followed her out the back kitchen door to a porch where an old electrical circuit box was bolted to the wall. Cables ran from above it to the steam generators, which were still chugging away in their shed. The fog had grown thicker; the sky seemed very close upon us. The wind had also risen yet further and was whipping at our clothes and hair as Mrs. Hudson fussed to hurriedly replace a vintage fuse. I was still breathing hard from barely escaping the unseen monster of my fantasy.

"Mrs. Hudson, what's that chamber behind the wine racks?"

The color drained from her face as though I had pulled a plug.

"What?" she said, low and very distressed.

"It looks like some kind of laboratory!"

Was it just the wind or had the lady begun to tremble? She stammered, "I . . . I don't know what you mean. Here—get the fuse in. We have to keep the electricity—"

We both jumped when the new fuse immediately blew out. I understood the problem. "The wires must still be crossed down there. Get me a flashlight, and I'll go back and—" I turned, but she caught my wrist in a startlingly strong grip. She pushed another fuse into my hands.

"No! Try again here! The electricity's never been out before! Hurry!" The wind continued to whip around us.

I would soon discover that the circumstances I had unwittingly set into motion were now progressing with a life of their own. For at that moment, yet unknown to me, in the secret chamber below, the massive lid on the bizarre copper coffin had begun to open. There must have been a hiss of decompression and a gushing out of vapors as the heavy cover was pushed upward by a quivering, deathly blue-white, frost-covered hand.

Outside on the porch, I was busy blowing yet another fuse. I could see this was going nowhere. I shouted over the rustling of leaves in the blowing wind, "It's no good! I'll go back down and uncross the wires."

But Mrs. Hudson was now nearing panic. She blew past me like a tornado through Kansas, saying, "No! I'll do it." I stood for a moment, blinking, befuddled by her strange behavior. Then I followed.

She had grabbed a flashlight and was hurrying down the cellar steps by the time I caught up with her. Fortunately, my arrival was just in time to help her as she lost her footing near the bottom. She stumbled, twisting her ankle, and cried out.

I shouted, "Mrs. Hudson! Wait! Let me—"

"It's okay, I'm alright," she said, but when she tried to walk, her ankle failed. She collapsed backward, plopping down on the wooden steps.

"Sure you are," I said, as I lifted and ushered her to a decrepit wicker settee. Behind her on the wall I noticed an old-fashioned life preserver bearing the name SS *Friesland*. "Now, you sit right there, and I'll—"

I was startled by a scraping noise coming from the direction of the secret door. Next, there came the sound of a bottle breaking from within the chamber beyond, shocking us both. I grabbed Mrs. Hudson's flashlight and moved toward the wine-rack entrance. I glanced back at her to be sure she was all right—and perhaps seeking a little moral support for myself. That glance proved to be a mistake, for when I looked forward again, I was staring into the totally white glaring eyes of a ghastly monstrosity.

Imagine a gasping, sickly gray, corpse-like face with flakes of skin dropping from it into a long, scraggly, dark beard. Imagine that face covered with frost and violently shuddering, with brown mucus draining from its nose and over its blue, cracked lips onto its yellow teeth. Imagine it with long dark hair sprouting in all directions and flecked with dead skin.

Imagine me screaming.

2

Indeed, I shrieked.

I also quickly realized that this hideous creature, standing before me with his eyes rolled back into their sockets so that only the whites were showing, was convulsing in a grand mal seizure in his tattered, once white but now disgustingly stained robe.

He had three-inch fingernails, curved like the talons of a great bird of prey, and his right hand was employing a huge 1890s syringe, such as I'd only ever seen in a medical museum, to inject something into his chest.

Then he collapsed at my feet.

Dead.

Or so it seemed. In spite of my revulsion at his appearance, my medical training kicked in. I knelt beside him and pressed the tips of my index and middle fingers against his neck, feeling for a carotid pulse. I couldn't find one. I pressed my left ear to the moldy, dingy garment over his foul-smelling chest. I heard no heartbeat. I shot a quick glance to Mrs. Hudson. She had risen shakily from the wicker settee and was staring wide-eyed with fear at this extraordinary figure, clutching her hands to her chest.

I shouted to her, "His heart's stopped! Help me!"

Mrs. Hudson responded by exhaling a limp sigh, then she passed out and fell sideways onto the settee.

"Oh, wonderful," I grumbled to myself as I overlapped my hands on the grotesque man's sternum and gave three sharp pumps. I was praying this would work. Fortunately, mouth-to-mouth CPR was no longer recommended. The notion of putting my lips to his drooling, mucous-covered mouth was beyond unappealing. I checked his carotid artery. Still no pulse. I pumped again, vigorously. This time he responded.

He coughed wetly, wheezed, and—thank God—sucked in a breath.

I saw that his tongue was still blue. His skin was icy cold to the touch. He was either in shock or headed that way fast. I turned an old trash can on its side and, lifting his legs, which I now saw were wrapped with gauze like an Egyptian mummy, elevated his feet onto it.

He coughed, sneezed, gurgled, wheezed some more, and then struggled to reopen his sticky eyes. He blinked, trying to focus. His skin had a sallow, corpse-like pallor. I tried to gain an idea of his age, but given his sepulchral, crypt-keeper appearance, I could only guess that he was somewhere between 30 and 130. His eyes appeared gray, his nose was thin and hawklike. His lips were thin but looked firm, even as they were covered with brown, slimy mucous.

Feeling that he was out of immediate danger, I grabbed a nearby stick and went back just inside the wine rack's secret entrance. I used the stick to separate the crossed wires overhead.

While there, I heard the faint sound of trickling liquid from the direction of the strange sarcophagus that I'd glimpsed earlier.

I ran upstairs to replace the fuse. This time it didn't blow. I grabbed my cell and dialed 911, but when I got their "due to unusually high call volume" computer voice, I decided not to wait and hurried back down to the cellar. Evidently, my fuse replacement had worked, because the single old-fashioned light bulb hanging from the ceiling was on.

Mrs. Hudson was not—still out cold but breathing adequately. I grabbed a nearby tarp and spread it like a blanket over the bizarre quivering man on the floor. He had a peculiarly foul reek, far beyond the sourness of normal body odor. His eyes still struggled to focus; they crossed and uncrossed themselves in a manner that I might have thought humorous in other circumstances. He brought his long, shivering, taloned fingernails up near his face and was trying to focus on them with some amazement, like an infant discovering its hands for the first time.

"Easy, just take it easy," I counseled, adjusting the tarp over him.

And then, with a rasping, unsteady voice and eyes wide and slightly crazed, he asked in what sounded like an elegant though inebriated British accent, "What . . . is . . . the year?"

"2022."

"*Ah!*" he emitted in a small burst of jubilation, then coughed badly again. Gasping, he spoke with a drunken slur, "Mmmm . . . three years sooner than I'd imagined . . . but I shall adjust."

I glanced back in at the Victorian laboratory and the now open steampunk sarcophagus he'd emerged from. Vapors were still rising out of it. "How long have you been in there?"

He smiled with a quirky smugness as he fingered and examined the length of his tangled beard, "Hmmm? . . . Since second November, 1899."

"Ah. Right," I said, humoring him as I took his pulse. "Well, that'd make you the world's greatest scientist."

He chuckled and coughed, still gasping. "Hardly. That honor . . . would likely still rest with my friend Louis."

"Louis?"

"*Pasteur* of course." He said it with a haughty flash, as though I were an idiot.

I stared at him, deadpan. "Of course." I nodded, continuing to indulge him. "So, you were friends with Louis Pasteur?"

"Until his death . . . four years ago. No, wait . . . 1895 would be—"

"One hundred twenty-seven years ago, yes." I saw a shiver run through him and felt his pulse rate increase slightly.

"Louis was a gifted man, although a fondness for garlic sometimes made his breath difficult to bear."

"Well, sure, naturally." I was still trying to get a sense of exactly how insane this disgusting individual was.

He was slowly regaining his breath. "Louis would have been . . ." (with his British accent he pronounced the word as *bean*) ". . . intrigued . . . by what I have accomplished."

"Oh, yes indeed, I certainly think he would have."

"Of course, he would have recognized that the biochemistry I created . . . was actually . . . very elementary." He took a deep breath. His respiration was becoming almost regular. "I'd found a man nearly frozen solid in a drift of London snow . . . whom I realized had miraculously survived . . . because he had been thoroughly inebriated." He wheezed and took in another long breath. "That gave me the idea . . . of lowering my body temperature and using brandy as an anti-freezing agent to keep my blood slowly flowing."

"Fascinating. Do go on," I said. Ever more certain that I was dealing with a madman, I was determined to keep him passive.

"I retarded my bodily processes through my long-developed skill at self-hypnosis," he continued, with growing enthusiasm for his perceived triumph. "A mechanical device cooled and cleansed my blood and administered vitamin E"—he pronounced it *vitt*-a-min—"as an antitoxin."

"Vitamin E. Well, it seems to have worked."

"The key element, however," he said with haughty pride, raising his taloned index finger to punctuate the importance, "is an extraordinary serum I derived from the blackfish of the Bering Sea, which every winter is frozen solid and then miraculously revives during the spring thaw. This serum also prevented my muscular system from withering by atrophy."

"*Annnnd* why were you so sure this whole process would work on you?" I inquired.

"Because I had meticulously researched it, experimented carefully—and primarily because it was all entirely *logical*." Again his tone was gratingly derisive, as though he were casting pearls of "*ob*-vious" wisdom before swinish me. He pulled some long, mud-colored beard hair out of his mouth. "*Ptoo!* And of course I fitted the apparatus with a fail-safe device to inject a stimulant into my body if the electricity failed before the year 2025, when my carefully crafted, electrically powered chronometer was set to trigger my revival. But upon awakening I still felt weak and injected myself with more."

"You injected too much," I said, picking up the large antique metal syringe and examining it. "You went into cardiac arrest. What, besides adrenaline, did you inject yourself with?"

He smiled coyly; his eyes twinkled between their gummy lids. "With a formula of my own devising. I'm sure it's all terribly antiquated by this modern age, but perhaps it might prove of some minor historical interest to the doctor for whom you nurse."

Still kneeling beside him, I leaned back onto my heels. "And just why do you think I'm a nurse?"

"The professional manner with which you've been taking my pulse; your knowledge of adrenaline," he rattled on with complete confidence, "the way you've elevated my feet to ward off shock; and the faint, but distinct, odor of medicinal alcohol on your clothing."

I frowned and tried to casually sniff the shoulder of my purple silk blouse. In doing so, I saw that Mrs. Hudson was just regaining consciousness. She struggled to pull herself into a sitting position. But when she saw the face of the man on the floor, her eyes went wide. She let out a small, fearful yelp, saying, "Oh dear God! It is him!" And she promptly fainted sideways onto the settee again.

I stared at her, feeling a bit nonplussed by everything. I looked down at my snot-covered patient. "Um, would you mind telling me just who you are?"

"Oh, come, come, my dear. No need to play games." The smelly man struggled onto one elbow, facing away from me. I was grateful since his breath was like a cesspool. "By the dust on the hem of your skirt, I can see you've been in my laboratory, so it must've been you that took out the tin box which contains my identification."

"What are you talking about? I was only in there to fix the electrical wires. I never saw a—"

He cut me off with a grumble, which, though gruff, also betrayed the first crack in his supremely confident demeanor. Getting unsteadily to his feet, he tottered past me on rubbery legs and went back into the secret lab.

"Hey! Wait a minute!" I called out, but he ignored me.

As I followed, his head snapped back toward me and he positively snarled, "Stop right where you are. Not another step!"

I did as ordered. He also stood unmoving, except for his sharp, beady eyes, which first flashed toward the dark brick wall to my left, then scanned up, down, and all around the strange cellar. He asked, "Was that entrance to the laboratory already open or obvious to you?"

"No. Not at all. I was getting a bottle of wine, saw the rack leaning forward due to an earthquake, and pushed it back until it slipped inward and—"

"Enough!" he angrily cut me off. Scanning the chamber again, he muttered to himself, "This is not good."

I stood in the secret doorway and got my first thorough look at his full stature. He was slightly over six feet, though his narrow neck, wrists, and ankles were so excessively lean that he appeared even taller. His eyes, darting around the chamber, were piercing. His nose was decidedly hawklike. Overall, he had an intense air of alertness, but as he began to move one careful step at a time deeper into the laboratory, I saw that his concern had increased. Apparently, he seemed to sense something deeply amiss; something untoward had occurred in this bizarre chamber.

"Not good," he mumbled again as he cautiously moved

toward a lab table, seemingly mindful of the placement of each footstep.

"We'll get it sorted out," I said, anxious to keep him calm. "But first tell me who you are. And I won't believe it if you say Captain Basil."

He snorted as he busied himself looking for some object on the lab table. "Of course I'm not Captain Basil!" His back was to me as he went on, "There is no Captain Basil, my good woman. I traveled to America under that name to conceal my identity."

"Which is?"

He turned to me, dramatically holding a large antique magnifying glass. "I am, of course, the gentleman whose name is known to the public as Sherlock Holmes."

He tried to look astute and collected, but his shaky legs failed him, and the momentum of his rapid turn to face me carried him into a pratfall on the dusty floor. I tried to stifle a laugh, but it came out anyway as I said, "Get serious."

"Madam," he snapped at me ferociously as he regained his wobbly feet, "I have never been more serious in my considerably eventful life." He then began a careful examination of the cobwebbed and dusty laboratory bottles and equipment. In spite of the draping of his stained and ragged nightgown, his body seemed lean and fit.

"Excuse me," I said politely—and carefully, so as not to antagonize him while analyzing his mental state—"but I've always been under the impression that Sherlock Holmes was fictional."

"And that is quite correct: Sherlock Holmes is *indeed* a fictional character. And I take it that people still read those little stories, eh?"

"Uh . . . yes, they do, but . . ." I was stumblingly trying to keep my grasp on reality while worrying that I might be dealing with a schizophrenic. "But help me out here—if Sherlock Holmes is fictional, then how can you possibly be standing there and—"

"My colleague Dr. John Watson is responsible for that sterling conundrum." He continued scrutinizing one of laboratory tables inch by inch as he went on explaining, "Watson was attending a medical conference at the University of Edinburgh. One evening in the delightfully ancient White Hart pub, which dates from 1516, Watson chanced to be conversing with a fellow attendee, a young physician of Anglo-Irish descent who had been struggling to sustain a medical practice that might someday make him a living. Unfortunately, he had far too few patients, which was diminishing his bank account but providing an abundance of spare time. As a result, he'd begun making attempts at becoming an author. That particular evening he'd reached an impasse with a story he simply couldn't work out."

"He had writer's block?" I volunteered, having no idea myself where *this* story was going.

"*Ha.* 'Writer's block,'" he said with some surprise, as though he'd never heard that phrase. "Rather a simplistic description I'd say, yet quite accurate." He stepped back from the lab table, turning his attention to gaze at a section of the dusty floor. "So the young physician had given up writing that story and was searching for some entirely different concept to pursue. Watson, always a reliably warm, generous, and supportive chap, mentioned that he might be able to suggest a subject and went on to describe how he'd recently become my helpmate in investigating a most remarkable mystery."

The ragged man turned slightly, lowered his head, and scanned slowly across a different section of the floor. His eyes seemed almost to bore into it, studying every millimeter as he continued. "The young would-be writer became quickly intrigued by the intricate details and the complexity of our exploration and analysis. It took Watson a full hour to recount the entire adventure, but he told me how the young man had sat listening, mesmerized. And when Watson reached the conclusion, telling the surprising revelations we had brought to light, the young doctor sat back and laughed heartily with great satisfaction. He asked if we might allow him to write it up as a story that he might hopefully get published."

I had begun to smile inwardly as he talked because the fledgling medical man's identity had become obvious to me. "And you're going to tell me that the young physician was named Arthur Conan Doyle."

"Mmm." He nodded, adding snidely, "Brilliant deduction, my dear." He looked back and forth between the first and second sections of the dusty floor he'd been assessing. "Doyle provided a few overly dramatic touches of his own and published the story, which he titled 'A Study in Scarlet.' It appeared in the November 1887 issue of *Beeton's Christmas Annual*, which sold for one shilling each. It was quite a success for him, selling out before Christmas." Still without moving, my newest patient then visually compared a third section of the floor to the two others. "Doyle did make one rather annoying alteration to Watson's original documentation." His voice took on an edge of sarcasm as he said, "He was satisfied with my surname because it reminded him of Oliver Wendell Holmes, an American physician and poet he admired. But he thought my Christian name a bit too ordinary and unmemorable. So he took 'poetic license,' changing it to a name that he felt would be, as he put it, 'a bit more cheeky, to better capture the public's fancy, stick in the reader's consciousness—and encourage more purchases.'" He shook his head with annoyance, causing a few more flakes of dead skin to drift down from his cheek. "Doyle was an aficionado of cricket, and one popular player of the day had a name that Doyle quite liked."

"Sherlock."

"Just so," he said offhandedly, still comparing the three sections of floor.

I nodded slowly, thinking it through. "*Okaaay.* So, the public came to know you by the fictional name of Sherlock, as in the stories, but your first name is actually . . . ?"

"Hubert."

My eyes widened. I swallowed a chuckle, maintaining a serious composure while thinking that Doyle had chosen wisely. "Your real first name was Hubert?"

"Was and is," he said dismissively as he lifted a particular small brown bottle from a lab table and sniffed its contents. "It having been my late grandfather's name."

I added it up: "Okay, so you, *Hubert* Holmes, were actually the *real* flesh-and-blood private investigator—"

His head snapped around. "The correct term, my dear," he said sharply, "is *consulting detective.*"

"Right." I nodded. "That. And you, Hubert, were the real 'consulting detective' who actually had the adventures and solved the mysterious cases that Doyle's stories attributed to a *fictional* Sherlock Holmes?"

"*Brava!*" he sneered in a condescending tone as he continued his meticulous examination of the room. "You have sorted it all out magnificently." Then he chuckled pridefully. "And I can tell you with surety that lot of criminals I sent to Newgate Prison certainly wished Hubert Holmes *had* been fictional."

He dropped to the floor—not from a loss of balance this time but rather to make a scrupulous inspection of the leg of a stool, which he then pushed along ahead of him as he continued. "But I was, and am, quite real. I am Holmes in the flesh." He brushed a few pieces of dried skin off the back of his hand. "Albeit rather flaky at the present moment."

"Mmm. Yes, quite flaky," I said, more to myself than to him, then asked, "And you allowed the stories about your cases to be published under that false name because . . . ?"

"Doyle proposed—actually, insisted—that Watson and I receive an appropriate percentage of the proceeds, which would help to underwrite the many pro bono investigations we undertook. And of course the stories helped spread the word to other potential clients who had the need—and sufficient means to pay—for my services."

While speaking, he climbed with tipsy gravity to perch precariously atop the stool, still weaving to maintain his balance as he inspected the top of a hanging metal lampshade. The shreds of his stained robe swayed like a hula skirt, adding additional absurdity to the surreal scene. I had somehow dropped into a Fellini movie, or perhaps one by Mel Brooks. But I tried to remain calm since I still didn't yet have a clue as to what kind of neurosis I was dealing with. "Naturally you have some iron-clad way to prove all of what you claim?"

He leered down from his perch, his voice dripping with sarcasm. "It would be rather foolish not to have, eh?" He climbed awkwardly down from the stool, then crawled toward the large sarcophagus across the floor, his chin nearly scraping while he examined it through his magnifying glass. From my perspective, the glass magnified and ballooned his face to look like a funhouse mirror.

"My aforementioned tin box," he articulated pedantically and without looking at me, "had been secured in the small compartment hidden in that wall just to your left, which has clearly been discovered and breached."

Glancing that way, I noticed that a twelve-inch square section of the dark brick wall was hinged open slightly. It was a small door with a wafer-thin facade of brick that would disguise its presence when closed. "And your tin box contains—"

"Photographs of myself with several notable friends of my day—Dr. Freud, George Bernard Shaw, P. T. Barnum, et cetera. I trust you have perhaps heard of at least one of them?"

I didn't dignify his insult by responding, but watched him creep across the floor, punctuating his speech with an occasional groan, whistle, or chirp of enthusiasm. I was incredulous but also amused as he went on. "All of those notables provided signed documents describing their personal meetings with me. In addition," he spat stridently, "my fingerprint records from Scotland Yard are in the box, as well as Doyle's fingerprints and records, plus a written statement by Doyle confirming all I have told you. Everything was duly notarized, signed, witnessed, and dated by Chief Inspector Layton himself. When Doyle began writing his stories, I had him change the inspector's name to Lestrade to avoid embarrassing Layton."

By now he had reached the elaborate copper sarcophagus, from which cloudy gasses still slowly wafted upward. I noticed that the inside of the open lid was also lined with shining copper. "I had anticipated that my sudden reappearance in a later era might be difficult for *many* people to comprehend and believe." He shot me a pointed glance, assigning me to the "many people" category—and he was right to do so. "It was therefore of vital importance for me to have unimpeachable proof of my identity so that skeptics would take me seriously and also be convinced that Doyle's writings were, in fact, based upon my casework. I knew if his stories continued to command even slight popularity a century later, it would greatly assist me in attracting new clients for my services." He had worked his way up the front of the sarcophagus using his magnifier, pausing several times to examine tiny details. He moved his eyes slowly along the lip of it as he said, "Also in the tin box was a quantity of jewels of considerable value to help me reestablish myself in this new day and age."

His stern conviction made him sound almost credible, though I was convinced I was dealing with a seriously delusional man.

"Ah! Eureka! Mmmm," he mumbled as he went down along one corner of the container and began crawling again across the floor and under another large oaken lab table. His nose was almost touching the floor. "Damn. Hmmph. Aha!"

I tried to maintain a natural, conversational tone. "Why exactly did you do all this?"

"Because I had already solved the major mysteries of the nineteenth century," he impatiently replied. "And after the death of my archenemy"—here he paused to look up and meet my eyes to emphasize the statement—"my nemesis, that evil Napoleon of crime, Professor James Moriarty, life ceased to hold any fascination for me." He briefly looked away as his thoughts turned inward. Then he dove aggressively again under the heavy oak table, moving across the dusty floor, not missing a millimeter in his examination with his magnifier. "Moriarty was the only man whom I felt to be my intellectual peer and a worthy adversary. With him gone, I suffered the most terrible ennui. I became increasingly morose and began succumbing more and more to my principal vice: cocaine, injected in a seven percent solution."

Now we were getting somewhere: a connection to drugs would explain a lot. And he was talking about a massive IV dose. As he raised his left hand to slide a wooden chair, his tattered sleeve dangled, and I caught a glimpse of his sinewy forearm and wrist, where there were scars and numerous puncture marks—something I had seen too many times in the trauma unit—the telltale signs of an addict. But before I could pursue that line of questioning, he went on: "Watson and Doyle actually began to fear for my life." He scrutinized the lower edge of a chair. "In an effort to stimulate and distract me, they introduced me to several intriguing thinkers, including Doyle's fellow writer Herbert George Wells." He glanced up to ascertain if I recognized that name.

I nodded, reciting, "*The Invisible Man, War of the Worlds . . .*"

His smirking expression implied, *Well, at least she's not an* illiterate *idiot.* Then he resumed his meticulous exploration of the dusty environs while saying, "Wells had just published his Martian book when we met. During dinner conversation, he mentioned an earlier novel of his that I hadn't read—about a machine that could travel through time. That concept sparked my imagination. I realized one of the greatest mysteries of life remained unsolved." He turned his face to look up into the distance before drawing in an enthusiastic breath. "The mystery of what would happen in the future! I knew that such a machine existed only in Wells' imagination, but I also realized I might be able to create a method of hibernation utilizing chemistry, of which I have considerable knowledge. I recognized that it would be a one-way excursion with no possibility of return, but I was nevertheless determined to turn myself into a time traveler and explore the future, hopeful that therein I might find intriguing new crimes to solve, perhaps even an adversary as stimulating as Moriarty had been. And it appears that I may have done so already."

He continued his survey, dodging cobwebs, to inspect a tiny piece of broken glass under a lab table. He emitted a pleasurable squeak regarding that fragment. I determined to ease him along until I could get adequate help or access to a straitjacket. I asked lightly, "Why San Francisco?"

"Distance. Moriarty's faithful minions are legion. I was concerned that one or more of them might attempt to discover my whereabouts and destroy me—which is obviously what they had sought to do."

He came out from under the table and stood. From the tabletop he retrieved the small brown glass bottle he'd earlier sniffed. "The housekeeper at my Baker Street residence in Marylebone, London, was a Mrs. Hudson. She had a son struggling to make a living in San Francisco. I came here under the name of Captain Basil, purchased this property, prepared this laboratory, and then engaged Hudson's family as caretakers."

As he strode past me out of the laboratory, he blew a puff of dust from the top of the bottle right in my face, making me sneeze.

3

He went directly to the unconscious Mrs. Hudson, unstoppered the small bottle he'd brought out of the laboratory, and before I could question his intent, waved it under Mrs. Hudson's nose. She snorted, coughed. And I caught a whiff of the ammonia.

"There now, my dear," he said gently to Mrs. Hudson with a far more empathetic and congenial tone than he'd used with me. "No reason to be frightened. But I do need some information from you."

As her vision cleared, Mrs. Hudson stared at him with astonishment, then glanced at me. "You—you saved him? But you said his heart had stopped! You brought him back to life?"

"Yes, yes, she's an excellent nurse," he said dismissively, anxious to get on with his questions. "Now tell me, madam—"

"She's not a nurse," Mrs. Hudson cut him off sternly. "She's a doctor."

His eyebrows shot up. "Ha!" He seemed entirely bemused by the concept. "Really? . . . Well, well, well." He glanced at me, then went on with a snide edge: "It seems as though I am in your debt, *Doc*-tor . . . ?"

"Winslow. Dr. Amy Winslow," I said, trying to look worthy of the title, then getting angry that I'd felt the need to impress this flaky lunatic.

"*Doc*-tor." He repeated the carefully separated syllables with cynicism as he gazed at me, then with a simpering smile he added a hard-to-believe "*Humph.*"

Honest to God, I wanted to slug him. But then I realized he'd be quite a bit behind the times—if indeed any of his outrageous fable were true. He glanced about, inquiring of Mrs. Hudson, "Is your husband nearby, madam?"

"No," she responded sadly, "he died last month."

"My condolences," he replied, without a trace of sincerity or empathy. "Then I will need *your* careful assistance to illuminate a detail or two. Here is what I have deduced." He dropped down rather forcefully into a 1920s wicker wheelchair—which his momentum promptly rolled backward, carrying him completely out of sight into the shadows. It struck me as very funny, but he maintained an entirely serious mien as he wheeled it back to us, crossing his mummy-gauze-covered legs and ostentatiously clearing his throat. Even if he was completely delusional, he was without a doubt a singular and commanding orator.

"In June or July, about sixty years ago," he began, "a robbery and a death occurred in that laboratory."

I noticed Mrs. Hudson go even paler than she had when I'd first told her about my discovery of the secret room. The blood drained again from her face, leaving her a ghostly white. I was beginning to get intrigued.

"An elderly gentleman," he continued, "who was stoop-shouldered and walked with a cane in his left hand, discovered this chamber with the help of a boy about ten, who wore a blue shirt and possessed very low morals."

"What?" I blinked. I could not imagine where on earth this was going.

He went on without missing a beat. "They opened the chest wherein I lay. Assuming I was dead because I was ice cold, they searched the room until they discovered the tin box containing my diamonds and my invaluable identification papers."

"And how did they find the secret compartment in the brick wall?" I inquired.

"Because the aged intruder had a brilliant skill set nearly matching my own. Since the laboratory has not been thoroughly ransacked, as an unskillful thief would have done, I recognized immediately that this was no average intruder, but one who instinctively understood I would not have left any valuables tucked onto a back shelf or even in an obvious safe. Nor did these thieves accidentally stumble upon the secret entrance through the wine rack into the laboratory. This old man and his young accomplice were nefarious people with ill intent. They were on a mission to find me and were well aware that I would have scrupulously secreted anything of monetary or other significant value. So, the old goat must have thought as I had: Where does one best hide an egg?"

"Uh . . ." He had lost me. I was missing the connection.

"One hides an egg among many other eggs . . . or in this case, bricks—in the wall." Holmes' eyes darkened, his jaw set, expressing frustration but also a grudging admiration for the old man. "He was clearly a highly skilled individual." Pausing, he pondered that a moment. "He might even have been a worthy adversary."

"Except that he'd be long dead by now," I noted.

"Actually, Winslow, he was dead just moments after he found my tin box."

"What?"

"He and the boy lit a torch, were about to set the place afire and leave, when they were surprised by a man about five feet ten inches tall with red hair."

Mrs. Hudson gasped, then whispered, "Yes! My husband!"

I looked sharply at her, stunned.

But to the crypt-keeper relating this fantastic tale it was all very matter of fact.

"So I supposed. The old man drew a pistol." The storyteller was on a roll now, saying to Mrs. Hudson, "Your husband scuffled with him until the old man was bludgeoned from behind with a wine bottle by a woman of approximately your height."

Mrs. Hudson looked stricken, glancing at me with a guilty expression before turning back to him and nodding in stupefaction. I realized my own jaw was beginning to slacken. Our gazes returned to this apparition in the wheelchair as he continued.

"The old man fell, striking his head against the brick abutment near the floor, dying instantly."

I looked at Mrs. Hudson for confirmation. Her voice was barely audible, "Yes."

As much as I tried to resist, I found myself getting drawn into this strange man's astonishing tale and was also becoming increasingly curious about Mrs. Hudson's own history.

"During the fracas, the bad boy bolted, running awkwardly and slicing open a nasty wound on the back of his right hand." He looked at Mrs. Hudson. "You and your husband saw my 'corpse,' but finding no identification and never having met

Captain Basil personally, feared opening a rather distressing and prosecutable hornet's nest. So you left the old man's body in the secret chamber for a few days."

Mrs. Hudson stared blankly as he went on. "When no police came around to investigate, you removed the old man from the site of his demise and buried him. Then you resealed the chamber, bricking up the edges."

White as a sheet, Mrs. Hudson's mouth was agape. "That's . . . that's exactly the way it happened!"

I looked at her, aghast, and found myself stammering, "But . . . but even if that's all true," I turned to the ragged, wild-haired man, "how could you have possibly pieced it all together after poking around that laboratory for only five minutes?"

"It was about eight and three-quarter minutes," he corrected, then sighed. *"Wir sind gewohnt dass die Menschen verhöhnen was sie nicht verstehen.* Goethe was pithy, wasn't he?" Then, as if to enlighten a schoolgirl, he began, "Goethe, you see, was—"

"A brilliant German writer, thank you," I said archly, "but *Ich spreche kein Deutsch.*"

"Ah. Then I shall translate: 'We are accustomed to the mockery of what they do not understand.'" He stared at me as though I were a fool for not recognizing and revering his august reputation. "And 'piecing together' a crime, solving a mystery—that, my dear doctor, is what I do. It is my *trade.*" I stared a moment longer and was about to speak when he was off again, summing it all up. "So, the bad boy who stole my papers and valuables would now be a dishonorable man of about seventy-two, who walks awkwardly and has a scar on the back of his right hand."

I was still staring. "Dishonorable because . . . ?"

"Oh come, come!" he blurted. "Because he never reported

the crime! Or returned the stolen valuables. And his ambulatory awkwardness results from his club foot."

I shook my head and laughed again. "After sixty years, how could you guess all that?"

"I never *guess!*" He bristled and practically jumped down my throat. "Guesswork is a shocking habit, destructive to the logical faculty. And the prospect of being your patient would fill me with concern, *Doc*-tor. Do you guess rather than observe?"

I was startled, insulted, and angry. But as I was drawing a breath to defend myself, he abruptly jumped to his feet, swayed for a moment to find his balance, and headed for the laboratory with a grunt. "Oh, very well, so you can begin to comprehend my methods."

Mrs. Hudson and I exchanged a concerned glance. She was chewing her upper lip and still looked exceedingly abashed. Myself, I was more than curious to see this peculiar man prove how he could have deduced all that information—if only so I could find fault with it and poke holes in his surly, annoying self-confidence. His snide comments had gotten my dander up.

His egoism was bolstered by the renewed vigor of his physicality. Seeming to have overcome his wobbliness temporarily, he walked straight-backed and chin up with an almost military bearing. Indeed, if there was ever a man of whom it could be said, both physically and character-wise, "He had a broomstick up his ass," it was him.

There were many times to come when I gladly would have shoved it there myself.

We reentered the secret laboratory, and he assumed the role of an impatient, oh-so-clever tour guide. "I realize of course that some of this may be difficult for your mind to fathom."

I muttered dryly, "No shit . . . *Hubert.*"

"One must not only see, Doctor, one must *ob-serve.*" He held up his magnifying glass to emphasize the point. "Before commencing my lengthy slumber, I carefully swept the floor of the laboratory clean, so any items that are now upon it have accumulated since. Particularly," his eyes brightened, "the dust!"

There was certainly a lot of that. Everywhere. On everything. He moved to one side, an errant cobweb catching in his stringy, matted hair. Pointing toward a shelf, he said, "You can easily see that the undisturbed dust on the shelf there is of a certain thickness." I could. "That thickness equals an accumulation of one hundred and twenty-three years. But here"—he knelt and indicated a spot on the floor—"is a footprint with an accumulation of dust only half as thick as that which is undisturbed, hence the footprint was made about sixty years ago. The same half-thickness occurs on the books that were thrown down at that time, confirming my hypothesis."

He had a point, but I wasn't about to give in so easily. "Alright, but—"

He gestured for me to keep quiet and look more closely. "In one of these footprints can be observed a dried peony petal, and in this Marin County clime, peonies blossom only in June, therefore specifying the approximate month in which the crime took place. This other set of footprints I indicate here was made by a man who shuffled slightly, indicating advancing age— the old man of whom I spoke. His advanced years are further evidenced by his use of a cane. See the cane marks in the dust?"

Well, yes, I did. "But 'stoop-shouldered'?"

He rose to his full height while showing irritation at the slowness of my wit, then demonstrated, assuming a slouching posture. "The cane of a stoop-shouldered man will come to rest ahead of his feet because his curved back puts his shoulders and arms forward!"

I had observed enough elderly patients to realize that he was correct once again. He sniffed, saying, "The rest is quite obvious to even the most casual observer." He pointed over my head. "The blackened circle on the ceiling right above you indicates a torch was lighted. Indeed, its remnants can be seen, stomped out, over there." He pointed, and I saw the blackened fibers. He steamed onward. "These larger footprints indicate the entrance of a man about five feet ten inches: the late Mr. Hudson. I deduced his height from the length of his stride. Was he not five feet ten inches, Mrs. Hudson?"

"Exactly," she said with a rasp. I could tell that her mouth was dry.

Again he knelt, identifying something I hadn't seen. "This tuft of red hair where the old man fell indicates he grabbed Mr. Hudson by the hair, pulling out some of it, and their struggle is evidenced by their intermingled footprints. Are you getting the idea, Wats—er, Winslow?"

I could only nod my head, overwhelmed.

"Alright." He scooted slightly to one side. "Now here is a much smaller footprint, and near it a hairpin exactly like the one Mrs. Hudson is wearing in her hair today." He held up a distinctive, very old-fashioned hairpin to Mrs. Hudson, whose own wrinkled hand reflexively lifted to touch an identical one in her white hair.

"And here are fragments of the wine bottle Mrs. Hudson had taken from among its fellows there in the wine rack and broken over the head of the old man." Now he stood and pointed up to the hanging metal lampshade he had examined while so ridiculously perched atop the stool earlier. "Had she been any taller, she would've struck this hanging metal lampshade, which is undented." He tapped it twice, wiggling his eyebrows, delighted with himself.

I glanced at Mrs. Hudson for confirmation. Her eyes told me this speculation was also true. When I looked back, our tour guide to murder was kneeling by the bricks at one end of the copper sarcophagus.

"Here fell the evil old man, having drawn but not fired his pistol. The outline of the pistol is seen in the dust. The dust also tells us that he made no further movement—therefore, dying instantly, as I stated. He was dragged away several days later—see the scuff marks over here?"

I nodded blankly. They were indisputably visible.

"The passage of a few days is indicated by the fact that much blood had time to be absorbed into the porous brick floor." He looked sharply at our host, "Mrs. Hudson, did the dead man have any identification?"

She drew a nervous breath and appeared sorry that she had to report "No, sir." This gave only a moment's frustrated pause to the odd gentleman, who moved to the large copper sarcophagus before beckoning me closer.

"The top edge of the chest wherein I laid has four distinct sets of fingerprints. They represent the old man, the bad boy, and Mr. and Mrs. Hudson." He looked me in the eye. "Do you recall Mrs. Hudson's comment today when she first saw me?"

I realized and reluctantly repeated, "It is him!"

"Correct. Confirming that she had indeed seen me before." Then he turned and strode back toward the secret entrance into the chamber. "This new brickwork along the seam of the wine rack is clearly of later construction than the rest of the house—therefore, added by Mr. and Mrs. Hudson. Careful inspection of this exposed nail"—he held his glass down to magnify for me the designated nail—"shows an accumulation of skin, dried blood, and a tiny piece of blue material from his shirt. The escaping boy held the tin box by its sides in front of him, like this." He mimed holding such a box. "He gouged a serious wound on the back of his right hand."

By now I was nearly breathless, sputtering, "And . . . 'clubfooted'?"

He threw his head back, exasperated by my stubborn stupidity. "Ob-*serve*! Look at the boy's footprints: the right one is curved in and under. Your diagnosis, *Doc*-tor, must be . . . ?"

"Uh, yes. CTEV," I said. When Mrs. Hudson glanced at me for clarification, I added, "Congenital talipes equinovarus. Deformity. Clubfooted."

"*Brava*, Winslow!" he positively sneered. "*Brava!* Is it not rewarding to use the senses the Almighty gave us?" He drew a deep breath, looking at our host. "Now then, Mrs. Hudson, might there be any mail for Captain Basil?"

She looked surprised that he would know to ask. "Why yes, sir, that there is!"

She bustled away, and he followed, leaving me alone and standing in the secret doorway. My mind was reeling. Could he possibly be who he said he was? No. That was ridiculous. But after the dazzling display I had just witnessed, I found myself wondering. How could he *not* be? My own powers of deduction were completely jumbled.

I quickly went upstairs and watched him approach the arched entrance to the charming Victorian sitting room where early afternoon light was now beaming in through tall leaded-glass windows. His gait was slightly off again, like someone trying to find his sea legs aboard a rocking ship.

The semi-mummified gentleman proceeded through the archway, apparently glimpsing something that made him jump and utter a startled yelp. It was his own horrific reflection in a mirror just inside the door. He cleared his throat and recomposed himself while still working to find his balance. I could tell he was trying to mask his embarrassment and hoped no one had witnessed this brief moment of surprise. And vulnerability.

As I entered the sitting room, again I drew a breath, recalling Mrs. Hudson offering me ownership of the estate. My eyes were drawn longingly to the mahogany bookshelf wall filled with many leatherbound volumes. I knew that many of my favorites must be among them, and I had a moment of yearning for my earlier fireplace fantasy of living there—shortly before life had become weirdly complicated by the appearance of this odd Englishman.

I saw that Mrs. Hudson was still limping slightly from her twisted ankle as she crossed the inviting room to the vintage rolltop desk, and I wondered aloud, "How did the intruders get into your house that day, Mrs. Hudson, without you knowing?"

She looked back at me, saying, "They must have taken note of our regular Saturday night dates." A sweet smile brightened her face at the memory. "For dinner and a little dancing. That particular night was our anniversary, June nineteenth, and the peonies had just blossomed."

"Indeed they had," Holmes said matter-of-factly. "Like clockwork." He shot me a haughty glance to emphasize his previous assertion that the laboratory break-in had taken place in June.

Mrs. Hudson's expression clouded over. "When we returned that night, we realized that someone had been searching through our rooms, then we heard them in the cellar." She lifted the cover, which rolled up and revealed a desktop with a wide, brown leather writing area set into the wood. Two inkwells were in evidence, and there were several pigeonholes and small drawers of varying sizes stacked up at the back. Mrs. Hudson opened one of the drawers and carefully withdrew a single yellowed envelope, holding it out to her cellar resident. "This was the only letter, sir. Dougy's grandfather showed him where it was kept, but it's never been opened."

He took it with some urgency, but his three-inch fingernails frustrated his efforts to open it. After trying for a moment, he impatiently thrust the envelope my way. I stared at the front of it in some confusion. "It's postmarked London, twenty-six October 1899."

"Yes." He was slightly bemused. "Posted on my birthday, actually. And it would have arrived on these shores shortly *after* I began my hibernation." He gestured impatiently for me to open it. "Do get on with it."

Very carefully, I unsealed the envelope and withdrew the fragile epistle from within. He had moved slowly away from me, around the room, gently touching various items. For the first time I saw a softer, more serene side of him as his long, thin fingers carefully touched the back of an 1890s chair, then a lamp, then the white queen of a marble chess set. It was as though he were greeting old friends of whom he was very fond. He sensed my eyes upon him, looked up, and raised his overgrown eyebrows, indicating for me to read the letter.

I looked at the handwriting on the thin, century-old paper.

The penmanship was graceful, evidence of a more elegant, lettered age than our own. Taking a hesitant breath, I began to read: "'I hope you don't ever again know such despair.'" I glanced up at him, but his face betrayed no emotion, and I resumed my oration, "'If you do, this letter perhaps will help you reach some peace. You always managed before when troubled. You can again. Slumber, rest yourself but also remember H and naturally M send support. Is there anyone in all of America whom you take as friend? Care for yourself.' And it's signed . . . 'My'?"

He smiled. "Mycroft. My brother." Then, for the first time, a tiny crack appeared in his tightly composed veneer as he realized, "My . . . late . . . brother."

His eyes grew distant as he seemed to reflect on the loss of his brother—and of all he had known in the past, if one was to believe his phenomenal tale. Then he snapped back into the moment. "Well! This, of course, explains everything!"

He eagerly rubbed his hands, and his eyes glistened as he came around the velvet tufted chair, sat down in it, and elegantly crossed his legs as though he were wearing formal afternoon clothes instead of tattered, foul-smelling, mummy rags. "The old man with the cane was Henry Moriarty, come to avenge the death of his despicable older brother, James Moriarty, who had died by my hand. It obviously took Henry sixty years, but he had finally tracked down my resting place. Even in his dotage old Henry clearly maintained the keen instincts and thievery skills of a Moriarty, all carefully honed and still razor sharp."

He put his fingertips together in what I would later recognize as one of his characteristic poses when pondering a situation. At this particular moment, however, with those three-inch nails, he reminded me of the Wicked Witch of the West.

"And knowing the evil ties that bind the dark Moriarty family," he went on with relish, "the clubfooted youth was perhaps Henry's grandson or great-grandson. Given his family background, he is not only dishonorable but outright dangerous."

I couldn't help chuckling. I was beginning to think there was more Don Quixote delusional thinking going here than anything else. The don was always able to extemporize and spin out of thin air a new and fabulous "logical explanation" for anything he couldn't understand. Hence windmills became giants until he was knocked to the ground by one of their swinging blades. Then the don would easily explain to his loyal sidekick, Sancho, how the giants had transformed themselves into windmills at the last second to escape his wrath.

I looked again at the letter in my hand, and said with faux-humble apology, "Please forgive my complete stupidity, but I'm mystified how you got any of that from this letter."

The ragged man sniffed and appeared to be talking to himself, rather than answering my question. "I'm rather surprised that Mycroft would've written in such an obvious code, knowing it might've fallen into the hands of the supremely intelligent Moriartys."

I registered that the "supremely intelligent" part was a thinly disguised dig at me. I tried to throw it back at him: "Excuse me, but what 'code' are you talking ab—"

"You really must learn to read between the lines, my dear," he interrupted. "Or in this case," he held up three of those flaky-skinned, taloned fingers, "Read every third word."

What the hell was he talking about? I looked back at the letter and began rereading it as he suggested, just to prove him wrong. "I . . . don't . . . know if this will reach . . . you . . . before you . . . slumber, but . . ." I felt my blood chill—there *was* a code! I forced myself to read on. "But H M is . . . in America . . . take . . . care."

I looked over at Mrs. Hudson, who was as flabbergasted as I. Our tattered friend, however, was invigorated. He leapt up from the chair, weaving a bit as he crossed around behind it, then leaned against the top of it as though at a podium, or perhaps to steady himself. "Well! Mrs. Hudson dispatched old Henry for us with a wine bottle to his cranium. My thanks and congratulations, dear lady. You did the world a great service. But I do have a theory that each person of a new generation becomes the epitome of his family heritage."

Mrs. Hudson swallowed uncomfortably. "Oh sir! From the way you've described the Moriartys, that would make this grandson of his the vilest, the . . . the . . ." She searched for words dark enough. "The most evil, most dangerous of all!"

"Precisely! Isn't it invigorating?" The shaggy man's eyes were positively flashing with enthusiasm. "First, it's absolutely vital that I focus on recovering my stolen identity papers."

"Of course," I agreed emphatically, though tongue-in-cheek, still refusing to wholly buy into all of this. I added, needling, "Oh, and don't forget all your stolen diamonds."

He waved a taloned hand dismissively, saying, "Far less important. Many other diamonds will follow once I am able to show proof of who I am and all my past accomplishments."

"Right," I said, nodding as if going along with his program, "But isn't recovering your ID papers going to be just a tad difficult?"

He laughed. "What most people perceive as *difficult* I can

sort out right away. It's only the *impossible* that can take me a little longer."

With that, he stepped around from behind the chair with such a bounce in his step that it disturbed his center of gravity, making him look like an inebriated man departing a saloon. He pretended to ignore his wavering and said, "Allow me to get cleaned up and more presentable." He strolled toward me and the door, endeavoring to stay in a straight line. "Then we shall resolve the inconvenience of my stolen papers, so I can proceed to tackling more demanding mysteries—such as," he said with an impassioned air, "yesterday's intriguing murder by a phantom tiger!"

Aha! Now I had him! "*Waaaait* a minute! Just stop right there!" I said, forcefully confronting him, completely certain of myself for the first time in hours. "If you've been in a deep freezer in the cellar since 1899, how can you possibly know about that?"

With an imperious twinkle in his eyes he whispered, "It's elementary, my dear . . . Winslow."

From a nearby end table he gracefully lifted a newspaper and placed it into my hands as he breezed on past me and out of the room. It was that morning's edition of the *San Francisco Chronicle*.

The banner headline was

MYSTERIOUS MURDER BY PHANTOM TIGER.

4

An hour later I stood in the mahogany-paneled foyer of Mrs. Hudson's house. In its center was a heavy circular oak table with a Victorian lace tablecloth beneath a round Waterford crystal vase containing some delicate pink and white sweet peas from Mrs. Hudson's gardens. I was pondering the front page of the *San Francisco Chronicle* that, in addition to the phantom tiger headline, included a photo of Lieutenant Ortega. I remembered the news photographer taking it just outside my ER. Even in the grainy black and white, it was easy to see the grief the officer was feeling over the brutal death of his mentor, Detective Donald Keating, whose covered body was lying on a gurney before him.

From up the ornate wooden stairway nearby came the Englishman's voice. "Winslow, are you present?"

"Yes," I spoke loudly so he could hear me, my thoughts returning to the enigma presently upstairs.

He called down, "So, because of the taxations and the various economic crises, the financial arrangements I made for the preservation of this estate are essentially gone?"

"According to Mrs. Hudson, they're completely gone," I called back.

"That is lamentable."

"I was thinking that your Rip Van Winkle hibernation process might perhaps be worth a fortune—but you said your 'key serum' was derived from the Bering Sea blackfish?"

"You are correct. And fascinating little creatures they are."

"They *were*. I just called the San Francisco Aquarium, who told me the blackfish were driven to extinction thirty years ago."

"How unfortunate. And careless." I heard his footsteps starting down the lovely old wooden staircase. "Well, my good friend Charlie Darwin said we were creatures of adaptation. I suppose I shall put his theory to the test."

The configuration of the stairway cut off my view right at the top step, so that the first things I saw were shiny black patent leather shoes. There were dapple-gray spats saddled across them. Then I glimpsed the pants, or in his case they should be more appropriately referred to as trousers. They were also a medium gray, cuffed, slim-fitting, and pleated at his waist, which rapidly became visible to me as he came further down.

Next into view came his black 1890s frock coat, with its long coattails swinging down to his knees as he descended step by step. Beneath that period jacket he wore a stylish silk vest with an understated paisley tapestry pattern in rich shades of burgundy. A gold watchchain with a sovereign attached to it hung in an arc across the lower front of the vest. His white shirt had gold cufflinks, of course, and the traditional Victorian high collar with those two little upward points of stiff material. His wide black tie was on the outside of the collar. I also caught the scent of cedar from the chest where he must have stored these garments.

His right hand was holding his gold pocket watch, which the long fingers of his left hand were adjusting when suddenly his balance seemed to falter again. His left hand clutched the banister as he stopped on the bottom step, and I saw his face. For the first time really.

As a child I'd always been completely confounded and amazed by the metamorphosis of a hairy caterpillar into something strikingly different. But I must say that no previous transformation I had ever witnessed was as thorough as the one now facing me. On the bottom step before me, in place of the macabre, gruesome, malodorous, stained, ragged, drooling— well, you remember. In place of that grotesque creature was the perfect example of what I could only describe as what the magazines of his day would have considered to be "the Compleat English Gentleman."

My God, I thought. He looked like he really could be the fictional Sherlock Holmes. Or a real-life, 1890s Hubert Holmes. (And for your ease of reading, I'll refer to him hereafter merely as Holmes.)

He was just over six feet, but his confident, upright bearing made him seem taller. His black hair was still shoulder-length but now clean and neat. His brows, now trimmed, were equally dark. The scraggly, filthy beard was gone. Vanished was his corpse-like pallor. He was squeaky clean-shaven, so I could better appreciate the strong jawline, which had a prominent squareness that suggested determination. His face was aquiline. He was a bit pale from lack of sun, but his skin was clear and appeared flushed with health. His teeth were straight and now, thankfully, very white.

I guessed his age to be late thirties or early forties. But I was unprepared for just how truly impressive he was. While not matinee-idol handsome like He Who Shall Not Be Named, he was nonetheless a man at whom women would look twice. I found myself a bit dumbstruck. I simply couldn't help it, so extreme was the difference between the fearful, ugly creature I had first encountered and this elegant, decidedly attractive gentleman now before me.

Holmes' left hand was still tightly gripping the banister, and he was blinking heavily, as though trying to clear his vision or his head. Finally, he glanced up, and his gray eyes met my mesmerized blue ones. He had caught me in the act: appraising him.

"What?" he asked, sensing some implied criticism in my gaze. He cocked his head questioningly. "You preferred the beard?"

"Uh . . . no. No," I managed to murmur, trying to get a handle on my confused emotions. "No, this is much . . . better," I stammered, then regained wits enough to express my concern. "But are you feeling okay?"

He blinked twice more as his eyes held mine. I thought I might have detected some curiously connective spark in them, but if so, he strove to dissuade that impression by abruptly looking away. "Yes. Indeed I do. Hale and hardy." I knew he was protesting too much, and he sensed this because he added, "Just reorienting my brain a bit, but otherwise tip-top." Eager to change the subject, he touched the length of his hair, asking, "By any chance, do you know of a barber in the vicinity?"

I was still trying to regain my composure, "What? Oh. No. I mean, I don't think you really need to—"

Mrs. Hudson entered just then, sparing me the embarrassment of feeling a bit like a college sophomore confronting a vastly popular senior quarterback / Rhodes scholar.

"Is this the one, Mr. Holmes?" she asked, indicating the heavy, hundred-year-old-and-then-some valise she was laboring to carry. It was black and rectangular, with thick leather protecting the corners and edges. Holmes' eyes brightened at the sight. He stepped off the final stair, though I noted he did it rather gingerly, as if worried about a misstep.

"Indeed it is! Thank you, Mrs. Hudson," he said, as he slowly crossed the foyer, seemingly reluctant to display any impediment. He bent carefully to help her lift and set it flat on the central, circular table. As he passed me, I caught a whiff of his fresh cologne. The subtle, pleasing lavender fragrance completed his transformation from entombed semi-corpse.

He gazed fondly at the valise. "The contents of this will help us bring the blackguard Moriarty descendant to justice." He was running his fingers around the edges of it, inspecting it for anything out of the ordinary.

"But even if you could find him," Mrs. Hudson asked, "hasn't the statute of limitations run out on the robbery and—"

"Retribution, Mrs. Hudson. That's what I shall have. And justice for the guilty, I should hope. But most importantly, I must regain the documents that attest to my identity."

I found myself still trying to bait him, "What about Scotland Yard? Wouldn't they still have your fingerprints? Copies of the other documents?"

"Precisely what I'd been recalling upstairs. They certainly should," Holmes agreed, "and I intend to wire them posthaste." He turned his head sharply toward me. "If you would kindly direct me to a telegraph—" He'd become suddenly woozy, apparently from his quick head turn. His legs grew rubbery again, and he threatened to collapse.

"*Whoa*," I blurted as Mrs. Hudson and I each took an arm to support him. "Maybe a little inner ear problem there." But he ignored me, brusquely grabbing at the table to steady himself. Also, I thought, trying to prove he could be self-sufficient. I ignored that idea.

"You really need to sit down," I said conclusively.

"No, no, I'm fine, I tell you. Just fine," he insisted with harsh, huffy determination. But I could see by his sudden paleness and eyes trying to focus that his brain was still swimming even as he rationalized, "You try walking around after sleeping one hundred twenty-three years."

As I hung on to his shaky arm, everything that had been churning in my head while waiting for him to "freshen up" came surging back again. In trying to sort out all the freakish elements that had been thrown at me, I knew only one thing for certain: I was in a major quandary. This strange man was most definitely off-balance—likely in more ways than just physically. However, I couldn't remain here in Marin to monitor his behavior. Nor could I leave Mrs. Hudson with that worrisome duty.

With considerable annoyance, I recalled the Chinese proverb which declares that when you save someone's life, you become responsible for them. That was a way bigger step than I wanted to take, but damned if I saw any other immediate alternative.

Reaching for a polite approach that wouldn't exacerbate the situation or ignite his potentially unhinged brain, I said offhandedly, "You know, I think it would be a good idea for you to come back with me into the city so I can try to help you sort things out."

"Very kind to offer." He breathed deeply, still trying to

steady himself. "But I prefer being beholden to no one, particularly not . . ."

A woman! Wow. He couldn't bring himself to say it, but I could see it in his judgmental expression. I immediately rammed my knee into his crotch. Mentally.

I decided to put the offensive remark on hold for now. "I'm sorry," I said, with a deadly smile, as the professional physician taking charge, "but I'm afraid you have no choice." He looked hard at me, which I rebuffed by presenting him with my most steely, mature, and formidable facial expression: *I'm a doctor, pal, so don't mess with my diagnosis.*

Holmes took it in, seemed to be weighing all his other options only to discover he had none. Finally, he sighed and mumbled in Latin, "*In rivo fimi sine remo sum.*"

"Right. You're up the creek without a paddle."

He was clearly surprised that I had understood. It pleased me to see *him* be the one gawking for a change. I grabbed his valise and headed out.

A few moments later I was putting the valise into my Accord when Mrs. Hudson brought out a suitcase of his clothing, which we also stowed in my trunk.

The dear lady looked at me with concern. "Amy, lass." Her hand gently squeezed my arm. "Of course I'm still sorry you're unable to take up my offer about the estate, but my goodness, I feel simply terrible that I got you into this, this—"

"It's alright." I placed my hand atop hers. "You had no idea. You didn't do anything wrong."

"Well, I did kill a man."

Her eyes expressed a painful childlike guilt. I tried to placate her, shrugging slightly as I stammered. "Oh, but that was just—Well, I mean, you know, yes, technically, I guess apparently you did, but that was just because—"

"I didn't intend to. I was desperate to save Dougy."

"Exactly!" I put my arms around her.

She leaned her snowy-white head against my chest, murmuring, "It's haunted me all these years."

"Believe me, I would have done the same thing."

She looked up at me, fighting tears, but hopeful. "Really?"

"Definitely. He was a very evil man who'd broken into your house. With a gun. He was threatening to kill you both. And probably would have. It was self-defense. And you saved your husband. Had sixty more wonderful years together."

She sniffed and wiped a tear. "Aye. That we did, Amy." Her face clouded again. "But what about now? What about the police? What about—"

We both saw Holmes emerging from the front door. He had donned a finely brushed black bowler hat. I grasped Mrs. Hudson by both her tiny shoulders and looked right into her hazel eyes, whispering insistently, "I will deal with him. And I guarantee that you have nothing to worry about. Absolutely nothing at all. Do you hear?"

She pursed her lips, forcing a tight smile. And then managed a tiny nod expressing the deepest, heartfelt gratefulness.

I responded with an earnest, reconfirming nod. But I was already worried that I'd just overpromised and might somehow underdeliver.

Then I watched Holmes make his way carefully down the front walk, seemingly mindful not to exhibit any signs of difficulty. He carried a dusty wooden case of his wine bottles from the cellar. An old violin case rested on top.

He inhaled the clean Marin County air deeply, "*Ahh*. Invigorating. Don't you love it here, Mrs. Hudson?"

She rose to the occasion, saying cheerfully, "Aye, sir. I always have."

There wasn't enough room in my trunk for the wine case and violin, so I put them in the back seat while asking, "What kind of wine is this?"

"*Extreeeeemely* rare vintage." He wiggled a snooty connoisseur eyebrow, then stepped back to inspect my car. "Interesting. Mr. Daimler and Mr. Benz were experimenting with self-propulsion in my day." He sniffed again, this time disapprovingly. "Hmm. Petrol. I'm rather surprised they didn't settle on using electricity instead. Seems that any thinking person would've."

"Yes, it's only taken a hundred years for people to have come around to that idea. This car is actually a hybrid of the two," I said, as I thought ahead to other things he was about to encounter. "You may be disappointed by quite a few developments in the modern age."

"Nonetheless, I'm exhilarated by the prospects. Shall we be off?"

We said our goodbyes to Mrs. Hudson, whom I hugged tightly to confirm all that I had said. As I drove us out, I thought of her sadly having to pack up and leave her longtime home. I deeply regretted my inability to buy the estate, but there was just no way I could manage it. I glanced at the lovely old place as it receded in the rearview mirror, then at the strange man sitting next to me. I had needed to show him how to connect his seatbelt, which he declared an unnecessary encumbrance.

I took the route back through the rich, green country of Mill

Valley and noticed my passenger's eyes darting about, birdlike, as he endeavored to take in as much as possible. As best I could while driving, I tried to keep a keen eye on him. I was still skeptical of his incredible story, though he gave every impression of a man trying to absorb a new world. He also watched carefully how I managed the gas and brake pedals, used the turn signal, and adjusted the inside temperature.

He broke the silence with a question, "Is anyone allowed to just climb aboard and drive?"

"You have to take lessons, then take a test about all the laws and a driving test. Plus have official identification."

"Ah. My initial and most important challenge."

The thought of Holmes at a DMV made me chuckle. "And even if you get that identification, I think it's unlikely they'll give a license to anyone who's a hundred and sixty years old."

"Mmm," he muttered, seeming more interested in the variety of vehicles around us. I watched him scrutinize a cyclist passing on a multispeed off-road bike, wearing tight biking shorts, a colorful tee shirt, goggles, and one of those mirror-shiny helmets. Then he looked ahead from side to side at the greenery surrounding us. "Might we encounter that telegraph office I require along this route?"

"No, we'll send your message to Scotland Yard when we get to my house. We have other, more efficient methods of communication now."

"Indeed you must. I'm most eager to become acquainted with them. It may intrigue you to hear, Winslow, that I made a list a century ago of logical predictions about the future. I'm curious how many will be accurate, and which entirely wrong."

I said, quite truthfully, "I'm curious about that too." There was one item in particular that I couldn't resist pointing out. "You know, society's attitudes toward women have also evolved quite a bit."

"Ah. Your talents have extended beyond the embroidery frame?" He smiled patronizingly. I wasn't sure whether he was merely teasing, but I knew for certain I wasn't going quite fast enough to push him out of the car.

He gave a long look to a passing billboard showing two athletic women climbing a sheer cliff.

"Yes," I emphasized, staying on point. "To get by in the modern world, you'll need to adopt a less condescending attitude."

"Mmm-hmm," he mumbled, as though he'd barely heard me and couldn't care less.

I managed to contain my temper, and after a moment decided to take a different, gentler approach. "It must be difficult to have left your brother behind." I glanced at him to gauge his reaction. I was rewarded only by the faintest flicker crossing his otherwise unconcerned face. I decided to press it, "Were there other loved ones?"

"Certainly not." Holmes chuckled sardonically. "Love is an emotion which I studiously avoid, Winslow, as it tends to bias the logical mind. The disadvantage of emotions in general is that they lead us astray, whereas the advantage of science and clear reasoning is that they are not emotional. Of course, I regret the absence of Mycroft, good old John Watson, and a few other acquaintances, but they are carefully filed and indexed in memory for future reference."

"But don't you feel the loss?"

"No," he said emphatically, with chilly candor. "I agree with Horace Walpole: the world is a tragedy to those who *feel.*" He put a trivializing snicker into that last word. His implication being that any of us who did commit the heinous crime of *feeling* were an inferior life-form roughly on the level of jellyfish. He went on, "Ah, but the world is a comedy to those who *think.*"

Now let's see, I wondered sardonically, *which of us present could be included in that loftier, Olympian category?*

"I prefer to think," he confirmed proudly.

"What a surprise." Just then another car pulled in front of me and slowed down. In my state of annoyance, I was tempted to lean on the horn but restrained myself.

"And most specifically about crime," Holmes continued.

"Because?"

"Because it represents the darkest side of human nature."

"Exactly. I mean, I know it's out there, but I don't like to dwell on it."

He looked at me as though I were a five-year-old. "Your head is in the sand, my dear. If unchecked, evil begets more and greater evil. Such as this new nemesis of mine, this clubfooted descendant of"—there was an unsettling glint of delight in his eyes as he slowly spoke the name—"Moriarty." He seemed to be relishing the challenge.

I shook my head. "Look, don't you think if this man were as terrible as you say, even I would've heard of him?"

"One is rarely aware of the viper until it strikes. But I'll ferret him out. And then focus on this delicious tiger murder!" There was that glint in his eyes again, a look of focus and enjoyment of the chase that I would come to know all too well. "You say the victim was a police officer?"

"Retired. And renowned. For years Detective Keating also

headed the police academy. Lieutenant Ortega told me yesterday morning that—"

"Wait," he interrupted sharply. I could feel his antennae telescoping out as he pronounced Ortega's rank in the British fashion, "*Leftenant Ortega?* Am I to understand that you spoke with the constable mentioned in the newspaper?"

"Yes. He was one of Keating's star graduates. According to Ortega's partner, Lieutenant Civita, they had almost a father-son relationship. Civita told me that Ortega and Keating even enjoyed calling themselves 'blood cousins' because they both had ancestors in the Paiute Nation. Ortega was grief-stricken at the hospital and—"

"So, you have a personal connection to this tiger murder?" When I nodded confirmation, he focused on me with new respect and intensity. "Did you actually attend Keating in hospital?"

I nodded. "Yesterday at dawn. But I couldn't save him." A wave of bleak emotion washed over me as I thought back on it. Perhaps I *was* a lower life-form in Holmes' exalted estimation, but I couldn't help feeling it. I described the horrible extent of Keating's injuries, then said, "Him dying in my care was painful enough, then seeing Luis Ortega's eyes showing his vast sorrow was—"

"Yes, yes," Holmes interrupted, not the least interested in my emotional interlude. "But what details did Ortega share? Tell me precisely."

"All they knew at that time was that a tiger had appeared, attacked Keating, then disappeared without a trace."

He blew out an impatient puff and snapped, "I shall need more data. I can't make bricks without clay. It is a capital mistake to theorize before one has all the evidence. It biases the judgment."

I was suddenly angry at his insensitivity to the pain and regret both Lieutenant Ortega and I had felt. I snapped right back at him, "Well, mister, you're about to run into a mountain range of . . . *data*." I tried to snicker the word *data* as effectively as he had demeaned those of us who *feel*. Then I pointed ahead to a sight I hoped would stop him in his tracks. And to my immense satisfaction it did.

Into his view was coming the southbound approach to the towering Golden Gate Bridge.

For once I was greatly rewarded by seeing his angular jaw drop in amazement. His eyes even widened as he took in the sweeping grace of the giant cables curving up to the top of the two gargantuan 746-foot pillars that provide the support for this magnificent architectural and engineering masterpiece.

My little Accord glided onto the bridge as though we were floating on a magic carpet. The day was perfect with the sky crystal clear. The late-afternoon sun glistened brilliantly off the expanse of the startlingly blue San Francisco Bay to our left, and to our right the expansive Pacific Ocean stretched to the horizon.

Holmes also saw the gigantic, just-commissioned nuclear aircraft carrier *John F. Kennedy* inbound toward the bay, with its attendant fleet following behind in the distance. He blinked as if he'd truly never seen or even imagined ships of such size. Staring at the magnificent supercarrier, he actually stammered, "What are those . . . those winged things atop it? Flying machines?"

"Yes. F-18s. Jet powered. Can fly over a thousand miles an hour. That ship carries a hundred of them inside it."

If the mighty *Kennedy* had amazed him, what he saw next

truly set him back. He looked to the left, across the beautiful bay, to San Francisco. The gleaming, distinctive skyscrapers of the city made him catch his breath. He stared at it in what certainly seemed like abject wonder, breathing through his open mouth.

As we reached the south end of the bridge, he recognized old Fort Point and called it by name. I decided that rather than driving directly to my house, I would take him along Marina Boulevard and around to the Embarcadero. I was curious to keep assessing what his reaction would be to it all, still looking in vain for some crack in his barely credible story. He continued, however, to show the utmost fascination. He smiled at the skyscrapers shining in the golden-hour light, rising above us at the Embarcadero Center, but frowned, as I always do, at the commercialized shopping malls and the graffiti on the walls.

He sniffed and raised a highly critical eyebrow at the more-revealing fashions of the day, taking particular note of two attractive young women rollerblading in cutoffs and sports bras. He continued eyeing their sleek, long legs until we were well past them. Men are men, I guess, no matter what the century.

He was assailed by advertising billboards, crowds, ghetto blasters, homeless people, and a crowd of protesters waving signs at passing cars while crying out, "Support gay rights!" That made him frown with perplexity. "I don't understand. They are demanding the right to be happy?"

I drew a breath to attempt an explanation, but he was already distracted by a landmark on the shoreline ahead. He cut me off with a surprised gasp. "Can that be Pier 7?"

I nodded. "Indeed, it is." It had once been the city's largest. The original had been rebuilt several times. The current, beautifully wood-planked, pedestrian-only pier was considerably narrower than the massive, actively working piers adjacent to it. Only about fifty feet wide, Pier 7 extends out eight hundred feet, like a thin finger pointing across the bay toward Yerba Buena Island and the midpoint of the Bay Bridge.

"It's been considerably diminished," said Holmes, frowning slightly as he surveyed it. "Might we pause here a moment?" He was so intent upon the sight of it that I slowed the car and eased us across the bike lane and onto the long curb cut, stopping with my blinkers on so he might have a longer look. He gestured toward the door handle saying, "Might I step out?"

The passing traffic was very light. "Okay. But not for long." He opened the door, but his exit was annoyingly checked by his seatbelt, which he fumbled with until I snapped it open. I got out and walked around to where he was standing but still subtly trying to maintain his balance.

As he took in the view he also drew in a breath and said with quiet amazement, "This is where I first arrived from England. In 1899 it was six or seven times broader. Down its central portion there"—he indicated straight ahead with a finger—"were large wooden customs offices and storage warehouses for incoming and outgoing freight. Running parallel on both sides of those structures"—he pointed to the right and left—"there were equally wide roadways to service the steamships and the myriad passengers of every class and language embarking or disembarking."

He spoke very convincingly, as though he really had witnessed the scene, but I wanted to dig deeper, to assess all the details. "What did they look like?"

He gazed back down the pier, seemed to be envisioning

it all. "Oh, it was just as one would expect in that year: male passengers wore bowlers or top hats and travel clothes, many in earth tones of brown or green, some in gray or black." He glanced down at his own clothing. "I arrived much as you see me today."

"And the women?"

"Their dresses were more varied in color, full-length to the ankle of course, and tailored to narrow waists in the style of the day. Most ladies wore small complimentary hats."

"Tell me more," I encouraged.

Seeming to focus his memory more sharply, he continued, "The passengers stood out in contrast to the legion of burly stevedores and old salts who were far scruffier in workaday clothes and knitted wool mariner's caps or fiddler's caps. They were busy manfully loading or off-loading the stately vessels that were moored." Then he extended his hand flat out toward the pier, palm downward, and wiggled his outstretched fingers, saying, "And intermixed with the crowds, Winslow, try to picture the dozens of horse-drawn cargo wagons, hansom cabs, or fancy private carriages of the well-to-do and— Ha!"

"What?" His small spontaneous laugh intrigued me.

He chuckled, saying, "I fancied hearing the sounds of the drivers whistling and shouting at their horses, all dodging willy-nilly past one another, traveling on and off the dock. The pier was positively bustling with all that boisterous humanity."

I was somewhat mesmerized and impressed by these vivid descriptions. "It really is like you'd just seen it all yesterday." He was still looking outward as I explained, "Well, for years Pier 7 has only been used as you see it now: for strolling, fishing, contemplating. It's one of my favorite spots to jog. From out there on it, the views of the city and bay are amazing."

He continued gazing out at the long, lovely pier, sparsely peopled just then with a mix of everyday twenty-first-century folks, but he seemed to be pondering his own, apparently well-etched memories of it. His voice grew softer. "The night before I began my long sleep, I took one last walk down this pier, past the tumult of passengers, laborers, horses, maritime activity. I stood quite alone at its far end, Winslow. I recall a slight breeze wafting in, rendering it surprisingly quiet. A three-quarter moon was over the bay, waxing brighter. I took that as a portent of encouragement for the strange— and, I dare say, unique—journey on which I was about to embark."

Half to myself, I whispered an understatement, "Unique, indeed." If true, I thought.

He continued gazing at the pier. "You must remember and truly understand, Winslow, how—*for me*—having awakened this morning, that night I've described was . . . quite literally just *yesterday*."

I stood silently, feeling the weight of that concept, trying to fathom the possibility of it.

Still not looking at me, Holmes inquired, "Jog?"

It took me a beat to come back into the moment. "What? Oh. Jog means to run. At a comfortable pace. For exercise. Aerobic purposes while building muscle."

"Ah." He continued studying the pier while I regarded him.

Finally, I blinked and shook my head at the incomprehensibility of it all as I turned back toward the car. He followed silently and got in. I eased us back onto the Embarcadero and headed home, more perplexed than ever.

Q

The Palace of Fine Arts is a neoclassical Romanesque landmark built in 1914 for the Panama-Pacific International Exposition. It stands just east of the Presidio and just below Marina Boulevard, which runs along the harbor waterfront to the north. The quarter-mile-long, crescent-shaped main building now houses a wonderful museum called the Exploratorium, where kids enjoy hands-on experiences to learn about science. Adjacent to the museum building is one of my favorite structures in the city: the 162-foot-tall domed, open-air rotunda on the banks of the large curved lagoon.

That reflecting pool comes almost up to the sidewalk directly opposite my house. I am blessed with one of the loveliest views in the city. Both the museum and the rotunda are surrounded by a green park with footpaths. Oaks and sycamores provide welcome shade in the summer.

The Palace, its classic rotunda, the lagoon, and the greenery are made all the lovelier in the evening twilight, such as it was when I turned left off Marina onto my street, which runs southward along the east side of the park. Holmes glanced up at the street sign and drew a small breath, considerably struck by it. Speaking in a low, uncharacteristically reverent voice, he said, "I think a certain destiny may be operating here."

Holmes had seen that I live on San Francisco's lovely old Baker Street.

5

Most dwellings in my Baker Street neighborhood are now multi-family apartments or condos. My house, where my late parents had lived, was one of the exceptions. And thank goodness they'd paid it off before their deaths. It was a two-story, single-family house above a ground-floor garage. It had been built in 1909 and lovingly cared for and refurbished several times over the years. It had exterior walls of smooth stucco finished in a soft rose-gray color. The north and south corners had carefully tended ivy climbing toward the third floor on top. Up there was the back bedroom I'd used as a kid as well as the modest master bedroom facing Baker Street, the beautiful Palace, rotunda, and lagoon. The second floor contained my living room with a dining area and kitchen, along with a small back bedroom. On the ground floor, beneath the living room, was a small garage that my father had used as his workspace.

There was a tiny driveway in front, not really long enough to park my car without it extending over the sidewalk, so I always parked on the street. My secondhand Vespa motorbike was kept locked to a plumbing pipe near the stairway that ran up the south side of the house to the covered porch.

When we arrived that evening, the streetlights had just come on and dusk was settling in. Holmes retrieved his well-worn valise and violin case from my car. I set the alarm with my key remote and the car responded with its familiar chirp. I saw Holmes' brow knit and explained, "That means it's locked up tight." He pulled on a door to satisfy himself, then I led him up the fourteen steps to the arched porch and proceeded to unlock my front door.

As we walked in, Lucie, my golden retriever, gave her typical little *woof,* which is more of a greeting than any kind of warning. I love Lucie, and she's a dear companion, but as a watchdog, forget it. I've always felt that if burglars ever came in, she'd woof once and then cheerfully lead them straight to the family silver—what little I have. Seeing me, Lucie panted contentedly and accepted my ritual kiss atop her head. Then she did what truly looked like a double take at the dapper, formally dressed Holmes, forming a skeptical expression that, I swear to God, implied, *Are you serious with this guy?*

"It's okay, Lucie. He's a friend," I said, and she greeted him as such. For his part, Holmes was reserved—obviously not a big animal lover, but he gave her a polite nod.

I noticed that Holmes was surveying my living room with those keen gray eyes of his. My house was brighter inside than Mrs. Hudson's, the walls a warm, pale yellow. The curtains were white and thin. I like light. The electrical fixtures on the wall had replaced their gas predecessors ages before I began living there but maintained the early San Francisco look. Out of necessity, my furniture was eclectic. Some of it was still my parents' furnishings, mostly cheery florals, with soft cushions. I have a lot of plants, which I talk to encouragingly as I water them.

"I haven't had the money to fix the place up much," I apologized. "And it's probably kind of sparse for your 1890s taste."

"A bit perhaps, but nonetheless quite revealing," he said, lightly rubbing his hands together while still scanning the room.

"Really?" My voice had a slight edge as I asked, "And what exactly can you tell me?"

"Oh, perhaps not that much." He shrugged. "After all, there have surely been changes in styles and fashions over the years which may affect, ever so slightly, my deductions."

I welcomed the opportunity of putting him to a serious test, so I gestured expansively toward the living room, saying, "Oh, pray, proceed."

"Well, first off, I should say you are the daughter of a passionate sculptor."

I blinked. He'd grabbed my attention. Then, while generally looking in my direction, he meandered back and forth across the room in front of me, like a lawyer presenting his summation to a jury. "You, however, followed your mother's example and swung toward the rigorous discipline of medicine, taking your degree at Mr. Stanford's University." He paused an instant, then said, "I extend my condolences about your parents' decease."

I drew a little surprised breath.

Then he continued, "In addition to your knowledge of Latin, you speak French and Spanish. You are highly intelligent and have an excellent bedside manner with children—who are the specialty of your medical practice."

Now I was surprised, but Holmes was just getting warmed up.

"You are affiliated with the Saint Francis Memorial Hospital at 900 Hyde Street," he went on while sometimes glancing downward or thoughtfully upward as though pulling his deductions out of thin air like a magician materializing a bouquet. "You have strong opinions but prefer to work through quieter, more circuitous avenues." I felt my jaw slackening, but clamped my mouth shut.

"Despite some lingering interest in unusual scientific experimentation here at home, it's obvious that you're not entirely consumed by doctoring any longer." He glanced directly at me, saying, "You are endeavoring to write a work of historical fiction, but are experiencing much frustration in your efforts, and thus far you are unpublished in that arena."

My perplexity was growing. I perched on the couch's round arm as he did a slow three-sixty while saying, "You enjoy wagering on sports." He came back around with his fingertips pressed together in front of him. "Despite your conservative appearance, you harbor a deep romanticism and a desire for adventure"—he spoke that word with a beguiling twinkle in his eyes—"in spite of the recent injury it's brought you."

He drew a breath. "You are intrigued by the bizarre, and—" Here he stiffened, clasped his hands behind him, and glanced away from me with some embarrassment and considerable distaste. "And apparently," he finally managed to say, "you find humor in the male . . . sexual organ."

My jaw dropped open. But then I clenched it—this time, because something was dawning on me and I was beginning to get angry. He paid no mind and steamed ahead, using his hands to shape or emphasize some words. "On holiday, you prefer exotic, tropical locales, particularly Panama, if I'm not much mistaken." Then he looked directly at me with his brow lowered and a darkly knowing gleam in his eye. "You sometimes require a heartier stimulant than tea or coffee, not unlike myself, although you prefer to inhale *your* cocaine, rather than injecting a solution as I do."

Unaware that I was beginning to fume, he proceeded with clinical coolness. "I also know without question that you are," he said with syrupy sarcasm, "*overly sentimental.*" A quality he obviously abhorred. He continued breezily: "And that you had a gray, short-haired, female cat named Twinkie, now deceased."

I gritted my teeth, jamming my right fist hard on my hip. Lucie glanced up, knowing that move signaled a storm about to break.

"Ah, but I also know you have excellent resiliency, Winslow. Granted, you did have a childish temper tantrum when your husband very recently abandoned you." My eyes went wide. "But," he continued pleasantly, "you've taken positive actions to create a new life without that man who has long blond hair, fancies himself a painter, and whose name is—"

"*Don't say it!*" I shouted, but he did.

"—Max."

I screeched with an explosive, furious, caustic-ironic laugh as I leapt to my feet! The *furious* laugh was at myself—because I'd sworn to never hear that damnable name again.

The *caustic-ironic* part was also at myself—because by saying that hated name, this Brit had triggered a light-bulb moment: in a flash I suddenly understood exactly what was going on! What I should've guessed all along. The truth! My rage was roiling because I realized that the devilish man he'd just named—my own personal "archnemesis"—*had obviously orchestrated this whole ridiculous, unbelievable circus and*— I started spewing out a string of vile expletives that startled the Englishman and were incoherent even to me until—abruptly—I sucked it up. Locked it in tight.

I stood unmoving. Turned to stone. At last, I allowed myself to slowly whisper, "How could I have been"—I scrunched my eyes closed as I shouted, full voice—"SO INCREDIBLY STUPID!"

"Winslow?" the bemused Britisher asked calmly, "Whatever in the world are you—"

"*Stop!*" My hands shot out with palms facing him. I glared at him. "Just. Stop. And you can drop that oh so *veddy, veddy propah* over-the-top accent, okay? I get it now: the whole scam. Clear as a bell." Now, I was the one pacing, thinking it through, grumbling about my despised ex. "I've heard that bastard brag about the elaborate practical jokes he'd played on people. Some funny, some shameful." I nodded because all the pieces were fitting. "And I sure know how badly he wanted to get back at me, to really stick it to me." I chuckled bitterly. "Well, I have to give him credit—this one was a *doozy!*"

"Doctor, I'd very much appreciate it if—"

I was deaf to him, off in my own world, still adding it all up. "He must've dipped deep into his damn trust fund to engineer this theatrical hoax." I shook my head at my blind naiveté, rambling, "I can absolutely picture that despicable rat and his gleeful cronies setting up that Frankenstein cellar, rigging the vapors rising, the freaky makeup, the letter in code from the 'poor dead brother' and—" That brought a sideways thought. My eyes narrowed. "I certainly hope he paid old Mrs. Hudson a bloody *fortune* to come out of retirement. To get back on stage again, lure me in, send me down into that cellar so I could 'accidentally' discover your funhouse!"

For a nanosecond I thought of her sweet old face and muttered to myself with honest respect, "And wow. She was really convincing."

Then I turned sharply on the "Englishman," saying with a smirk, "But where did he dig *you* up?" Suddenly I knew: "Probably down at the Improv, huh? Pretty good performance. You really studied your part. Completely sucked me into the possibility of—" The anger suddenly surged volcanically back up, and I went wild-eyed as I shouted-laughed, furiously shaking my fists at the ceiling. "God! How could I have been so *gullible* as to fall for the whole 'asleep for over a century' routine?"

"My dear woman," the Brit said patiently, quietly amused, "why on earth would you make such an unfounded supposition?"

"Why?" I turned on him, shouting, "WHY?" Then I began my frontal assault. "Because with the exception of a few obvious errors, everything you said about me was absolutely dead on! And there's no way you could possibly have known it all without being told!"

"Errors?" His eyebrows arched in curious disbelief. "What sort of 'errors' are you—"

"Oh, will you please drop all the Sherlock-Hubert crap. The show's over, pal. Now get the hell out of my house!" I pointed dramatically toward the door.

He remained unruffled, saying with smug, patronizing assurance, "But you have left out the critical fact—the one that is *obviously* the most important, because it undermines your entire hypothesis."

"I haven't left out anything. Now go."

"Yes, you have," he insisted emphatically. "The fact that you, *Doc*-tor, pronounced me *dead*—from an adrenaline overdose."

"Well, *obviously*"—I glared—"I was *wrong*! Now move it, mister."

Still entirely cool, he drew himself up imperiously. "Madam, if you'll kindly quell your feminine hysteria for one brief moment—"

I saw red and snarled at him with focused vitriol. "This is *nonsexist* hysteria, *goddammit*!" And with that, I grabbed his funky old violin case and bowler hat, pushed them against his paisley silk vest, and pressured him backward across the small foyer toward the door, which I flung open.

As I herded him out onto porch, he was still insisting, "I assure you, Winslow, that this person named—"

"*Don't say it!*" I snapped with deadly menace, fist raised, ready to stop his clock.

"This . . . person of whom you speak . . . is entirely unknown to me. And I never even imagined your existence until I awoke today. Everything I just deduced is perfectly obvious to the trained, observant eye and—"

"Well, you can take your 'trained, observant eye' and stick it up your pseudo-Victorian *arse*!" I thrust the violin case into his hands and slammed the door in his face.

I stood inside, quaking with seismic anger. After stomping into the living room, I pulled out my cell phone and hotly punched in the cursed number that I had kicked out of my speed-dial contacts.

I saw sweet Lucie looking out mournfully through the thin drape on the narrow window of my front door frame at the performance artist who remained standing on my porch. Lucie glanced at me with her woeful hound eyes, seeming to plead his case.

"Forget it, Lucie. Don't go there. Don't make me try to explain *charlatan* to you." I heard a knock at the front door and that British voice saying something unintelligible outside. But just at that moment my call was answered by an outgoing message from that oh-so-velvety-smooth, smoky baritone voice I now detested, and I blasted it.

"Hello, *you, you*—" I barely held back all the blistering, profanities I could have branded him with. "Well, you know exactly what the hell you are—and you're damn right I'll leave a message for you! How dare you drag that sweet old Mrs. Hudson into such a warped, nasty, lowlife scam!"

I smacked the phone off and stormed upstairs toward my bedroom, where I kept my emergency stash of See's chocolates.

6

It wasn't until later that I learned exactly what transpired after my furious outburst and my expulsion of the man in question, but having now researched it thoroughly, I can recount it to you.

In point of fact, there were several occasions during this adventure when I was not actually present with Holmes in the midst of a situation. In such instances, he later provided all the details, or I pried them out of him.

In addition to having Holmes' meticulous accounts to guide me, I've interviewed in depth most of the involved parties, whom you're about to meet, regarding the specifics they witnessed. By cross-referencing those with my debriefings of Holmes, it became clear to me that he had not editorialized his recollections and had essentially stuck to the truth. The result is that I have collected all the considerable facts. The only embellishments I've allowed myself are a few small touches that I know to be consistent with Holmes' character and behavior from my personal involvement with him. I'll endeavor to present it all to you in a straightforward, linear fashion, which will hopefully keep the narrative flowing more smoothly.

Now back to the matter at hand. After I slammed the door on him, here's what happened:

Holmes stood on the porch a moment, looking back in at Lucie. He was left quite off-balance by my seething eruption. He knocked on the door and said loudly, "I am not seeking reentry, Winslow, but it is absolutely vital that we get that inquiry sent off to Scotland Yard."

Getting no response, he shouted, "Winslow?" but still heard nothing in response. Frustrated, he raised his hand to knock again on the door, then stopped himself—he had too much pride. He saw that Lucie was still offering her sympathy through the narrow vertical window beside the door, but he stiffly refused it. He squared his shoulders, turned, walked down the steps, angrily muttering, "Ridiculous!" Then he crossed the sidewalk to my Accord.

Night had fallen some time earlier, but when Holmes peered through the car's back window, he could see his dusty case of wine resting on the back seat. He tried the car door, but it was locked. He was not about to come back and ask me to open it. Instead, he uttered an angry puff of irritation, then looked around and spotted a bench across the street in the Palace of Fine Arts Park opposite my residence. A punked-out kid with green, spiked hair and a nose ring lumbered past him. Holmes sniffed to himself, "Herbert Wells was prophetic: the Martians *have* landed."

Penniless, friendless, but nevertheless the absolute master of himself, he walked toward the wooden bench, behind which reflections of streetlamps glittered on the surface of the rotunda's placid lagoon. Facing his destitution with much more than merely the traditional British stiff upper lip, Holmes' self-confidence was extreme. His possession of unique and extraordinary skills set him apart from his fellow *Homo sapiens*. This made him feel superior to just about all of them.

Except perhaps one. Even in his own thoughts he referred to that person merely as "the Woman." She was like a saucy gadfly who flitted up occasionally from his subconscious. She had been cocksure of her own abilities and more than a match for him. Over a hundred years later, he still found the memory of her deeply unsettling. I would learn much more about this intriguing lady, but not for a while.

Holmes sat on the bench in the dark park, and despite the curious glances that his Victorian attire attracted from several passersby, he assumed the confident attitude of a neighborhood regular. He had found his briar pipe and matches in his frock coat's inner pocket along with a bit of his favorite black shag tobacco. Being over a century old, it was stale, but to him it was very pleasant. The blue smoke curled slowly upward into the lamplit darkness.

It was his first moment of actual solitude since awakening. He leaned back, spread his left arm out along the top of the bench, and began processing this new world he'd crossed over into. London and all his experiences in the past seemed like a dream to him now, though not in merely a will-o'-the-wisp fashion. Not simply fleeting images, instead it was a long dream, richly, intricately detailed, day by day, night by night, for forty-one years. Here was his childhood, his brother, his education, insights, humor he'd enjoyed, tragedies he'd endured, plus dangers, adventures, a great many successes, and yes, he admitted to himself, an occasional minor failure. The Woman's beautiful visage flitted through his brain again, gazing deeply into his eyes with a puckish twinkle in her own violet ones.

Surely, he knew, even she would have been appropriately impressed with his crowning achievement: traveling forward through time to sit on a bench in twenty-first-century San Francisco. He smiled to himself, thinking how intrigued and envious H. G. Wells also would have been. Holmes thought back on that autumnal evening in 1898 when Wells had joined Watson, Doyle, and himself in the sumptuous, gaslit Hotel Connaught dining room.

Wells was thirty-two, yet when wearing a dark, high-collared sweater and white shirt but no tie, as he did that night, he still had the youthful air of a recent Oxford graduate. Fine-featured, with sandy-brown hair and eyebrows set widely apart above his light eyes and crescent mustache, he had a boyish lick slanting across his smooth forehead, which Holmes had noted attracted the attention of several young women Wells passed when crossing the dining room. His smile was warm as he gripped Holmes' hand. Wells expressed delight at meeting him and Watson, being well acquainted with, and a fan of, Doyle's chronicling of their casework.

And now—thanks to Wells' mention of his time-machine novel on that inspiring evening—here was Holmes, in a stimulating new future full of mysteries to unravel.

He inhaled deeply. He'd immediately noticed how much clearer the air was than it had been in the midst of England's coal-fired industrial revolution. He scraped a toe of his black patent leather shoe across the sidewalk and noted there was not a bit of soot on the streets as there often was in his London. He had also noted the total absence of horse manure, which had been so ubiquitous in the city streets of his era. There were the familiar sounds of crickets and distant boat whistles from the nearby bay, but he was also cataloging new and unanticipated sounds. He heard a rhythmic *boom boom boom* growing ever louder as a dented, rusted automobile approached and cruised past with what sounded to Holmes like nothing less than a dozen bass drums pounding in unison. That booming was accompanied by a man's voice shouting a patter of poorly rhyming words so fast as to be unintelligible.

Soon afterward, he heard a similar but much louder *whump whump whump* that seemed to come from overhead. Looking up, he saw an automobile-sized vehicle several hundred feet in the night air suspended beneath a single huge propeller carrying it forward. Holmes smiled, thinking, *Of course!* He comprehended immediately how the craft had evolved from ideas he'd seen in seventeenth-century sketches by Leonardo da Vinci. He also noted the much smaller vertical rotor on the tail, recognizing it as a necessity to prevent the craft from counterrotating. Holmes was delighted by how the airborne vehicle had been logically conceived and realized.

For almost two hours he sat observing passersby with fascination and accumulating a myriad of fantastic novel aspects of this modern world. He paused to recollect the remarkable events of this first day, and then his thoughts drifted back to his final evening in 1899.

He'd quadruple-checked the elaborate equipment he'd fashioned in his secret laboratory. Before proceeding as planned, he paused one last time to reconsider his entire theory. His agile mind went back over every minute detail in his research, including the thorough experimentation he had undertaken, in which seven rats had been put through the complete process. All had survived in suspended animation for over a month; they sailed through with flying colors and were revived as healthy as ever. Except one. And upon performing an autopsy on that notable exception, Holmes discovered it had an abnormally enlarged heart, to which he attributed the failure. Satisfied with his success, he took his remaining rodent colleagues out into the gardens and happily set them free. His experiments had removed any doubt that his life-extending process was well within the margins of safety and had a high probability of success.

After returning from his walk on Pier 7 that final evening in the nineteenth century, he went into the estate's sitting room, put a favorite cylinder on Mr. Edison's marvelous new phonographic invention, and listened to the scratchy music emerging through the large horn. He thought his selection was most appropriate for that special night. He slowly breathed in, appreciating and absorbing the strains of Johann Sebastian Bach's *Jesu, Joy of Man's Desiring.*

Afterward he went to the upstairs bedroom and exchanged his clothes for a simple, ankle-length sleeping gown. He used a roll of gauze to wrap his right leg like a mummy from toe to knee and did the same on his left. Finally, he donned a pair of soft slippers.

Returning to his cellar laboratory, Holmes carefully and securely closed the thick secret door. He used a small stool at the head of the sarcophagus to step up and into it. After inserting intravenous needles into his femoral arteries and veins, he set the preservation process in motion. He administered a final large dose of cocaine into his arm and settled into the copper chamber.

Last of all, he activated the mechanism that slowly lowered the heavy lid just as he felt himself slipping into the darkness.

Sitting on the nighttime park bench in twenty-first-century San Francisco, Holmes cocked an eyebrow, feeling inflated with pride. He'd always been impressed by himself, but this achievement surpassed even his most intoxicating experiences with opiates and intravenous cocaine.

He drew a thoughtful breath, set his violin case on the bench beside him, and opened it. He carefully took out his beautiful Stradivarius, smiling slightly at his dear old friend. He plucked the strings, adjusted the tuning, and eased it onto his shoulder. He held the violin in place with his chin as he rubbed a bit of rosin on the catgut of the bow. Then he softly put the bow to the violin and began playing a plaintive Puccini melody.

Later, I remembered hearing it faintly inside my Baker Street bedroom, but at the time I didn't realize that it was him.

Violin-playing soothed Holmes. He closed his eyes as his bow smoothly drew out the beautiful melody.

After a few moments he sensed someone approaching, and while still playing, Holmes opened one eye to espy a scruffy seventyish fellow. The man wore clothing that was secondhand but clean and a crush cap. A threadbare bedroll and apparently all else he owned was slung over his back. In his left hand he carried what looked to Holmes like a battered black cigarette case emanating pictures and a woman's voice. The old gent had in fact been viewing the evening newscast on his cell phone but paused as he drew nearer to Holmes playing the violin.

A smile warmed his kindly, weathered face. He sighed. "How I love *La Bohème*."

Holmes glanced up at him and nodded pleasantly. The

septuagenarian settled on the other end of the bench, caught up in the melody and even humming along as a nicely dressed friendly-faced woman in her fifties passed. She leaned down to drop a few coins into the open violin case. Holmes paid no attention. He brought the musical piece he was playing to a gentle melancholy conclusion.

His ragtag benchmate nodded his approval. "Pretty nice interpretation." Then he gestured toward the coins in the violin case. "You must do okay busking, huh?"

"I've never conscientiously endeavored."

"You'd do great. I heard a lotta would-be musicians out here on these streets. Most of it's just plain dog shit. But you got real talent. That vintage outfit you got on is also a smart eye-catcher. If I was you, I'd try down in the financial district, along Battery or Davis. You get a better-quality audience down there. They'll appreciate the classics."

"Thanks for your advice, Mr. . . . ?"

"Lefty." He extended a clean hand in greeting.

Holmes nodded and took the offered hand. "Holmes."

"Ah, like the old detective."

"Yes," Holmes chuckled. "Precisely like that."

"I loved them stories," Lefty said as he firmly gripped Holmes' hand.

Holmes nodded politely. "I found some rather too melodramatic for my taste."

"Well, I thought they were great. Loved all the Sherlock movies too," Lefty said smiling.

Holmes inclined his head in curiosity. "Movies?"

"Yeah. Them old films they made about him back in the '40s are still my faves. But there's been a bunch since then."

"Films?" Holmes was trying to coax out the meaning without sounding uninformed or daft.

"Yeah, you can still catch 'em on TCM or streaming. I even watch 'em on here sometimes," Lefty said, referencing his cell phone. "But it's always better to see 'em in a theater."

It was beginning to dawn on Holmes what Lefty might be talking about, and he said, "I saw some moving picture films in 1897." Lefty glanced curiously at Holmes, who quickly clarified, "That is, which had been *made* in 1897 by a Frenchman named Georges Méliès and also the Lumière brothers."

"Can't say I caught any of their movies. Were they about Sherlock?"

"I shall have to investigate that." Holmes changed course and ventured, "But tell me, sir, isn't Lefty an odd name for someone who's right-handed?"

Lefty chuckled. "It comes from my political sympathies. But how'd you know I'uz a righty?"

"Oh, I once wrote a trifling monograph on the subject." Holmes was carefully adjusting a string on his violin. "I was able to illustrate how seventy-four different occupations could be deduced from the observation of hands. I also analyzed the specific detection of dominance by scrutiny of size, muscle, calluses—that sort of thing."

"Oh, yeah?" Lefty's eyes narrowed as he decided to test Holmes. "So, what's my line?"

"Mariner." Holmes stated, without a moment's hesitation.

Lefty blinked, amazed, "Y'could tell that from m'hands?"

"And from the fine lines around your eyes that sailors get from squinting on a bright sea. Also, the corner of a tattoo visible on the back of your wrist, which I take to be an anchor."

Lefty nodded and turned his hand over to reveal the entire design of the anchor.

Lefty appeared fascinated by Holmes' observational powers. But Holmes was even more intrigued by the cell phone in Lefty's hand.

The tiny video screen was at that moment carrying a picture of police at a crime scene. Holmes leaned tentatively toward the small screen. "Do you mind? May I?"

Lefty generously offered it up. "Sure, turn up the volume there."

Holmes looked at Lefty curiously, unfamiliar with that use of the word. "Volume is . . . ?"

Lefty looked at this odd character curiously for a beat. "It's, y'know, the sound? Here." Lefty adjusted it louder.

Holmes was intrigued by the moving picture visible on the tiny color screen—and by the police who were shown. Several were milling on the broad terrace outside the four-story glass entrance of a modern, museum-like building. On an equally tall red monolithic sign in the foreground Holmes could barely read California Academy of Sciences.

A voice coming from the small video device was saying, "And another bizarre death was reported tonight at San Francisco's Steinhart Aquarium here in Golden Gate Park."

Holmes watched as the tiny cell screen displayed video of a chubby, middle-aged man in a security guard uniform, sitting on the back of a fire engine and being attended to by paramedics. The newscaster continued, "Night watchman Tom Walsmith had apparently been drugged. When he awoke an hour later in his office, he immediately went through the aquarium to investigate."

The broadcast next showed the view from a handheld camera inside the museum, moving among the tanks of octopuses, eels, and other aquatic animals. "Walsmith was unprepared for what he discovered, however . . ."

Holmes watched as the night watchman pointed out to police a specific tank in the aquarium that was about four times the size of a bathtub. Around it was yellow police tape and gathered members of the coroner's office.

"In one tank," the newscaster dramatically intoned, "thickly clouded by blood, was all that remained of a woman's body." The screen displayed a momentary glimpse of a shredded, bloody hand floating inside the tank before a police officer pushed away the inquiring camera. "A woman's body had been partly chewed to pieces . . ."

Holmes' thin nostrils flared, as though catching the scent of something important. He watched and listened even more intently as the newscaster continued, "This tank contained vicious, voracious piranha."

Holmes' head snapped back and an eyebrow raised sharply as something fell into place for him and he repeated, "Piranha!"

Lefty noticed his strong reaction and intently watched Holmes, who remained keenly focused on the cell screen showing Lieutenants Bernie Civita and Luis Ortega standing out in front of the aquarium building, surrounded by other press people.

Clearly fighting off grief, Ortega spoke to an off-camera reporter, "Yes, the coroner's initial assessment is . . ." He swallowed painfully. "There were signs that she'd struggled against her attackers at some other location, where she suffered a skull fracture, and—" Ortega's voice broke slightly.

Civita stepped forward and continued. "The victim's body was brought here and dumped into the piranha tank. The victim has been identified." Holmes noted that Ortega's pain seemed to intensify as Civita said, "Her name is Louisa Chang. She was a judge, as well as a criminology professor at San Francisco State. Many of us on the force had been her students."

Lieutenant Civita exchanged a pained personal glance with Ortega as another nosy reporter jabbed a microphone at the silent officer, saying, "Lieutenant Ortega, this is the second extremely unconventional murder in two days. Do you feel this crime is connected to Donald Keating's death by the tiger?"

Ortega spoke quietly. "It's too early to tell. Both victims were related to the police department. Both were brutally attacked by animals. We will update you when we know more."

Lefty saw Holmes draw in his chin with surprise, as he muttered, "Oh come, come, Leftenant Ortega. Surely you realize there are at least two more connections than that. It's so obvious." Holmes' voice hissed as though he wished Ortega could hear him and take note. "It was right there in front of you!"

Lefty leaned closer to the screen, completely baffled. "What is?"

Holmes didn't answer, but rather looked up with newfound vigor. "This city really does have need of my services."

Lefty grew a little wary. "Uh . . . you a cop?"

"No." Holmes sniffed. "Merely a student of crime." He took a long look at Lefty, having a sudden idea and nothing to lose by taking a wild shot. "Tell me, Lefty, did you ever happen to know an incredibly evil, clubfooted man?"

Lefty drew a startled breath. Holmes saw the old man's eyes

go wide and his face turn pale as a ghost's. A shiver ran down Lefty's spine as he sputtered, "Oh, Jesus save me! Yes! I did!"

"You did?" Holmes was astonished at his luck. And instantly attentive.

"Aye," said Lefty, his frightened eyes riveted on Holmes. "Kill ya soon as look at ya!"

"Yes, yes! Do go on, old boy!" Holmes was greatly enthused.

"I seen him stab a friend of mine in the back—and twist the damn knife! Splayed him wide open. And it wasn't the first time he got away with murder. Threatened me too. And lotsa other guys I knew."

Holmes was sharp-focused. "Tell me more about him."

"Big Chinese guy, he was."

Holmes sagged.

But Lefty steamed right on, "Everybody on our crew hated him." Then with a wink and a meaningful look that implied a bit of foul play by his shipmates, he added, "One night when we were down under, off Nuku Hiva in the Marquesas, the bastard got accidentally swept overboard—if you get my drift."

Holmes nodded, indeed understanding, but was frustrated that Lefty hadn't known the specific clubfooted man he sought. Then he tried another approach. "Did you ever come across an evildoer named Moriarty?"

Lefty shook his head. "Just in them old Sherlock movies. Otherwise it don't ring a bell. Sorry," Lefty then nodded toward the violin. "You really kick ass with Puccini. Know any Waylon Jennings?"

Holmes put the violin to his chin, "No, but if you hum a few bars . . ."

Lefty began singing a rasping, throaty rendition of a song: "Mommas, don't let your babies grow up to be cowboys."

Holmes grinned. "Ah, a country waltz!" He picked up the melody and played along with sprightly ease. "How jolly."

Lefty was delighted, "That's it! Y'got it, brother!"

Even as Holmes continued his rather brilliant violin accompaniment, his mind was elsewhere. He was analyzing the intriguing information he'd just received about the murder.

He was thinking that it must be a clever fiend indeed who would incorporate the use of horrific needle-toothed piranha into such an evil, serial-murder plot.

7

By midnight, I'd changed into my very faded Greenpeace tee and gone to my kitchen for a carrot, which got overruled by a warm oatmeal raisin cookie. My enjoyment of this was interrupted when my cell rang, labeling it "Potential Spam." It had to be You Know Who returning my irate call.

As I stared at that spam warning, I pictured him in that old greenhouse off Fillmore that was his artist's loft. He was wearing one of the paint-spattered tight tank tops that flattered his fullback shoulders and quarterback waist. I pictured that clever leading-man's face and those soft, dark eyes, those full, dangerous lips, envisioning him standing in front of a half-done canvas, pouring two glasses of our favorite Mondavi Reserve merlot. But instead of me, a voluptuous redhead stood nearby, her long curls cascading down over her tacky black Frederick's of Hollywood teddy, which barely concealed her more-than-ample breasts, the cleavage of which she had just highlighted with whipped cream from a can in her hand. It was all too easy to imagine.

Because that's exactly the scene I had stumbled into a week before.

So, standing in my kitchen, I answered his call with a blistering hello, skipped over last week's infuriating *in flagrante* debacle, and cut right to the chase: I wanted him to confirm his disgusting complicity in the outrage I'd endured today. I really uncorked on him, ripping into him like a chainsaw for two minutes straight until I took a deep breath to go on and he managed to jump in.

"Amy, Amy, Amy will you calm down and listen?" He was pleading over the phone. "I have no idea what you're talking about!"

I slammed my hand on my kitchen counter. "Don't do this to me, goddammit!"

"I'm not doing anything, Ame! Really. I didn't do any of that wacky stuff! I did nothing. I'm *doing* nothing! Except—" His deep voice turned softer, more vulnerable. "Except missing you."

No way would I get sucked in. "Oh, yeah. Right. You've probably got some candy in your hand right now."

"That's not fair, Amy," he murmured, sounding hurt. "I told you last week it wasn't what you thought. She was just a model I was using to work out a new concept for a—"

"Don't start with that," I snapped. "Just tell me the truth about today!"

"I swear to God, Amy, I don't know any Mrs. Hudson or anything about the crazy story you just told me. Honest."

"Coming from you, that's not a reliable word."

"But it's true. I had nothing to do with any of what you said happened to you today."

He sounded unusually sincere, even contrite. Like a shamed

little boy. His voice was almost a whisper as he said, "And listen—I miss you so much. Can't sleep. I've been thinking about you every second. I promise that—"

"I'm hanging up now."

"Amy, wait! Please just . . ."

I listened for a second with annoyance to what sounded like his anguished breathing. I was about to click off, when I heard another sound. Even over the phone, it was unmistakable: it was the distinctive sound of an aerosol can applying whipped cream onto something.

I flared up and laughed angrily. "Never gonna happen. You've been *busted*!" Suddenly envisioning his voluptuous model, I chuckled at my unintentional pun. "And I can hear you're about to be again. Go enjoy your banana split! We are *done*."

I clicked off, then banged the counter again, hurting my fist. I gritted my teeth. As much as I just wanted to go firebomb his studio, I made myself stop and examine the important aspects of the call more carefully.

Personal bullshit aside—and there was plenty of it—he had nonetheless seemed genuinely confused and baffled when I confronted him about my Mrs. Hudson adventure. Maybe he wasn't lying—about that, anyway.

I walked into the living room frowning, my brain twisting in turmoil, my eyes flitting around distractedly, searching for some kind of tangible answer. I found myself looking at the old valise that the Brit had brought in with him.

I walked slowly over to it and, for the first time, examined it carefully. It had seen much use. I lifted it and set it onto the couch. The black leather covering the surface was battered and scratched and cracked from years of wear and tear. There were two light brown straps that encompassed it and buckled in the front. They were as weathered as the rest of the case. I sat beside it and undid the buckles, then eased up the lid.

A musty aroma arose from inside it. Everything within the case was from a time long past. Fastened to the underside of the lid, facing me when it opened, were half a dozen false mustaches, sideburns, and two beards. Stuffed into a special compartment within the lid were four wigs of varying colors and lengths. Like all the hairpieces, the wigs were professionally and finely woven. I was sure that if properly applied by someone skilled in the art of theatrical makeup, they would be completely convincing.

There were seven different styles of eyeglasses, most of them the thin wire frames so popular in the Victorian era.

There was a beautiful antique brass microscope and a compass. There were several pipes, including one made of black clay and another of cherrywood. There was a small leather pouch with tiny tools, almost like you'd see in a dentist's office. It occurred to me that they might be for picking locks. There was a pistol: a classic nineteenth-century revolver. It was loaded. I carefully extracted the cartridges and put them in the back of a nearby drawer.

What startled me the most was within a small, finely tooled wooden picture frame displaying a fading Victorian photograph of a striking woman.

She wore a lace blouse and a dramatic hat with a lengthy feather in it. Her dark hair was drawn back, but a long serpentine wave of it came around her from behind and down in front of her right shoulder. This woman seemed to gaze right into my eyes. Her enigmatic expression made her appear much like a real Mona Lisa. The light in her eyes conveyed a strong spirit. Perhaps it was my romantic nature, but I had the distinct notion that she and I could have been cut from the same cloth and would've liked each other if we'd had the opportunity to meet. I looked into her eyes and wondered who she was. What secrets did she keep behind those intelligent, entrancing eyes? And what had she meant to this man who carried her picture?

Continuing my investigation of the valise, I lifted a Moroccan leather pouch, which could be opened like a small book. The wear on it showed that it had been opened and closed hundreds of times. Inside was a surprise: an 1890-vintage hypodermic syringe, several needles, and a stoppered vial of honey-colored liquid.

I took out the vial and held it up to the light. I had only seen it in this liquid form once before, but I recognized it as cocaine. I was pondering it, when the trill of my cell phone made me jump.

I saw that the caller was Mrs. Hudson. I took a breath, then quietly answered. She said, "Dr. Winslow? Is that you, dear?"

"Yes," I said warily, still unsure about her role in this bizarre drama.

"I called to apologize."

What? Was she going to *admit* having done something nefarious? Being part of a hoax?

Her Scottish voice continued, "I should have told you about that old laboratory from the beginning, lass, but I was so frightened by what had happened in there all those years ago."

She sounded completely sincere and penitent, but still, I had to know for certain. "Mrs. Hudson, I'm sorry, but this is very important to me: have you told me the absolute truth now? About that man in your cellar? Told me the *whole truth* about everything?"

"Why yes, Amy, I have. What do you mean?"

"Please forgive me"—this was really tough—"but would you be able to *swear* to everything you said in a court of law?"

The lady paused an instant, likely considering the consequences she might face, then she said firmly, "I would, Amy." And added, "I'd swear to it on my Dougy's grave."

Whoa. Her response had been so thoroughly heartfelt that I released a huge sigh. But then my throat tightened with concern. It seemed I'd made a gigantic mistake by kicking that man out of my house. I could hardly breathe.

"Amy, lass? Is something wrong?"

"No, no. And thank you. You've taken a huge weight off me. It's just all been so hard to believe."

"For me too, lass! Dear God, I never dreamed that anyone could possibly be alive inside that, that whatever it was!"

"Yeah." I was still trying to breathe. "Who would have thought it was possible?"

"What an experience today was! My heart starts pounding whenever I think about it."

"Yeah." My own heart had started pounding now too.

"And I haven't been able to stop worrying about poor Mr. Holmes. Is he alright?"

The sincere concern in her voice made me feel so unbearably sheepish that I found myself lying to the dear old lady, "Oh. Yes. He's just fine. He's, uh, resting just now but seems to be doing okay."

"Well, please give him my regards."

"Oh, I will, Mrs. Hudson. Just as soon as . . . as I see him."

I thanked her again, hung up, and bit my lip. My heart was positively fluttering. Along with my nerves.

All I could think was, *Oh my God. What have I done?*

I quickly pulled on some jeans, grabbed Lucie's leash, and rushed out the door. She was confused about taking a walk so late. But walk we did. I circumnavigated the entire park and the Palace of Fine Arts itself, but the few people I encountered were very un-Holmes-like.

Lucie and I headed south on Lyon along the Presidio as far as Lombard, then crisscrossed the entire neighborhood back up to Marina. There was no sign of him. I inquired of the few people we passed, but no one had seen the unusual man I described.

With great frustration at our lack of success, Lucie and I headed home, making one last pass along Baker Street. A police car was cruising slowly around the far side of the park on their usual rounds as I looked again into the now dark greenery. All the park benches were empty, including the one directly opposite my house.

Lucie and I went inside, where I sat in the living room, feeling miserable. I considered calling the police, then remembered that a missing-persons report couldn't be filed until twenty-four hours after someone disappeared. I was at a total loss.

I was not aware at the time, but behind the shrubbery near that last bench across from my house were two men crouching. They were an odd couple: one in the mismatched garb of the homeless and the other in Victorian day clothes and a bowler. They hadn't seen me either. Instead, their eyes were fixed upon that police car in the distance. They were both intent upon avoiding unwanted contact with the law.

Lefty smiled at Holmes regarding the police car. "It's okay, the heat's past. They won't be back around this way until about 4:45 in the morning."

"Thanks for your help, Lefty."

"No problem, mate." He indicated the vacant bench. "Make yourself at home. Or if you prefer, you're welcome to join me in my small suite across the park."

"Ah!" said Holmes, looking across at the glorious old classical rotunda and appreciating Lefty's wry humor. "Tempting, but no. I need to remain hereabouts, Lefty. Very kind of you to offer, however." Holmes placed his bowler on the bench and then shook Lefty's hand with a formal bow. "Bon voyage, my friend."

Lefty smiled and gave him a comradely little punch on the shoulder. "Ya ever need any more help out here, you know where t'find me, mate." Holmes nodded, and Lefty sauntered away.

Holmes turned to look at my house across the street. I normally turned the porch lamp off at night, but I'd turned it back on, in hopes he might return. I had already gone up to my room and pulled down the shade. Had I been looking out, I might have seen Holmes sniff scornfully in the direction of my house. He parted his frock coat and took a seat once again on the bench. He drew a breath of night air, stretching out on his back, and arranged his bowler as a pillow.

As his head came to rest, he was looking skyward and chanced to see among the stars overhead something he'd never seen in his life. It would have been a commercial airliner about two thousand feet directly above him, outbound from San Francisco International for Seattle. He watched the big jet craft with intense fascination and pleasure and found himself quietly quoting Miranda from *The Tempest*. "O brave new world . . ." A satisfied smile developed on Holmes' face as he again considered the huge accomplishment he had achieved. Even he was impressed.

At that moment, I was up in my bedroom, lying in my four-poster, wearing the faded blue plaid flannel man's pajama top I like to sleep in. But I wasn't sleeping. I was staring at the ceiling. I was going over the extraordinary events of the day, the horrifying moments as well as the comically absurd ones. I was disappointed with myself for not being more open-minded about the prospects and possibilities of a genius scientific intellect. Wherever this remarkable man had come from, he was certainly a singular character. And I had thrown him out. I was feeling very guilty.

About two o'clock in the morning, I was awakened by a noisy row outside my window. I later learned exactly how it had transpired.

Unknown to me, Holmes had still been camped out on the bench across the street from my house. He'd been unable to sleep, perhaps in part because he'd just awakened from the longest nap in human history.

At any rate, he was reclining on the bench, with his head on his bowler. That spring night was balmy and clear, and Holmes was enjoying the air. He had relit his briar pipe and was reading a copy of the *Chronicle* that Lefty had left behind.

Holmes scoured it, digesting all manner of new ideas, products, attitudes, personalities, and statistics. He was gathering "data, data, data" as I would so often hear him say later on. More particularly, he was examining the articles regarding crime in

San Francisco. And most specifically of all, he focused on the small amount of knowledge available regarding the two recent murders. The front-page headline—MYSTERIOUS MURDER BY PHANTOM TIGER—most definitely prompted an echo for him of his adventure with that equally mysterious and monstrous Baskerville hound.

He had just begun thinking over yet again those details I'd given him about Lieutenant Ortega when his attention was diverted by an electronic chirping sound. He looked up to see a gang of five teenage street toughs moving down Baker Street toward him. They were being systematic, proceeding car by car. One of them, a sixteen-year-old, particularly caught Holmes' attention.

Holmes felt the boy clearly had Hispanic blood in him, but, like his mates, he also represented the melting pot that was America. They each had varying degrees of Anglo, African, and Asian heritages. The boy in question combined an appealingly innocent face with an Artful Dodger grace and dexterity. He wore a black BLM baseball cap backward atop thick curly black hair. His eyes were brown, large, and expressive. He had dark eyebrows and a strong forehead. His nose was small, and his features were fine, almost delicate. His rounded face and the deep dimples in his cheeks gave him a particularly innocent, boyish appearance. In his left ear was a tiny gold stud.

He was the smallest and likely youngest of the group, only about five feet eight or nine. Like the others, he preferred to make his fashion statement with the latest hip-hop, hodgepodge look. He wore baggy pants and an oversize tee shirt, with a blue, hooded, zipper-front sweatshirt on top. Like his compatriots, he wore a large backpack.

Holmes retreated into the shadows as, with silent admiration, he observed the carefully orchestrated operation of this clever gang of young thieves. Despite his smaller stature, the Artful Dodger boy seemed to be the focal point of the group. He operated a small remote control, adjusting and transmitting chirps until he was able to neutralize the alarm system of each car they approached.

Then another beefy teen, with slicked-back, wet-look hair and shoulders like a rhinoceros, used a thin, flat metal jimmy strap to pop open the car door. His size alone indicated that he had probably muscled his way to overall leadership. Once he had opened the car's door, the others swarmed into the vehicle like scavenging hyenas. In about twenty seconds, they emerged with the radio or whatever else of value was inside. After slipping these items into one of the backpacks, they continued on to the next car. Holmes heard them speaking in urgent whispers to each other, and later related their dialogue to me.

"Awright, man! Cool!" said mountainous Slick. "A Blaupunkt! We strikin' it, Rancho!" He was speaking to a tall, wiry youth with light brown hair and bad skin. Slick held out the radio to the smaller Artful Dodger type. "Check it out, Zapper!"

The Artful Dodger, whom Holmes deduced was called Zapper, spoke up sharply. He had a streetsy, Latino-tinged dialect. "Yeah. But we ain't takin' this haul to Pavon's guys."

"C'mon, Zapper," Rancho urged, "Pavon'll cut us the best deal in town."

"That's bullshit, man," Zapper snapped. He used his adjustable remote to chirp open the next car, and his partners in crime dove in to strip out any worthy prizes. Zapper continued angrily, "Pavon stiffed us royal last time."

Rancho came out of the car, waving a leather jacket that the owner had left behind and a half-full bag of ranch-flavored Doritos. "Lookie! My favorite flavor! We got leather and munchies!"

But Zapper was still under a dark cloud. "And I told you before about Pavon, man—it was Pavon had 'em do the hit-and-run on Billy."

Rancho munched on the Doritos, crumbs falling out of the corners of his mouth, as he shot back at Zapper, "C'mon, bruh, you don't know that for sure."

Zapper was hovering beside the next car, which happened to be my poor, defenseless Accord. "Hell I don't. It was Pavon called the hit, and Billy was blood."

Slick was impatient, hopping from one foot to the other. "Okay, okay, we won't fence it with Pavon. Just zap the car, will ya?"

Zapper leaned down and looked in at my Accord's dashboard, saying, "That radio ain't worth it." And was he was right.

Rancho, however, had spotted something else in the back seat of my little red car. He dropped his Doritos and focused the beam of his heavy flashlight to see in more clearly. "But hey, check out the case o' booze! Looks like primo vino, man!"

"May be worth lots more than a radio. C'mon, Zapper," Slick whispered, prodding urgently, "zap it, man!"

Zapper grunted, adjusted his remote, sent a signal, and got my car to chirp unlocked. It was at that point that the gang was startled to hear a proper English voice speak up loudly saying, "I beg your pardon, gentlemen."

The teens jumped, quickly turned, ready to fight or fly, and saw an elegantly dressed shadowy figure silhouetted against the distant lights of the park, who said, "I can see from your profession that you might have contact with a man I'm looking for."

Slick puffed up. Not only did he have his four comrades around him, but he could hold his own in a fair fight with almost anyone—because Slick never fought fairly. He sneered at this man in the ridiculously antiquated costume. "Who the hell are you, rando?"

His face shadowed and unseen, he replied, "You would likely know me as Holmes." Then he took a dramatic step into the streetlight so they could see his lean face. "Sherlock Holmes."

All the boys laughed.

"Yeah?" snickered Slick. "Well, I'm LeBron James. Pleased t'meet ya, mofo. But just turn your skinny ass around and get outta here before I bite your head off!"

Holmes continued as if Slick hadn't even spoken. "The man I am seeking would be about seventy years old, an archcriminal." He strolled over to the street gang, "And he would walk with a pronounced limp."

Holmes had eyes sharper and more foolproof than a polygraph. He caught the slightest trace of reaction from Zapper. Holmes was about to pursue it, but Slick crowded him. "You better move on, Jack, 'fore *you* walk with a limp."

Holmes ignored Slick and spoke over Slick's shoulder directly to Zapper, who stood several paces behind. "It's important you tell me what you know, Zapper."

The boy reacted again, this time with concern that Holmes knew his name.

"He don't know nothin', okay?" said Slick, "Now I'm tellin' ya, get your fancy ass outta here." He shoved Holmes in the chest.

But Holmes remained rooted to the spot, gazing into Zapper's uneasy eyes.

Slick was getting annoyed, and a bit embarrassed in front of his cronies, so he presented a tougher attitude. "Didn't you hear me, sucker? Are you deaf?" Holmes still ignored him. Slick was angry now. "I said beat it!" He punctuated his demand with a vicious, two-handed jab at Holmes' chest.

That was a mistake. With the grace of a seasoned toreador, Holmes deftly pivoted aside, grabbed Slick's passing arms, and used the boy's momentum to propel him headfirst against the fender of a car. Slick rebounded down to the ground, stunned.

Holmes correctly anticipated an additional attack by another. He turned to see Rancho swinging a roundhouse right fist at him. Holmes easily ducked under the incoming blow, and again using the assailant's momentum, he allowed Rancho to fall off-balance and right over Holmes' shoulder in a posture similar to a fireman's carry.

Holmes stood up with a snap, hurtling the boy off and sending him crashing onto the hood of the same car with which Slick just had his own encounter.

Rancho's crash onto the car's hood is what startled me to wakefulness in my upstairs bedroom. I sat up with an alarm usually reserved for earthquakes. Lucie was beside me on the bed and equally unnerved. She jumped off and started barking.

I leapt—or more accurately, stumbled—to my window, flipped back the curtain, and raised the roller blind. I drew a quick breath of surprise and delight as I saw Holmes standing beside my car on the street below. But then a wave of concern swept over me as I realized that he was facing off with a bunch of tough-looking street teens.

Holmes seemed totally calm and unruffled, however. He was straightening his cuffs as I heard him say to the young toughs,

"I should give you proper warning, I studied Japanese baritsu with Master Barry himself."

One of the gang had picked up a length of broom handle and swung it devastatingly at Holmes as he shouted, "Study this, sucker!"

To my amazement, Holmes casually sidestepped the arc of the wooden rod, planted his hand firmly on the boy's passing shoulder, and shoved him mightily into the rear fender of my Accord. The boy's head dented it and he, too, crumpled to the ground, dazed.

In that encounter, Holmes had taken possession of the length of broomstick, which was about four feet long. I blinked with awe as I watched him twirl and brandish it like a dueling sword. And just at the right moment too, because the scruffiest member of the gang had flipped open a switchblade knife that flashed with a six-inch blade.

Still, Holmes proceeded confidently and attacked with the exquisite grace of a master fencer. I swear to God, at that moment Holmes reminded me of Cary Elwes dueling Mandy Patinkin in *The Princess Bride* or even Errol Flynn as Robin Hood, fencing through Nottingham Castle as he battled Basil Rathbone. I had a brief flash of confused and ironic memory: Rathbone had also played Holmes in the old movies. And now on the street below me was a man who claimed to be Holmes using a broom handle to duel with some twenty-first-century street thug and— My mind was reeling.

Holmes thrust and parried forward against the threatening youth, batting the dangerous knife from his hand. As Holmes pressed closer, the kid tripped backward over his own feet.

Holmes brought his broom-handle sword down on the

youth's head, hard enough to make a point but not so fiercely as to do any permanent harm. The teen toppled backward onto the pavement.

Holmes, smugly savoring his easy triumph, lowered his "blade" and turned slowly, 360 degrees, the back of his left hand pressed against the small of his own back, in a formal dueling position. He haughtily surveyed the battlefield and his fallen opponents, who were slowly regaining their dizzied senses.

It should be pointed out that throughout this confrontation, the youngest boy, Zapper, had made no move to attack Holmes. If anything, his attitude was one of wishing the fight would cease.

Holmes glanced at Zapper, then gallantly tossed down his weapon and spoke to the group, "Have you no leader?"

Slick was still kneeling beside the car, leaning against it to steady himself and seeing butterflies. He muttered, "What you talkin', man?"

Holmes peeled off his frock coat, folded it neatly and laid it atop the trunk of my car, saying, "Mano a mano. If you dare. Though I must warn you that I once went three rounds with famous prizefighter Shamus McMurdo before ending the match with a cross-hit under his jaw."

He assumed that classical, Victorian boxing pose you may have seen in old period photographs: arms extended in front, elbows bent so the forearms and fists were vertical. All he needed to complete the picture would've been a waxed handlebar mustache. I realized I had seen a false mustache exactly like that earlier in his valise.

By then I'd managed to shake off my fascination with the scene below and had realized its true danger. I grabbed the phone and dialed 911.

Outside, another of the gang took up Holmes' challenge. This boy was stocky, of Pacific Islands descent, perhaps Samoan, with the long, straight black hair associated with Polynesian-Asian physiognomy. He was also apparently familiar with the Oriental tradition of martial arts, for he brought up his hands into a posture worthy of Bruce Lee. He accompanied this with a series of growls and guttural threats like I'd once seen Jackie Chan do—as a joking send-up of himself and over-the-top chop-socky movies.

Holmes blinked. He had never heard such a noise or seen anything like this posture, of course, but nevertheless, he was prepared to continue. He reached forward with the toe of his black patent leather shoe and drew an imaginary line across the pavement between. It was then the beefy boy's turn to blink. "What the hell are you doin', man?"

The teen then resumed his best karate stance, slowly rotating his open-palmed hands in front of him as though they were lethal weapons—which they may well have been. As he did this, he slowly moved in an arc around Holmes, who remained facing the line he had drawn on the street. Holmes looked at the boy with considerable consternation. "What on earth are you doing?" he asked with an air of abject astonishment and social criticism. "Can it be that you are ignorant of the Queensbury Rules?"

In an effort to educate the obviously disadvantaged youth, Holmes turned with a sigh to face him again, and drew another line on the pavement with the toe of his polished shoe. The boy regarded him with a blank look.

Then Holmes snapped back into his formal boxing position and nodded sharply for the boy to do the same. Instead, the kid glanced with leering amusement at Slick, and mimicked Holmes' formal fisticuffs position. Then he threw a serious punch at Holmes.

And punishing it might have been but for Holmes' lightning-fast reflexes. He easily parried the fist, startling the young man with a brisk uppercut to his chin. He saw stars, I'm sure. Both he as well as his comrades were thunderstruck by Holmes' unexpected skills.

The boy recovered and reattacked. Fists flew, but only Holmes connected, landing a powerful left hook with such intensity that the boy was spun around and thrown to the ground.

By now I had given up on getting through the voice menu on 911—"If you are reporting a fire, please press one now. If you are reporting a—" et cetera. I ran downstairs and grabbed the pistol out of Holmes' valise. I flung open the front door, forgetting that I was wearing only my pajama top. Lucie rushed past, barking in an uncommonly fierce manner for her. I brandished the pistol and shouted from the front porch at the gang. "Hey! Leave him alone!"

My intrusion had an unfortunate result. Holmes turned at the sound of my voice. The boy called Rancho used the distraction to blindside Holmes by bashing a heavy flashlight hard across the back of his head, taking the Englishman down.

Zapper reacted angrily to the cheap shot, yelling, "Hey, no, bruh!"

Rancho saw my gun. "She's got a piece! C'mon!" They all took off, headed back into the darkness of the park, with Lucie barking after them.

Rushing to the street, I knelt beside Holmes. "Are you

okay?" I lifted his bloodied head onto my knee. He looked up at me with dazed confusion, perhaps unsure who I was.

"My violin," he mumbled.

"What about it?"

"It's under . . . under the bench."

"Yeah, yeah, don't worry, I'll get it."

We looked toward the fleeing street gang. Zapper paused in his flight to look back at us. He appeared genuinely concerned, trying to ascertain if Holmes was indeed okay.

Slick dashed back and grabbed his sleeve, "Zap! Come on, bruh! Let's blow!" He pulled the reluctant Zapper on, into the darker section of the park.

As I watched them disappear, I found myself saying, "Welcome to San Francisco, Mr. Holmes."

And that gave me pause. Looking down at the strange man leaning against my knee, I realized I was actually coming to believe that his remarkable story had to be true.

8

Shortly thereafter, about 2:30 a.m., Holmes was sitting in the overstuffed easy chair in my living room while I attended to his cuts and scrapes. Lucie was at his feet, with her chin resting on his right knee, watching these goings-on with attentive concern. I was on the floor beside his left foot. His trousers had a small flap torn in them where he had landed on the pavement and the skin on his knee beneath was badly abraded.

"This may sting a bit," I warned before applying the antiseptic. He nodded that he was suitably prepared. As I proceeded, only because of the slightest tightening of his facial muscles did I perceive that he felt any pain. He glanced away from me, toward the foyer.

His case of wine was now safely on the floor inside my front door along with the old leather suitcase containing some of his clothes. He had insisted on lugging the wine inside so it would provide no further temptation in case the young thieves or any others decided to break into my car. He caught me watching him gaze at it.

"Vintage, huh?" I surmised.

"An extraordinarily *rare* vintage," he said by way of explanation. That was obviously why he was so protective of them. Those bottles could have considerable monetary value that he might need to rely upon.

I continued medicating his abrasions, saying, "Thanks for defending my car."

"It was nothing." He sniffed as he rubbed his lean neck, which must have still been aching from the blow of that heavy Maglite. His torn shirtsleeve draped open slightly, and I saw the bleeding scrape on his left wrist—as well as the telltale injection scars on his forearm.

"Yes, it was quite gallant of you," I insisted. "Particularly after I'd tossed you out on the street. Let me clean up that wrist too." He laid his hand, palm up, across his leg. Lucie licked his fingertips as I folded back the cuff to sponge his current wound while referencing his older scars. "You weren't exaggerating about your cocaine use."

"No," he said matter-of-factly. "Initially I found it so transcendentally stimulating and clarifying to my mind that its negative influence on me physically was merely secondary and a matter of small moment." His face clouded. "But after the death of my archenemy, Moriarty, whose evil genius had been a challenging match for my own skills at intellectual combat, I found myself sinking into depression."

"You no longer had a worthy adversary," I said, studying his face as I applied the dressing on his wrist.

"Correct." He inhaled sharply. "Give me problems, give me work, give me the most abstruse cryptogram or the most intricate analysis, and I am in my element. Then I can dispense with artificial stimulants. I do not tire from work, but idleness exhausts me. I abhor the dull routine of everyday existence. I crave mental exaltation. I cannot live without brainwork, and with Moriarty dispatched, what challenges were there to live for? Hence the cocaine."

"What finally prompted Dr. Watson to intervene?"

"He came to feel that I was dangerously overdoing it. Bear in mind that seeing someone taking cocaine intravenously was no more alarming than watching someone have a cigarette. But being my closest friend, and a physician, he'd grown increasingly concerned about how often I indulged."

"Which was how often?"

"Three or more times a day." He saw me draw a reactive breath. "However, I had ceased to get satisfaction. Instead, a growing malaise and indifference to living settled over me. Watson grew evermore irritated at me until his conscience swelled one night after a glass of Beaune. He was watching me thrust the sharp tip of my syringe into a vein. He saw how eager I was to press down the tiny piston and then sink back semiconscious into my velvet-lined armchair. Watson suddenly snapped at me, 'Which is it today, Holmes? Morphine or cocaine?' When I made some dismissive jest, he sprang angrily to his feet. 'It is a pathological and morbid process, you fool! Usage of these chemicals causes tissue changes and may leave a permanent weakness. Or even lead to your death!'" Holmes shook his head at the recollection. "The good doctor snatched up his greatcoat and top hat with a fury I did not know him capable of, declaring, 'I will no longer stand by and watch you kill yourself!' He stormed from my flat, stomping loudly down the inner stairway and slamming the outside door."

Though Holmes sat silently there in my present-day living room, I assessed from his unfocused intense gaze and strained expression that he'd been thoroughly reliving that difficult night. After a long moment, I volunteered quietly, "And then, being such a close and caring friend, he and Doyle set about trying to find healthier ways to stimulate your 'everyday experience' by introducing you to the likes of H. G. Wells."

Holmes drew a breath. "And Bernard Shaw, Joseph Conrad, Gilbert and Sullivan, Marie Curie, and—"

"Watson saved your life."

He nodded. "Yes, bless his soul." Then a wistful shadow passed across his face as he realized, "*Rest* his soul."

I paused in my doctoring and looked up. "I'm sorry about the way I lost *my* temper tonight." He shrugged as if it hardly mattered, but I tried to explain myself further. "It's just so hard to believe this could be happening, that you're who you say you are. I mean, how could you possibly know all you said about me?"

He didn't look at me, but rather gave a flippant wave of his hand—a gesture I would become quite familiar with. "From a drop of water, a logician such as myself can infer the possibility of the Atlantic Ocean without ever having seen or heard of it." He drew an expansive breath. "I simply observe the facts around me and deduce logically from there."

"But I still don't understand how you could have possibly 'deduced' all those tiny details."

"Then let me illustrate, Winslow." He rose, pointing to a small sculpture on a stand across the room. "That bronze bust over there is easily recognizable as yourself as a child. It was sculpted in the romantic, passionate style of the Parisian Rodin, and the bronze is signed 'Dad.'"

Indeed it was. Holmes touched Dad's signature, which also had quite a flare to it and was on the base of the sculpture. Holmes continued walking slowly around the room, following the same route he had taken earlier when reeling off the details of my life. He pointed toward my shelves.

"On your bookshelf there is a tankard with the California redwood tree emblem of the Leland Stanford University and the word *Alumnus*, although it should properly say *Alumna*." He ran his fingers lightly along the shelf. "Your shelves also contain these several books written in French and Spanish, which indicates an ability to understand those languages. Three of the books are on the subject of philosophy, which attests to your . . . *intelligence*." He swallowed the last, managing to slip a slight editorial edge into the word, as though still unconvinced that I possessed any meaningful brain cells at all.

Nonetheless, I was enjoying his performance. I settled into the armchair near the window, pulling my legs up under me.

He picked up from my desk a child's painting with bits of popcorn and dried macaroni glued onto it. Also, he lifted up a little "ghost" made of Kleenex, with a crude face drawn on it.

"These objets d'art fashioned by young hands, some signed 'Thanks, Dr. W.,' indicate children's fondness for you," he held them up for my examination and went on. "The sizable quantity of them suggests the pediatric specialty of your practice."

He set down the trophies from my kids and picked up a small plastic card, turning it over in his long fingers. "This personalized parking pass amid your mail shows that you are affiliated with the Saint Francis Hospital, and its location on Hyde Street." He chuckled to himself, "I wonder if San Francisco has gained a corresponding street named Jekyll."

I was about to tell him that most everyone I'd ever known at Saint Francis had asked that obvious question, but he paused not a second, steaming on, holding up a paper containing notes I'd written. "From this sample of your penmanship, even the most casual student of handwriting analysis would deduce that you're a woman of strong opinions tempered by quieter, more circuitous approaches. Would you agree with that assessment?"

Though I tried hard, I couldn't suppress a sheepish smile and nod.

"The white physician's jacket hanging on the back of your desk chair has your name tag pinned on it. There is a similar name tag on your bookshelf displaying the name 'Elizabeth Appling-Winslow, MD,' and beside it is a framed photograph of a smiling man and a woman who much resembles you. On one corner of that frame hangs a thin gold chain holding two wedding rings, one smaller than the other. That placement, and the fact the rings would otherwise be on your parents' fingers, indicates your loss. The small votive candle, which generally signifies a memorial, sits directly adjacent and underscores my conjecture."

Then he pointed at an object of stainless steel and black plastic across the room, half out of its box, where I'd left it. "Despite that unusual scientific apparatus over there, it's obvious that you're not consumed by doctoring."

"Why would you say that?"

He paused, inviting me to look down at a side table, "Because I noted the unthumbed quality of your current medical periodicals."

He was right again. My *AMA Journal* and *Pediatrics Quarterly* were still in the same pristine condition they had arrived in.

In truth, they'd gathered a bit of dust, which I made a mental note to clean up.

"You are endeavoring to write," he went on, "using what I presume to be some manner of electrical typewriter here." He touched my computer keyboard, then moved on to indicate the paperbacks of *Les Misérables*, *The Count of Monte Cristo*, and *Tess of the d'Urbervilles* lying nearby as he said, "These several works of historical literary fiction on your desk indicate your preference for that style of literature, and that you were likely using them for reference."

With his elegant, black patent leather shoe—unfortunately scuffed during his encounter with the street gang—he kicked lightly at something on my floor. "These crumpled papers in and around the rubbish basket are the classic indicators of a frustrated writer."

I chewed the inside of my cheek, trying to keep a straight face. Because he was dead on.

His hand swept in the direction again of the bookcases. "There are, however, no books on these shelves bearing your name as author, and I have never yet known any published author who could not resist displaying his books."

"Or *her* books."

"Yes, of course, *Doc*-tor," he sniffed, still with lingering incredulity about me being one.

I suspected, therefore, that the notion of a serious female author was barely possible in his estimation. He might not have known that George Sand was a woman. Perhaps he'd never given the Brontës, Jane Austin, or Mary Shelley any consideration. And his smug pronunciation of "*Doc*-tor," dripping with skepticism about my intelligence and abilities, was clearly employed to assert his perceived, egoistic superiority. But I decided to blithely ignore it, and not call him out on it until he'd gotten more situated in this century.

And in this specific instance I did have to admit, "You're correct. I haven't had a book published . . . yet." In spite of his annoying sexism, I was truly amazed by his perceptiveness.

"Yes, exactly as I said." He continued with his typical haughty air as he picked up a folded section of the *Chronicle*. "This newspaper, with teams marked by you, suggests you enjoy wagering on a sport called *hoe-key*."

"Hockey."

"Right." He snapped back, as though that was *exactly* the way he'd pronounced it. He glossed over his error, took it completely in stride, ignoring my correction. "Your manner of dress is decidedly more conservative in appearance than others I've glimpsed today, and you are apparently a *physician*—a traditionally conservative profession. But your relatively short hair betrays you as what I believe your American writer Mark Twain called a 'tomboy.' This suggests you have the adventurous spirit more appropriate to the masculine gender."

Wow. He was definitely a piece of nineteenth-century work when it came to gender equality. Not unlike men in too many countries of this century, I sadly realized.

He paused beside another small table. "That desire for adventure is further substantiated by the numerous travel magazines lying about. They, quite unlike your medical journals, have been well thumbed. This indicates to me that you enjoy looking through them again and again, which could only mean you harbor a romantic desire for faraway places and *adventures*."

He drew a breath and gestured toward the front door.

"When we first arrived. I noticed your motorized bicycle outside. That in itself would seem a rather adventurous mode of transportation—particularly for a woman—and a dangerous one as well, judging by the recently acquired scratches on its right side and the corresponding abrasion and bruise on the outside of your right knee."

Glancing down, I realized that I was still clad in only my pajama top, and he was looking at the still-healing scrape on my bare leg.

"Have you not had a minor accident in recent days?" he said confidently, baiting me.

"Well, yes," I tried my best to downplay it. "No big deal, really. Some jerk cut me off down on Marina. While he was texting."

Holmes waited patiently for the sound of my voice to stop. Beyond my admission that his deduction was correct, he wasn't even listening to my words.

He drew himself up rather formally, about to speak of something that was obviously quite distasteful to him. "Your amusement with the . . . the male sexual organ is suggested by the license plate on your car: BG WILLY. *Willy* being common, vulgar slang for the male . . ." He struggled to find a word and then to let it pass his lips. "The male . . . *membrum virile.*"

I swallowed a smile. He would not acknowledge my amusement but rolled onward. "Your preference for tropical vacations is made clear by the number of folk items, several of which are woven in a style that is, if my memory serves correctly"—and I saw he was absolutely certain it did—"peculiar to Panama." He pointed to a brightly colorful handmade wall hanging picturing South American peasants in their native garb, leading llamas over a sunny mountainside.

Growing more serious, he tilted his head lower and raised an eyebrow, like one talking to a fellow addict. "Your use of cocaine is obvious from the fine, white powder on your glass table here," he indicated the coffee table in front of me. "Along with the straw you use for inhaling it."

Then he pointed at my left hand. "On the ring finger of your left hand, there is a thin white line which has not been tanned by the sun. My deduction would therefore be that a wedding band has been recently removed. And your bitterness at your husband's departure is obvious from these photos of him cast carelessly aside. One of which shows his blond hair."

I glanced in the direction he was looking and saw the pile of photos I had gathered to give—or rather throw back at— He Who. The topmost was one I'd taken at Rockaway Beach. He was shirtless and mugging with a bodybuilder pose. I was embarrassed that Holmes had seen it.

"His paints and canvases, two of which bear his name, are stacked haphazardly by your front door. And your childish outburst of angry temper is clear from the bent nails on the walls where you pulled down those paintings, and also by the way you apparently smeared paint across his canvases, defacing them."

Holmes tapped the floor with the toe of his shoe, drawing my attention downward. "Marks on the rug suggest you're taking positive action, rearranging your furniture to start afresh." Reaching down with careful fingers, he retrieved something from the front of the couch. "These few short gray animal hairs along here and those thin claw scratches on the leg of the couch tell of the cat. And this small collar"—he picked it up from the table in front of me—"has a tag labeled Twinkie—*i-e* being the female suffix. The collar's lack of occupancy affirms that Twinkie is, alas, no longer with us. That you *kept* Twinkie's collar testifies to your excessive sentimentality, does it not?"

He held the collar out to me. I took it from him with an annoyed expression that also indicated I could not deny the truth.

He settled, like a monarch, into the overstuffed chair in front of the bay window, looking smug, like the cat who'd eaten the canary. He crossed his lean legs and seemed unaware that the flap of his torn trousers had opened, exposing the pale, scraped, bony knee beneath.

He smiled grandly and sighed. "You see how truly elementary it is, Winslow, if one only trains oneself to *observe*?" Then with a flourish, as though he'd done it a thousand times before, he flipped the piece of trouser material back to cover his exposed knee.

Putting his elbows on the arms of his chair, he touched the tips of his index fingers together, forming a triangle in front of his face, looking at me while cocking a superior eyebrow.

I stared a moment, then broke into giggling laughter. "I cannot believe I am really sitting here and saying this: You have now convinced me that you really are Holmes!"

"And what was your first clue?" he simpered derisively. Leaning his right cheekbone casually against his right forefinger, he took on the air of a learned college professor, and pontificated. "Actually, most women don't possess logical minds, so it's natural that you would have difficulty in—"

"Hey!" I bristled. This time he'd gone too far. "You're brilliant, okay? I acknowledge that. But my being female has nothing to do with my abilities. Or lack of them."

"Actually, you are quite right," he said with certainty, pointing that long, thin forefinger at me for emphasis. "My friend Watson, as well as Inspector Layton and all of Scotland Yard, also seemed slow-witted to me. I had to constantly exercise great patience with them."

"Well, I'm sure the exercise of patience worked both ways." I smiled with a sharpened edge of my own. "Considering your incredibly irritating arrogance."

He blinked at my straightforwardness. I enjoyed seeing him put off-balance and was eager to rub his nose in it a bit more. "And hard though it may be to believe, given the general accuracy of your deductions, you did make a few errors which I should probably clarify for even such a brilliantly logical mind as yours."

I got up and moved toward the stainless steel and black plastic object he'd pointed out earlier. It was partly out of its box and in the living room because I had been planning to return it. "What you referred to as an 'unusual scientific apparatus' is a cappuccino maker." His blank expression revealed he had absolutely no idea what I was talking about, so I elaborated, "For making an espresso-based coffee drink."

"I see." His eyes had narrowed, his mind was working. "A coffee beverage with perhaps an equal amount of milk in it?"

I was surprised. "Yes. You know about them?"

"No, but I deduced from the specific name you gave the concoction. A 'cappuccino' would most likely derive from the monks of the Capuchin order, and the only distinguishing aspect of them which might be mirrored in a coffee-like beverage would be the color of their traditional robes."

"You know, I never thought about it, but you may be right."

"I'm sure," he said dryly.

Boy, this guy didn't give an inch. But I had him for certain on the next one. I sat on the arm of the couch to tell the story. "My license plate, BG WILLY, does not refer to the male . . . *pe*-nis." I stuck it to him in the fashion of his snide "*Doc*-tor" and enjoyed seeing him shift uncomfortably and recross his legs, so I played into it. "Your incorrect assumption might instead indicate that you, sir, have a mind fixated on sex." He squirmed ever so slightly. I was delighted. Then I smiled, to let him a little off the hook, explaining, "Big Willy was the name of a dimwitted guy from my teenage hippie years. Big Willy was permanently stoned on marijuana and was always so confused that I started using his name to define confusion. If someone is 'Big Willy,' it means they don't understand. Like you didn't, for example. Get it?"

"I do indeed." He nodded, grudgingly. "I am no longer 'Big Willy.'"

I raised an eyebrow. "Well, not about that, anyway." I walked back toward the folk items on my wall. "Panama, yes. Tourist, no. I worked there with Doctors Without Borders—a wonderful international aid organization my mother also worked with. I was down there during the 2017 cholera crisis that unexpectedly turned into an armed protest."

I picked up a small piece of lead from the mantle and held it proudly between my thumb and forefinger. "I took this bullet in my right leg."

I saw, with pleasure, that he appeared positively startled by the prospect that I'd been at a battlefront. "A woman in a military skirmish?"

I cocked my head at him. "Oh yes. And women are also

part of the crews aboard combat naval ships like those in the fleet you saw today. Some women are admirals, generals, vice president. Times have changed, Mr. Holmes." I held the bullet out to him.

He took it and turned it thoughtfully between his lean fingers, then cocked his head right back at me. "Ah, but only a romantic would've kept it, Winslow."

He was right. But I pressed on, crossing to my desk. "I am trying to write a novel—you are correct. But what you called an 'electrical typewriter' is actually a computer that allows me to record, store, cross-reference, and alter the work. The computer can also find other resource material via the internet, which is a wireless communication system, a worldwide web, initially created by our United States Defense Department. That digital network can be accessed, searched, and used by anyone with a computer or a smart phone"—I held mine up—"from just about anywhere in the world."

Now *that* concept caught his attention in an electrifying manner. His eyes lit up. Holmes keenly studied my cell phone and computer. I could sense that he felt an immediate kinship between my PC and his own computerlike mind.

I sat on the couch opposite him. I tried my best to look contrite regarding my "habit."

"My cocaine," I began with an attitude of confidential confession that, I was pleased to see, drew him in, "is actually an artificial sweetener that I spilled here. It is a sugar substitute. Taste it."

He put the tip of his finger in it, smelled it, and touched it to his tongue. The intense sweetness turned his face positively sour.

"I add it to my iced tea," I went on, "which I drink with

a straw, such as this one." I looked at him intently. I wanted to be certain he got the point. "In your day, the casual usage of opiates and narcotics such as cocaine was more acceptable. Now, these drugs are deemed dangerous 'controlled substances.' Illegal possession of them is a serious criminal offense." He was thoroughly startled. "And addiction to them remains just as debilitating."

I held up my ring finger. "This white line does not indicate the absence of a wedding band. It was just a friendship ring. We were not married, we only lived together. And only long enough for me to diagnose what an insincere, disgraceful ass he was, which was a very short time. I was not the one who was abandoned. It was *I* who threw *him* out."

Holmes shifted uncomfortably. It was clear that an empowered, independent female represented a challenge to his Victorian perspectives.

"I broke it off with him when I caught him 'playing doctor' with a model in his studio. And those so-called smears you detected on his canvases are not my vandalism but—*brace yourself*—his style of painting. They look that way because he painted them that way. It has nothing to do with my tantrum. A tantrum which, I admit to you, I did have."

Holmes' brow furrowed, elbows propped up, his fingertips touching, processing it all like my computer when that spinning blue circle indicates it's hard at work.

"Thank you, Winslow. Most educational. Now, if you don't mind—" He jumped to his feet, grimacing slightly with stiffness from his injuries. Though he tried to hide his discomfort by pretending to stretch then shake out his arms, I knew better. Finally, he took a rejuvenating breath, saying, "I am most eager to begin exploring new opportunities." He handed the bullet back to me with a wink. "Be sure to keep it in a safe place, so you can show it off again."

He crossed toward my desk. "Now then. If you've no objections, I'll continue my schooling. I'm most anxious to get in touch with the twenty-first century. First, I'd like to clear up this problem with my clubfooted nemesis and regain my identity papers—after which I will turn my focus to helping Leftenant Ortega solve the two strange murders involving a tiger."

I was confused. Had I missed something? "*Two* murders involving a tiger?"

"Mmm-hmm," he murmured. He had seated himself in front of my open laptop and was studying its keyboard. "So, how do we go about getting in touch with Scotland Yard?"

"Oh, no, no. Not tonight." I was exhausted. This killer day had caught up with me. I hauled myself up off the couch and walked toward the desk. "We'll do it first thing in the morning."

He glanced searingly across at me. "I thought I'd made it quite clear, Winslow, that regaining my identity papers is of—"

"Utmost importance. Yes! I *know*. All of it. I also know that *you* just slept for a hundred and some years, but *I* haven't. I can barely see straight and—"

"But you agreed to—"

"Yes!" I stomped my foot. "Tomorrow. First thing."

He saw my determination and sputtered, "Oh, very well then." He looked back at the keyboard, and his tone became slightly more reasonable. "May I impose upon you to at least tell me how to—"

"Just touch the Enter key. The big one on the right side." He did so and was surprised as the fifteen-inch flatscreen came to life in front of him. I paused beside the desk, frowning. "But I only know about the one tiger murder involving Detective Keating. Has there been—"

He raised a hand to dam up any further inquiry. "That must wait, Winslow." Then he needled me with "Particularly as you are so exceedingly tired."

I chuckled at his petulant tit for tat, then I touched the external trackball, saying, "You'll need this too. See?" I demonstrated how to maneuver the cursor. I brought up a web search box and showed him how to click into it. "It's menu-driven, so just—" He'd glanced at me for further clarification, I groped for an explanation. "Uh . . . user friendly?" He still wasn't getting the drift. "Type in any question you have—like 'how to use a computer,' then left-click on any results that look promising."

He did so and a how-to list appeared on-screen. He was enthralled. Little smiles were chasing each other over his lips. He inhaled energetically as I added, with a definite sarcastic edge, "I'm sure someone as brilliant and intuitive as you will figure it all out soon enough. Just please don't *erase* or *delete* anything." I always kept my files completely backed up, but I didn't want the hassle. "There's a guest room and bath down the hall there."

He pulled out his pipe, but I interrupted that move emphatically. "No, no. You can only smoke on the porch."

He appeared affronted, but I didn't care. I was completely tapped out and headed off, but I did pause a moment at the foot of the stairs to glance back at him. He was leaning closer to the screen, poring over the on-screen instructions. His concentration was so intense it seemed I had ceased to exist for him.

Wondering about this strange man, this clearly singular

individual, I stood and watched him, the bluish light from the screen glowing on his dark hair.

In spite of the startling way he had entered my life and how he had certainly shaken it up so far, I was even more intrigued by—and considerably concerned about—the prospects of what might lay just ahead.

9

The morning arrived only a few hours later and way too early for my taste. The birds in the trees outside my window were far too cheerful. For a moment, I laid there staring at the slanted, beamed ceiling over my bed, playing with the idea that it all had been a dream. But I knew better. Mr. Holmes had clearly become my responsibility, at least for the time being.

I rolled out of my four-poster with a sigh, clipped my hair back, and slipped on loose gym shorts, a tee shirt, and the short robe I wear for my morning tai chi routine. As I went through the sharp thrust and parry strokes, I would not have held out very well against Holmes' assailant last night. But I worked at the tai chi chuan not with any thought of combat but rather to focus my energies. I was deep into that mode, when my concentration was shattered by the sound of an explosion from below. I yelped, then shouted, "Holmes?"

Scrambling down the stairs, I saw a cloud of smoke billowing from the kitchen. I raced into the doorway and faced a shocking sight: there was a spattering of blood on the front of the counters and floor where Holmes was sprawled out, barely conscious. Bright red blood was covering his face and the collar of an elegant green silk robe he wore over his white shirt.

"Oh my God!" I exclaimed as I slid down beside him to assess the damage and stop any profuse bleeding. But when I grasped the hand he held up to his bloody face, I got a good whiff, and my tension became annoyance. "Tomato sauce?"

Holmes looked up at me, wheezing with disorientation, "Mmmm, yes. To mix with my eggs." He pointed toward the saucy countertop. "Before opening the can, I was just heating it in that little—"

"Microwave oven." I sighed with relief but plenty of exasperation. "Yeah. I get it." As I climbed to my feet and began cleaning up the mess, Lucie wandered in and began lapping up the "blood," which was everywhere.

"My apologies for the disarray," he said, as he shakily raised himself up and took a seat on one of the pine chairs at my kitchen table. "You must allow me to repay you for any damage that may have resulted and, indeed, for your hospitality here."

I was feeling ornery and decided to stick it to him. "Thanks for the offer, but you don't really have any money, do you?"

"Not presently," he admitted, without the slightest hint that I had challenged his ability to sustain himself. He dabbed tomato sauce off his face with a paper towel. Then he asked, "Are there still pawnshops in this day and age?"

I told him there were. He breathed a long, melancholy sigh and speculated, "I suppose I could endeavor to pawn my Stradivarius. I imagine it's worth quite a reasonable amount by now."

I hate it when anyone tries to manipulate me, so I paused in my cleaning and turned it right back on him. Smiling broadly,

I said, "Oh yes! What a great idea! I can tell you several places where you could get a good deal." I was rewarded by seeing a bit of color drain from his face. I let a pause hang in the air, allowing him to be troubled by the prospect.

"Yes. Well, I would, of course"—he fidgeted—"have to be certain that the proprietor and his establishment were of the highest, most unimpeachable character and—"

"Oh yes, of course you would," I agreed with utmost sincerity. I'm embarrassed to admit how much I enjoyed seeing him squirm.

"Very well." He saw that he was trapped. "If I could enlist your aid, then, in finding such a shop that—"

"Holmes," I finally grumbled, "I won't let you pawn your—" I blinked. "Is it really a Stradivarius?"

He gave one precise nod. "Of course." Then shot my way a snooty expression implying he'd never condescend to an instrument of lesser pedigree.

"Well, I won't let you pawn it." He showed a hint of relief, until I added, "Not immediately anyway."

That brought the faintest glimmer of new respect for my ability to confront him. That was likely quite different from many of the beleaguered women of his own era. Except perhaps for one of them.

"Who was the woman in that photo in your valise?"

From the way his scalp tightened back, I saw I'd hit paydirt— of some sort, anyway.

His eyes shot at me like lasers, but seeing my inquisitive, suggestive smile, he quickly managed to reestablish a cool veneer. "I hadn't realized that you'd taken advantage of casting me out on the street to pillage my personal belongings."

"There was no pillaging involved. I was just trying to figure out who you were. And I must say I was intrigued by your disguises and your stash of intravenous cocaine. But the photo of that striking woman was unexpected."

He was trying to avoid the issue by glancing around at the floor for something else to discuss. "She was merely a client."

"Did you often keep pictures of your clients? I didn't see any others in—"

"Ah, there it is," he said, determined to change the subject. He reached down and from under the table he retrieved a small red silk slipper that looked like it came from a sultan's harem.

"And what, pray tell, is that?" I asked. "A memento of that same lovely lady?"

He was appalled. "Certainly not. It is my Persian slipper." He proudly held it out for my examination. "I keep tobacco in the toe."

"Well, it smells like you've been smoking a Persian's socks. Be sure you do it outside." I pushed the slipper back in his direction and returned to cleaning up the tomato sauce. I was about to pursue the question of the mysterious woman when I glanced over at him. He was looking at my legs, which were bare below my short robe. I felt at once self-conscious and could see he was turning something over in his mind. "What?"

"Difficult to imagine you ever having a . . . large posterior."

I glanced down at my lower body, then at him. "What are you talking about?"

"You mentioned your 'hippy' days?"

I laughed. "Not that kind of hippy." I searched for an appropriate explanation. "*Hip* is a word that means 'in touch with the times.' By *hippies*, I mean the counterculture—people who felt they were in touch with the best of humanity, human consciousness, and the Earth itself. A lot of young people still go through such a phase, just like I did a dozen or so years ago. When the term originated back in the late '60s, they were also called flower children. Their big things were peace and love—and for too many of them, drugs."

"Drugs?" His eyes brightened.

Way too much, for my taste. "Yes, drug usage destroyed many minds and lives, which is why I have put away your own cocaine supply."

He was highly offended. "I beg your pardon!"

I grasped his wrist to check his pulse. "As I already told you, it is what we now designate a controlled substance, and as a physician I can't have it lying around my house."

"I understand. However, I am perfectly capable of keeping it securely in my own—"

"Holmes," I interrupted quietly but sharp as an axe. "It is locked in my safe. Along with your pistol." His eyes held challengingly on mine. Until he finally looked away. Then I lightened my tone. "So, aside from recovering from the explosion, are you feeling alright today?"

"Quite," he said briskly. I could see the blue circle in his mind was already working on something, then he hit on what he was searching his memory for. "Ah, yes. I saw illustrations of flower children last night on your CP."

"PC. For *personal computer*."

"Right!" he blurted as though he'd known it all along. His face was as enthusiastic as a kid on Christmas morning. "There's an entire encyclopedia in there!"

"Lots more than that." I was enjoying his eagerness.

"Seems to contain a good deal of information on crime, which is my primary interest."

"Also, a world of *misinformation*. You have to check sources very carefully."

"One of my specialties," he gloated. "I was amazed by the high price of illegal cocaine."

"Yes, large amounts can be worth millions."

"Mmm." He grew even more exuberant as he got to his feet. "And I was delighted by how I could communicate with other computers. Your hospital link indicated that your patients are all doing well."

"*What?*" I turned sharply, looking at him with disbelief and anger. "That is private information, Mr. Holmes, and—"

"I was frustrated, however," he steamed on, more to himself than to me, "by my inability to access Scotland Yard and search for my records. Neither could I penetrate your city hall or police computers to gain additional information about the tiger murders or explore birth records for Moriarty's and—"

"Well, you'd need access codes."

"Or a good pair of . . . legs." I caught him glancing furtively at mine again. I realized that he'd probably seen more exposed female flesh in the last two days than in all his nineteenth-century existence. Having been caught gawking, he glanced away self-consciously, changing the subject. "So . . . um, tell me, Winslow, is city hall still where it used to be?"

"Yes, it is, but first let me get dressed and we'll take a stab at contacting Scotland Yard."

"Excellent!" He rubbed his hands together. "And I shall do us up some scrambled eggs, if that would suit."

"Fine," I said heading out. "But go easy on the tomato sauce."

While getting into jeans, I called the hospital and shifted my schedule a bit. Holmes made the eggs, then traded his tomatoey silk robe and shirt for a different ensemble. I provided a white shirt that had been left behind by He Who. Holmes turned the collar up, Victorian-style, and adorned it with a crimson cravat. Over that, he wore a black vest and matching trousers. His gold watch chain with that sovereign attached hung in an arc across the vest's lower front. A Harris Tweed jacket, shorter than his previous frock coat, completed the look—still Victorian but less formal. It was an eclectic fashion statement, but after all, we were in San Francisco, so why not?

Eating his very acceptable eggs while working at my laptop, I quickly realized that Holmes had been right: the process of getting information out of Scotland Yard was like jumping through hoops of fire. But I persevered because I knew that it would be nice to have Scotland Yard on our side. I finally initiated an inquiry and was startled when I received an instant auto-email answer of, "Thank you for your request to New Scotland Yard and the Metropolitan Police. Please be patient because we have an unexpectedly high volume of inquiries. We will assess yours as soon as possible. Whilst you await a reply, you may find answers at our FAQs link . . ." et cetera. I told Holmes why FAQs wouldn't help, and we were both frustrated, but at least it was a start.

Before tromping off to city hall, I did a quick online search of San Francisco and environs, which turned up scores of Moriarty references. We narrowed the field of search considerably and efficiently by age and gender. Holmes was amazed and enthused by how swiftly we accomplished this.

Just before we left the house, I took his vitals, which looked mostly nominal, except that his pulse was still as irregular as his character. I was glad to be keeping a careful eye on him.

As we finally headed out, I made sure Lucie's doggy door was in good order while she sat patiently awaiting her traditional Mommy's-going-away cookie.

Outside, in place of his black bowler, Holmes donned a brown herringbone newsboy-style cap with a button crown and a short bill.

As I drove us south from Baker Street onto Divisadero, I glanced at him, asking about the original Moriarty. Holmes' eyebrows flicked up in reaction.

"His anglicized family name originated in County Kerry as Ó Muircheartaigh. The Irish word *muir* means *sea*."

"A cognate of the Latin *mare*," I noted.

He glanced over, slightly surprised. "Yes. And *cheàrdach* means *skilled*."

"So 'sea-skilled' might mean what—*navigator*?"

"Just so. And indeed, Professor James Moriarty skillfully navigated the seas of crime for decades."

"He was a professor?"

"Oh yes. He'd had a first-rate education and was endowed by nature with a phenomenal mathematical faculty. At age twenty-one, he wrote a treatise upon the binomial theorem, tracing it from Isaac Newton back to Euclid. On the strength of that, he attained the mathematical chair at Cardiff and had, to all appearances, a brilliant academic career before him." Holmes' face clouded. "But the man had hereditary tendencies of the most diabolical kind. A darkly criminal strain apparently ran in his blood, which instead of being *modified* by his extraordinary mental powers, was *increased* and rendered infinitely more dangerous. Sinister, disturbing rumors about him were whispered at Cardiff just before he departed university and ventured into the lucrative career of master criminal."

"At which," I said as I turned left to head east on Bush Street, "he was obviously successful."

He nodded. "Sometimes going by the name Adam Worth, Moriarty was the organizer of half that was evil and of nearly all that went undetected in London, Winslow. He became the focal point of countless criminal enterprises." Holmes' hands shaped a funnel in the air, saying, "It all channeled back to him: robberies, burglaries, brothels, blackmail, kidnapping, smuggling. Though he rarely committed crimes personally, Moriarty used his intelligence and network of resources to provide criminals with strategies for their misdeeds and sometimes protection from the law—all in exchange for a healthy fee or a share of the profits."

"So, you were the consulting detective, but he was the 'consulting criminal.'"

"Yes, an ironic parallel." Holmes' eyes narrowed as he stared into the distance, seeming to picture Moriarty. "He was like a poisonous spider in the center of its web, but that web had a thousand radiating threads, and he knew well the meaning of their every quiver."

"Amazing," I said, contemplating it. "He sounds positively Machiavellian."

"But far more potent. He was a criminal mastermind, a champion gamesman, but also a philosopher, an abstract thinker. His brain was of the highest order. Exceptional. Ingenious."

"So, obviously," I said slightly tongue-in-cheek, "he was the perfect foil for you."

"Yes!" he agreed emphatically, totally missing—or possibly ignoring—my sarcasm, while taking his own exalted stature as a given. "James Moriarty was the singular individual truly worthy of testing my skills and my ardent opposition."

Wow. We could all wish for having the tiniest percentage of Holmes' stunning, egoistic self-confidence. But I also remembered his vast reputation for brilliantly delivering the goods time and again. No wonder he was eager to recover his identity papers: they would be compellingly impressive on a CV.

San Francisco's city hall is old but nevertheless postdates Holmes' time. Constructed in 1915 on Van Ness and McAllister Streets, it fills two city blocks and was in the same neoclassical Romanesque style of my neighborhood's Palace of Fine Arts. At a glance, it looks like the US Capitol in Washington, with the same high vaulted dome. It's a Beaux-Arts monument to the City Beautiful movement that epitomized that era's high-minded American Renaissance.

After finally finding a parking place, we climbed its broad marble steps to the glass doors at the front entrance. Holmes was startled when the doors opened automatically to admit him.

Once inside, we located the City Records room, and were allowed to pore over microfilm records—now thankfully digitized and searchable on the building's computerized system. Holmes hoped to get a lead on Moriarty's lineage. I'd brought my iPad so we could further refine our earlier search. It wasn't an easy process, but I was impressed by Holmes' tenacity and his astonishing ability to cross-reference data in his head.

In our search for the descendant of Henry Moriarty, the bad boy who had scarred his hand while stealing Holmes' ID papers and diamonds, we came away with a list of several possible

Moriartys who might help us locate our quarry. The first was a photographer. Her office told us she was that day engaged in a photo shoot at the top of San Francisco's serpentine Lombard Street at Hyde Street. I understood why that would be an excellent location for such a photo session: from there, in the crystal clear, bright sunlight, the city spreads to the northeast with a spectacular view all the way out past Coit Tower on Telegraph Hill to the sparkling bay and Treasure Island.

En route to that beauty spot, I mentioned how Treasure Island had a manmade enlargement expanding it into a naval station during World War II.

Holmes was troubled, "Which implies there had been a First World War?"

"Yes, and unfortunately it had not been 'the War to End All Wars,' as promised. Millions lost their lives."

He was appropriately aghast. When I told him that the second was even worse, he bowed his head slightly, shaking it slowly, saying, "How monumentally tragic. I'm so sorry, Winslow, to hear how the drumbeats of such wars continued across the twentieth century." Then he drew a breath and looked at the city around us. "I trust there also have also been brighter, more positive developments that offered some counterbalances." He spotted a jetliner outbound from Oakland climbing into the blue sky. "Like the flying machines I've glimpsed. Simply marvelous!"

"Yes," I said smiling. "I've had breakfast in London, hopped on a plane like that, and gotten home to San Francisco in time for tea. The same day."

His fascinated eyes followed the jet. "Remarkable!"

"But imagine this: two very clever bicycle mechanics

hand-built the first powered airplane, which they flew in 1903. And only sixty-six years later we landed men on the moon."

His jaw actually dropped in pleasant amazement. Then he needled me. "What? No women?"

"A lot of females have been to space." I smiled. "There are a couple up on the International Space Station right now, orbiting two hundred twenty-seven miles above the Earth every ninety minutes." His eyes widened. "Astronauts of both genders have been the norm for decades. We haven't returned to the moon in forty years, but the Artemis mission with a standard female/male crew will soon be back on it walking around together."

"My, my," he begrudged, "So, there's just no stopping you ladies."

"You're right. It's taken us longer than it should have to catch up because of"—I shot him a pointed glance—"*old-fashioned attitudes.*"

He received the barb, responding, "Well, I must salute your fortitude, Doctor."

"And speaking of: medicine is just one of many areas where humankind has made great leaps. We've conquered many diseases; created artificial hearts, replacement legs, arms, hands. I perform dozens of operations nowadays with minimally invasive robotic surgery."

"'Robotic?'" He was puzzled. "*Robota* is an old Slavic word meaning drudgery, and the root of their word for serf or servant."

"*Ha.*" I smiled, admitting, "I never knew that. But *servant* makes sense because robots today are engineering devices that 'serve' in thousands of ways: they can be remotely controlled to assemble automobiles, explore other planets, or in my case, perform complex surgery through an incision the size of a pea instead of cutting the patient wide open or—"

"'Explore other planets?'"

"*Ohh,* yeah." I smiled. "I've got a whole lot of videos to show you."

He gazed back out at the city, seeming to ponder the enormity of all the myriad developments and events he had missed by being unconscious over a hundred years. It wasn't merely this present-day "future" he must acclimate to but also so much history he had yet to discover.

I told him, "I do have concerns that your head might explode with such a fire-hosing of input."

"Not likely," he snickered confidently. "I have a rather large storage attic in my brain, which I generally endeavor to keep uncluttered by useless material. But at this juncture, Winslow, I am still gathering the threads with which to weave tapestries. I am allowing more absorption than usual so as to best determine what is valuable then dispense with what isn't. And I'm quite enjoying the process. I would, however, like to focus more specifically on my overriding interest: criminality."

"Unfortunately, that is not my strong suit, but I will help you dig deeper into the internet, which holds a goldmine of law enforcement data."

On foot after reparking my car, we dodged past a cable car at Hyde and Lombard, and I asked what Professor Moriarty had looked like.

"He was slightly taller than me," Holmes responded. "Very lean, clean-shaven, pale, and ascetic looking. His shoulders were rounded from much study. His forehead domed out into a white curve. His face narrowed triangularly with hollow cheeks and protruded forward, slowly oscillating from side to side in a curiously reptilian fashion. He had thin lips that gave the impression of a permanent haughty sneer."

"What about his eyes? I've always felt they display the most hints about a person's character."

"And indeed, his did. They were pale and deeply sunken, but with sinister pinpoint pupils that seemed to lacerate whatever they gazed upon, Winslow. His overall demeanor presented an air of subtly malicious danger that demanded respect and extreme caution."

"Clearly not someone to trifle with."

"Only at your own peril," Holmes said with deadly seriousness. Then he had a startled reaction to something just ahead, mumbling, "Good lord!"

We reached our destination on the top of Russian Hill, where Holmes was definitely getting an eyeful of the twenty-first century. He wasn't the only one. The eyes of many other people passing by the photo shoot location were pausing to focus on eight nubile female and male models who were wearing—barely—undergarments you might see in trendy fashion magazines, on the Victoria's Secret website, or almost any giant billboard nowadays.

If Holmes had raised his eyebrows at my bare legs that morning, I could just imagine how he was inwardly reacting to his first exposure to *real* exposure. I must say he presented a remarkably coolheaded and detached attitude after his initial exclamation, though I did catch him sneaking peeks at the well-supported and blooming breasts of the striking female models.

At one point he leaned in to me, privately asking, "And the authorities have no problem with allowing this sort of . . . this lack of . . . ?"

"Holmes," I said with a smile, "this is tame. Believe me."

Between lighting setups, we were able to speak briefly to the photographer, Maxine Moriarty, who bore no resemblance to Holmes' description of the professor. She was a wiry, alpha-personality woman in her early thirties with short black hair teased straight up as if she'd stuck her finger into an electrical outlet. Though preoccupied with the details of her photo session and answering questions from several crew people simultaneously, she did manage to also field our questions about any relative she might have who would be a seventyish male with a deformed foot and a scar on his right hand.

Unfortunately, Maxine could give us no lead, so we headed for the next Moriarty on our list.

We tracked him down in the seedy, adult-theater section of Broadway below Russian Hill. En route, we came upon an alley in that downtrodden area where a number of makeshift tents had been clandestinely set up by homeless folks. Holmes noted them with an uncharacteristic touch of melancholy, saying, "I see that in spite of a century of advancements, the poor are still with us."

I nodded, sighing. "Sad to say, despite our best efforts."

As we walked past, Holmes carefully eyed the alley's inhabitants, many wearing shoddy, ill-fitting clothes. "Reminds me of people I encountered in Benthal Green—a dismal area which had not the slightest bit of greenness. It was like so many of the decrepit streets I traversed in London's East End." I studied him as his eyes lingered on the unfortunate people. Though I'd accepted the bizarre reality that was walking around with the actual, original Victorian Holmes, I was still trying to fathom him being right here beside me yet also having walked those

Dickensian streets—perhaps even alongside Dickens—over a century ago. Sometimes I needed to pinch myself.

We arrived outside a small run-down theater that we'd learned was owned by Charley Moriarty. The burly, red-faced, long-haired man looked like a sixty-five-year-old Hell's Angel, complete with forbidding tattoos and a black leather Harley-Davidson vest.

But Charley proved to be an entirely friendly, approachable guy. I'd learned over my years in medicine—particularly working the ER—how deceiving first impressions can be. Charley was helping to unload amplifiers from a rock band's tour bus for a one-night benefit stand at his theater. He was happy to talk to us, even shared his business card for the theater and the small twenty-four-hour storefront mission he operated next door, where he lived and also fed, clothed, and ministered to the destitute. As we talked, a well-dressed woman dropped off some used clothing, setting it atop a small pile of similar clothes on a nearby collection table.

We were disappointed to learn that Charley had never known or heard of a Moriarty matching our description.

"Sure sorry I can't help y'all," Charley said in his gravelly voice as he took a pack of gum out of his pocket, "but if you guys wanna come back for tonight's concert, I'll give you the house seats."

"Thanks," I said, "but we're kind of on an important mission."

"Well, consider it an open invite." When he noticed Holmes eyeing the gum, he asked, "Wanna stick?"

I smiled, watching Holmes take and scrutinize the wrapped piece. "Uh, thank you, Charles, but what exactly is it?"

"Juicy Fruit." Charley popped a stick into his own mouth and started chewing. "My fave."

Holmes glanced at me, saw my encouraging nod, then delicately unwrapped the little stick. He sniffed it, let the tippy-tip of his tongue taste it, then somewhat awkwardly folded it sideways into his mouth. Charley found the performance a bit odd, and when he glanced at me for some guidance, I provided a little shrug and tried to say with my eyes, *Yes, he is a little odd, but all is well.*

Holmes chewed slowly a moment, murmuring a noncommittal "Mmmm." He forced a wan smile, saying, "Much obliged, Charles."

I shook his hand. "And thanks again for talking to us."

"Anytime." Charley grinned and turned back to thank another woman for her donation.

As we walked away, I whispered to Holmes, "Congratulations. You got your first piece of chewing gum."

"Is chewing all that one does with it?"

"Yes. It's preferable not to swallow, so—" I said just as his chin lifted and his Adam's apple bounced out from peristalsis as the gum went down. "*Ooop.* Too late." Then I said very seriously, "Now I'll have to rush you to the emergency room!"

He went pale. "What?"

"Just kidding."

He glanced at me with annoyance. "Not humorous, Winslow, for a man in my circumstances: unfamiliar with current mores and good manners. I thought perhaps it had all been part of a peculiar ritual that people nowadays sometimes engaged in when parting."

"Nope." I giggled. "Just a stick of gum, Holmes, which—let me guess—was far too sweet for your refined taste?"

"Indeed it was," he responded stiffly as he swallowed again, trying to disperse the disagreeable flavor. "Let's just get on to our next interviewee."

Visits to three subsequent Moriartys also did nothing to advance our search for Holmes' clubfooted prey. As we walked past a small bookstore on Sacramento Street across from Lafayette Park, a newspaper headline caught his eye, and Holmes reached for the door handle, startled once again when the door opened automatically.

He rushed toward the newspaper rack but was momentarily distracted by the bargain book cart near the door, snatching up a small volume to glance at it. With an amused little puff, he dropped the book back onto the cart and moved on to the papers.

In his wake, I paused to examine the book: a used paperback of *The Adventures of Sherlock Holmes*. I looked up from it toward the living, breathing subject of the book, complete with his nineteenth-century clothing, now embroiled in checking the latest details about the murder involving piranha.

As we left the bookstore, I asked why that newspaper headline attracted his attention.

"Because," he responded, "Judge Louisa Chang's murder by piranha is obviously connected to Donald Keating's death by the tiger."

"What? How could you possibly—"

"I prefer to have clearer proofs before I speak," he said dismissively as he indicated the book in my hand. "Curious, are you?"

"Actually, yes." It was the battered copy of Doyle's stories. "Looking for some additional *data* about you. And how could I go wrong for only five dollars?"

"Why on earth is that ear-flapped traveling cap on the cover?"

I was confused. "It's the deerstalker cap that you were famous for wearing."

"*Ha.*" He was genuinely amused. "I only wore one a handful of times, mostly to please Watson's wife, Mary, who gifted it me on Christmas in '90, shortly before we investigated the Boscombe Valley mystery."

I laughed. "Really? Only a few times? Then why in the world does everyone think— It must've been the movies." I clicked on my iPhone, saying, "Siri, show me Basil Rathbone as Sherlock Holmes."

Siri's voice came back, "Here's what I found for Basil Rathbone."

On my screen appeared the classic image of the actor in his tweed deerstalker, which had a bill on both the front and back and ear flaps that folded up from the sides and were secured together at the top. He was holding a large pipe.

Holmes looked closely at it, asking, "Siri is . . . your secretary?"

"Sort of, yeah. Anyway, Rathbone was a wonderful actor who played you in a dozen movies made in the 1930s and '40s—"

"And still available on TCM or streaming," he interjected.

I blinked with surprise, but before I could form a question, Holmes said, eyeing Basil's face, "From his keenly intense gaze and the native intelligence present in his sharp eyes, I should judge him to have been quite an effective actor. Not a bad choice for me. And the cap looks rather becoming." He stood up straight. "But one thing I can tell you assuredly: I never smoked that style of pipe."

At that moment, my text alert sounded. I read it and told Holmes, "The hospital needs me to check on one of my patients."

"Well," he said dryly, glancing away with his nose slightly upraised, "if you find *your* cases more interesting than *mine* . . ."

"What?" I was astonished, glaring at him. "Listen, *Mr.*—"

"Just 'kidding,'" he said mischievously, as I tried to hold on to my mad. "Come, come now, Winslow, 'twas merely a jest."

He smiled sincerely and I couldn't help but relent, admitting. "Good one, Holmes. You really got me."

"I shall take that as a compliment." He nodded graciously. "And allow me to return one: I'm truly grateful for your mentorship, Winslow, and especially for your assistance today. But of course, when duty calls, you must adhere to your Hippocratic oath and respond, *Doc*-tor." This time he spoke that formerly arch word with something bordering on respect. I nodded with an expression that acknowledged I had noticed the difference.

Then he took an expansive breath, saying, "By all means, see to your patient. I shall carry on our investigation on my own and—"

"No, no, no." I wagged my head. "I'm not comfortable with that."

"But *I* am completely comfortable, Winslow," he said with confidence. "Rest assured I am familiar with the basic street layout of downtown San Francisco, which, I have ascertained, has not altered drastically since 1899. I often utilized the cable cars and trams back then, and I'm convinced I will be perfectly fine on my own."

I studied him with trepidation, then fished out my backup iPhone, showing him how to call me if he encountered difficulties. I gave him twenty-seven dollars, all the cash I had, saying,

"Cable cars are six dollars now, and when you're finished you can catch a cab back to Baker Street."

Holmes glanced at me curiously, then around busy Sacramento Street. "I haven't seen any hansom cabs, Winslow. Do they still—"

I smiled. "No hansoms anymore, but they're still called cabs." I pointed out a passing taxi. "Like that one. They won't all be yellow, but if the roof light is on, that indicates they're available. And you should pay about fifteen percent more than the fare as a tip. A 'tip' means—"

"Gratuity." He nodded. "I'm familiar with the concept."

I headed for my car and Saint Francis Hospital—so naturally, I missed the excitement that ensued and was later described to me in exacting detail. Additionally, as previously noted, I had ample opportunity later to interview other participants in this unfolding drama.

After we separated, Holmes headed back south on Larkin to revisit city hall, just to be certain there was nothing else we had overlooked. He was puffing contentedly on his briar pipe when his keen eyes chanced to spot the street kid Zapper walking north on Larkin toward the Main Public Library with a book in hand. Holmes was delighted with the opportunity to question Zapper further about why the boy had reacted so noticeably to Holmes' mention of a limping archcriminal.

Unfortunately, at precisely the moment Holmes saw Zapper start up the library's front steps, the boy also spotted *him*—and instantly took off, running back the way he had come.

"Zapper! Wait!" Holmes shouted, but the boy kept running full tilt.

Holmes gave chase.

Zapper cut across the vast civic center plaza on the west side of city hall, and turned right onto Grove Street, dodging pedestrians with a well-practiced athletic grace.

I later had the opportunity to see Holmes running and that his style was very different from Zapper's. If running could ever be described as formal, then that's how Holmes does it. His back was held straight, his chin up, and his fists pumped in careful synchronization with his pistonlike legs. It's somewhat comic to behold, but believe it or not, he's quite fast.

Holmes was gaining ground on Zapper when the boy artfully dodged through the heavy traffic that had stopped, awaiting a green light at the corner of Grove and Van Ness. Holmes saw Zapper aim a small remote device at the box above the stoplight—which bus drivers can use to activate a change in the light—and the light instantly switched from red to green.

The traffic took off, providing an effective river of cars barring Holmes' pursuit, but Holmes was determined. He stepped into the street, heard a horn blast, and was nearly run down by a motorbike speeding even faster than the cars, weaving around and through the heavy traffic.

Holmes wasn't hurt, but when he looked up, he saw Zapper in the distance glancing back with a delighted laugh at his own skills. The young man turned the corner past the ultramodern Davies Symphony Hall and disappeared onto Hayes Street.

Though frustrated and angry, Holmes was undaunted. He went back to city hall and, using their computer searching system, managed to turn up one additional Moriarty that hadn't made it onto our previous printout.

Holmes rode the cable car up Geary, taking in the vistas of the city and ignoring the curious looks of several people on the trolley eyeing his odd Victorian clothes.

He hopped off the cable car as it slowed at the top of the hill at Van Ness, hoping to perhaps find some luck in an unexpected place. He crossed the intersection toward the lofty, neogothic bell tower that rose above the large late eighteenth-century redbrick church. To the casual eye, it bore a slight resemblance to one of the towers at Notre Dame in Paris. This was Old Saint Mary's Cathedral.

Holmes entered through heavy wooden front doors, leaving behind the noisy busyness of Van Ness and entering into the serene calm of Saint Mary's interior. He looked up at the Gothic-arched white ceiling towering four stories above him, then focused his eyes on the altar with its three neo-Renaissance paintings set into the wall above it. Holmes breathed in the cool air of the large chamber, whose quiet was then softly interrupted by the low, haunting strains of a slow passage of Bach being practiced on the pipe organ. Stepping deeper into the central aisle, he looked around the white marble choir balcony that ran around three sides of the cathedral. He saw the organist above the rear balcony, facing the keyboard, her back toward him as her fingers traversed the stately instrument's keys.

Just seven congregants were seated or kneeling in the pews or at one of the shrines to the side. Holmes caught the attention of an altar boy, and after inquiring, was directed toward the person he sought.

The priest stood in subdued light beneath one of the tall stained-glass windows. He was replacing votive candles at the shrine of Saint Francis of Assisi, a statue of whom, dressed in his simple brown robe, stood above, looking pacifically down upon the votive candles and those who stopped to light them. There was a single white rose in a bud vase also on the dark wooden candle tray.

The priest was as tall as Holmes, with a lean, almost gaunt look and a high forehead accentuated by his receding hairline. Holmes thought he bore a family resemblance to James Moriarty. He wore rimless glasses and appeared to be in his early fifties. Holmes' senses came alive, feeling he might at last be on the scent. When he asked the priest if he might make a personal inquiry, the man responded warmly. The flames of many votive candles lit both of them from beneath, creating a subtly sinister feeling, Holmes thought, and was in keeping with the nature of the mystery he was pursuing. And the moment Holmes described his clubfooted quarry, the priest went pale and glanced away.

"Ah!" Holmes' nostrils flared, his instincts confirmed. He whispered with urgency, "Then you do know of such a man, Father Moriarty?"

The priest continued staring intensely down at the candles. Holmes felt the man was carefully considering his answer. Finally, the priest drew a breath, his head remaining tilted down, but his eyes slowly raised, almost menacingly, to Holmes. "May I first ask, do you believe in God, sir?"

"Yes," Holmes answered without pause. Then he elaborated. "I have deduced there must be a merciful Providence, by observing a rose." Holmes lightly touched the soft petals of the white rose before them, saying with absolute sincerity. "There is no *need* for the rose. Its fragrance and color are not a necessity but rather an *embellishment* of life. It is only goodness which gives extras, so who but a Great Beneficence would have created it?"

Father Moriarty's face warmed upon hearing Holmes' conjecture. The two men gazed at each other for a respectful moment before Father Moriarty grew more serious. "Would you then agree to the existence of a darker, antagonistic force?"

Again without hesitation, Holmes sternly nodded. "I am certain of it."

Father Moriarty appreciated that response, then he looked slightly aside and said with frustration, "Such a dark force has dominated my extended family for over a century. I personally chose the cloth in an effort to fight such evil." The priest's eyes lowered once again to the candles. With noticeable remorse, he said, "I only wish I could have been more successful."

"Perhaps I can help you to be," encouraged Holmes.

Father Moriarty looked back up at Holmes, studying him. Then he decided to put faith in this man. Holmes could see the multicolored stained glass of the window high on the wall behind him reflected in Father Moriarty's glasses as the priest spoke. "The man you seek is a consummately evil human being who has cleverly eluded the police for decades. *His* cathedral is the dark tower of organized crime, wherein he is an archbishop." He swallowed with bitter distaste, then continued, "I'm ashamed to say"—the priest paused, glancing down, which emphasized his humiliation to admit—"that he is my cousin."

Father Moriarty continued looking down, seeming to have second thoughts—as though weighing Holmes' earnest desire to know versus the priest's responsibility for whatever darkness might envelope Holmes. Finally his head lifted, his eyes looked keenly into Holmes', saying, "I would urge you, sir—most strongly—to proceed with the utmost caution."

Holmes' eyes conveyed that he understood the warning. He took the responsibility.

Still the priest hesitated. But finally he said, "His name is James Moriarty Booth."

10

In 2015 the San Francisco Police Department Headquarters moved from its former Stalinesque, monolithic Hall of Justice building on Bryant Street to a new facility at 1051 Third Street. It was a few blocks below Oracle Park and just one block from the waters of the East Bay. It consisted of three interconnected, seven-story, glass-fronted buildings that filled the blocks between Mission Rock and China Basin Streets. It was pleasingly modern and, to Holmes' eyes, strikingly different from the weathered coal-dust-blackened stones of Old Scotland Yard in 1890s London.

Holmes had decided it was time to pay the SFPD a call. He walked briskly up the three short steps from the Bryant Street sidewalk, never breaking his stride as he marched toward the glass door, which he naturally expected to open automatically for him.

Unfortunately, this one wasn't automatic—and he did a hard header right into it, knocking off his newsboy cap and giving him a lump on his forehead. It was an inauspicious beginning, but Holmes quickly collected himself and pressed on, unaware that it was an ill omen of the shape of things to come.

Having no picture identification—nor any other kind—it took him nearly an hour to acquire the pass necessary to be admitted deeper into the building. Only after explaining to numerous stone-faced security guards that he had pertinent information related to two recent murders was he given temporary permission. Then he was guided through the pristine corridors by an athletic, engaging rookie whose name tag read Faheem.

"Got some info on Jimmy the Gimp, huh?" she energetically asked, "That's great, Mr. . . . uh . . ."

"Holmes, Hubert." He had decided against using his famous literary first name out of concern he would not be taken seriously. Clearly that was a wise choice.

"I'll tell ya," the rookie chuckled, "Detective Griffin's one of our top guys, but he can use all the help he can get to bring old James Booth down."

"Well, I am certain that together we can achieve that aim."

They turned a corner and came into a section with a wide double door numbered 304 that looked newer and smelled of fresh paint. The young officer said, "This section's all been redone, you seen it before?"

"I'm afraid not."

"Totally state of the art now." Faheem was jazzed about it. She pointed proudly through a glass wall. "Check out down there—a whole wing for pathology and forensics. Best SID in the country."

Holmes glanced at her, "And SID would be . . . ?"

"Scientific Investigation Division. They're like total aces, man! They can take the tiniest, most obscure detail or drop of blood or DNA, then make the most amazing connections."

Not wanting to appear out of touch or behind the times, Holmes did not inquire as to the meaning of DNA. But he looked with extreme curiosity through the glass into the busy police laboratory. He saw a dozen people working with computers, tablets, and all manner of sophisticated biological and electrochemical lab equipment. Holmes was intrigued even as a vague, uneasy feeling began to gnaw within, as though his own unique capabilities might somehow have been eroded.

He turned and followed the rookie into the main police bullpen, which was crowded with desks and file cabinets, where Faheem asked him to wait by the door. Holmes looked around the noisy place, bustling with witnesses, suspects, handcuffed perpetrators, riffraff, and numerous cops, some in uniform, some not. Of course, Holmes had seen such a place many times before in Scotland Yard. But the contrast here was startling. In 1890s London, virtually all constables Holmes had ever seen were appropriately uniformed white males. Holmes knew that there were sometimes one or two uniformed white women, called police matrons, but they were only used for searching and escorting female prisoners. The few civilian female office workers in the Victorian Yard wore conservative, secretarial, white blouses, and full-length skirts.

The nonofficial civilians present in such an 1890s room—whether they were innocents being interviewed or seeking help or suspects being questioned or held in custody—those civilians were more of a mixture of races and nationalities. Nineteenth-century London was a melting pot of society, yet still majority Caucasian.

But this noisy, hyperanimated, present-day San Francisco "cop shop" was for Holmes decidedly a horse of many different colors. Virtually every race and ethnicity or combination of both that Holmes could imagine seemed to be represented among the mass of civilians present. Taken as a group, they were *not* majority Caucasian. Gender was also confusing to him. There were several whose sex Holmes could not positively identify.

The most startling aspect for Holmes, however, was how that same diversity existed among the uniformed and plainclothes police personnel. His normally crystal-clear mind was swirling as he observed this noisy, jangling, world-upside-down, surreal human carnival.

A shirtless, tattooed bodybuilder with a bleeding ear was led past in handcuffs, drawing Holmes' eye to a nearby showcase containing precinct sporting trophies and photographs of diverse currently serving police personal. One photo was of Lieutenant Bernard Civita, and next to it Luis Ortega. As Holmes studied it carefully, he thought he heard someone nearby say Ortega's name amid the room's hubbub.

Glancing around, he saw a thirtyish Latina with thick black hair and a sweet but troubled round face sitting beside a sergeant's desk. She was leaning toward the sergeant, and her body language also displayed much anxiety. Holmes stepped a bit closer as the woman was urgently saying to the gray-haired Asian American cop, "Luis told me he was just getting the last of some major new evidence that was going to put Enrique Pavon away. That's got to be why he's missing!"

The mention of Pavon focused Holmes' attention even more sharply.

"Mrs. Ortega," the sergeant spoke gently, trying to comfort

her, "it hasn't even been twenty-four hours. We know he's been following a hot lead and—"

"But Luis always checks in with me." Holmes saw her bravely fighting back tears. Her fortitude impressed him. "He hasn't called since last night and he always—"

"Hey, Karen," the empathetic sergeant gently touched her arm, "you think I want to lose the best shortstop on our softball team?" He smiled warmly, trying to console her. "We're on it, believe me. And Civita's got Pavon in there right now, grilling him. Look."

Holmes glanced in the direction which the sergeant had indicated. An inner office door had opened and a smartly dressed, smiling man—presumably Enrique Pavon—sauntered out. Two Colombian bodyguards who'd been waiting outside the door came to attention. Holmes saw that Pavon had the confident gait and steady eyes of a man whose pleasant lot it had ever been to command and be obeyed. He wore an Armani jacket over a white silk tee shirt. His black hair was pulled back tightly. Holmes observed his heavy gold watch and two large-stone rings—one a diamond, the other an unusual semi-precious quartz, which particularly caught Holmes' attention.

Following him from the office were what looked like Pavon's advisers, presumably a legal entourage of three expensively dressed lawyers: one male, one female, and one whose gender Holmes could not determine. They were all smiling as Pavon spoke.

"Please don't bother us again, Lieutenant Civita, or we'll be forced to serve you with harassment papers. Unless you have something substantial to discuss—"

"I am gonna nail your fat ass, Pavon," Civita angrily interrupted. Holmes recognized the detective from the TV and his news photos. Civita's voice was low and deadly: "And I'll do it with or without Ortega!"

Holmes witnessed how Mrs. Ortega reacted as though she'd been hit in the chest. Civita's harsh words seemed to confirm all her fears about her missing husband. Pavon smirked as he smoothly glided past with his entourage in tow, all of whom were unaware of Mrs. Ortega and Holmes.

Holmes later told me how he'd immediately connected Pavon with the tiger and piranha murders. But at that moment Holmes was observing Mrs. Ortega's glare of hatred toward Pavon, then her desperate look toward Lieutenant Civita, who was now terribly embarrassed at how he'd spouted off about continuing the case without her missing and possibly dead husband.

The cheery rookie Faheem stuck her smiling face in front of Holmes. "Sir? Detective Griffin can see you now. His office is number 306—just down the hall there."

Holmes approached the indicated door, which was ajar. Looking in, he saw Detective Darryl Griffin Jr., an overworked, underpaid African American cop in his late forties who chewed Gelusil tablets like some people chain-smoke. He was leaning back in his chair with his shiny shoes propped up on his desk, reading a report that he finished, wadded up, and lobbed into a wastebasket as Holmes observed him while standing just outside the doorway.

Then Griffin noticed his oddly garbed visitor. But Griffin had seen all kinds and said offhandedly, "Yo, Mr. Holmes, how's it going?"

"Detective Griffin?" Holmes questioned tentatively. He was surprised to see a man of color in a position of such authority.

Griffin picked up on that vibe, but let it pass, gesturing for him to enter. "They told me your first name was Hubert, but I sure could use your ancestor Sherlock around here."

Holmes privately enjoyed his secret as he glanced around Griffin's office. "Yes, I daresay you could, Detective. Particularly in the case of James Moriarty Booth."

"Oh yeah, right, right," Griffin remembered, "Moriarty was Sherlock's big, bad boogeyman, huh?"

"Yes, indeed." Holmes enjoyed the memory of that triumph. "Until Sherlock did away with him at the Reichenbach Falls in Switzerland. You are correct."

"That what happened?" Griffin yawned. "I quit reading those stories 'cause Sherlock was such an unbelievable character."

Holmes' interest was snared. "Oh really? How so?"

"Well, shit, man." Griffin chuckled. "No dude could really walk into a room and scope out all the crap Holmes supposedly could in ten seconds. I mean, c'mon. I got twenty-seven years on the force and a pretty good eye for picking up clues, but that Sherlock?" he said with a smirk. "Gimme a break."

Holmes raised an eyebrow. "You don't believe that someone such as"—he tried to look as modest as possible, which was a major accomplishment for him—"myself, for example, could walk into your office and immediately tell that twelve years ago you left Detroit, where you were very much in the public eye but not well liked."

Suddenly, he had caught Griffin's interest.

Holmes continued, "Or that your father still operates a plumbing business in Detroit and that he has a female secretary with a fondness for cocoa."

Griffin stared at him blankly, a not uncommon occurrence among people meeting Holmes for the first time.

"Or that you worked your way up from policing the streets," Holmes went on, "and are meticulous in your habits, but stubborn and vain about your age. That you're a crack shot, Detective Griffin, and sight your pistol with your left eye even though you happen to be right-handed. And within the last hour, you were in room 304, down the hall."

Griffin paused thoughtfully, realized that he had been in 304. But he was even more amazed as Holmes said, "You also enjoy helping short people; you had pasta for lunch, which is perhaps why your nickname is Noodles, although your favorite fruit would appear to be watermelon; and—"

"*Whoa!* Hey! Hang on, man." Griffin pointed a finger of warning. "Before I get pissed."

Holmes looked askance, "You drink on duty?"

"No man, not pissed as in drunk," Griffin snarled. "Pissed as in riled, angry. You feel me? Where are you pulling this crap out of?"

Holmes smiled coyly. "I can see you're Big Willy."

Griffin blinked, startled, and glanced down at his crotch.

Holmes slid gracefully into his overly patient, tour-guide mode, "Please allow me to explain." He gestured over his shoulder toward the wall behind him, "The front page of the *Detroit Free Press* framed on the wall behind me gives your departure date and the public's unfortunate attitude toward you."

Holmes moved closer to Griffin's desk, rather grandly. He relished these moments of revelation to us astonished plebeian philistines. "The nameplate on your desk indicates that you are Darryl Griffin *Junior*, and this envelope leaning against your lamp has the return address of a Detroit plumbing firm operated by a man with the same name. Therefore, I deduce that the correspondent is your father."

Holmes lifted the envelope and showed it to Griffin. "Your father's secretary spilled a bit of cocoa on the envelope before sealing it—see? The flap hides part of the spill so we know that she did it—and a touch of her lipstick on the envelope indicates her gender."

Holmes replaced the letter and stood back up smartly. "Your military bearing, well-polished shoes, combined with your earthy style of speech attest to time spent on the force in the streets, whilst the tidiness of this office suggests meticulous habits."

Griffin was clearly impressed, while also put off by Holmes' erudite, confident attitude as he continued, "When I entered, you were reading a paper by holding it at arm's length, stubbornly denying the spectacles you obviously need but are too vain to admit needing even though they are there on your desk within easy reach. Your marksmanship, obviously, is indicated by that trophy." He indicated a small brass figure of a man firing a pistol with Griffin's name on the base. "And I observed that when you tossed that wad of trash as I came in, you used your right hand, but aimed with your left eye."

Holmes sucked in an expansive breath, rolling toward home. "There's a Wet Paint sign on the door of room 304, which I passed en route to see you, and the color matches a fleck of still-damp paint on your right elbow."

Griffin looked down at the spot of paint.

"Your helpfulness to short people is made clear by the commendation from them framed on your wall," which Holmes indicated, then pointed his long, lean index finger at Griffin's chest. "A tiny piece of pasta clings to your lapel, and the cup, of which I can see a portion in front of you, has your nickname,

Noodles, printed on it. The ceramic sculpture of a slice of watermelon atop your filing cabinet there—"

"And why don't they like me in Detroit?" Griffin interrupted gruffly.

"Ah." Holmes smiled, indicating the wall behind him without looking. "The framed newspaper headline: GRIFFIN LEAVING; LOSS TO NO TOWN."

"That's MO-town, Jack!" Griffin bellowed. "You got it exactly backwards, asshole. They *loved* me in Detroit. And that commendation is from my Little League team. That's baseball, in case you haven't heard, not *Wizard of Oz* munchkins—" His eyes narrowed, "And nobody calls me Noodles! That's what I ate for lunch!"

He rotated what Holmes had thought was a personalized cup to reveal the full imprint: Cup o' Noodles. Holmes realized, uncomfortably, that it was a commercial product's brand name.

"As for the watermelon, that's called *irony*, man. It's a joke. A freakin' joke—Hello?—Jesus, what the hell time zone are you from anyway?"

That gnawing in Holmes' stomach that had begun when he saw the police laboratory had now twisted into a knot.

Griffin stared at him a moment, furrowing his brow upon a closer examination of Holmes' odd clothes and generally peculiar demeanor. Griffin was a smart man who had risen to his current position by listening to people and never refusing their help when needed. But he was also nobody's fool and could spot a wacko across Oracle Park, and Holmes was just across the desk. Griffin went brusquely back to business, saying, "Now, they said you had something for me on Jimmy the Gimp Booth, so what is it?"

Holmes was struggling to regain his mental balance as he uneasily took a seat in the wooden chair opposite Griffin. "Uh, yes, that is correct. Actually, I'm hoping for information about him from you, as well. I was robbed by him."

Griffin grabbed a pen and note paper, "Okay, what'd he take?"

"My identification papers—and about a million dollars in precious stones."

"Really?" Griffin whistled, making notations. "When did this occur?"

"About sixty years ago."

Griffin stopped writing. He slowly raised his dark brown eyes, his expression blank. "Say again?"

"Approximately sixty years back, give or take a year," Holmes replied. "I'm aware, of course, that the statute of limitations has expired, but if you could provide me with some important information, I've no doubt I can be of assistance to you in capturing—"

Griffin threw down his pen and glared at Holmes. "Let me show you something, man." He angrily spun his chair to face his computer. "Check this out." He tapped out his access code and opened a file on the screen. Photos of James Moriarty Booth at various ages scrolled past, the most recent showing him to be about age sixty-five or seventy. His face was broad and full, and his graying but still-ginger hair clearly reflected his Irish heritage. Pages of writing also scrolled past as Griffin popped a Gelusil tablet.

"Booth has smuggled drugs, robbed, cheated, money-laundered, hustled, and killed all over this city for fifty years but managed to keep his hands just clean enough to avoid going down.

He's fenced all around with safeguards so goddamned cunningly devised we've never gotten any hard evidence that would convict him." He gestured toward the outside office. "Just like that dickwad Enrique Pavon we dragged in here again today. And that son of a bitch has always walked too."

"Yes, I saw Mr. Pavon," Holmes chimed in fraternally. "And actually, I must tell you there's a good possibility that—"

Griffin cut him off. "Whatever racket Booth doesn't operate, Pavon does. They've been huge rivals for years. Their flunkies will never testify 'cause they're afraid of getting whacked." He leveled his eyes at Holmes. "I have personally been after Booth's ass for twelve years. The only assistance I need is something airtight in the way of hard evidence." He paused to glare full bore at Holmes. "Now, you got anything solid or not?"

"Nnnnot yet." Holmes drew himself up, readying to provide Griffin the incredible benefit of his extreme expertise. "But you may be keenly interested in my theory about the recent tiger and piranha murders."

Griffin closed his eyes. Then he opened them with a deadly smile. "Gee, Hubert—NO. You may be Holmes, but you'll never be Sherlock. Now get the hell out of my office!"

As Holmes slowly walked back through the busy police headquarters lobby toward the exit, he later confessed to me in a moment of rare candor, there was a dark cloud over his head. His face was a tight mask. His insides churning. Not only had he been blocked from getting deeper information on Booth, he had been ridiculed. *Ridiculed!*

But far worse, he'd been dismissed. That was an even deeper wound. His brilliant talents—of which he was so justifiably proud—had been blithely disparaged and disregarded.

Holmes was infuriated over it all but didn't know where to go with that anger. It kept swirling round and round in his roiling brain. When he'd given himself this challenge of solving mysteries of the future, he'd never even considered that the future might be unreceptive. He felt spiteful.

And as he walked out the entrance of police headquarters, being brutally honest with himself in that moment, he was at a loss regarding what his next step might be.

Holmes later said that Fate can sometimes smile, for had he exited the building a moment or two earlier or later, he could well have missed a valuable encounter. The rookie Faheem was standing on the wide entrance steps listening with rapt attention to an older cop who'd paused in telling a startling tale to take a drag on his cigarette. As Holmes was passing by unmindful of them, embroiled in his own troubles, a few words caused his ears to prick up.

"Yeah," the cop continued relating his story, "that tiger killing was plenty weird enough." Holmes slowed down. The cop went on, "Then the one at the aquarium, shit. But this new one—*whoa!*"

Holmes stopped.

The rookie eagerly prodded the older, "What new one? Tell me!"

Holmes stood silently nearby as the cop, whose name tag read Hernandez, rested his butt on the edge of a planter and went on. "You know that hot assistant DA, Jacob Weiss? Ortega's buddy?"

Faheem nodded, "Yeah, sure. I've seen Weiss and Ortega working through cases together. Heard 'em finish each other's sentences a lot. Seemed like really close friends."

"Yeah, for years," Hernandez confirmed. "So I roll in Code 3 to Weiss's neighborhood street answering a 911 for a 243."

The rookie struggled to remember. "243 . . . isn't that battery with a dangerous—"

"Weapon. Right." The veteran smiled, impressed by the young woman. Then Holmes saw his face turn dark. "But lemme tell ya, kid, I'd never heard of a weapon like this. A buncha neighbors were gathered around but were keepin' their distance 'cause it was one weird crime scene. The eyewitness, a soccer mom who'd called it in, she ran up to me and described what'd happened." Hernandez took a breath and said very slowly to Faheem, "Now, you've got to really try to picture this."

Holmes, also listening carefully, did exactly that: mentally envisioning the crime as Hernandez described it. "She's coming home from her morning walk on this residential street and notices a cement truck stopped in the right lane with its blinkers on. Weiss is coming outta his house. He sees soccer mom and trades a friendly wave with her. Then he gets into the old VW bug in his driveway, facing the street." Holmes correctly assumed the cop was speaking of a car. "He starts the VW and slides the sunroof back. The neighbor says she'd seen him do the same routine every morning. He puts on his seatbelt and drives about halfway outta his driveway . . . when a big black SUV sweeps in and smacks his bumper, blocking him. The witness sees Weiss start to get out, but then he's struggling with his seatbelt—which we later discovered somebody'd rigged so it wouldn't unlock—meanwhile, the cement truck backs right up to the VW and dumps its load right through the sunroof onto Weiss!"

"Holy shit!" Faheem's eyes went wide.

"Yeah. But guess what—it ain't cement." The older cop swallowed uneasily, then with a sickened expression said, "It's *beetles!*"

Holmes reacted sharply. As did the stunned rookie. "Beetles?"

Hernandez nodded, "Yeah. Picture that."

Exactly what Holmes was doing.

"The witness said it was like a waterfall of a goddamn zillion bugs! She says it was a horrible sight, one she'd never forget: Weiss screaming as these millions of creepy bugs fill up over his shoulders then his face and head. Finally, she sees his hands come sticking up outta that ocean of insects, clawing at the air like crazy, his hands crawlin' with them. Then the cement truck and SUV both take off. The woman didn't make any plates but called 911. I was there in less than two minutes with backup right on my six. When we finally got the seatbelt cut and pulled Weiss out, he was dead, drowned in bugs. They'd swarmed down his throat. Up his nose. Killed him."

"Oh my God," the rookie said low, horrified.

"And they were mean little bastards. Bitin' the shit outta us too as we dragged him clear. They musta been starvin' because they chewed Weiss up somethin' awful. Shredded his face, his eyes. Right down to the bone."

"Geez." Faheem grimaced. "Does Ortega know?"

Hernandez shook his head. "We haven't found Luis yet," then he added grimly, "if he's even still around to find."

He and the young cop shared a worried glance as Holmes spoke up, "What kind of beetles?"

The older cop glanced over at the odd-looking Englishman. "How would I know, pal?"

The rookie spotted something coming up the street toward them, "Jesus! Is that the car?"

All three looked toward a passing police tow truck pulling the old VW bug, empty now, except for a few dozen beetles. Several dead ones fell onto the street in the vehicle's wake.

Faheem and Hernandez watched curiously as Holmes walked into the street and picked up one of the insects. He studied it with care before nodding as he muttered to himself, "Of *course*."

He glanced back at the tow truck as it pulled the VW into the station's parking lot, driving past a tearful woman.

Holmes recognized the distraught Karen Ortega, who was getting into her car. He saw her angrily wipe her eyes, clench her jaw, and gaze straight ahead into an uncertain future, fearful for the fate of her husband, Luis. Then she summoned just enough courage to start her car and drive away.

Holmes observed her departure. He would have liked to offer his help, but there was nothing he could do for her at that moment. He sympathized with her, however, feeling as frustrated and stymied about his own problems as Mrs. Ortega did about hers.

So he drew a breath, refocused, and took from his pocket a small gold snuff box. He carefully secured the dead beetle within it, then squared his shoulders and marched off.

Since the police were unwilling to take his counsel, Holmes had decided it was time for him to take direct action.

11

It was getting dark by the time I arrived home from work that evening. I'd stayed longer than expected at the hospital because at the last minute a six-year-old ringlet-haired tomboy named Katie, suffering from a burst appendix, had been rushed into the ER by paramedics. She was trying to be brave but was tearful and terrified. We eased her under sedation, and I successfully performed an emergency robotic appendectomy, but I waited to leave until Katie had fully awakened in recovery so we could talk a little about her whole experience.

Talking personally to my young patients was important to me because lots of kids can be fearful of hospitals and doctors. That's why my mom, also a pediatrician, liked to visit elementary schools. I was so proud when she came into my kindergarten classroom. The other kids were surprised when she sat right down face-to-face with them in a kindergarten-height chair just like ours. To the other kids it looked funny to see a grown-up sitting on such a tiny chair. To me it was typical Mom.

She reached out and shook hands with the closest kids.

"Squeeze firmly," she said smiling. "Always shake like you mean it." Mom never talked down to kids. She always talked to me or any kid like we were grown-ups. She'd confide that *she* used to be scared of doctors when she was our age, but she'd learned to trust them, to understand that all doctors wanted to help.

Then she'd put her stethoscope on the ears of each kid and let them listen to *her* heart. Her sincerity made them comfortable. With her grace, her humor, and her professionalism, Mom was an ideal role model. I didn't just follow her eagerly into medicine, but all the way to becoming a pediatric surgeon myself. Back when I was still a kid, she told me, "If you find a job you really love, Amy, you'll never work." That confused me till I realized she meant that if your job brought joy and fulfillment, it would never feel laborious. She was right. I've tried to pay it forward ever since, passing along to kids like Katie my mom's lessons of sincerity, spirit, and "Always shake hands like you mean it."

I was smiling, thinking about Mom, as I opened my front door. I had given Holmes a key to the house, so he was already inside and pacing my living room with his brow furrowed, lost in thought as I entered—whereupon he sprang to life like my hybrid Accord after the engine's been sleeping at a stoplight.

"Ah, Winslow, at last!" he said, rubbing his hands together.

"What . . . *What?*" I stammered as he put on a water-repellent Victorian coachman's cape in a gray houndstooth pattern that went over his frock coat and extended below his knees. It had no sleeves, but armholes that were covered by a small winglike cape on the outside that fell below his waist.

It looked strangely familiar, then I realized why: it was exactly like one I'd seen Basil Rathbone wearing in those old black-and-white movies.

"I need you to accompany me on a little drive."

"Accompany you?" I said with an arched eyebrow. "Really? Did you get a driver's license today?"

"Well," he backpedaled, "you, of course, would do the actual driving."

"Yeah. No kidding," I said, not hiding my annoyance. I tossed down my bag and kicked my shoes off. "Listen, I will do my best to help you, Mr. Holmes, but we've already had quite a long day. I'm tired. I'm hungry and—"

"Of course!" He headed directly into the kitchen and took something out of my fridge. "Allow me to prepare for you one of these bury-toes from the Trader Joe person. They're quite delicious. Additionally, I have studied the instructions and now understand how not to explode your macrowave."

"Microwave."

"Right!" After punching in various beeps, he watched the burrito revolve inside the oven. "You can eat it while we're driving."

My head collapsed onto my chest. "Please, Holmes, can't it wait until tomorrow?"

"For some investigations, Winslow, the cover of darkness is essential."

"It can also be useful for sleeping. I'm sorry, but I am just not up to—"

"When you met Leftenant Ortega, you felt his grief and that he was a most worthy person, did you not?"

"Of course I did, but what does—"

"He has gone missing."

"What?"

"Dangerously missing. I saw his wife at police headquarters this afternoon and—"

"Wait, wait. You were at police headquarters?" This was the first I'd learned of it. He nodded smugly as I stammered, "How did you— What did they—"

"It was . . . an enlightening experience, which I will expound upon hereafter." There was an awkward flavor to his utterance of the word *enlightening* that I found worrisome. He was also dodging my questions while absolutely determined to plow ahead. "Far more importantly, Winslow, I witnessed firsthand why Mrs. Karen Ortega was appropriately distraught and fearful for her husband's life." He raised an index finger to emphasize: "I also spotted a clear *connection* between Ortega, the tiger murders, and an underworld chieftain named Pavon, who was just then waltzing out the station after avoiding arrest."

I said cynically, "So, naturally, you brought all this to the attention of the police and . . . ?"

"I *tried* to tell them my theories, Winslow," he said heatedly. "But before I could expound, they cut me off—tossed me out!"

I feared I could guess the answer, but asked anyway. "Why?"

He looked away, reluctant to admit, "'Twas a painful lesson, Winslow. Bitter tea to swallow, but I learned that no authorities will give a shilling about my opinions on face value, nor even *listen*"—he looked squarely at me—"until I can conclusively *prove who I am*. Only then will anyone fully grasp and respect the enormous body of successful detective work I've accomplished in the past. Only when I have such proof will they appreciate all that I have to offer, that I am *eager* to offer." He blew out an angry puff. "It was made all the more ironically, insanely frustrating because the moment I set foot outside the building I gained *additional* insights, saw more pieces of the puzzle and logical reasons to believe that the good Leftenant will not long remain alive." He lowered his brow, his eyes locked onto mine, his voice low and insistent. "Unless you and I intervene to help."

Ding. My burrito was ready to go.

Five minutes later I was starting up my Accord as Holmes put a cylindrical canvas duffel bag into the back seat. Rain was imminent, and it was already misting.

Wearing his newsboy cap, he climbed in front with renewed energy as I activated the nav unit and the screen lit up. "Okay," I asked him, "what was the address?"

"196 Dardenelle Avenue, Pacifica, California."

I input it and the map showed our location as Siri's voice came on, "Calculating directions to 196 Dardenelle Avenue." Holmes blinked with delight. Siri added, "Drive time by fastest route, thirty-four minutes."

He whispered aside to me as though thinking Siri could hear us and he didn't want to be rude, "Is she always on call for you?"

I nodded. "Actually, she is."

"But how in the world can she determine with such alacrity that—" Then he deduced it. "Ah. She is using a computer."

"No, Holmes." I smiled wanly, as tired as I was. "She *is* a computer."

Holmes stared at the screen, saying quietly, "Miraculous."

Siri's voice instructed, "Head south on Baker Street for three hundred feet then turn right onto Bay Street." I made a U-turn following Siri's instructions while I asked, "What exactly is down at 196 Dardenelle Avenue?"

Holmes was watching the map display on my dashboard screen and spoke distractedly, reiterating, "Possibly information that will help me recover those damned identity papers." Then he frowned when Siri guided us north onto Richardson. "Is she confused? Pacifica is south."

"She's taking us by the fastest possible route."

"How is she aware which way that is?"

"She's constantly getting input from GPS—Global Positioning System satellites that—"

"Satellites, as in moons?"

"Very small ones that have been launched on rockets up into orbit."

"Ah. Jules Verne lives!"

"Yes." While driving, I was fumbling with the wrapper on my "bury-toe" and finally handed it to him. "Would you, please?" He unwrapped it with his long fingers as I went on, "Siri also gathers information from traffic cameras and sensors and even other drivers. She's your kindred spirit, Holmes, always looking for data, data, data." I saw his eyes twinkle at the concept.

By then we'd merged onto the 101 freeway and were crossing through the Presidio when Siri interjected, "In a quarter mile, take exit 438 toward California 1 south."

Which I did. I'd also taken a couple of bites of my Trader Joe's entrée and of course gotten salsa on my fingers. I pointed down toward the floor by Holmes' left leg and asked, "Hand me a tissue, would you?"

He retrieved it, but also noticed on the floor the book of Doyle's Sherlock stories just inside a small shopping bag. He cast an inquiring look my way, prompting an explanation. "I had a couple hours to glance through it at the hospital while I waited in recovery for a young surgery patient to wake up."

"Had you never read any of them?"

"A little bit, long ago, but I was immediately reminded why they've had such popularity for so long. I was surprised to read that *A Study in Scarlet* was actually rejected four places before being accepted for the 1887 *Beeton's Christmas Annual.*"

"Quite true." Holmes nodded. "Then Doyle received twenty-five pounds sterling for the copyright of the story. Quite a nice amount in those days."

"Well, put this in your pipe: I discovered that a copy of that *Beeton's Annual* sold at a Sotheby's auction in 2007 for one hundred fifty-six thousand dollars."

He was stunned. "You're joking!"

"Making it the most expensive magazine in the world."

"My, my," Holmes pondered that. "Reviews were favorable but certainly not *that* enthusiastic. Although our exploits proved quite popular, particularly in America. Partly because anyone outside of England could print it without paying the author. And the story's great success caught the attention of an American publishing house, which then commissioned Doyle to supply a new tale, for which he would be properly and amply rewarded."

"So he came back to Watson and you, hoping to hear about more cases."

"Indeed, yes. Watson supplied him with material and case notes, from which Doyle crafted a new story that he eventually titled—"

"*The Sign of the Four*," I said. "Published in *Lippincott's Monthly Magazine*, 1890, to great acclaim."

He was surprised by my specificity. "Why, Dr. Winslow, when did you become such a wellspring of Sherlockiana?"

I smiled, delighted to be one-up on him. "Just surfed the web a bit today for more *data*."

"I see. You have been gargling."

I glanced at him curiously.

He frowned and tried another word. "Gurgling?"

"Googling?"

"Right!" He said it as though that's what he'd said the first time. "And your Mr. Google is correct." I drew a breath but decided to let "Mr. Google" go by as he continued, "*The Sign of the Four* was received with even more positive notoriety and enthusiasm than *A Study in Scarlet*. Thus, Watson and I extended our arrangement with Doyle, allowing him to scour our numerous case files to form the basis for additional stories."

"Those were the ones that got published in that other magazine, *The Strand*?"

"Yes." His nose turned up a bit. "A periodical which could occasionally be a bit lurid. And sometimes Doyle would 'enhance' our case files with romanticism, which for me had much the same effect as working a love story or an elopement into the fifth proposition of Euclid."

"But Mr. Doyle's stories were wildly popular," I said while feeling a bit of envy, wondering if my own writing might someday be published. "Is it true that people began to believe that his Sherlock was a real person?"

"Absolutely."

"And would-be clients really came looking for 221B Baker Street and were frustrated to discover that it existed only in the stories?"

Holmes nodded. "Watson soon put up a small sign near where 221B would have been situated, suggesting that they instead call a few doors away at 236 Baker Street. That was where I had actually taken rooms. Where Watson and I made our headquarters."

"And then what? You'd explain to potential clients that Sherlock was fictional but Hubert was real and could do the job?"

"We began that way, but quickly realized that it was easier and—as good old softhearted Watson always noted—kinder to simply say, 'Yes, I am Sherlock. How can I help you?'"

"And no harm done," I said, "since you obviously had the skills they were seeking. Besides, lots of writers have taken a nom de plume."

"Of course, like Amantine Dupin, who wrote under the name—"

"George Sand." I was surprised that he actually did know of the female writer.

"Precisely. And it was also a common occurrence for an actor or actress to assume a stage name. Sometimes this was done so their relatives might avoid the embarrassment or shame of having a thespian in the family. Thus, I slipped into using the name Sherlock for my public persona while I simply went on being exactly whom I'd always been. That allowed Watson and me to avoid repeated explanations to new clients and a lot of irrelevant chatter so we could get on with solving whatever mystery they presented us."

Siri spoke up, "In a quarter mile, turn right onto Sloat Boulevard, then bear left onto Skyline Drive."

As I made the turn toward the west, Holmes gazed at the

dark road ahead through the windshield, on which a misty rain was being swept by the wipers.

"But Inspector Layton—whom you said Doyle renamed Lestrade—and his fellow officers at Scotland Yard would have known you by your real name, right?"

"Yes," Holmes said sardonically. "I often had to endure their clever little gibes and jests about my dual identity. But whatever his given name, Consulting Detective Holmes had been so helpful in a great many of their difficult cases, solving so many intricate mysteries which had left them baffled and confounded, that they went along with my charade. Even so, Layton was not overly fond of me 'interfering,' as he put it, in police matters."

"Doubtless annoyed that you often solved cases which he and Scotland Yard could not."

"Correct. So, in 1899, when I told Layton I was leaving England, bound for exotic foreign climes, and that he might never hear from me again, you can imagine how eagerly he agreed to fingerprint me and supply me the official papers verifying my identification as Mr. Holmes, Hubert, a.k.a. Sherlock in the Doyle stories."

"He was probably happy to get you out of his hair," I said, with a slight shading of my own current feelings.

He smirked. "How tastefully stated, Winslow."

"I read that the *Strand* stories were very popular."

"Frightfully so. Young Dr. Doyle received quite a financial windfall from them. So much so that he was able to completely abandon his medical practice and, to his delight, focus entirely on his burgeoning career as an author."

"Then why in the world did Mr. Doyle kill off Sherlock in only the twenty-fourth story? Did he tell you he was going to?"

Holmes looked greatly taken aback. "I'm astonished you would even ask the question. Of course he informed me. He would never have wished me to just read about it along with the public at large. Doyle was honest, honorable, and a thoroughgoing gentleman. He was extraordinarily appreciative of how Watson and I had given him open access to our files, to the raw material that provided the foundation of his literary accomplishments. Material to which he had added his own editorial artistry and made a success, from which we had all three benefited financially." He looked off into the distance, recalling, "As I sit here with you, I can vividly picture sitting there with him that night in 1893 in the handsomely furnished old Savile Club." He glanced at me. "Considering your fondness for historical novels and environments, you'd have been impressed by it, Winslow. Its walls were ornamented with the choicest French paper, enriched by an elegantly designed, gilded cornice. A maroon carpet covered the floor. Two superb mirrors—one above the chimneypiece, extending to the ceiling, and the other at the opposite end of the room, reaching floor to ceiling—multiplied the length and spaciousness of the room while reflecting the flames of the crystal chandeliers. The padded leather chairs were marvelously comfortable." He shifted in the passenger seat of my Accord as though recalling the preferable feel of the Savile's vintage chairs.

"I love London." Just thinking about that great city always made me smile. "Whereabouts was the Savile?"

"Overlooking Green Park. It commanded a generous view with Buckingham Palace in the distance." He chuckled slightly, his eyes narrowing as though focusing on well-remembered images. "I can absolutely *see* Doyle's sturdy round Anglo-Irish face, with its crescent mustache illuminated by the gaslight, Winslow. We three were talking over snifters of Courvoisier, Watson smoking his cigar, Doyle enjoying the shag cut tobacco in his bent billiard pipe as I drew on my favorite old briar-root. Doyle told us of the tremendous delight he had taken in publicizing our investigations. How he would have loved to continue writing about them ad infinitum, but that lately he'd felt a yearning to move on to other 'more serious' writing he had long been delaying. And now, in order to do so, he planned to bring the stories of our exploits to a dramatic and irreversible conclusion wherein Sherlock would meet his end while fulfilling his destiny. He assured us of his gratitude and fondness for us, which we never doubted, and also that our percentages of any revenue he might yet receive from the existing stories would continue."

I asked delicately, "Did you have any concerns that ending the stories might affect your livelihood?"

"No. At the time, I still had former clientele returning for assistance with new problems and also fresh inquiries for help. Watson had satisfactory earnings from his medical practice to support his family. And we both did receive minor earnings from our percentages," Holmes drew a breath. "But yes, Winslow, over the next several years, my services were less frequently sought, and my caseload dwindled."

I nodded. "Because people thought Sherlock was indeed dead."

"*Requiescat in pace.*" He chuckled sadly. "Alas."

"Weren't you able to explain the truth to prospective clients? Who you really were?"

"I attempted that for a time, even showing them an affidavit Doyle had volunteered, but my veracity was increasingly questioned, some even presuming I was a charlatan, a pretender endeavoring to cash in on the amazing reputation of a well-beloved but now sadly deceased hero. The irony was amusing, but it was also . . ." He paused, and I sensed that he was searching for a word that would not make him sound too vulnerable. He finally sniffed dryly, and said, "It was somewhat debilitating. Work had always been the antidote for any frustrations, but with less and less call on my services, my life grew ever more empty."

I spoke softly, "I'm certain that was very hard. Particularly for someone of your abilities and worth to find himself in forced retirement."

Holmes turned his head slightly away to look out the side window toward the dark ocean that was now on our right.

"But Inspector Layton knew the truth, knew of your tremendous value. Didn't he ask for your help after that?"

"On a few occasions, yes. But he was a proud, ferret-like little man, protective of his own esteemed position. When he did seek my counsel, he did so privately and often as though he were going out of his way to do me a favor."

By then we were driving through Lake Merced Park, several miles above the town of Pacifica. "Nowadays, someone might go to a media outlet or newspaper to get the truth out to a broader public," I said. "Did you ever consider—"

Holmes sat up stiffly. "Never." He glowered at me. "Neither Watson nor I ever expected or requested any public credit be given us for supplying our cases that inspired Conan Doyle's stories. Besides, the general public would likely have dismissed me as an impostor. And also"—he grew more introspective—"it seemed an appropriate time to bring his chronicling of our investigations to a close, because it came within a few weeks of my return from Switzerland."

"Where you dispatched James Moriarty to his death at the Reichenbach Falls." I glanced at him.

Holmes paused, with a thousand-yard gaze through my rainy windshield, as though recalling that moment of "dispatch." He finally said slowly, "Yes, he fell into the abyss." Holmes sat, staring down the foggy, dark road ahead.

"I actually jumped ahead and read that story today," I admitted. "*The Final Problem.* Doyle wrote that there was clear evidence of the struggle between the two of you and that you had tumbled off together . . ." As I spoke the next five words, Holmes whispered them along with me. "'Locked in each other's arms.'"

"Yes," Holmes said quietly, "That's what Doyle wrote." After an introspective moment, he added, "Perhaps the way it should have been."

"You mean, because that left no one who was a worthy challenger to your skills." I understood. "That brought on your depression and heavier addiction to opiates and cocaine."

Without looking at me, he gave a single nod.

I weighed whether I should ask. When I did, it was a whisper. "What really happened that day at the falls?"

"Moriarty and I did struggle ferociously, hand to hand, fired by our mutual hatred. We fought so intensely that I was barely aware of the narrowness of the ledge on which our combat was engaged." Holmes glanced at me. "Try to envision it, Winslow: a torrent of plunging water roared downward right beside us into the glistening, black rock chasm with its flickering spray hissing upwards." Holmes' intense eyes wandered as he described the scene. "The constant, thunderous whirl and clamor were dizzying as we clutched at each other's throats with extreme exertion and the wafting mists soaked us to the bone." I glanced over and saw that Holmes' respiration had increased, he was deeply into the memory, saying, "Moriarty was a physically powerful adversary. I felt my strength waning. We were both near exhaustion when I managed to shove him backwards"—Holmes thrust out his hands—"against the sheer wall of the black cliffside, and in doing so, I recoiled a step back toward the precipice." He paused, blinked. "Oddly, I remember having a fleeting thought of Newton's third law of motion: action causes reaction." Emotion flooded back into his description as he continued. "Then I chilled, having felt nothing but air below my left heel. At that moment"—Holmes unconsciously acted out the moves as he spoke—"Moriarty's right hand drew from within his greatcoat a dagger—the classic secret weapon of the sinister—which he plunged straight toward my heart, putting his full weight behind the mighty thrust. But my Japanese baritsu training protected me. I turned sharply to the right, pivoting on the toe of my right foot to barely avoid his blade as my right hand parried and grasped his oncoming wrist. I pulled him onward, pivoting further to my right, onto solid ground, while using his own inertia—Newton's first law—to propel him past me. And off the cliff."

Holmes was panting. He seemed lost in the moment, unaware that he had been performing all the actions as he replayed them in his head.

"I watched as he fell nearly a thousand feet, like Lucifer cast out from heaven. He was clawing at the misty air, flailing madly with an expression of hellish terror on his face, and with a hideous shriek of abject fury, he disappeared into a dreadful cauldron of swirling water and seething foam far below."

Holmes paused, slowly transitioning back into the present-day moment, forcing himself to breathe more calmly, then finally inhaling through his nose. He continued to gaze out into the darkness, frowning. He glanced at me momentarily, seeming very self-conscious. "Of course, Winslow, those events transpired much more quickly than it takes me to describe them."

I shook my head with wonder. "What an extraordinary moment of triumph you must have felt. But also confusion?"

"Indeed so," he said quietly and now devoid of emotion.

I understood why. "Your principal adversary so suddenly gone. It was a well-earned victory for you yet also a monumental loss."

He nodded, once only.

"Did you feel that emptiness right away?"

"Perhaps." He was still deeply immersed within that moment over a century ago as he whispered, almost to himself, "Beware what you wish for."

Siri said, "In a quarter mile, bear to the right to merge onto California Route 1."

Her voice drew Holmes back into the present. Or, in his case, back to the future.

Something we were passing caught his eye. "That is the strangest tree I've ever seen."

I glanced at it and smiled. It was tall, slender, and had a dozen dish antennas peeking out of the faux green foliage. "It's actually a tower and those dishes are transmitting signals to these." I held up my cell and also indicated my dashboard screen. "They try to disguise them as trees."

"I'm afraid they missed the mark." Then he glanced in my

direction. "Tell me, Winslow, what became of Conan Doyle? Was he able to write those 'more serious works' he wanted to?"

"He did write a couple of novels. But the public's outcry over the loss of Holmes put continuing pressure on him to bring back Sherlock and Watson. And he was certainly aware that his later novels hadn't sold nearly as well as the mystery stories. So in 1902 Doyle created a new book to revive Holmes, which I haven't yet read: *The Hound of the Baskervilles*."

"*Ah*," Holmes reacted with a smile of pleasure. "Now that was indeed one of our more fascinating adventures. And I know that Watson had kept a detailed accounting of our investigation. I recall us telling all the specifics to Doyle one long evening that began over dinner at the Eclectic Club."

I smirked. "Sounds like the perfect club for you."

"It was. Always invigorating, eccentric company. After dinner, Watson and I continued relating the adventure to Doyle as we walked together uptown through the chill, damp streets of Mayfair, past Grosvenor Square, and into Marylebone. We ended in my lodgings on the second floor of 236 Baker Street where they two shared the enjoyment of tobacco, while I took a small injection of cocaine."

It struck me how offhandedly he said that, reminding me just how much that casual sort of drug use had been a completely legal, everyday occurrence in those times and in his life.

Then he asked, "Was his Baskerville book successful?"

"Resoundingly. But he'd written it as though it were a later memoir of Watson's, so he hadn't actually *revived* you. It was so popular, however, that a couple years later—1904, I think—Doyle published another story, called *The Empty House*, in which he actually brought Sherlock back to life."

Holmes chuckled. "And just how, pray tell, did the dear old Irishman deign to resurrect me? Some elaborate biochemical process such as my own?"

"No. He simply said that you hadn't died in Switzerland. That after doing away with Moriarty you faked your own death and went into hiding in Europe because you knew several of Moriarty's minions were pursuing you to avenge their leader."

"As indeed they were," he acknowledged. "Which you've now witnessed yourself. But there was no European excursion. Watson merely sequestered me in a family cottage outside London whilst I endeavored to face the loss of the archnemesis who had been the focal point of my crime-fighting existence. He'd become my raison d'être, and the subsequent ennui and depression was such as I'd never experienced."

"Certainly, your seven percent solution wasn't truly a solution."

"No. The effects of cocaine and opium were fleeting. The days got continually darker. And the lack of clients to distract me was further dispiriting."

"You were fortunate that Watson's and Doyle's concerns prompted them to introduce you to stimulating people like H. G. Wells."

"It was a gift of life. And certainly inspired a sea change in me."

"Did you tell them what you were going to attempt?"

He glanced at me mirthfully. "If anyone told you such a thing, Winslow, how would you react?"

I nodded. "Right. I'd have you sequestered for being a danger to yourself."

"Precisely. I feared my benevolent friends would render me that same service."

"But the letter I read from your brother shows that—"

"Mycroft was the only one I told," he acknowledged. "But I made him take a vow of silence before I revealed my proposed undertaking."

We both smiled at him using that word. I said, "Had anything gone wrong, you would have *needed* an undertaker."

"But everything went exactly right! And chancing the adventure has led me forward—in every sense of the word—into this very evening." A fond smile slowly formed as he gazed ahead while reflecting on his success. Then he drew a breath and asked, "So, when the public read Doyle's new story, were they happy to have Watson and me back in their company?"

"*Ohh,* yes. And Doyle followed up with a series of additional stories. He became Sir Arthur, incidentally. Knighted by Edward the Seventh for his patriotic efforts in the Boer War—and also for all his stories about you."

"*Ha.* Bravo, Lord Doyle. He must have dug back into the treasure trove of many other previous case files that Watson had supplied to him."

"Apparently so. Because the world's most famous consulting detective remained alive and well through to 1917 when the concluding story appeared, *His Last Bow.*"

"The final, final curtain. And then he killed me off again?"

Before I could answer, Siri interjected, "In one mile, turn left onto Reina Del Mar Avenue."

"No," I said to Holmes. "The story was set three years earlier in 1914, at the beginning of World War One. Doyle wrote that you had retired from being a consulting detective and—"

"Retired?" Holmes was incredulous.

"Yes. You were contentedly enjoying beekeeping and—"

"*Beekeeping?*" His face screwed up in such abject astonishment that I couldn't help but chuckle.

"Yes." I reported, smiling. "In the English countryside. But you and Watson were recruited by the British government to help the war effort by recovering vital documents stolen by a German spy."

He nodded. "Similar to that assignment we undertook for the king of Bohemia."

"Oh," I reacted to that with a touch of delight, which I tried to hide, saying, "You know, Holmes, that was the *first* story I read today." I kept my eyes focused on the rainy road and turned left as Siri directed, but I was smiling slyly to myself as I prodded, "Isn't that the case where you encountered a certain American woman?" Out of the corner of my eye, I detected a slight squirm. Perfect. Exactly the reaction I'd hoped for.

"It . . . may have been." He was dismissive and definitely vamping. "There were so very many cases that it's hard to remember all of the minor details, the supporting players that—"

"I'm sure it was her. The opera singer? 'The stunning diva who'd dazzled audiences at La Scala'?" I needled him. "How was it Watson described her? Oh yes, the 'well-known adventuress'?—the one with the sparkling eyes who had a fling with the king of Bohemia. They exchanged clandestine love letters, with which he feared she would blackmail him. Doesn't sound like a minor detail or a supporting player, Holmes."

"Well, she certainly must have been, because I really don't—"

"Oh, come on, Holmes," I chided. "You know damn well who she was. Watson said you always simply called her 'the

Woman'—and the photo in your valise must certainly be the one that the Bohemian king gave you. So naturally I'm curious about—"

"I've never quite forgiven you, Winslow," he interrupted. "Nor have you apologized for rifling through my personal belongings without my permission." He suddenly inhaled a huge breath and seemed revitalized—or he wanted to appear so in order to change the subject. "But enough of the past, Winslow." He glanced at me sharply. "And I can tell you this . . ."—he heaped great derision on his next word—"*retirement* is clearly *not* among my plans."

He leaned down to slip the Doyle book back into the small bag. "While you're down there," I said, "there's something in that bag for you." He glanced at me curiously, then felt inside the bag, becoming truly wide-eyed as he extracted a brown tweed double-billed deerstalker cap.

"Ha! Wherever did you find this?"

"This afternoon I also read *The Boscombe Valley Mystery*, which contained an original drawing by Sidney Paget that showed you wearing what Doyle described as an 'ear-flapped traveling cap.'"

"Just so," he said, mildly amused while turning the cap over in his hands. "Good old Sidney. He was a fine fellow with an easy laugh. Quite a talented artist and an aficionado of these peculiar toppers. Thinking back on his other illustrations I believe Sidney put that cap on my head many more times than I ever did. He might even have shown it falling off my head into Reichenbach Falls."

"I'll check on that. But seeing it in the book reminded me that one of my actress patients had been in a theater production about Sherlock. She dug it out of their wardrobe."

"Well, perhaps a bit misguided, but—" He paused, looking at me with the warmest expression I'd yet seen, then said quietly, "Very thoughtful of you, Winslow."

Our eyes held for more than a second. Then Siri's voice told us, "In one hundred yards, turn left onto Dardenelle Avenue. In two miles, you will reach your destination."

"Well done, Siri!" Holmes said with enthusiasm. "Tonight's journey may be of immeasurable help to conclusively prove my identity, fully resurrect me into this new world—and hopefully save the life of the good Luis Ortega." I saw a thought strike him pleasurably. "I'll tell you what, Winslow, in honor of our inaugural adventure together . . ."

He removed his newsboy's cap, gave me a meaningful glance as he straightened his shoulders ceremoniously, then fitted the deerstalker snugly onto his head.

I inhaled with unexpected revelation. For the first time he completely fulfilled the image of truly being Sherlock Holmes.

I will always remember that being a magical moment.

My mind kept trying to process the whole astonishing situation as I drove us further up into the hills above Pacifica, a small upscale town on the ocean. The fog had thickened, and rain was still sprinkling. Dardenelle Avenue curved up between the many posh residences, which became increasingly larger and farther apart until we were finally into an area with nothing but old-growth trees on either side of the road.

He was squinting to see ahead. "Stop just up there, Winslow." He was pointing to the corner of a ten-foot-tall stone wall that paralleled the dark road ahead. Another angle of the stone barrier went southward into the forest. I pulled partly onto the mossy shoulder of the road as he said, "Excellent."

"Excellent why? What are we doing here?"

As he surveyed the secluded forested area, he said, "In addition to the information I gleaned at police headquarters today, I found my way to a certain priest at old Saint Mary's Cathedral. One Father Moriarty."

A chill ran through me. "Did . . . did he know—"

"The identity of the clubfooted boy who sixty years ago had stolen my jewels and identity?" His eyes flashed with delight. "*Yes!*"

My blood was freezing up entirely as I looked out warily at the wall extending off into the dark forest. "Holmes, surely you are not telling me that this—"

"Is the southwest corner of number 196 Dardenelle Avenue, the estate of underworld chieftain James Moriarty Booth."

I was startled. But emphatic. "*Ohh* no. No, no, no!" I began to turn the car around, but Holmes had already popped his seatbelt, opened the door, and was stepping out.

12

"Wait a minute!" I said urgently with a hushed, stunned voice as I stopped, grabbed his discarded newsboy cap for my own head, and jumped out of the car into the light rain. "You're really certain that man Booth lives here?"

"Correct." He had opened the car's back door and was fishing something out of his small cylindrical duffel bag.

"How in the world did you find that out?"

"I saw the address on Detective Griffin's computer screen. Then back at your residence I scouted it out on your computer. What an amazing research asset. Of course, it has its limitations, which is why I need a closer look." From the duffel, he extracted a coil of rope and what looked like a stack of small boards bound together.

Numerous fierce concerns tumbled out of my mouth, one on top of another. "Are you out of your— In the history of bad ideas this is the worst I've— You *cannot* just go right up to his front door and—"

"Does this look like the *front* door?" His eyes twinkled

devilishly. He turned dramatically and headed for the ten-foot wall.

I was right on his heels, saying forcefully, "Stop! I will not let you do this! You could get—we could *both* get—*arrested!*"

"Should that happen, which I assure you it won't," he said while uncoiling the rope, "I shall assume full responsibility."

"*Ha!*" I laughed ferociously. "Big help *that* would be. You just bring that whatever-it-is and get back in the car!"

"Calm yourself, Winslow. I'll merely be exploring quietly to see what I can discern."

I was emphatic: "No, Holmes!"

"May I remind you," he grumbled, while working with the rope, "that this man stole and likely still possesses my identification and valuables. I also hope to find some incriminating evidence that will bring down the mighty Mr. Booth and—most important to Luis Ortega—I hope to gain the insights needed to save his life!"

With that he tossed a small grappling hook onto the top of the wall and pulled down hard on it, making certain it was reliably secured.

"Forget it!" I was apoplectic and determined to take charge. "We are out of here!"

I reached for his arm, but with the grace of a ballet danseur, he adroitly avoided my grasp and held up his right index finger, saying, "Wait. Allow me to demonstrate that I am an excellent cat burglar, my dear—always in a moral cause, of course." He was pulling on a second rope, which ran through a pulley on the grappling hook at the crest of the wall. That second rope was raising the pile of boards up to the top of the wall as Holmes continued his lecture. "My tutor was Charles Peace, the best cracksman in London. He gifted me with this little gem. Behold!"

He pulled a small trip cord hanging from the boards—and they dropped down toward the ground, spaced about a foot apart. It was a collapsible ladder. Quite ingenious.

Holmes enjoyed my surprise, proud of his criminal toy. "Now then, if you'd be so good as to secure the base for me."

"I won't. And you are not going to go up there!"

But he'd already started climbing as he sneered back at me, "Thanks ever so for your support."

At my wit's end, I grabbed for his cape with both hands, but he leapt two rungs higher with feline dexterity. I jumped to catch hold, but he was a millimeter out of reach. I shouted. "Come back here!"

"Winslow!" he whispered loudly, shooting me a dark look over his shoulder. "If you're not going to help, would you at least keep your voice down!"

I choked down my volume but ramped up the intensity. "I will not! Holmes!"

He shook his head at my stubbornness and scampered atop the wall. I called to him in one last desperate attempt, but he just pulled the ladder up, slipped it down the other side, then dropped out of sight. Only the trip cord was left dangling on my side. I gritted my teeth, trying to figure my next move.

Holmes later told me that on the far side of the wall he had "landed like a panther." Probably not a complete exaggeration, given his general nimbleness. He quickly surveyed the lush, expansive grounds sloping uphill toward the large estate and began moving.

Keeping a stealthy profile, he trod through the dark,

foggy compound, the master cat burglar sneaking closer to his quarry—for all of seventeen seconds, when he was blinded by bright xenon emergency lights. A blaring alarm sounded, and Holmes found himself nose-to-fangs with a giant Baskervillian hound: a two-hundred-pound, snarling English mastiff, straining against its leash, eager to bite his face off.

Holmes also felt the muzzle of a .357 Magnum tap him on top of his deerstalker.

On my side of the wall, I could see the bright lights, hear the alarm, the ferocious dog, and the deep growling voices of at least two other men, who were clearly taking my houseguest into custody.

I slapped my forehead down into the palm of my hand in frustration. Cold rain ran down my face and neck as I tried to decide what—if anything—I could do now.

Inside and out, James Moriarty Booth's exceedingly contemporary estate consisted of broad, curving expanses of poured concrete in the I. M. Pei style of architecture. The giant mastiff was led off by its handler while the other two guards, one with a shaved head and the other a curly-haired redhead, trundled Holmes across an outdoor terrace and through a tall sliding glass door into the great room of the house.

Inside, Holmes saw that the walls were white, with many works of modern art and sculpture displayed. The ceiling of the great room was twenty-five feet high. Light reflecting off the large swimming pool outside flickered, giving shimmering blue movement to the ceiling. A large, ancient, hanging tapestry covered part of one wall in contrast to the contemporary chrome and black glass tables of various sizes, including a large gaming table and one for dining with twelve guests. There were two separate sitting areas with black leather couches and chairs.

Holmes took in all of this while being thoroughly frisked by the muscular guard with a shaved head. Holmes was being made to spread his legs and lean with both hands flat on top of a side desk, which held some paperwork, a calendar, and couple of file folders labeled with bold numbers. Hanging on the wall over the desk was the most garish painting Holmes had ever seen—as though a human face had been scrambled. It had a large eye, a small eye, two equally mismatched ears, a strangely triangular nose, and huge lips, all rendered in brilliant and conflicting clownish colors and juxtaposed in the most peculiar, nonhuman, geometric manner. He assumed it to be a purposely outlandish cartoon. It was dated 1913 but the artist's scrawled signature was unclear. It was later determined to be a rare Picasso—stolen, of course.

The curly redhead had gone quickly up a broad, polished wood stairway and was now walking back down with cold eyes focused on Holmes.

"Did you inform your master who I am?" Holmes asked him with stern formality. In spite of his capture and being at the mercy of these men, he refused to concede a milligram of confidence.

Curly nodded darkly and directed Holmes' attention upward toward a balcony overlooking the living room. On the wide white wall near the balcony, Holmes saw a large shadow slowly approaching like a dark cloud. A man appeared, looking down over the balcony railing with an air of menace. He stood above, assessing Holmes, who could not see the man's face because of the light silhouetting him.

After a moment, the man withdrew from the balcony and descended the stairs. He had apparently attended a black-tie affair earlier but had removed his tuxedo jacket and untied his bow tie, which draped around his neck atop his formal white shirt.

James Moriarty Booth was seventy-two, though he looked several years older. Holmes recognized him from the photos he'd seen in Detective Griffin's office and online, but in person it was clearer that Booth's face and physiognomy diverged considerably from Professor Moriarty's balding, tall, lean, and hungry looks. Booth was sturdy and an inch shorter than Holmes. His graying red hair was thick and perfectly trimmed. His face, rather than gauntly triangular, was oval and well fed. His thick Irish nose had apparently been in more than one fistfight. He walked with a slight limp due to his deformed right foot, but Booth's countenance and presence were nonetheless imposing; he looked every bit a forbidding and powerful crime baron.

Though Booth was quite different physically from Professor Moriarty, Holmes noted their unifying genetics and lineage in Booth's thin, sneering lips and particularly his pale eyes with their sinister glint and piercing pinpoint pupils.

Upon seeing Holmes' face more closely, Booth reacted sharply and stared with studied amazement. He then broke into scornful laughter.

"Ah," Holmes said with satisfaction and a raised eyebrow. "Of course you recognize me, Mr. Booth. And I see you still have the scar on the back of your hand from that night sixty years ago."

Booth crossed the polished oak floor, circling Holmes to get a closer look. His voice, like his features, was strong. "I didn't know that Holmes had any offspring. My great-grandfather thought he was gay."

"Indeed I am!" Holmes said with pride, grandly sweeping his cape-like coat as he turned to face Booth full on. "And never gayer than when confronting a clever enemy."

Booth came to a stop in front of his black marble fireplace. The light from the fire flickered, outlining Booth—rather satanically, Holmes thought.

"I am not a son or grandson, however," Holmes stated. "I am the original Holmes."

"Not possible." Booth eyed him cynically. "I saw his cold corpse."

"Cold, yes," Holmes acknowledged, then smiled and continued authoritatively. "Corpse, not even close. I am the very man whose valuables you absconded with sixty years ago. Perhaps you'd care to refresh your memory by comparing my face to the photographs you stole—if you still possess them."

Booth eyed Holmes coolly, keenly scrutinizing him for a long moment. Then he took up the challenge, saying, "Actually . . ." Booth stepped over to a seven-foot-tall chrome curio cabinet with clear glass doors, saying, "I think I did keep them. Among some of my family's souvenirs." Inside the cabinet Holmes could see on thick glass shelves a strange assortment of items including a blackjack, an old Brink's money bag, a 1930s tommy gun, an elegant twelve-inch Lladró figurine of a woman with the head broken off, as well as a framed—and autographed—mugshot of someone named Alphonse Capone. Amid other interesting heirlooms Holmes noted a bell jar containing what looked disturbingly like a shriveled human foot.

Booth had opened the cabinet doors. "That hit up in Marin was my first big score. Those diamonds of yours set me up in business." He looked on one shelf, then reached up to a higher one, moving a vintage axe and a tarnished set of brass knuckles to get at something behind them.

"An evil empire," said Holmes, "which includes drug smuggling, thievery, murder, and money laundering—whatever that is."

"What can I say?" Booth smirked. "Business is good." He brought down from the shelf a rectangular metal box twelve by eighteen inches and nine inches deep. Holmes knew the dimensions specifically because it was, indeed, his stolen tin box. He felt a surge of emotion, but artfully concealed it within.

Booth placed the tin box on a table near the fireplace, then opened its lid.

Holmes maintained a level expression, but his mouth went dry as Booth lifted out several of the photographs that lay on top of a sheaf of other papers. The crime baron paused as he looked incredulously at the black-and-white photo in his hand. It showed George Bernard Shaw with his hand resting comradely on Holmes' shoulder.

Holmes drew a controlled, but internally tense breath. Everything he needed to conclusively prove his identity was there, barely six feet away.

Booth held the photo up and compared it to the living, breathing Holmes in front of him. There was no denying it was the same person. At the same age.

Booth spoke with low bewilderment, "I'll be goddamned."

He laughed. "I guess I *do* have you to thank for all my success. But how the hell can you be alive?"

"Merely a trifling bit of chemistry, but also a huge determination to bring villains like yourself to justice."

Booth stared at him, still awed by the uncanny circumstances. He was slowly absorbing the impossible yet undeniable reality of the Victorian man standing before him. Finally, he smiled. "Mr.—" Booth still had difficulty acknowledging it. "Mr. Holmes," he inadvertently chuckled, glancing around incredulously, speaking aside to himself, "I can't even believe I'm having this conversation." Then his pinpoint pupils zeroed in again on the detective. "Within these seriously secure walls, Mr. Holmes, I'll admit certain things to you, but I run a very careful business. So while the cops—and the feds—have been after me for years, they've never even gotten close to succeeding."

"But *I* was not on the case . . . until now."

"And perhaps not for much longer," Booth said with a cunning grin.

While Holmes was in the midst of his potentially lethal close encounter, I had hurriedly pulled his nifty ladder back over the top and thrown it in my trunk. I sped my car on up Dardenelle Avenue to the front entrance of the imposing Moriarty Booth family estate. Then, standing in the misty darkness, talking fast through the ten-foot-tall wrought iron gate to the wrought iron, steely-eyed guard behind it, I said, "I'm terribly sorry to bother you. I'm Dr. Amy Winslow from Saint Francis Hospital in the city." I handed one of my business cards through the wet fence.

"One of our mentally disturbed patients escaped tonight, and I'm afraid I saw him climbing over the wall into your estate."

The guard turned the card over in his thick fingers, considering it for what felt to me like an endless moment. I had put on my best smile, playing it as calmly as I could, and trying to suppress my fears of what they might be doing to Holmes while I stood helplessly out there in the drizzle. Finally, the guard moved slightly away from me and took a cell phone from his jacket.

Inside Booth's living room at that moment, Holmes had managed to inch a small step closer to Booth. He clearly saw the Scotland Yard paper with his fingerprints on it beneath the photos in Booth's hand and saw his other documents in the box. Holmes desperately wanted to lunge and grab them, but he was wary of the two unpleasant security guards hovering behind him.

Booth was saying, "My great-grandfather Henry was obsessed with finding you." His soft, precise fashion of speech carried a conviction of sincerity and imminent danger. "It took him decades, but his perseverance paid off. He told me you'd killed his brother James. That's who I'm named for."

"The easiest deduction I ever made," Holmes said sharply. "I also have since discovered that you have been carrying on the family's corrupt business and criminal traditions."

Booth held Holmes' eyes. "You know, pal, I really liked Great-Grandpa Henry."

"Apparently not enough to report his death or reclaim his body from my laboratory."

"Didn't matter, and he would have agreed. What was important was the education he'd given to my grandfather, to my father, and to me." His eyes focused on Holmes with forbidding dark humor. "And one of the most important aspects of

212

that education was instilling in us the Moriarty commitment to *vengeance*." Booth imbued the word with biting vitriol as his eyes bored into Holmes.

But as they gazed at each other, Holmes observed Booth's deadly expression unaccountably begin to transform.

Slowly, Booth's face became less and less menacing as its taut muscles relaxed. His left thumb and forefinger pulled slightly on his thick lower lip as he glanced again from Holmes to the photos in his own right hand and then back at Holmes. A more enlightened thought had apparently dawned on Booth. He seemed to be mulling over an idea as he eyed Holmes narrowly. Finally, he said, "An equally important lesson I learned from him, however, was to never miss a golden opportunity." Booth drew a breath, glancing once more at the photos and documents while pondering. "If you actually did manage this, this what?" He searched for the words. "Incredible *hibernation*? By God, that's a mind-bending, astonishing achievement! Worthy of congratulations and tremendous respect. It marks you as a highly valuable man of extraordinary genius."

Holmes knew that was all true, but his brow remained tightly knit, gazing steadily at Booth, curious about the tack that the crime baron was shifting onto.

"It marks you, sir," Booth continued slowly, "as someone to whom I might even be willing to extend professional courtesies. Perhaps even a helping hand."

Holmes blinked in abject amazement. Booth caught it, saying with a wise grin, "Yes, yes, your knee-jerk reaction is negative, naturally. That's to be expected. But take a breath. Like I have." When he continued, his voice was softer, lower, with Mephistophelian smoothness. "Allow yourself to think on it just for a moment, my friend. Assuming you are who you say you are—as you do indeed seem to be—that makes you a total newcomer to this present-day world. A time very different from the one you left behind. But perhaps if you could see your way to leaving that past behind, to let bygones be bygones." His voice grew even more cordial and confidential. "I can offer you insights, counsel, guidance, and invaluable opportunities. Into the hands of someone as clever and resourceful as you, I am capable of bringing unimaginable fortune. If you were to consider allying yourself with me, I would—"

"Well," Holmes interrupted, laughing darkly, as though he'd had a sudden unanticipated epiphany. "*That* is certainly something I'd never have contemplated a century ago."

"I'm sure not." Booth smiled, urging, "But those who can't keep up with changing times have little chance of surviving." It was friendly but also a thinly veiled threat. "Those who do adjust, however . . ." He proudly indicated the grandeur of the great room and all the wealth it represented.

Holmes paused, seriously thinking it through then acknowledging, "And you are correct that under current circumstances I am slightly compromised."

"In more ways than one, Mr. Holmes," Booth pointed out, and let that sink in. "However, my offer is quite serious and sincere." He saw that Holmes seemed to have relaxed slightly, which gave the impression he was allowing himself to carefully weigh the proposition. Holmes lowered his head until his chin rested on his chest, as though giving deepest consideration to Booth's offer.

Holmes was actually doing something else entirely: he was looking downward and back to determine exactly how many inches behind him the guards' feet were and their exact lateral placement. He was making a final assessment of the playing field. From the moment of his capture, Holmes had been formulating how to still achieve his goal and escape with his papers. He'd initially been disadvantaged by the bestial dog and the gun at his head, but now he had much better prospects. While his legs were being frisked, he'd glimpsed the pistol now resting in a shoulder holster beneath the guard's jacket, and he'd noted the sliding glass door through which they had entered was still open. With the element of surprise also on his side, he was confident that it was now "advantage Holmes" to win the game, set, and match.

Standing there, facing Booth, Holmes knew he could eliminate the guards behind him. His scuffle with the street teens had been but a mere trifle compared to the lethal force he could unleash when necessary. His full-blown baritsu attack could be debilitating, even deadly. One night in South London, two brutal leaders of the notorious Peaky Blinders gang had him in exactly the same compromising position, but Holmes had ended their careers in a flash. He knew that with the knuckles on each of his hands sharpened into flat, axe-like wedges, he could pivot around and devastatingly pile-drive them into the throats of both guards, crushing their Adam's apples in the blink of an eye. As they crumpled, stunned and choking, he could snatch the gun from the holster, spin back around, and have Booth at bay to use as a hostage in tow while escaping out the open door with his identity papers secured inside the pocket of his cape.

While Holmes was locking in his plan, he glanced up as Curly walked past him toward Booth with a fingertip touching his right earbud, indicating to Booth he was getting a message. Then he whispered something into Booth's ear. The underworld chieftain listened, then seemed greatly amused. Curly walked back behind Holmes, who sensed that the moment of truth was near at hand. Holmes looked down and behind again to reconfirm Curly's exact position, then looked up to see that Booth's shrewd eyes had leveled on him.

"Someone's at my front gate, Mr. Holmes," Booth said with quiet humor. "Declaring that you're a mental case."

Holmes laughed, as best he could. Booth laughed along with him like hale fellows well met. Then Booth pretended to frown as he contemplated, "Of course, if they saw these photos and this identity information, they might think again." Holmes steadily met Booth's gaze. "But listen," Booth resumed in his generous, comradely tone, "let's get back to my proposition. I'm really hoping you'll accept the opportunity to gain for yourself a future of unlimited wealth—and power. I guarantee you won't be disappointed." He shifted Holmes' identity photos into his left hand then slowly extended his right hand toward Holmes and nodded encouragingly.

The tall Englishman nodded back appreciatively, then explained, "Sorry, but I would be disappointed with myself." Internally Holmes was coiling his muscles, readying to strike like lightning and disable the minions. Success depended upon exquisite, precise timing.

Booth kept his inviting hand extended a moment longer, finally saw it was useless, and withdrew it. "Okay," he said, exhaling a sincerely disappointed sigh. "Then let's just save everyone a lot of trouble."

Less than a half second before Holmes could launch his

attack, Booth jumbled the timing by abruptly scooping up the rest of Holmes' papers and blissfully tossing them all into the fire.

Holmes leapt forward shrieking, "*Noooo!*" but he was tackled to the floor by the guards, who immobilized him facedown as he struggled, bellowing, "No! Confound you!"

He tried to wrench himself free, but there was a two-hundred-pound knee pressing down painfully on his back and the thick-handed grips of the men were viselike. With his cheek pressed against the oak floor, Holmes was forced to watch helplessly as flames wrapped around his precious papers, curling the corners upward, inward, searing up through the images, engulfing all of the vital information and sending it up in smoke. He felt as if a hand of ice had grasped his heart.

Booth watched the flames complete their work and diminish, then smiled down at Holmes with pleasure over his accomplishment. "Well, look at that. I seem to have succeeded where my great-grandfather failed. I have just destroyed the famous Mr. Holmes." He nodded to the men, who pulled Holmes to his feet while maintaining their iron grip. Then Booth leaned closer to Holmes' face, saying sweetly, "You—whoever you are—are nothing but an escaped lunatic."

Holmes' hatred was white-hot, but the underworld baron's sly grin was undiminished as he said with cheerful politeness, "Have a nice day."

He indicated for his men to throw Holmes out. Muscular as they were, it took quite an effort on their part to drag him away. As they did, the outraged Holmes managed a final, anguished look back over his shoulder at the fireplace. He saw that beneath the burning logs nothing remained of his irreplaceable papers but glowing ashes.

As we drove back along the dark coastline, Holmes only gave me the awful headlines, barely able to speak through his fury and the humiliation I knew he felt over what Booth had done to him. From his rigid face and glaring eyes focused dead ahead, I sensed he was mentally leaning forward, feeling there might yet be one faint last hope, but he maintained his impenetrable, silent reserve throughout our return to the city. Though I was angry at him for acting so impetuously, I kept it to myself. Nor did I mention what I'd learned while waiting outside Booth's front gate.

Not until we were back in my house did I show him the email on my phone.

Scotland Yard "regretted to inform" us that records dated prior to 17 September 1904, including any that might have existed on a "Holmes, Hubert, a.k.a. Sherlock, DOB 26-10-1858," as well as many thousands of others, had all been lost in a fire at the Yard on that date.

The email concluded, "Unfortunately, the Yard cannot verify whether or not the information you sought was ever a part of those records."

He endeavored to maintain an imperious air, but I monitored him closely because I knew he was now entirely devastated. As he sat there in my living room chair, he tilted his head back, letting his eyes trace blankly across the ceiling as though seeking a solution. Finding none, he avoided looking at me as he finally chuckled bitterly, forcing some gallows humor. "Well, one must admit, Winslow, it is rather a singular, ironic achievement. I don't know of anyone else who, in one night, has been so completely *burned . . . Twice!*"

He breathed a long sigh of resignation, still looking away as he said, "On this extraordinarily catastrophic evening of evenings, I should be most especially grateful if you would open your heart, and your safe, so that I might retrieve my syringe and cocaine."

I spoke gently. "I hope you know that I understand all the pain you're suffering through, but I can't in good conscience—"

"*Oh, damn your conscience!*" he spouted hotly as he stood abruptly, storming toward his room. But he stopped dead at the hallway entrance. He stood for a moment with his back to me, then bowed his head slightly. "I was very rude, madam. You have my apology."

"That's okay," I said quietly. "But I do have something milder which might help if—"

"No. No thank you, Doctor. I shall require no further assistance of any kind."

Then he continued off down the hall to his room in the back, and I heard the door close.

Soon after, I was lying in bed, turning through the pages of Doyle's stories. It was startling how accurate his portrayal was of this man now living under my roof. I heard the melancholy sound of his violin begin echoing up from below. As I drifted to sleep, I was feeling sad for him, and for myself, because I had no idea how to help him or what might happen now.

13

I awakened at 2:00 a.m. with a sense that something was wrong. Going downstairs, I discovered that Holmes was gone. Having concerns about his mental state, I threw on some clothes and launched upon a search through the area on my motorbike, grateful that the rain had stopped. The air was clear as I cruised the dark, wet streets of my neighborhood. But I had no luck. I was on my way back toward Baker Street, thinking about the first time I'd driven Holmes into San Francisco and amazed to realize that had only been three days ago. Suddenly I remembered something else about that day. I turned my bike around and headed toward the waterfront.

I rode to the base of Broadway and turned right at Embarcadero for a dozen yards to Pier 7, where Holmes had described to me how different it looked in 1899 when he had taken a walk there on the night before he began his long sleep. That original Pier 7 was ruined by a fire fifty years ago and the current wood-planked pier was built. It extends the length of two and a half football fields out into the bay, but being barely fifty feet wide, it has always reminded me of a long, thin finger. It's built upon twenty-four concrete pillars, each of which is topped with a semicircular alcove about five feet wide to accommodate people fishing. Its entire perimeter is lined by a lovely wrought iron fence. Several dozen streetlamps along both sides, reminiscent of San Francisco's gaslight era, provide warm illumination at night. Pier 7 is one of the most picturesque spots in the city, with expansive views in all directions.

Looking inland from the pier, a viewer sees the landmark Transamerica Pyramid rising up from amid the city's sparkling nighttime skyline. That's what was behind me as I guided my motorbike to a slow stop on the wooden decking and looked out across the pier. In the distance was the Bay Bridge with its suspension cables extending like three enormous roller-coaster waves across to Yerba Buena and Treasure Island. Their lights twinkled in the dark waters below. At the pier's far end, I saw a pair of lovers enjoying the romantic place and each other. Between them and me, running the length of the pier, were parallel rows of benches facing outward toward the perimeter fence. They had wooden seats and graceful wrought iron backs and armrests.

Sitting on one of those benches about halfway along, turned slightly to his left and facing the bay with his back in my direction, was the person I sought. He wore the coachman's cape but had forsaken the deerstalker for the simple newsboy cap, which diminished his overall persona. His body language was listless. He appeared disconsolate, but I determined not to join in his low spirits but instead present a positive attitude.

Out over the bay a slender, horizontal wisp of fog was drifting in, catlike. I walked up casually, marveling at the panoramic view, and said quietly, "It's really beautiful, isn't it?"

If Holmes felt any surprise at hearing my voice, he covered it up. I walked just past him to the far end of his bench. When I turned around, I saw he was scowling. I had never before seen his face so grim or his brow so dark. He glanced dismissively toward the spectacular nighttime San Francisco skyline behind him, and grumbled, "*Ach.* I cannot look at that city without seeing the leering face of James Moriarty Booth hanging over it like an evil specter." He blew out an angry puff. "And that *my* valuables were used to found his nefarious empire is . . . is . . ." He laughed resentfully. "It's beyond ironic." He rubbed his temples with both hands. "It lays siege to my brain! How can vermin like Booth—and Enrique Pavon and other evildo-ers—continue to spread their diabolical poison and pestilence throughout the city, whilst I am helpless, useless?"

I waited a moment, hoping this wave of frustration and despair might subside. I noted how ashen he looked. The muscles of his face seemed flaccid, almost as though he'd phys-ically melted a bit in the last few hours. He was clearly in the midst of darkest depression. I spoke, softly and hearteningly. "You know, you're an amazing man, Holmes. You've given yourself the opportunity to do something no one's ever done before—travel over a hundred years into the future. And you are definitely the all-time great *ob-server*," I acknowledged with a delicate, encouraging smile. "But at the same time, you miss so very much!"

He glanced at me, frowning, as though unclear about what I meant.

"You're so focused on the dark side of life," I went on as I settled onto the other end of his bench, "that you miss its beauty. You're so preoccupied with tiny details that you overlook the bigger picture. You miss the rich tapestry of life, of the world around you. And also the comfort of relationships."

"That sounds like Watson's old description of me," he said sourly. Quoting his longtime companion, he intoned, "'Holmes is an automaton, a calculating machine, there is something positively inhuman about him. A brain without a heart, as deficient in human sympathy as he is preeminent in intelligence.' But"— Holmes pointed at me—"at least that was in a time when my intelligence was unique and useful. Now"—he made a sweeping gesture toward the city behind him—"now there's an entire *wing* down at police headquarters possessing something called DNA which apparently gives them the power to make the kind of analyses and assessments that I *alone* had once been capable of."

I didn't want to push him further into depression by corroborating the usefulness of DNA, so I held off as he continued bitterly. "What is the use of having extraordinary skills and powers when one has no field upon which to exert them? Even my deductions are often absurdly out of date, as you yourself have enjoyed pointing out."

"But overall," I said warmly, determined to stay positive, "considering that you've catapulted yourself into the twenty-first century, you've still been brilliant, Holmes! And no one can always be right."

His eyes met mine. "But I almost always *was*." His gaze drifted to look out over the dark water. "Until now."

He sat still, mulling over his defeat. "The greatest irony was hearing from you how Doyle had resurrected Sherlock—shortly *after* I began my sleep. That I had given up on the nineteenth century too soon. That more stories collected from Watson were published, which, had I still been awake and in London, would have led to an immediate resurgence of clients seeking my services . . . True, none would have been as challenging as Professor Moriarty, but at least I could have continued to ply my trade. I could have continued to be a man who was ahead of his time, instead of jumping into this new age that has no use for me."

He laughed with exasperation. "I have been hoisted by my own petard, Winslow. Been too 'brilliant' for my own good. Well, I got exactly what I deserved. I have been laid low by my own self-confidence—that is the very definition of classic hubris: when one sets one's ego above nature's gods."

He paused a moment, feeling the burden of it. "And yes, I have now realized my foolish mistake—but it's impossible to correct it. I cannot go back. It's impossible to change the circumstances or the punishment to which I have condemned myself. I brought down onto myself the worst kind of cursed damnation for a man such as I: as a detective," he chuckled with resentful irony, "I am defective."

I sat silently, trying to figure out the best approach, to find some words that might help him. But before I could, he sighed listlessly. "It *would* have been better if Moriarty hadn't been the only one who plunged into the abyss. Booth is right: he has now destroyed me."

I could see he'd reached his lowest ebb, was feeling a vast emptiness, that he had no future here in the future. And then he put the seal upon it, saying with finality, "There's no way I can recover. It's impossible. Simply *impossible*." He shrugged slightly and opened his hand toward me. "I truly need you to give me back my vial and syringe."

That did it—I saw red. "*Oh right!*" I snapped, standing up

and turning away hotly. "That's the answer, huh?" I turned and came back at him. "Shooting up is going to fix everything, is it?" I glared at him. "I've treated my share of addicts, mister. I know exactly what cocaine does. So tell me, is the short burst of euphoria really worth what follows? The paranoia, the hallucinations, the fresh depression deeper than the one you started with?"

He was unresponsive.

That made me angrier. "You know what? I'm sorry you're having a hard time, but come down to my hospital and I'll introduce you to some people who have *real* problems. The world was not put here for your 'gaming pleasure,' Mr. Holmes. You can't just drop out when the game goes against you."

I forced myself take a breath and tried to calm down, in hopes of discovering a way to get through to him. I came closer and sat on the bench facing him. "Listen, my mom always said a person only grows by facing challenges. By going through them and coming out the other side, better for the experience."

He glanced flittingly at me, then away. I decided it was best to face the main issue head-on. "There may not be a Holmes from the nineteenth century anymore, but there clearly is a Holmes here in the twenty-first: a genius of a man who can create and control his own destiny—if only he doesn't wimp out!"

He seemed to at least be listening, so I went on. "And as far as Booth or Pavon are concerned, I happen to believe in karma: what goes around comes around. The pendulum swings slowly, but it tends toward justice. Sooner or later they'll screw up— or get screwed up. Eventually someone will provide damning evidence against them—and they'll be condemned."

Holmes' simpering expression implied my thesis was idiotic, and I was forced to admit, "*Orrrr* maybe they won't. But there are plenty of other crimes out there for you to solve in this day and age, plenty of other hurting people who could use your help, if you're not too busy wallowing in your own personal problems."

His eyes had gone distant, vacant. I saw he'd tuned me out. I got mad again.

"Fine," I huffed as I stood up to leave, flashing both palms in his direction. "I've got no interest in hanging out with someone who's up to his eyeballs in self-pity."

I angrily stalked back up the pier and climbed onto my bike. While putting on my helmet, I said, "I'd be much more interested in a detective like the one I was reading about tonight. 'When he was at his wits' end was when his energy and his versatility were most admirable.'"

Holmes looked over his shoulder, and our eyes met.

"A detective who himself said, 'There is nothing more stimulating than a case where everything goes against you.'" I kickstarted the bike and revved it. "And that same detective said to me, 'What most people perceive as *difficult* I can sort out right away. It's only the *impossible* that can take me a little longer.'"

I glared at him a final moment, then rammed the bike into gear, did a tight one-eighty, and roared off. I tried not to look back but couldn't help glancing in my rearview. From the dark pier, he stared after me.

I went home, angrily pulled my old pajama top back on, and got back into bed. I was still frowning from my encounter with him and his damned reticence. Long-suffering Lucie was patiently lying beside me as I tossed and turned for an hour or so. At length I heard him come in downstairs.

I listened carefully, and after a few minutes I heard the

sound of his fingers tapping my keyboard. My tension eased. I lay there listening for a few more minutes, but then I grew concerned that he might be composing a letter of farewell to leave behind for me. To my surprise, that was actually a painful thought. In spite of the difficulty he had brought into my life, he was such an extraordinary man. Such a rare, brilliant, attractive— I blinked and stopped myself. That particular line of thought was somewhat unexpected.

Nevertheless, I did not want to face the disappointment of discovering in the morning that he had left with no way for me to locate him. So I headed downstairs.

My bare feet were quiet on the wooden steps. I peered into the living room and saw him at my desk, his back to me. He had taken off his coachman's cape and his frock coat. He was reaching into its pocket and removing a small snuff box made of gold, with a large amethyst set in the middle of the lid. Still facing away, he spoke quietly, "I sense that you are staring, Winslow."

I whispered, "Yes, I'm sorry."

"This was another small gift of appreciation from the king of Bohemia."

"Very nice."

"Quite so. But what's important at this moment is its contents, which I collected today." He opened the box and took out not tobacco but a small black bug.

I remained in the doorway. "What is that?"

"A beetle."

"Dead, I hope."

"Conclusively. And yet a matter of paramount importance." He still had not looked at me. He began tapping again at the keyboard.

I waited, then asked gently, "What are you doing?"

He answered softly, "Taking your suggestion, Winslow. Working on behalf of my first clients of the twenty-first century: Luis and Karen Ortega." He tapped on the keyboard, then paused to say, "Let the weight of the matter rest upon me for now, and do not let your mind dwell upon it further."

I stood silently for a moment. He turned slowly to look at me in my faded flannel pajama top, my tousled hair and no makeup. I saw that his face had regained some color. Though he was still far from the flush of energy and eagerness he'd displayed when I'd first driven us into the city, at least his mood seemed slightly improved.

But something else was going on. His eyes focused onto mine in a way they never had previously. There was a subtle expression of what might possibly be sincere gratitude.

And there was a hint of something even deeper. I was experiencing it too: a sort of mutual discovery. As our gaze held steadily, taking on a life of its own, I sensed, and sensed that he was also sensing and trying to comprehend, an unexpected stirring, a faint awakening of—what? An emotional connection? As I tried to comprehend what was happening, he blinked, seeming to take in for the first time that my legs were bare. Then he looked away—though not instantly, I noted. But he was clearly self-conscious, and his gentlemanly eyes could not meet mine again.

Instead he nodded officiously, which I took to mean "Good night," and turned back toward the computer. He sat like that, not moving. He knew I was still standing behind him, gazing at him.

And I knew that he knew—and that he knew I knew he knew.

It was a very complex and resonating moment that I have often reflected upon.

At length, he drew a breath and began typing again. I eased into the shadows and padded upstairs, trying to process the remarkable exchange that had just passed between us. I got into bed with a ghost of a smile on my face, snuggled in comfortably, and slipped soundly asleep.

14

Coming downstairs the next morning, I discovered that except for Lucie I was alone in the house. My chest tightened with concern and grew tighter when I saw that Holmes *had* left behind a note on my desk. I rushed over to look, my heart beating faster. It was handwritten, and its forward-slanting penmanship evoked Victorian elegance.

It read, "I am appreciative for your counsel last evening, Winslow. My spirits are reasonably reconstituted. I shall be out and about today, likely not returning until quite late this evening, but I make sincere assurances that you have not the slightest reason for any anxiety."

It was signed with only a gracefully executed *H*.

So for the detailed description that follows, I am again indebted to Holmes' mostly astute recollections, as well as the insightful reports of a clever, engaging young man named Julius, whom you already know by another name.

Zapper, our Artful Dodger, walked cheerfully into the main entrance of the San Francisco Public Library, carrying a book. He was dressed in the same slouchy style as when Holmes encountered him two nights previously on Baker Street. His BLM baseball cap had been replaced by a tight knit cap, part of the standard uniform of his hip-hop generation. He had an iPhone with yellow Skullcandy earbuds in his ears and was bouncing to the rhythm from them as he waved and grinned at the middle-aged security guard, who recognized him as a frequent visitor and smiled back.

Zapper performed a little show-offy pirouette for her benefit as he passed through the metal detectors and walked across the broad, circular, gray marble floor of the atrium. He dropped off the book he'd been carrying in the main "Returns" area, then glanced up at the glass dome towering seven floors above. It was a skylight with a unique design that always fascinated him because it gave the optical illusion that the dome had been twisted to one side. Concentric circles spread out across it like ripples in a pond when a pebble is tossed in. A librarian had told him that the architect wanted to project the idea that when anyone walked into a library in search of one thing, it very often led to discoveries of many other unexpected things.

Zapper was about to have that exact experience.

On the second floor, he moved in among the neatly organized shelves, with a clear idea of exactly where he was headed: a section with volumes about electronics. His head was nodding in time with a thumping rap tape unheard by others around him.

He walked past a library ladder, continuing down to the dead end of the row of shelves. He was unmindful of the man who trailed behind him, taking a place beside the ladder, thus blocking any easy escape.

"Good morning, Zapper."

Zapper turned, dumbfounded that this weird guy dressed in an 1890s tweed jacket, black vest, and trousers had found him. The boy drew a quick breath, then puffed up. "Hey, you better watch your ass, dude. I got like fifty megabytes of brothers with me."

"On the contrary." Holmes winked. "You're alone."

"All I gotta do is yell," Zapper warned, shakily.

"Oh, not in a library," Holmes chided. "Bad form, old boy."

Zapper eyed Holmes suspiciously, thinking that maybe he was some kind of deviant who was stalking him. "How'd you know I'd be here?"

"Late yesterday afternoon I saw you heading up the front steps of the library carrying a book with a Dewey decimal label on its spine. You obviously had not come *out* of the library but were en route to return the book. This morning I arrived when the library opened and since that time have been watching the entrance from a concealed vantage point within—that is, until I saw you enter and return said book."

It was Zapper's turn to stare at Holmes. It seems everyone who encounters Holmes has that reaction. Often more than once.

"I also know a few other things about you," Holmes went on. "You're an electronics wizard, with handmade devices you use to break into cars and change stoplights." Though nervous, Zapper couldn't suppress a little smile of pride. His expression grew darker, however, when Holmes continued. "Your father is a petty thief currently in Folsom Prison. Your mother is doing the best she can working at a bakery. You've been arrested seven times for minor infractions." Zapper glanced grudgingly at the floor with guilt. "The first when you were only eleven years old, for stealing a case of electrical components. Your given name is Julius, and your surname Castaneda."

Zapper smirked, thinking he now understood something about Holmes. "Yeah, okay. So you're a cop."

"No. But I delved into the police computer and read your rip sheet."

"Rap sheet."

"Right." Holmes said decidedly, as though that was precisely what he'd said the first time. Then he softened his tone as he partially perched upon one of the ladder's steps. "So I know a fair amount about you, and I pass no ill judgment, my boy. But there is someone I'd sincerely like to hear more about: your late friend, Billy."

Zapper shot a sharp glance at Holmes. He'd struck a nerve. Zapper tried to gloss it over with a shrug, but he kept a leery eye on this strange guy in weird clothes. "What's Billy got to do with anything?"

"Perhaps quite a lot," Holmes said with uncharacteristic gentleness, "I heard you say that 'Billy was blood'—meaning a relative?"

The boy looked away, frowning with the onset of disturbing memories. "Nah, but he was like one."

Holmes waited patiently.

The boy's eyes remained diverted, lost in thought. Finally, he took a breath and said, "Billy was a really good guy. Six years older than me. Lived down the hall."

Holmes understood. "He was a close friend."

"Like a big brother. After my dad got sent up." He paused, and Holmes patiently waited. "And Momma was so busy workin' to keep food on the table, Billy just kinda leaned in, watched out for me. For other kids in our 'hood too. But for me in particular." A memory stirred a faint smile. "He could be a pain in the ass sometimes. He was workin' to be one of them community organizer dudes. Always tryin' to steer us younger bruhs away from big trouble and all. Away from running drugs and shit. Away from getting hooked into the really bad guys."

"Like Enrique Pavon."

Zapper's eyes snapped to Holmes.

"You seemed certain that Pavon was responsible for Billy being killed."

"Damn straight he was, man. He was pissed 'cause Billy was slowing down Pavon's takes from street action." Zapper's blood was suddenly up and boiling. "I heard two of Pavon's guys laughin' later on about how they did Billy."

"I heard you say Billy was killed in a hit-and-run. Did you witness that happen?"

"From right 'cross the street." The boy was pained, remembering. "This muscle car swerved on purpose up onto the sidewalk to plow into him, sent him flyin', then burned rubber outta there. I jammed over to Billy, but he was already—" He closed his mouth tightly.

Holmes was understanding. "That must have been terrible." Zapper stood silent. Then Holmes spoke softly, "So I would be correct in assuming you bear a considerable grudge against Enrique Pavon."

"'Considerable' ain't even close," the boy said.

Holmes nodded as his eyes narrowed at Zapper. "Then how would you like the opportunity to get even?"

"What're you talkin' about?"

Holmes stood up tall and laid down the gauntlet. "How would you like to help bring down Pavon once and for all?"

Zapper regarded Holmes quizzically a moment, then Holmes saw the boy's eyes turn fiery, making it clear that he was good to go.

By that night, however, Zapper was getting acutely nervous as Holmes led him toward the same back wall of Booth's estate in Pacifica that Holmes and I had visited so disastrously twenty-four hours earlier. It wasn't raining this time, but the fog was swirling in thickly off the dark ocean. Zapper had borrowed a primer-patched car from his friend Rancho and driven them down there, arriving just after dark.

Holmes was concerned that Zapper might turn them around if he heard the details of their mission any sooner, so he had waited until they arrived to reveal his plan and why he'd asked Zapper to bring along all of his sophisticated electronic equipment. They would use Zapper's unique skills and tools to gain secret access to Booth's estate.

Upon hearing all this, Zapper was understandably freaked out.

Holmes, however, was rejuvenated and full of gusto as he approached the wall. Zapper was wearing his black backpack and a photographer's cargo vest, one of those with a lot of pockets, which were bulging with many of his own handmade electronic gadgets. His stomach, however, was swirling with butterflies.

"I'm tellin' you, man, this is like dive-bombing the Death Star." Zapper whispered fearfully. "You know, Pavon don't mess around—he killed one guy I used to know with a *steamroller*! I like see 'Fatal Error' flashin' here."

"Julius," Holmes said, loudly enough to make Zapper cut him off.

"Shup, man! Keep it quiet! Jeez!" Zapper whispered, vibrating with nerves.

"Julius," Holmes continued more softly, "we have an opportunity to permanently dethrone Pavon." He encouraged his accomplice by thrusting into Zapper's hands the collapsible ladder that I had barely managed to recover after Holmes had been captured and hauled off by Booth's henchmen.

Zapper was thoroughly confused, completely Big Willy. "If we're tryin' to bring down Pavon, then what the hell're we doin' here at *Booth's* house? That's one barracuda too many!"

"I'm convinced there is a connection, that Booth and Pavon are both integral parts of a deadly plot that has left three people murdered in the last three days and another targeted now."

"Naw, man," Zapper contradicted, "those two big honchos ain't workin' together. They're *rivals*. Only connection they got is they'd both cut your heart out and eat it raw. Sorry, but I'm outta here, man."

He turned away, but Holmes yanked on the rope that was attached to the ladder Zapper held. It jerked the boy back face-to-face with Holmes, who said in his firm, crisp way, "Julius, we'll also be saving the life of a good man: Detective Luis Ortega."

"A cop? What do I care about a—"

"Listen!" Holmes grabbed Zapper's sleeve. "Ortega wants justice for Pavon as badly as you do. He was about to accomplish that until he disappeared two nights ago. Do you want Pavon to keep on going? So he and Booth can brutally kill more worthy people like Ortega?" Zapper wasn't convinced until Holmes riveted his eyes and said pointedly, "Like Billy?"

Zapper's jaw set. "Alright, alright. Let's just do it quick, 'fore I change my mind."

"Excellent." Holmes gave him a comradely nod and tossed the grappling hook to the top of the wall, where it bit in with a clang. Zapper flinched. His expression also suggested he still had grave misgivings about the whole operation.

But when Holmes deployed the ingenious ladder, it made Zapper blink, form a crooked smile, and pronounce his ultimate praise and respect. "That is sick, man! Can I have it when we're done?"

Zapper read Holmes' expression as "perhaps," and about five minutes later they were both atop the wall, straddling it like riding tandem on a horse. Zapper sat behind Holmes as the detective gingerly lowered the ladder down inside the estate.

Zapper was edgy again, his mouth dry. "Now, which side of the house you want to get to?"

"The southwest side, about three hundred twenty-one degrees—" From his vest, Holmes took out a small gold compass. "—according to the blueprint designs I viewed at the Building and Safety Commission."

Zapper was digging for something in a vest pocket. "They let you do that?"

Holmes was haughty. "I sought it out on the Interweb."

Zapper paused but went with the flow. "Right. The good old Interweb. *Natch.*"

Holmes checked his compass and squinted his eyes toward the distant estate, trying to pierce the darkness, then pointing. "I should say we need to travel in that direction."

Zapper pulled out homemade night-vision binoculars. "Well, let's really lock in on it, man," he said to Holmes. "Turn your cap around." Zapper was used to making this move with his baseball cap, and to put the device on Holmes, he needed the brim of the detective's hat to be in back. But when Holmes turned his around, Zapper realized that move wouldn't work with a deerstalker.

"Uh, right. How 'bout we try sideways, dude," Zapper suggested.

Holmes complied, rotating his traveling cap ninety degrees. The brims were now over each ear, making him resemble a floppy-eared bloodhound. Zapper would've laughed if he hadn't been so stressed. He was struggling to stay professional as he slipped the optical rig into place atop Holmes' head. Binocular tubes extended out six inches from Holmes' eyes. Holmes saw the bright greenish view of Booth's house in the distance and exclaimed, "Ah! It's like daylight!"

Zapper flinched at the volume of Holmes' voice. "Yeah, yeah, but *shhh*, okay? Jeez!"

"What sort of optics are employed to intensify the light?"

"Point five lux. Night-vision gogs, man, specially modified by yours truly," Zapper explained. "So, you see any eyes?"

"Eyes?" Holmes turned to point his long binocular eyes at Zapper.

"Security cams, Holmesy. Turn around. Check the roof."

Holmes looked back more carefully at the fortresslike ultramodern house, focusing the image more sharply. "Yes. *Hah!* There. On each corner. Panning slowly. Thirteen second cycles, judging by my pulse."

"Okay. Let's see what else we got." Zapper fiddled with another gadget.

"What is that device?"

"Sort of a modified radar detector, man."

"Ah, yes." Holmes contemplated a moment. "And what is radar?"

Zapper looked up. "What's what? Are you shittin' me?"

Holmes was highly offended. "Certainly not, Julius!"

Zapper shook his head. "Well, it's kind of an involved concept to go into right now." A light blinked on Zapper's gizmo. He nodded, pleased. "Alright. One twenty-watt tomato."

"To-*mah*-to?" Holmes glanced again at him.

Zapper thought Holmes looked pretty ridiculous with the goggles' tubes sticking out where his eyes should have been and the twin bills of his deerstalker hanging like Goofy's hound ears. "Infrared, man. Probably what trashed you last night."

"Have you any means to circumvent it?"

"Yeah. We throw our own 'to-*mah*-to' back at it. No signal interference, we're like invisible men, man."

"Outstanding! My friend H. G. Wells would have loved to see that." Then Holmes chuckled at his faux pas. "But of course, if we were invisible, he wouldn't have been able to see us."

Zapper blinked, trying to catch up. "Uh, wait . . . your friend . . . H. G.—?"

"These devices of yours are superbly conceived, Julius." Holmes was excited. "They are all extremely cold."

"What?"

"Cold. Isn't that what you say, meaning 'very good,' or 'fine'?"

"I think you mean *cool*?"

"Quite so. Cool!"

Zapper shook his head, muttering to himself, "What the hell am I doin' here?"

Holmes swung a leg over onto the ladder, "Prepared for the drop?"

"No." Zapper said honestly. He'd suddenly felt shaky all over. His heart was fluttering in his chest. "I mean, it's not exactly like I've ever gone up against guys as stone-cold bad as Pavon or Booth. These are seriously dangerous dudes, man. Like deadly."

Holmes drew a breath, facing the boy. "I understand. And that's exactly the fate Billy suffered, and that I fear for Luis Ortega—unless we take action to save him." Seeing the boy's continued reluctance, Holmes zeroed in. "Let me tell you something, Julius: you only grow by facing challenges."

"Yeah?" His mouth was dry from fear. "Well, then by the time this is over, I'm gonna be the size of Mo Bamba." He flipped on the tiny switch of his infrared generator. "Alright, I'm jammin'. Do it! Go!"

Holmes quickly glided down the unstable ladder with the smooth skill of a trapeze artist, born of having done it countless times. Zapper had a much shakier climbing experience. At the base of the wall, goggle-eyed Holmes paused to reconnoiter. His vision-amplified eyes swept the grounds before he whispered, "One guard with his Baskerville hound at the south corner."

"Copy that, workin' on it," Zapper said as he fished in one of his myriad pockets and produced yet another device. He fanned out a tiny dish antenna. "Gimme a vector."

"I beg your pardon?"

"Aim me, man, tell me where to aim. You can see him way better than me."

Holmes pulled the boy in front of him facing the same direction, then leaned across Zapper's shoulder to point out the specific direction. Zapper aimed the small dish.

"Like a dog whistle, is it?" queried Holmes.

"But in reverse and times a shitload!"

Holmes tilted his head, learning and cataloging on the go. "A 'shitload' being an extreme amount?"

"You got that right. Watch!" Zapper grinned as he triggered it, saying, "Kiss my ultrasonics."

Holmes felt a slight sensation in his own inner ear, but the giant mastiff in the distance reacted like someone had thrown ice water on him. He started, then shook his head and rubbed his ears along the ground. The guard who was leading him had no idea what was happening.

Finally, the gargantuan dog decided that discretion was the better part of valor. He turned tail and ran, dragging the flustered guard along behind.

"Well done, Julius," said Holmes. Then he looked up through his goggle-night-vision rig at the scanning security cameras. "Alright, runners take your mark." He was carefully timing the cameras panning away from them. "Set. And . . . now." Holmes glided swiftly along the base of the wall toward the estate.

"Stay low!" Zapper cautioned as he slunk speedily along behind Holmes.

The two of them hurried through the blowing fog across the dark, lush, heavily wooded grounds, soon approaching the main house. They came to a low hedge. Holmes rose up and carefully peered out. Through his night-vision binoculars, he could see directly into the house through a window of Booth's great room and also into his study.

"Yes. The blueprints were correct. This should do nicely," Holmes said with a dark smile.

KENNETH JOHNSON

"Okay, here's your long eyes." Zapper handed Holmes a pair of modified higher-power binoculars, with a shotgun mike jerry-rigged in between its lenses. "It's seven by fifty mag and . . ." Zapper paused, observing Holmes trying to hold the binoculars up in front of his night-vision goggles.

"No, man," Zapper said, still trembly and struggling to stay patient. "You gotta lift up the night scope first."

"Yes, of course." Holmes flipped the night-vision goggles upward, exposing his eyes. Zapper stuck the yellow Skullcandy earplugs into Holmes' ears.

"That feel okay?"

"What?" Holmes said, much too loudly.

Zapper quickly pulled the plug out of Holmes right ear and whispered, "I said, does that feel okay?"

"Mmm. Yes. Quite comfortable, thank you, Julius." He looked back toward Booth's windows. "No one there yet."

"Well, when they do show up, you'll be able to see and hear 'em." Zapper was fiddling with a small radio rig of his own and still very edgy. "What are you hopin' to find out?"

"Anything at all that might help us, Julius," Holmes said, carefully surveilling the house through the more powerful binoculars. "Sometimes even the tiniest clue can be the key to a treasure trove." Holmes glanced at the boy curiously, impressed with him. He whispered, "How'd you get so interested in these marvelous devices?"

"Billy, man. He pushed me." Zapper put in an earplug of his own, which was attached to a radio scanner. "He seen I had a feel for 'lectronic stuff. Told me the streets was a dead end, man, 'less I developed a real skill."

"But you're still on the streets, using that skill for illegal purposes," Holmes scolded.

Zapper bristled. "And what you're doin' right now is legal?"

"We're trespassing, yes. A minor violation. But investigating for a noble and moral cause."

"Well, just get it done as fast as you can, so's we don't get offed like Billy."

Holmes studied the talented boy appreciatively for a long moment, then refocused his attention on the house.

They stayed on this stakeout for nearly two hours, with the fog drifting around them and Zapper growing increasingly distraught and uncomfortable. Finally, he said, "I gotta take a whiz pretty soon, man."

"To be successful on such a mission as this, Julius, one must exercise Zen-like self-control of bodily functions and also patience, my boy. Those are the most vital— *Ah!*" Holmes had finally seen Booth and two of his henchmen cross through the great room and enter the study.

"Here he is!" Holmes whispered. "The camera?"

Zapper focused his small but very high-end digital camcorder. "We're rollin', man. I see 'em."

Holmes watched as one man unfolded what looked to be a map of San Francisco's waterfront and the bay, which he laid atop the desk.

Holmes tapped his ear, whispering to the boy, "And the sound I'm hearing from them will be recorded on your camera?"

Zapper nodded, "Yeah, yeah, whatever you hear. But I'm keeping *my* ears out for the bad guys. I'm scannin' other audio channels." Through his viewfinder Zapper saw Booth activate a speakerphone and initiate a conversation that looked friendly but also very businesslike.

Holmes smiled, watching through the binoculars while

listening to every word as Booth pointed out several locations on the map and spoke to his associates while Zapper recorded the scene on video.

"Can you hear 'em okay?" Zapper asked, "Gettin' any good stuff?"

Holmes nodded and strained to listen carefully for a full seven minutes, which to fearful Zapper felt like seven hours. Several times, he saw Holmes nod with a grave smile.

Zapper was pleased, but still scared silly. Then he went pale, pressed his earpiece tighter into his ear and listened carefully. He had heard an unsettling communication between Booth's guards. He tapped Holmes urgently. "Hey, hey, hey! Red alert! The guards are headed out again. We gotta get back to the ladder. Move it, or we're dead! *Go!*"

As they dashed into the darkness, Holmes wore a satisfied smile.

15

It was about 10:15 p.m., an hour after the scene just described above took place. I was in my kitchen, where I'd pulled a dusty bottle of Holmes' wine out of its old wooden case and was fishing in my junk drawer for the corkscrew. I was talking with Lucie, who was, as usual, sprawled in the middle of the kitchen floor.

"After all he's put me through, the least he owes me is a taste of his special wine, don't you agree, Lucie?" She whimpered back at me. "Okay, you can have some too, but only if you tell me where you hid the stupid corkscrew the last time you used it."

Suddenly my back door burst open. Lucie and I jumped out of our skin, and she started barking like crazy as Holmes breathlessly entered. He grinned at me. "A clean getaway!"

"Speak for yourself, man," said the teenage boy who followed him in, the left side of his face stained with dried blood.

"Oh my God! What happened?" I dug into a lower cabinet where I kept my emergency gear and first aid kit.

"Oh, merely a superficial wound. His feet got tangled in my ladder because of his rather ungraceful exit from Booth's."

"*What*? You went back there?" This was the first I'd heard of their foolhardy escapade.

Holmes was beaming. "We undertook a second and far more successful expedition. It came off splendidly! Julius here has what he would colorfully describe as a shitload of the most ingenious devices I have ever—" Holmes interrupted himself, frowning. "What is a bottle of my wine doing out here?" He grabbed it off the table.

"Oh," I stammered guiltily, "I was just going to sample a little."

"Uh, hel-lo?" the boy said, holding his head. "Like, I'm bleeding here."

I had opened a sterilized wipe and turned to assess the teenager's injury, which was just a minor cut at his hairline, but head wounds often bleed excessively. I was also really looking at him for the first time. He was no more than sixteen. His smooth, brownish, round face still had hints of baby fat. He had deep, adorable dimples and— "Wait a minute." I did a double take, my eyes narrowing on him. "Weren't you the kid trying to break into my car?"

"Uh . . . that was . . . kind of a mistake, yeah," he said, offering up a wan smile.

Holmes was still focused on his precious bottle. "This is an extremely rare 1879 Imperial Tokay from the personal cellar of the Emperor Franz Joseph's Schönbrunn Palace, a bottle he gifted me with after I prevented an attempt on his life. I have saved this entire case for a particularly special occasion—for which your *whim*, Winslow, does not qualify."

He pointedly jammed the bottle back in its case, kicking up a puff of dust.

"Of course," I snapped at him, "And I'm really looking forward to the emperor dropping in for happy hour." I looked back with steely eyes at Zapper. "You sit right there. I'll get some antiseptic."

"Will it sting?" he asked with a grimace.

I'm quite sure they were unaware I could hear them as I looked for the antiseptic in the nearby bathroom. I heard Zapper say, "She your squeeze, man?"

"If I understand you correctly, Julius, no. She is certainly not." Holmes answered.

"She's kinda hot. Nice booty."

I shook my head, then heard Holmes say, "Booty? Well, I hadn't thought of her as a *treasure* exactly."

"No, no, man," Zapper began. "When I say *booty*, I'm talkin' about—"

"I do admit, however," Holmes interrupted, "to having a sneaking admiration of fearlessly independent females like Winslow, but I'm also rather apprehensive in their company."

"Oh yeah? How come?"

"I've always felt that they're never to be entirely trusted," Holmes replied.

"Oh," Zapper said cynically, "but you think guys *are*?"

Peering down the hall, I saw that while Holmes' back was turned to him, Zapper was slipping pieces of my old family silverware into his pocket.

"Women are naturally secretive," Holmes philosophized. "Their hearts and minds are insoluble puzzles to the male. Even to this male. Kindly replace the silver, Julius."

Zapper was amazed, "S'up wit'chu, man! You got eyes in the back o' your head?"

"No," said Holmes, "but there's quite a good reflection of your treachery on the glass of this macrowave."

"Microwave," I reiterated, coming back in.

"Right," he snapped briskly, as usual.

"Thanks for saving my silver," I said as I focused on the boy who was replacing the stolen wares. He smiled a sheepish apology as I went to work on his cut.

"I don't get this," I said. "Yesterday you attack him, tonight you risk your skin for him."

"T'get back at Pavon and— *Youch!*" He deserved to have the antiseptic sting after trying to boost my silver.

"So why'd you go to *Booth's?*"

Zapper puffed up importantly, informing me, "We're convinced there's a connection."

Holmes deigned to bless me with a minimal explanation. "When I first learned of the tiger murders, I suspected the evil genius mind of a Moriarty might be at work. Then when Booth's henchmen were searching through my pockets in his great room, they pushed me forward, making me lean with my hands on a desktop. At that moment, I confirmed my belief that the two cases consuming my interest—pursuit of Booth on the one hand, and the mysterious tiger murders on the other—are intricately linked to one another."

"How did you know that?"

"Because right beneath my hands on that desk was a thick file labeled with a large number: D61977—which I recognized as the badge number of Leftenant Luis Ortega."

"But how in the world would you have known what his badge—?"

"Because," Zapper interjected with Holmesian pedantic

emphasis, "he had ob-*served* it earlier yesterday beside the cop's picture in a trophy case at the precinct. Pretty cold, huh?"

Holmes interpreted: "He means 'cool' of course. Or perhaps 'sick.'"

I was struggling to keep up. "Okay, but that doesn't explain a connection between Pavon and Booth. I don't—"

We were interrupted by another man's smoky-smooth baritone voice. "Amy? Hey."

I looked up—and felt an icy wind blow in. I couldn't believe that You Know Who stood in the archway to my living room. Complete with tight, sleeveless tee shirt barely containing that muscular chest, his long blond hair like a romance novel cover, his leading-man face, and winning smile—all of which was just a front for a thoroughly duplicitous nature. He said, "I didn't mean to inter— *Hey!*" He pointed at Holmes. "Is that one of my shirts?"

Without even looking his way, Holmes raised a cagy eyebrow. "Did you enjoy the Italian meal you dined on when last you wore it?"

"Don't start, Holmes." I wasn't in the mood. Instead, I made a full-court press and backed He Who across the living room toward the foyer.

"Amy, honey, wait."

"Don't start. And definitely not with the 'Amy, honey' bullshit." I was angry—also embarrassed to have Holmes see him and think that I'd been an idiot to have been drawn in for more than five minutes by such a louse. As we approached the front door, I grabbed some of his remaining paints and canvases and shoved them into his arms.

He was trying to get a longer look past me at the Englishman in my kitchen. "Who is that guy, Amy?"

"We're not getting into it, okay? So just—"

"Is he living with you?"

"Yes!" I shouted, flustered. Then, "No. I mean, not like we're— Never mind, it's too complicated, and you don't deserve to know."

"C'mon, Ame, we had a good thing going and—"

"No, what *I* had going was an *idealized* thing—got drawn in by an engaging, witty, charismatic artist who I mistakenly thought reminded me of my father, except of course my father had integrity, loyalty, and was trustworthy. Meanwhile *you* had a better—or at least a flashier—*thing* going on the side. And she was probably just Thing One of God knows how many." By now I had backed him outside onto the porch. "Good night, asshole."

He tried to take a step toward me, saying, "I don't know who that putz is, but—"

That's when I gave him a huge shove. He dropped a canvas, stepped on it, then slipped and went tumbling backward down the porch steps in a pratfall worthy of Buster Keaton, yelping as he landed in a confused heap on my front lawn. I couldn't help chuckling as I went inside, slammed the door, and leaned my back against it.

"Sounded like a slight violation of your Hippocratic oath, Winslow." I saw that Holmes was seated at my desk, focused on my computer screen. Zapper was sauntering in behind him, eating one of my Fuji apples. Without diverting his attention from the screen, Holmes continued, chiding, "'First, do no harm.'"

"You have no idea how many oaths that . . . *person* violated."

Holmes casually asked, "Had you been involved with him very long?"

"None of your business! But no, just long enough to make a diagnosis." I walked toward them and couldn't keep myself from asking with a slightly crazed smile, "Italian meal?"

Holmes was intently typing on the keyboard as he responded, "Mmmm. A bit of tomahto sauce on the inside left sleeve of this shirt." He held up his left elbow to display the spot for a nanosecond, "With flecks of oregano and basil and the unmistakable scent of garlic . . . His dinner date was a woman with long, curly red hair who wears too much makeup, has a fondness for whipped cream, and—"

"Stop." I held up my hand for him to cease and desist. "I've seen that show. Don't need a replay. But between you and bleeding Zapper and He Who on my front lawn and *murders*, I'm getting just a tad frazzled. Will you give me some inkling of what's going on?"

He glanced my way arrogantly. "Until I'm in possession of all the facts, Winslow, I prefer not to divulge—"

I cleared my throat so sharply that he glanced up and received my look, which unmistakably conveyed that I was *not* to be trifled with.

"Oh, very well." He sighed with annoyance. He picked up and handed me the black bug I'd seen the night before.

"The beetle? That's old news."

He rolled his eyes. "Brilliant, Winslow, I *told* you that much. But obviously, it's not just any beetle. This one is an accomplice to murder. What do you observe, *Doc*-tor?" He handed me his magnifying glass.

Zapper and I used it to look closely at the creepy bug. "Well, extremely long mandibles."

"Yes, which clearly identify it as a cicindelid. See?"

He brought up a Wikipedia page on my computer screen that showed an image of a beetle exactly like the one I was holding. I read, "Cicindelidae . . . Commonly called . . ." I inhaled. "*Tiger beetle?*"

"Mmm. Making the death of Assistant District Attorney Jacob Weiss the third murder linked to tigers."

I was confused, "Third? But the piranha—?"

"Are also called 'tricky fish.'" He sniffed. "Or . . . ?" He dramatically wiggled his eyebrows encouraging me to answer.

"Not 'tiger fish'? Really?"

Holmes drew a long-suffering breath. "How quick you are . . . Now, yesterday during my visit to police headquarters, I got a glimpse of Enrique Pavon. I saw, among many other things of course, that he was wearing a certain ring." Holmes' eyes went distant as he recalled it. "It was a semiprecious quartz with a vertical luminescent band—called tiger's-eye!" Holmes looked at me with enthusiasm and gestured toward the computer. "So I've done a 'global search'—a miraculous tool!—to connect *tiger* and *Pavon* using . . ." He tapped a key, and to my amazement, the menu of the San Francisco Police Department's proprietary computer network appeared on-screen.

"Wait, wait, you're into *internal* police files?"

Zapper laughed. "Yo! You're a hacker, Holmesy!"

"Oh yes, indeed," I acerbically confirmed to the boy. "Holmes has become a pro at 'gaggling.' Or was it 'giggling'?"

"Make sport of me if you will, Winslow," Holmes replied with a sniff. "But I am quickly learning the fine art of utilizing the assistance of Mr. Google."

Zapper's face twisted up. "Mr. Google?"

"Right, Holmes." I winked at the boy to just go with it.

"You and Mr. Google are best buds. But how did you figure out the police access code?"

"Elementary, Winslow. Detective Griffin was kind enough to enter his access code in my presence. And look what my search turned up."

A rap sheet with the photo of a bare-chested, muscular young man appeared. He had a cocky look. I read the name beneath it. "Antonio Pavon? Related to Enrique?"

"He was Enrique's younger brother. Look here." He pointed at a line of text. "Antonio was a wrestler in Colombia and known as . . ."

Zapper leaned in to look. "*El Tigre!* Get outta here!"

"Tony the Tiger, okay," I said, "but I'm still Big Willy. I don't understand how the missing Lieutenant Ortega fits into this."

"All three murder victims—Detective Donald Keating, Judge Louisa Chang, and Assistant District Attorney Jacob Weiss—were Ortega's closest friends, colleagues, or mentors. And why were they killed, you ask?" Holmes tapped a key that took the screen to the end of Antonio Pavon's file. It featured a page from the *San Francisco Chronicle* with the headline TONY THE TIGER PAVON KILLED IN DRUG ARREST.

Zapper read a line in the text before I did, blurting out, "'When Antonio Pavon opened fire on police, he was shot and killed by Lieutenant Luis Ortega!' Check it out!"

"And there is also this." Holmes brought up another picture of Antonio dressed for a night on the town, then zoomed in on his right hand. "Antonio is wearing the signature ring he was fond of."

I saw that it was a gaudy crystal ring. "Is that a tiger's-eye?"

Holmes nodded. "Exactly like the one I saw decorating

Enrique Pavon's finger. It might well be the very one his late brother was wearing when he died."

I pieced it together. "You think Pavon is killing Ortega's closest friends for *vengeance*?"

Holmes cocked his head. "So it might appear . . . to the casual observer. Revenge can be a powerful motivator, as you know I am keenly aware of from personal experience." The manner in which Holmes narrowed his eyes at me telegraphed that there was more that he wasn't sharing. To me, however, only one thing really mattered.

"Okay, but where's Luis Ortega? Is he dead too?"

"Not yet," said the detective, conclusively. "But we have only until 2:30 p.m. tomorrow to rescue him."

Zapper nudged Holmes' shoulder. "Oh, so that's what you heard Booth talkin' about tonight, huh?"

Holmes smiled with a secretive gleam in his eye. "Part of it."

"Wait. 'Heard at Booth's tonight'?" I was struggling to process the breaking news as fast as it was coming in. "But how does Booth have anything to do with Pavon's revenge murders?"

Holmes wiggled his right index finger at me. "All in good time, Winslow. Right now, we must go directly to—"

"The police! Yes!" I said, standing up.

"Definitely not," said Holmes.

"What?" I said, sinking back down, desperate to understand.

Holmes continued, "Detective Griffin is unlikely to be appreciative of my efforts or receptive to my theories—not yet, anyway." He stood up and shook Zapper's hand. "You were brilliant this evening, Julius." The boy beamed with pride. "Take the rest of the night off, and I shall contact you on the morrow."

Holmes was pulling on his coachman's cape. "Winslow, it's time for us to visit Mrs. Ortega."

I glanced at my watch. "We can't do that, Holmes, it's almost midnight!"

"Quite right. So time is of the essence." He leveled his gray eyes at me. "Leftenant Luis Ortega will be facing a brutal death in just over fifteen hours."

16

It *was* midnight by the time I had driven Holmes over to the Sunset district, south of Golden Gate Park. The middle-class neighborhood was quiet, most of its residents tucked into bed. The night was cool, but the fog had cleared.

As we walked up the steps of the modest Ortega house and onto the porch, I saw inside through thin curtains. Karen Ortega sat on her couch, her cell phone resting beside her. Clearly, she was hoping it would ring and dispel her fears.

She was about thirty years old, her thick black hair was long and, likely due to her distress, a bit unkempt. Her six-year-old son was curled up asleep on her lap. The tense woman was robotically staring at the television, which we could see was playing a home video of her and her husband and son kicking a soccer ball in a city park. Glancing over at Holmes, I saw that he appreciated her solitary vigil, even if he might've denied feeling the poignancy of it. He tapped lightly on the front door, and I saw Mrs. Ortega jump.

"Who is it?" she called out nervously.

"Friends who want to help," Holmes said in a low but straightforward tone.

Mrs. Ortega eased her sleeping child to one side and approached the door. I couldn't see her now, but I could feel her cautious presence on the other side of the door. "At midnight?" she said, her voice quavering. "Who are you?"

Holmes drew himself up fully. "Madam, I assure you—"

I poked him hard and whispered angrily, "Put a lid on it, Holmes." I knew what this woman was feeling and made a softer approach. "Mrs. Ortega, my name is Dr. Amy Winslow from Saint Francis Memorial Hospital. I'm sticking my business card into your mail slot."

She pulled it on through as I tried to speak as gently as possible. "I met your husband when Donald Keating died in my emergency room. I'm sure that having people you don't know appearing at your door at this hour must be alarming, but my friend and I have some information about your husband, about the danger he's in, and we truly want to help."

"So go to the police," she said.

I was pleased to hear Holmes pick up the tone of my milder approach as he said, "I'm afraid that's not an option. The matter is extremely delicate, and involving the police just now might do more harm than good. I can tell you one thing, Mrs. Ortega. I know with certainty that your husband is alive. A bit of information from you might help us to ascertain his precise whereabouts."

After a pause, I added, "Mrs. Ortega, you must be going through agony with him missing. Please let us try to help."

After a moment, we heard the deadbolt unlock. She opened the door and studied our faces. Her own looked weary and emotionally drained, with dark circles under her large brown eyes.

After Karen Ortega slipped her sleeping child into his bed, she returned to where Holmes and I sat in their cheery, inviting, lived-in living room. She sat on the edge of a chair in front of us. "Losing Donald Keating was a terrible blow to Luis," she began, trying to hold her brimming emotions in check. "Then Mrs. Chang killed by those fish, and Jake Weiss by those terrible insects, and—" Her throat tightened up with emotion. I saw her hand quivering.

I placed my hand gently on her arm, saying, "I can't imagine how hard all that must have been for both of you."

Holmes allowed a moment to pass, then started in. "At police headquarters, I overheard that your husband was in the midst of gathering evidence against Enrique Pavon."

"Yes," Mrs. Ortega said, attempting to recover her composure. "Luis said he'd finally have enough to bring down Pavon. That it would be a huge step toward cleaning illegal drug traffic out of the city. Luis had been after Pavon forever. Almost caught him in a drug raid two weeks ago—"

"Where Antonio Pavon was killed." I interjected.

"Yes. Soon after, Luis heard rumors of a huge cocaine shipment coming in. Said he could finish off Pavon if he could intercept the goods and make the bust." She looked from Holmes to me with pleading eyes. "Do you really have an idea where Luis is?"

"I have solid information that no harm can befall Luis before 2:30 tomorrow afternoon," Holmes said. To Mrs. Ortega, that was clearly both good news and bad. Holmes went on. "Has it been established where exactly your husband was abducted?"

"No, but he told me he was working on a stakeout somewhere on the south side."

"Might I see the last clothes he wore?"

She hesitated, so I said, "This gentleman is quite a brilliant detective." I tried to assure her, hoping we seemed less like ghoulish lunatics dropping in at midnight.

Mrs. Ortega looked from me to him, then nodded, "Of course." As she went to get them, I followed Holmes' gaze to the home videos still playing silently on the TV. I watched a smiling, handsome Luis Ortega rolling around the backyard playfully with his young son. It made me want to cry. Holmes was probably critical of my emotional empathy, but I just couldn't remain as detached as he usually seemed to. This time, however, I did note his frowning brow and compressed lips as he pondered the Ortegas' situation.

A few minutes later, the three of us had moved to the small kitchen table, where the light was better. Mrs. Ortega had brought out the clothes her husband had worn the night before he disappeared: jeans and a blue chambray shirt, telling us she had just washed them yesterday. Holmes began by checking the pockets, and upon inserting his long fingers into the third one, his eyebrows raised as he said, "Hello. What have we here?" Using his right index and middle finger like tweezers, he carefully lifted out a two-inch-long folded paper that had survived the wash cycle.

He held it out for me to unfold.

Mrs. Ortega frowned, saying, "How did I miss that? But maybe it's good I did."

Holmes leaned closer, eagerly. "What do you make of it, Winslow?"

I saw what it was and showed it to Mrs. Ortega, who nodded, saying, "Three days ago."

"What?" Holmes was focused on us like a hawk.

Mrs. Ortega said, "Our son, Raul, saw how sad his daddy was about Detective Keating's death. He wanted to cheer up Luis and asked if the three of us could go get a Baskin-Robbins together."

I knew Holmes was clueless. On two levels. "It's just a receipt for their ice cream cones."

"Ah," he said quietly, adding a small nod expressing sympathy, then returned to business. "But we shall continue undaunted." He took out his trusty magnifying glass and began going over every square inch of the clothing. He also examined a pair of Ortega's usual type of sneakers.

Karen Ortega watched him carefully, then glanced at me, "Why is it that you two are trying so hard to help?"

"Because your husband is an extremely worthy man," Holmes said while continuing his close scrutiny of the clothing.

"And also," I added, glancing toward the home video still on the TV, "obviously a loving father and husband."

She nodded, but her breathing was shallow. I knew she was barely holding back tears as she glanced at the pendulum clock over their hearth, aware of time ticking away for her missing husband.

Holmes lowered his glass and sighed. "You're an excellent laundress, madam. I'm afraid even I can find no clues as to where your husband was 'staked out.'"

That seemed to trigger an idea for Mrs. Ortega, and I prodded, "What?"

"It's against protocol," she said, "but if you can't go through the department, why don't you ask Bernie—Lieutenant Civita? They were alternating nights on the stakeout. He's often Luis's partner, would do anything for him, one of his best buddies."

I felt a chill of concern. I glanced at Holmes, who knew exactly what I was worried about. Over the last few days, Ortega's close friends had tended to meet gruesome ends.

Karen told us Civita's home address and also gave us his private cell number. She tried to call him herself, but the call went to voice mail. Karen tried a text but still got no response. She told us he lived alone and she had no other way to reach him. That prompted us to hurry our departure.

I traded cell numbers with Mrs. Ortega, then at the front door I pressed her hand, assuring her that we'd be back in contact the moment we had any news. She was trying hard to be brave, her chin trembling. I was distressed for her. Squeezing her hand, I promised that we'd do everything possible. She held tightly to my hand for a moment, looking into my eyes. I saw the silent messages of deep gratitude and hope in hers, but also her desperate fear.

We hurried away and drove north through the dark expanse of Golden Gate Park into the Richmond District near the Lone Mountain Campus of San Francisco University.

As we arrived on Civita's street, I again encouraged Holmes to alert the police. While walking from the car toward the cop's house, he explained his reluctance. "Do understand, Winslow, it is not my usual style to involve any of the authorities until I'm certain of—"

"Forget your usual style, Holmes," I snapped, digging out my cell. "A good man's life is at stake."

"Perhaps two men's lives." He had noticed something ahead, which put me on alert as well. Something was amiss.

Civita's porch light was out, as were the inside lights, but the front door was ajar. Holmes bolted ahead and entered. He quickly glanced around, squinting into the darkness, then ventured a few steps down a hallway to the right, calling out, "Leftenant Civita? Hello?"

There was no answer. I was about to dial 911 as I eased the door wider, stepped to the left into the dark foyer, and tripped— falling flat on my face, right on top of Bernard Civita.

He lay on his back, his blank, wide eyes in a permanent state of shock. "Holmes!" I called, then instinctively I pressed Civita's carotid artery with my left fingers while my right thumb punched my cell and I said, "Siri, *lumos!*"

My cell phone lit up as brightly as Hermione's wand. I shined it in Civita's staring eyes. They were unresponsive, and he had no pulse.

I sat up, with that subdued feeling in my heart which the presence of death inspires.

Holmes returned and knelt beside the corpse. "As we feared?"

"Yes." I was examining the body. "But it couldn't have happened long ago. He's still warm and— That's odd." I frowned as I tried again to bend Civita's arm.

"What? Speak up, Winslow."

"His limbs are in extreme contraction. He shouldn't have this much rigor mortis yet."

"Really?" he said with a faintly sly smile. Then he glanced at me sideways, adding, "And tell me, *Doc*-tor, what might account for that anomaly?" It was clear he thought he already knew the answer.

But so did I. Looking confidently into his eyes, I said, "A powerful alkaloid or some strychnine-like substance could produce tetanus."

His remarkable gray eyes remained locked upon mine, but his left eyebrow gave the absolutely subtlest twitch upward—betraying his surprise that I had delivered such a specific answer.

He couldn't prevent the trace of a condescending smile to emerge. His voice was subdued as he said, "Well done, Winslow," accompanied by a minimal nod of approval. "Quite right. That would cause it." Before I could draw a breath to fully enjoy the moment, he added, "However, that is not what was responsible for Leftenant Civita's demise."

Though I tried to hide my slight frown of confusion, he noted and enjoyed it as he took a penknife from his vest pocket and handed it to me. "Kindly make a small incision in his radial artery."

My brow knit a bit more, I was unsure of where he was going with this. And concerned about something else: "That would be tampering with a crime scene."

"But the clock is ticking toward Ortega ending like this. Do get on with it, Doctor."

I took the lieutenant's stiff wrist, slid his sleeve up to reveal the artery, which runs along the lateral aspect of the forearm just above the thumb. Using Holmes' razor-sharp knife, I cut into the artery. I blinked. "No bleeding! It's completely clotted!"

Holmes smiled and nodded. It seemed exactly as he'd expected, but I was confounded and said, "That accounts for the stiffness, but what could've—"

"Venom!" Holmes hissed. "From a snake of the Elapidae family. Note two tiny dots on the back of his hand." And indeed, there were the apparent fang marks that would result from a snakebite. Holmes drew a breath, "I should say that he was bitten by an Australian *Notechis scutatus*, commonly known as—"

"Don't tell me," I said, staring. "Tiger snake?"

"Just so. It flattens its head and neck, cobra-style, just before it strikes." His voice grew quieter as he continued. "The particular one that bit the late Leftenant is black and yellow and four feet six inches long; its right eye is larger than the left, and it has one partly broken fang."

"Oh, come on!" I blurted. He'd gone too far this time. "How can you possibly know that?"

His voice became a whisper. "Because, Winslow, *I am looking at it.*"

My blood froze. Holmes' eyes were focused directly over my shoulder, so I assumed—correctly—the deadly reptile was hovering right behind me. I drew in a panicked breath, and he saw my eyes widen.

"Do not move." Holmes said barely audibly but urgently. "It has coiled on the stairs. In striking distance. Right . . . behind . . . your neck."

I was terrified, especially with the extremely dead Lieutenant Civita lying right in front of me as a concrete example of this snake's lethal bite. Through gritted teeth, I whispered, "Holmes?"

He was slowly reaching his left hand toward a nearby umbrella stand. Reaching much too slowly for my taste at that moment.

I heard the snake hiss. It could not have been more than a foot behind my right ear.

Even more frozen and petrified, I whispered, *"Holmes?"*

"Steady, Winslow." He had gradually wrapped his long fingers around one of the folded umbrellas and was slowly drawing it from the stand. "Do not move a muscle. It is flattening its head." At the same time, his right hand had reached out inch by inch to grasp my lapel. His eyes never left the snake. He spoke quietly, "Now then, Winslow, on three you will dive directly towards me. One . . ."

He jerked me violently to him, smashing the umbrella powerfully onto the snake's head, dispatching it with the single blow as he fell backward, pulling me along.

I landed directly on top of him. We were chest-to-chest, face-to-face, both breathless on the floor of the dark foyer. I glanced quickly aside toward where the snake lay motionless. I gasped, "You sure it's dead?"

"Very." He was thoroughly confident, though still breathing rapidly. I felt the rhythmic swelling of his chest against my own.

I turned my face back above his, still out of breath myself. "You said 'on *three*'!"

"I lied. I was afraid you'd flinch."

"Thanks for the vote of confidence, Holmes." My heart was racing, I knew adrenaline was pumping in both of us, but I caught my breath enough to add, "And thanks for saving me."

"You're quite welcome, Winslow."

His dark eyes avoided mine. Neither of us moved, still tense, hearts pounding, his respiration as rapid as mine. We'd never been so physically close. Yet our sudden intimacy felt unexpectedly comfortable. Was it my imagination, or did he seem to be having a similar feeling? A full fifteen seconds passed, then a bit longer, without either of us moving.

He seemed to be considering how to say something. Finally, he spoke haltingly, saying, "You're . . . actually quite worth saving . . . Actually."

He was the most disconcerted I'd ever seen him. Our faces were barely three inches apart, my lips hovering just over his. He seemed noticeably unsure of himself.

I've admitted previously to enjoying and even prolonging his rare moments of discomfiture as but brief respites from his normal presumed superiority. This time, however, something deeper and more meaningful was going on within me. With the only light coming from a streetlamp filtering in through lace curtains that cast delicate shadowy patterns onto the face of this supremely intelligent man who had just saved my life in such a dashing, heroic manner, it had surprisingly become an extremely intimate moment. He seemed more accessible.

I was breathing slower now. "I'm worth saving? Really?"

"Mmm." He glanced around. Avoiding my eyes. After a pause, he added, "And your perfume . . . suits you perfectly."

"Oh?" I was wary, but curious. "How so?"

"Roses, with just a hint of citrus . . . Rather like your personality."

I squinted at him, asking quietly, "Is that an actual compliment?"

"It . . ."—his voice also grew quieter—"could be . . . so construed. I suppose."

We were pressed full-frontally against each other. His body was stiffer than ever before. Much stiffer. Every part of him, I suddenly realized. My eyebrows raised on their own, inquisitively. "Uh . . . Holmes?" I whispered, with the shadow of a smile percolating.

He seemed to understand exactly what I was feeling. His eyes finally met mine and lingered. Then he murmured, "Winslow . . ."

I answered softly, "Yes?"

". . . Might you . . . possibly consider . . ."

I felt visceral emotions stirring in me and realized they were a strengthening of what I'd felt the night before, when we'd gazed so profoundly at each other. Leaning a half inch closer, my lips almost touching his, I whispered softly, "What might I consider?"

His eyes held mine. His breath was warm as he whispered, "Thinking about . . ."

"Yes?" I breathed.

His voice was barely audible. "Our case?"

I blinked.

Of course. Our case. Right. That was what we were supposed to be doing.

I slowly—dare I admit reluctantly?—rolled off him. I noticed that he drew an uncommonly long and deep breath. Still avoiding my eyes, he rolled onto his knees, seemingly forcing himself to gather his thoughts and refocus on the matter at hand. We both crawled to the nearby late lieutenant.

"We must investigate his clothing," Holmes said, trying to sound as businesslike as possible after the highly unusual moment we'd just shared, "That may help our search for the stakeout location."

"Yes," I stammered, still trying to reconstitute my own professionalism. "Absolutely." We began going through Civita's pockets.

KENNETH JOHNSON

"Check his trouser turn-ups, if you please, Winslow. Always invaluable."

I slipped back into the grim reality of the moment as I deciphered "trouser turn-ups." "You mean cuffs?" I pointed to the bottom of Civita's jeans. "Don't see a lot of those anymore, Holmes." I couldn't help looking with sadness at Civita's face. I reached out and closed his eyelids. Holmes sensed how I was feeling.

"Come, come, Winslow. Regain your physician's composure. I, too, deeply regret that we were unable to save Detective Civita, but unless we proceed with utmost alacrity, Leftenant Ortega will also be— Aha!" He'd found something in a pocket. "A ticket. Apparently to see a performance by someone named Bart Daly."

"Close," I said, "Daly City is a South Side station on the BART." I saw his blank expression and explained, "The Bay Area Rapid Transit—BART."

"I see. A logical descendant of the cable cars and the London Underground, of course." He stated this as though he'd known it all along and merely forgotten. "So, did you discover any evidence of where his 'cuffs' might have recently been?"

I did so at that moment, reporting, "Just some white dust? Or is it powder?"

Holmes touched his fingertips to it, brought some up to his hawklike nose, and sniffed. His expression reminded me of a computer in search mode, flipping through a thousand possibilities. "Chalk? . . . No." He used his magnifying glass to examine the talc-like granules. His eyes narrowed as he eliminated numerous ideas, then they flashed with recognition. "It's cement!"

Holmes insisted that we drive to Daly City, but I refused to do anything until we had reported Lieutenant Civita's murder to the police.

"Quite so, Winslow. It would be rude to leave the worthy detective lying there unattended." I was surprised he agreed. But of course, there was a caveat. "For the sake of Luis Ortega's safety, however, it's vital that you contact the police anonymously."

"What? Why?"

"The situation is at a delicate stage, Winslow. Even the slightest incorrect move, no matter how well intentioned, might cost Ortega his life." He looked directly into my eyes with the most sincerity I'd yet seen from him. "I recognize that I am asking a great deal for you to put your faith in me about this. But I earnestly entreat you to do so."

It was a decision I dearly hoped I wouldn't live to regret, but I drove us to a twenty-four-hour public computer café and sent an anonymous email to the SFPD about Bernie Civita's death and his whereabouts.

Then we headed south, with Siri guiding us down Nineteenth Avenue. The traffic was light, and I was hurrying just over the speed limit. I was also sorting through my confusion about what I'd felt while lying atop Holmes, so closely face-to-face. I'd felt how his heart rate and respiration were equal to my own, triggered in both of us by a rush of adrenaline.

But there had been an undeniable physical spark of something else in that moment. And I was certain he had felt it as well. I glanced over at him in my passenger seat and saw that he seemed focused intently ahead. I wondered if he was perhaps internally exploring the same feelings as I. I decided to come at the issue sideways by pursuing a different question I'd been curious about. "Her name was Irene Adler, wasn't it?"

Holmes tightened up slightly but continued gazing forward. "Whose name?"

"The 'American opera singer and well-known adventuress' whom Watson said you always referred to as 'the Woman.'"

"Hmm?" He was trying very hard to sound vague. "It may have been, yes." He glanced out his side window. "Quite an interesting section of town this, and—"

"In the *Scandal in Bohemia* story, Doyle—and Watson—made Ms. Adler sound like quite an intriguing woman of the world. And strikingly beautiful as well. Quite a package. She certainly seemed that way in the photo you keep of her." He was doing his best to ignore me, so I took the plunge. "Are those the reasons why you were smitten?"

"Ha!" he laughed. A little too hard? "I have never been smitten by—"

"Oh, come on, the king of Bohemia was about to be married, feared blackmail by Irene, which would cause a scandal, and offered you a fortune for reclaiming his incriminating love letters, which—"

"Just so," he eagerly interrupted, but I steamed ahead.

"Which actually you *failed* to reclaim because the wily Irene saw through your disguise and your subterfuge, and she one-upped you. The great Holmes' clever plans were undone by a woman's wit."

"Well, it didn't happen quite like that—" he began defensively, but I was undeterred and plowed right on.

"Irene had a change of heart and saucily put the letters into your hands. But when you were returning them to the grateful king—who gave you that gold snuffbox and was ready to reward you with half of his kingdom—you declined his generosity.

Instead, all you asked for was the photo he had of the divine Ms. Adler. Sounds terribly sweet and lovesick to me."

He blew out a puff of derision, then pontificated dryly, "Love and the sickness it generates are unknown to me, Winslow."

"Plus, Irene gave you a gold sovereign, a memento which you still display right there on your watch chain." When I pointed to it, he tried to look surprised.

"Oh. Was it she who gave it to me? Just the other day I was trying to remember how I—"

My sardonic chuckle stopped him dead, and he endeavored to regroup, pontifically.

"You must understand, *Doc*-tor, how I strongly believe that emotions in general, and particularly those of affection and sentimentality, are the enemy of clear, rational logic and are abhorrent to a precise, admirably balanced mind."

"Then what was it about her, Holmes, that so captivated you?" I sincerely wanted to know. "Was it the mere fact that another human being had outsmarted you? Particularly a *female*? That must have been galling. Left your admirable mind just a wee bit off-balance?"

He continued staring out the car's passenger-side window, but he put his left elbow on the armrest between us with his forearm raised so he could rest his cheekbone against his index finger. He seemed to be genuinely mulling over my statement. Finally, I was rewarded by what seemed a rare moment of candor. "I cannot deny your innate insightfulness, Winslow." He paused, measuring his words carefully. "I think what I felt was a deep . . . respect for Miss Adler's mental acuity and her devilish cleverness."

"And that made her attractive?"

"Well, I should not characterize it quite so dramatically."

I let the silence hang, keeping my eyes on the road as I asked, as casually as possible, "Has there been anyone since Irene Adler that came close to creating her effect?"

He seemed to consider a possibility and finally said, "No." But then, after a beat, he added quietly, "Not really."

I felt a flicker in my chest but couldn't be sure if it was disappointment, relief, or just frustration at his ambiguity.

Very soon after, I steered the Accord into the industrial warehouse section of Daly City. Holmes had my backup cell phone in his hand and had been scrolling down through a list of companies in the area.

"This is completely marvelous!" he said with delight. "You can just let your fingers do the walking."

"What an *original* concept," I said wryly, wondering if the Yellow Pages still existed.

"The only cement company within walking distance of the Daly City BART station is at the address I gave you."

"I don't know why Siri couldn't find that company name." I looked ahead along the dark street. "Okay. I see why. To the left up there. It looks out of business and abandoned."

"Yes. And over there is what we're looking for." Holmes pointed to the right at something I couldn't see because of the angle.

I pulled the Accord to a stop near the derelict cement plant. One door was hanging on a single hinge and partially open. Holmes got out and his eyes swept the area, which was dusty with fine white cement powder.

"If Civita and Ortega were staked out inside there"—he pointed toward the broken door—"then the object of their surveillance, something to do with Pavon's criminal activities, obviously would be across the street."

He indicated a six-story, windowless storage building opposite with large doors for unloading freight. Above the doors was what I hadn't seen from in the car. A sign on it read Peacock Trucking.

I turned back to see Holmes grinning at me expectantly as he said. "Peacock being . . . ?"

"*Pavon* in Spanish!" I gushed, then felt a bit of embarrassment at my effusiveness.

"Well done, Winslow. Now you're getting into the spirit of the chase. Seeing Mrs. Ortega seems to have had an energizing effect." He turned and headed into the dusty, abandoned cement works with a flashlight he'd taken from my car door's pocket.

I glanced back at Peacock Trucking and pondered what he'd just said. It was true. For the first time, I'd understood how people like Holmes and Lieutenant Ortega could have such a strong personal commitment toward crime fighting and solving mysteries. It was unquestionably rewarding and exciting. But I also suddenly felt the sobering responsibility—particularly when someone's life was hanging in the balance.

Holmes slowed his approach as he neared the plant. "Winslow, what's that yellow tape on the building?"

My excitement deflated. I positively sagged. "Oh, no. It's a police line. Marking off a crime scene. It means they've already checked this lead." I was disappointed.

But Holmes was not the slightest bit daunted. "Don't despair, Winslow, it's been my experience that even the most astute police officer often overlooks an item or two." He smiled encouragingly at me and whipped out his trusty magnifying glass. "Stay close to the walls so we disturb as little as possible."

I followed him through the broken door into a cavernous room with concrete floors and walls, mostly empty except for broken crates and rusting machinery. A couple of pigeons flapped around in the rafters, and a rat scurried away along a wall where we noted some fast-food wrappers that suggested a police stakeout.

Holmes pointed out how the dusty floor revealed a scuffle, confirming how this could have been the spot where the abduction of Ortega had taken place. We carefully explored the large premises for half an hour, then I finally heard his characteristic squeak of pleasure.

I hurried to where he was kneeling beside a small crate next to the wall.

"Look, Winslow. Here, near the floor. See the right and left heelprints in the cement dust against this box?"

"Someone sat on the box," I said. Then my eyes widened as I blurted, "And look at their imprints in the dust! It's the same design as Luis Ortega's sneakers!"

"Yes, the Leftenant sat here."

Holmes displayed suppressed excitement while I was tingling with a sort of half-sporting, half-intellectual pleasure.

"Whilst it is true, Winslow, that you have missed everything of importance, you have indeed hit upon the method and have a quick eye for comparative design."

I chuckled to myself: Holmes giveth, but then Holmes swiftly taketh away. "So, what was more important?"

"Notice these rusty nails atop the box." He was picking one up. "With Ortega's hands behind him—even if they were tied—he could've used a nail to scratch a clue on the wall as to where he was being taken." Holmes made a small scratch on the wall to demonstrate, then glanced at me as a professor or Socrates might have done when encouraging a student, "So what do you make of this?"

He focused his flashlight on the wall just above the crate. There were some small scratches I hadn't noticed. I squinted. "It looks like a *P* then maybe a *1* and *5*? With a sort of wavy line under it?"

"Yes, Winslow!" Holmes' eyes glittered, "We're on the scent!"

Annoyingly but typically, Holmes stubbornly refused to tell me what he'd deduced until after he'd attained further verification. He asked me to drop him off uptown in the seedy area below Russian Hill, near where we'd met Charley Moriarty.

"I'm really not thrilled about leaving you in this area," I said, glancing around the squalid locale as I brought the car to a stop.

But Holmes smiled as he opened his door. "Absolutely no reason to concern yourself. I have spent many of my most fruitful nights in such environs, and I expect tonight will be equally so." As he closed the car door, he continued brightly, "And definitely, do not wait up. I'll see you anon, my dear . . . Winslow." He paused to give me a final look through the window that seemed to silently acknowledge appreciation for my presence and collaboration. His gaze held for a moment longer than it ever had. Then he seemed to catch himself. He sniffed and turned to hurry down the dark street, disappearing around a corner.

Back at home, I tossed restlessly in my bed through what

was left of the night and kept listening for the downstairs door to open as he came back. But he never did.

At the hospital the next morning, I was bleary-eyed as I tried to put on a cheerful face while talking to my young patients. But I kept glancing at the clock, getting increasingly nervous with every passing minute. Given the dreadful details of the three previous murders, all I could think about was what bizarre homicidal horror Luis Ortega might undergo in a few short hours.

I was kneeling beside six-year-old, ringlet-haired Katie, who was departing by wheelchair after her appendectomy and happily showing me a thank-you drawing she'd made for me to add to my collection. I saw the approach of slender, forty-something Susan, an RN whom I loved for her bright blue eyes, smiles, and sharp sense of humor. Today she was *not* smiling, which telegraphed that something was up.

"I'm sorry to bother you, Dr. Winslow," Susan said with an exasperated tone unusual for her, "but we've got a problem in the ER. There's an older woman who refuses to talk to anyone but you."

One older woman came to mind. "Did she say her name was Hudson?"

"We couldn't get her name," Susan said. "She was mostly just muttering gibberish."

I followed to investigate. We walked through the double doors into ER Reception, and Susan pointed out the woman— although there was no way I could have missed her.

She had a filthy scarf pulled over matted, stringy hair that hung partly across her gaunt, smudged face, which was missing a few front teeth. She wore cheap, scratched sunglasses. Mismatched, stained clothes hung loosely on her frame, and she smelled like a brewery. She was truly off-putting. Her painful, stooped posture suggested a hard life, and it might have aroused genuine sympathy in me under normal circumstances. But not that day.

I took one look at her and pointed harshly toward an examining room. "Go in there. Now!" I saw Susan blink with surprise at my unusually callous attitude.

The woman shuffled ahead of me into the room, her voice raspy, "Thank you very kindly, Doctor."

I followed, then slammed the door shut for privacy and spun around, furious. "What the hell are you doing?" I grabbed the woman's ratty scarf and pulled it—and her hair—right off her head.

"*Yowwww!*" Holmes yelled. "That hurt!"

He stood up straight now, his large faux breasts ballooning beneath the worm-eaten, seedy sweater as he ran his lean fingers through his own long dark hair. He was thoroughly shocked. "How on earth did you recognize me?"

"Your patent leather shoes."

"Really?" He planted a hand on his hip. "I thought I'd slovened them up rather well."

"Not rather well enough," I said, narrowing my eyes and doing my best to look as acerbic and cocky as he often did. "I also *ob-served* the configuration of cocaine injection scars on your left forearm as well as the two moles on the back of your right hand, the faint but distinct smell of your pipe tobacco, and—" I caught myself. "Goddammit, I've been hanging around with you too much!"

"Upon my word, Winslow," he said with a hearty laugh, as he scraped the blacking off his front teeth, "you are coming along wonderfully!"

"Why the hell are you in this *ridiculous*— Did you find Lieutenant Ortega?"

"Yes!" he said with the greatest exuberance I had ever seen from him. "He has yet to be rescued, however. Now what I need from you are twenty dollars."

"What?"

"For our tattooed and fascinating friend Charley Moriarty. Come, come," he beckoned impatiently. "You have my word I shall pay you back . . . as soon as I have the means."

I fished for the small billfold in my scrubs with annoyance. "Oh right. And when might that be exactly? And Charley Moriarty because—?" I cut myself off as it came to me in a flash. "Because he runs that storefront mission, where you got this stunning ensemble."

"Well deduced again, Winslow! Indeed, Charley became my clothier," he said, cheerily displaying his squalid attire. "He gave me the pick of his hand-me-down haberdashery, even provided my delightful hairpiece." Then in a very serious, confidential voice he said, "Thus accoutred, I could—and did—prowl about the Embarcadero waterfront last night without attracting any notice while pursuing our investigation. I promised Charley a donation to his mission." He snatched from me the twenty and then another ten. "Excellent, that will give me trolley fare as well. My thanks."

"But what about *Ortega?*"

"He shall soon be safe. At one this afternoon, you must meet me at the restaurant La Serre on Washington Square to witness the successful completion of our case!" He grabbed the ratty wig and with a flourish swept past me out of the room.

"Wait a minute!" I shouted, heading into the hallway.

To the consternation of patients and staff alike, Holmes was parading hastily down the corridor toward the ER exit as I tried to catch up.

He shouted back at me, "Be there promptly at one o'clock!"

"Holmes!"

But he hurried grandly on. "And it's *imperative* that you come on your motor-bicycle! Do not fail me on that. Now I have a busy morning, as I'm sure you do also, Doctor, so adieu!"

At the ER's wide exit, he turned to look back while swinging the wig jauntily in a little circle over his head and gave me a courtly bow, then he disappeared out the door.

The stunned patients, doctors, and nurses he had passed by all stared after him, then they slowly turned to look at me.

I didn't know whether to laugh or scream.

17

La Serre was a sunny, classy French restaurant on Filbert Street, across from Washington Square. On the inside, white lattice-work panels airily divided the place into variously sized, inviting alcoves for dining. Elegant table settings with white and French blue linens abounded with delicate fresh flowers in centerpiece vases. I was at a table for two, far too much on edge to think about eating. I sat, nursing some San Francisco water in a fine crystal glass. Per the master's request, I had arrived promptly at 1:00. By 1:20, my stomach was in knots.

Then I realized with trepidation that across the flowery room, sitting at a more secluded table with a couple of well-to-do people, was the imposing figure of James Moriarty Booth.

I'd seen a picture of him on a police report that Holmes had printed out, but being in his actual presence was more than unsettling. I studied him as he was offered a bottle of wine by a white-gloved, painfully obsequious blond waiter. Booth took the bottle, turned it over in his hands to examine it, and dismissively refused it. The waiter shrugged and moved off.

After waiting another eleven minutes, I was getting really fearful, when God's gift to crime detection arrived at my table. His spirits were as buoyant as when he'd left the hospital a few hours earlier. Apparently dressing in homeless drag bolstered Holmes' mood. Now he was outfitted in the dapper afternoon frock coat and silk vest he'd worn when he first walked down that stairway at Mrs. Hudson's house. His deerstalker was in his hand.

"My apologies for the tardy arrival," he said breathlessly. "I had some final details to attend to."

I had stood up to face him and said sotto voce, "Did you see who's here?" I indicated with a nod of my head the far end of the restaurant, where Booth was cheerfully engaged in conversation with his cronies, entirely unaware of us. Holmes glanced for only an instant, then turned back to me.

"May I suggest," he said with a sour expression as he snagged my jacket from the back of my chair, "that we find a place where the air is less polluted?"

As requested, I'd arrived at the restaurant on my motorbike, and once outside I walked quickly to it, grabbing my helmet, asking, "Where are we going?"

"Up there." He pointed at Coit Tower atop Telegraph Hill, two blocks east of us.

"What? Holmes, do you know what time it is?"

"It is 1:34," he said, waving away the spare helmet I was trying to hand him. "No, thank you."

"It's the *law*," I snapped. "And what about Ortega? You said at 2:30 he'd be—"

"All will be well, Winslow." He reluctantly donned the helmet over his ear-flapped cap as he climbed on behind me. "Do get along now."

I started the bike. "But why are we going up—?"

"I have my reasons, Doctor. Off we go now."

With a taut, worried face I drove us up curving Hill Road as hurriedly as was safe. Reaching the top of the hill, I parked the bike and he hopped off saying, "Let's go up there, Winslow."

"Holmes," I began as I locked the bike, "I want to know exactly why we had to come all the way—" I turned to see that he was already on the move. With a grunt of irritation, I followed him up the wide steps beneath Coit Tower.

As we reached the small terrace beside the westerly base of the tower, he appeared not to have a care in the world. "Will you please tell me what is going on?" I said.

"Everything that should be, I guarantee you. There's nothing to be done for a while, so we may comfortably enjoy the view." He took off his deerstalker and, taking pleasure from the breeze, looked northwest across the glistening bay to the Golden Gate and beyond, then back in the northerly direction of Sausalito. "That island in the bay is where the Alcatraz prison sits, eh?"

"Yes," I said tersely.

"How ironic that its evildoer inmates should have had such a tantalizing view of a golden city that was inaccessible to them."

I was in no mood for his Tripadvisor philosophy, and I lit into him. "Holmes, I reworked my entire schedule so I could help you today. I deserve to be told what is going on."

He glanced my way. "Oh, please don't take it personally, Winslow," he said with a prissy smile as the brisk wind stirred his long dark hair. Then he sighed, admitting, "I'm afraid it's just my own damnable nature. *Omne ignotum pro magnifico est.*"

I knew lots of medical Latin but had to puzzle that out word by word. I guessed at the proper translation: "Everything unknown . . . for magnificent . . . is? – Everything unknown is . . . *taken for being magnificent*?"

"Exactly. Brava," he said. "The magician gets no credit for magic once he's explained his trick. I think—" I could see that he was struggling to continue, that what he had to say wasn't easy for him to confide, but finally he did. "The one thing I've always feared is that if I reveal too much the inner workings of my methods, people may conclude that I'm exceedingly . . . ordinary."

Was he pulling my leg? It was impossible to think that anyone—particularly the egoistic man himself—would ever consider Holmes ordinary. But his deeply thoughtful expression and slight frown gave the impression that he actually believed his thesis, that he truly harbored that insecure dread.

I sat with a huff on the low stone wall, my nerves on edge. I was still annoyed with him for not sharing everything with me but was nonetheless curious where he was going with this.

He remained standing and said, "Winslow, you do deserve to hear me acknowledge . . . formally"—I could see how he was forcing himself to say this—"that I am actually . . . somewhat . . . impressed by you."

I kept my voice level. "Don't patronize me, okay?"

"Certainly not." Then he went on, his eyes brightening, "But you must understand that one test of a true detective, of a sharp intellect, is penetrating a disguise. As you did with mine. Watson never managed it."

"But Irene Adler did," I sharply reminded him.

"Correct. And you are the first since her to accomplish it." He flinched slightly as though instantly sorry that revelation had escaped his lips.

I, on the other hand, took a breath as my ego inflated, but I refused to let any pride show, and I wanted to get some answers. I stood up to face him. "Well, bully for me. But listen, Mr. Holmes—"

"And a true *friend*," he interrupted, sitting down on the wall himself with an appreciative expression, "is one who helps when you're depressed." He looked up at me. "You're a whetstone for my mind, Winslow. You stimulated me out of my doldrums. You put me back in contact with . . . my mistress!"

"Your what?" I was stunned. "Who is she?" I realized that I'd said this as though he'd cheated on me.

"No, no, no," Holmes chuckled. "Women have seldom been an attraction to me, Winslow. My brain has always governed my heart."

His eyes met mine directly and with such an unusual softness that I almost expected him to say, "Until I met you."

But he didn't. Not out loud, at least. Not then.

He drew a breath and went on, "My mistress is my *work*." He pumped his fist for emphasis as he said, "Casework, not cocaine, is my real drug." He looked at me and repeated the quote I had read about him from a century earlier: "There truly *is* nothing more stimulating than a case where everything goes against you."

"Alright then," I said, trying to set aside my confused personal emotions and make him focus. "What about *this* case?" I pressed. "You've gotten on top of it? Luis Ortega is out of danger or—?"

"He shortly will be," he said with a damnably private grin as he stood up and walked casually toward the gentle grassy slope on the eastern side of the tower. I followed with my annoyance rising toward fury.

Holmes gazed out over the city. The air was crystalline, the view spectacular. He could see all the way across the lengthy span of the Bay Bridge to Oakland beyond. San Francisco sparkled like the Emerald City. But I was entirely riveted on him.

"Listen, Holmes—"

"Ah, what remarkable changes in over a century." His eyes scanned up the tower beside us, which rose 210 feet above our heads. "This tower certainly wasn't here when last I stood on this hilltop. Looks rather like a nozzle, doesn't it?"

"Exactly, Holmes," I said, quickly to dispense with exasperating small talk. "Old Mrs. Coit loved riding on fire engines, so she 'beautified the city' by leaving us with a big *nozzle*. Now, you listen to me." I poked hard at my watch. "It is 2:11, a man's life is on the line, and you're up here—"

"'When one has done all one can, it is wise to calm the mind by quiet contemplation.'" He glanced professorially. "That is a tenet of the Buddhism of Ceylon."

"It's not *Ceylon* anymore," I snapped, "it's *Sri Lanka*. Now, will you please—"

"Even the names of *countries* have changed?" That startled him into a nanosecond of reflection about the challenges he'd created for himself. He took a quiet breath, then said, "Winslow, please accept my deepest apologies for the inconveniences I've caused you."

"Then stop *causing* them and tell me—"

"I promise to vacate your premises soon. Perhaps, by way of recompense, I could offer some insights for the Victorian novel I've observed you're writing."

"You'll stay long as you need to, okay? That's not the issue!" I stepped closer to him, trying to look him straight in the eye.

But he kept glancing down at the streets below us, ignoring me. That did it: My extreme concern for Luis Ortega boiled over. I exploded, shouting with rage.

"You will tell me right this instant what the hell is—"

"*Aha!*" he bellowed even louder, went wild-eyed and scared the wits out of me.

"What?"

"Come quickly, Winslow!" He grabbed my hand and pulled me along, running back toward the base of the tower.

"Holmes, what is it?"

"Hurry! No time to waste!" He had me running flat out to keep up as we raced around to the front of the tower and down the steps toward my bike as he clapped the deerstalker onto his head.

I was now worried that his violent mood swings might indicate a truly unbalanced mind. He grabbed his helmet from the back seat, pulled it on over his cap, and quickly climbed on behind me, shouting, "Start the bike, Winslow! Down the hill at once!"

I dropped the bike into gear and almost did a wheelie as I peeled out of the parking lot. Hill Road is steep as it curves down around Telegraph Hill, but I was fairly skillful with the bike and had driven this road many times.

Holmes' surprisingly strong left arm was tightly around me from behind as he urged me on. "That's it, Winslow! Around that vehicle!"

I had to violently weave around a slow pickup truck that was headed downward, then I quickly cut back in before an oncoming bus made roadkill out of us.

"Would you mind telling me where we're going?" I shouted over the noise of the bike and the traffic I was dodging.

"Our destination is the Embarcadero! Pier 15!"

"That's what Ortega's 'P 1-5' meant? That he scratched on the wall at the plant?"

"Yes. I suspected Ortega meant the wavy line as the universal symbol for water, hence my logical deduction. Hurry now, Wats—er—Winslow! The game's afoot! There's not a moment to lose!"

I continued to weave rapidly through the slower-moving traffic.

"Is Ortega at Pier 15? Did you see him last night?"

"Of course." Holmes said like it was a given. "No one paid any attention to a stoop-shouldered, shaggy old woman poking about, pushing her rickety shopping cart along among rubbish bins. I approached a rundown waterfront warehouse near Pier 15, where a sizable cabin cruiser was moored. Moving stealthily closer, I peered in through a broken board and saw a man sitting on a chair. It was Leftenant Ortega, unshaven and fatigued. His hands were tied behind him. His forehead was glistening with perspiration as he leaned back against the greasy brick wall. His eyes were focused upward, reflecting deep grief. Three burly men were in attendance. One had long hair pulled back in a ponytail. He was saying to Ortega, 'After the snake bit him, your buddy Civita just laid there in some serious pain, let me tell you. He was pissed, staring at us, but he couldn't do nothing.' Then with a nasty laugh, he added, 'Civita's never going to arrest anybody again.' I witnessed Ortega's grief transform to fury, but it was impossible for him to act against them."

That made me shout back ferociously at Holmes over my shoulder as I steered the bike, "And why didn't you just call the police right then and there?" I was seething. "I can't believe you'd use Ortega as a pawn!"

"The good leftenant is no pawn, Winslow—he's a *knight* at the very least, a valiant warrior in the battle against crime. I believe he'd approve of my tactics."

"Not if your tactics get him *killed*!"

"That shan't happen. Watch out! Onto the pavement."

He had seen the car in front of us on Lombard come to an abrupt stop for a pedestrian. I swerved sharply to the right and jumped the curb onto the sidewalk, dodging a man carrying an armful of boxes. I managed to just miss a fireplug as I bounced us off the curb and back onto the street.

"In one hundred feet, turn left," he shouted.

"No. That's the wrong direction!"

"Yes, but the fastest route." He held my other cell in front of me, saying, "Siri is also on the case."

I made the sharp left and dodged more cars as I shouted back at him, "So Ortega's still at the warehouse?"

"Yes. He's being held there until 2:30, when he will be personally handed over to Pavon by James Moriarty Booth!"

"What?" My brain flip-flopped. "It's *Booth's* men holding Ortega?"

"Of course. Take the next two rights, then left onto Lombard."

"But the Tiger Murders all point to Pavon!" I shouted as I made the right turns and sped us faster down the street. "To avenge his dead brother, Tony the Tiger!"

"Yes. Devilishly sinister. An elegant motif, is it not?" he said. "Far too fiendish, elegant, and insidious a scheme to come from the crude-natured Pavon. I recognized it at once as a product of the aesthetically twisted mind of a Moriarty."

"Are you sure?"

"Absolutely. Pavon's usual style is far more brutish. Julius told me Pavon kills with steamrollers."

After I made the left onto Lombard Street, we were only a few blocks away from where it met the Embarcadero. I drove quickly, weaving between slower cars. "So, you're saying that *Booth* committed these Tiger Murders? Why? In honor of Pavon's brother, Tony?"

"Yes, to avenge Tony's death at the hand of Leftenant Ortega, but also to bring agony to Luis Ortega by first horribly murdering his four closest friends. Most importantly, however, Booth did it to gain Pavon's deep appreciation."

"And now Booth's going to hand over Ortega himself, so that what? Pavon can kill Luis personally and complete the vengeance?"

"Precisely my deduction." Holmes' left arm still held tightly around me. I felt a little encouraging squeeze as he said, "Well thought out, Winslow." Then he shouted, "*Oops!* On your right!" I swerved to pass a lumbering street sweeper.

Once I had the bike under control again, I yelled back to Holmes, "But why is Booth, who's Pavon's biggest *rival* in the San Francisco underworld, doing all this for him?"

"Why would someone like Booth do anyone a favor?"

That made me think of *The Godfather*, and then it clicked. "To get something in return? Okay. But what?"

"More, Winslow. People like Booth always want *more*."

"And you've told the police all this, right?" No answer. I screamed at him. "Right? . . . Holmes, answer me, dammit!"

He said calmly, "When I have spun the web, they may take the flies, but not before."

"No, Holmes! We—"

"Look out!" he cried. "Lady with a baby! Go that way!"

I barely missed the mother and child, but I refused to let him dodge the issue. "We cannot handle this alone!"

I heard his cell beeping. "Oh, Winslow, you're such a worrier." He was pulling out his iPhone. "Certainly, we cannot." He answered the call. "Yes? Holmes here . . . Oh, hello, Julius!"

"Zapper? That's our backup?" I was livid. "Holmes, hang up this instant and dial 911 or—"

"Winslow, please, it's difficult enough to hear on these devices," he said peevishly. "You're on Pavon's *what*, Julius? . . . 'Ass' meaning tail? . . . Very good. And he should be approaching . . . What do you mean Pier 27? That's not right. It should be Pier 15."

"I don't want to hear that." I said with dread, then demanded, "Holmes, hang up and call 911!"

"Everything is still well in hand, Winslow. Fear not." Then he shouted into the phone, "Julius, alert the others of the change in piers, then proceed as planned." He clicked the phone off, saying, "No, Winslow, don't slow down!"

"I've got a red light, Holmes."

He whipped out Zapper's handheld remote, reached his arm over my shoulder, and activated it. The stoplight flashed to green.

"Now, do proceed swiftly, Winslow, to Pier 15!"

I sped us along, turned left onto the Embarcadero and then right onto the aging boards of Pier 15, which held an obstacle course of cargo crates, barrels, and nautical gear. We saw a large, forty-foot cabin cruiser untying from the near end of the pier and getting underway.

"Blast!" Holmes blurted fiercely.

"That's *definitely* not what I want to hear!" I shouted.

Holmes had just been reminded that Fate can also be fickle. Even the best laid plans of mice and Holmes can go awry. He verified that by grumbling loudly, *"Damn!"*

"What's wrong?"

"That's the boat I saw docked here last night."

We saw that on the rear the deck of the yacht was a large cube, about five feet on a side, underneath a tarp. But more importantly, we saw two burly enforcers, one of them a redhead. "Booth's men I saw last night," Holmes confirmed. They were manhandling a tall hostage with his arms tied behind him toward the boat's cabin.

Even from fifty yards away, I recognized him. "Ortega!"

"Of course." In my rearview, I saw Holmes' eyes narrow. "Very clever of them. And why Julius and I observed Booth looking at a map including the bay. Now I understand: it's to be a rendezvous *on the water*. Drive that way, quickly!" He pointed for me to continue out onto the pier.

I gunned the bike, and we were able to overtake the yacht as it moved parallel to us in the water beside the long pier. "Get ahead of them quickly," Holmes urged. "Keep going till I tell you."

I maneuvered around stacks of pallets and boxes along the way, which helped block any view of us from the boat. I was about twenty yards from the end and barely ahead of the boat when Holmes said, "Stop here!" I braked the bike, and he was off in a flash, shedding his helmet and calling back to me as he ran, "Get to Pier 27, Winslow! I'll ring you up!"

"Holmes?"

He dashed across the pier, running in that formal way of his, fists up, arms pumping. To my astonishment, I realized he was running right toward the end of the pier.

The tide was in, but the water level was still about eight feet below the deck of the pier. I saw that the boat had begun to turn slightly, bringing it to within about ten feet of the pier's corner.

Holmes ran like a champion and seemed to be timing it perfectly, but my heart stopped as he leapt off the end, waving his arms for balance and landing hard on the yacht's back deck.

Though the craft was moving away from me, I saw that in the course of his skillful landing, something fell from his pocket and skidded across the deck. The noise attracted the attention of the curly-headed thug who was just then coming up from below decks. In an instant, he'd see Holmes.

But Holmes heard the man coming. In a flash, he flipped up the edge of the canvas nearest him to hide beneath it. I drew a sharp breath when I glimpsed what that tarp was covering: a cage containing a Bengal tiger. Holmes was under the tarp now, face-to-face with the beast.

The curly-headed man spotted the object that had fallen from Holmes' coat. He picked it up and looked around and then up at the sky, wondering where it had fallen from. I realized he'd found Holmes' cell phone.

Our communication was now cut off. I sat on my bike, near panic, breathing hard, puzzling over my next move. Then I remembered Holmes' telling me to go to Pier 27.

I decided to get over there fast, and if Holmes hadn't summoned the cops, I'd call them myself.

I snagged Holmes' helmet and gunned the bike, turning so hurriedly that I nearly ran straight into a large pole and dumped myself in the harbor. Somehow I managed to stay upright and raced back toward the Embarcadero.

18

Swinging my bike onto the near end of Pier 27, I saw ahead of me two hefty, intimidating SUVs, their darkened windows suggesting illicit activity. Parked next to them was a sleek charcoal-gray Cadillac limousine. There was a commotion on one side of that vehicle. Five men—all with that wise-guy look of organized crime—were trying to break up a scuffle between a bunch of scruffy street teens. Fists were swinging and punches hit flesh as the mobsters shoved their way into the melee and pulled apart the scrapping teenagers.

I skirted past the disturbance, catching only a quick look but surprised to recognize at least one of the brawling boys: the teen called Slick who'd attacked Holmes that night on Baker Street. As one of the heavies slung another of the kids away to separate him from the others, I heard the boy shout, "Hey, man! Ain't you never heard of the Queensbury Rules?" For a second, I thought I saw Zapper duck down on the far side of the gray limo.

Leaving behind that puzzle, I drove farther onto the pier,

hoping against hope to be rewarded by seeing a group of San Francisco's Finest. But once past a large pallet of packing crates, I instead found myself in the presence of the top echelon of San Francisco's Worst.

With no space to turn and exit gracefully, I was forced to pull to a stop directly in front of four dread-inducing criminal lieutenants and their respective commandants, James Moriarty Booth and Enrique Pavon.

The two underworld chieftains looked my way as if I were a total nonentity that had unwittingly stumbled into their royal presence—which, of course, would be perfectly accurate. Their alert lieutenants, however, moved smoothly to encircle me at a respectful but no-nonsense distance.

With icy indifference as to whether I would live or very soon die, Booth asked, "Who the hell are you?"

"Oh. Uh. Nobody," I stammered, shrugging and trying to smile. "I mean, I'm just out for a little ride. I sometimes come here to think, you know, get a little perspective. Is that a problem?"

The two crime barons glanced at each other, then eyed me with menace. I felt their enforcers drawing closer around me. Two of them reached inside their jackets—unlikely they were reaching for business cards.

At that moment out on the yacht in the bay, Holmes was in a precarious position himself. After facing the angry claws of a caged killer tiger only inches from his face and managing to maintain his composure, he'd waited for the curly-red-haired man to leave the deck. Curly finally disappeared up onto the flying bridge, where the cabin cruiser was being driven by the ponytailed man who'd been holding Ortega captive at the warehouse.

At last sensing that he was alone on the rear deck, Holmes carefully peered from under the tarp and eased himself over the side of the boat. But not into the water. He held onto the gunnel, hanging with his feet dangling just above the passing current. In that position he knew he wouldn't be seen by the men on the bridge as he eased himself along, hand over hand, toward the bow of the speeding yacht. His shoes were precariously grazing the top of the rushing water beneath him. While running along the pier to leap aboard, he'd noted that the portholes were open. He was now looking into each of them as he passed. It wasn't easy, but Holmes finally managed to reach and peer through the third porthole.

Down inside the cabin Holmes saw the man he was seeking, sitting on a bunk facing away, his hands bound behind him. Holmes whispered to him, "Leftenant Ortega, I presume."

Ortega was confused. He looked around to discover where the very proper English voice had come from.

"Hello! Up here!" called Holmes.

Ortega was amazed to see Holmes dangling outside the porthole, bouncing in the ocean spray. He was even more befuddled when Holmes stated, "I've come to rescue you."

Ortega blinked as Holmes let go with one hand so as to retrieve something small out of his vest pocket. "Now then, Luis, take this," Holmes offered it in through the port toward

Ortega, who reached his head up and took Holmes' penknife in his teeth.

"Good," Holmes said. "Now you must do exactly as I tell you."

On Pier 27, I had been enervated by the withering stares of Enrique Pavon and James Moriarty Booth. My bike's engine was still idling, and I was weighing if I could just gun it and peel out of there until one of Pavon's henchmen ended my fantasy by turning off the ignition and taking my keys.

One of Booth's bodyguards who'd been eyeing me whispered something to his boss, which caused Booth to raise an eyebrow. I had a sudden flash that a cement overcoat might be in my near future. I decided to face the tiger—an ironic metaphor given Holmes' current situation—and I summoned my courage, squared my shoulders, and switched into "professional physician" mode.

"Sorry to have interrupted you, gentlemen, but I'm a pediatric surgeon at Saint Francis Hospital, and I have to perform an operation there at 3:15, so—"

"My associate tells me he just saw you at La Serre," Booth said with a cold smile.

My stomach dropped, but I sucked it up and smiled at the intimidating bodyguard with curious surprise. "Why yes! Were you there? I didn't get a bite though because the woman I was meeting canceled, so I decided to take a quick ride before heading to surgery." I looked at the brute who had my keys, then held out my hand with all the bravado and annoyance I could muster. "So, if you wouldn't *mind* . . ."

Booth wasn't buying. So neither was anyone else. The bodyguards closed ranks, blocking any possible exit. I was quite sure I could hear the sound of cement being mixed, so you can only imagine the thrill I felt when instead I heard the scream of police sirens approaching.

Four black-and-white patrol cars swarmed the scene, red lights flashing. A police helicopter noisily swooped in, circling above as a dozen or so uniformed police deployed. Out of an unmarked car jumped a tall plainclothes cop. Quickly scoping out the scene, he strode my way, glancing sourly at Booth, who appeared entirely cool and at ease as he said, "Having a little outing with the boys and girls, Detective Griffin?"

Griffin pulled me aside and asked, "Did you call in this tip?"

"No. It was . . . probably a friend of mine." I knew he wouldn't be happy to hear it, but I had no choice, so I whispered, "Named . . . Holmes?"

Griffin closed his eyes, and murmured, "Oh, please, God, not *that* loony toon."

Booth had overheard Holmes' name, and now his steely eyes were riveted on me. Griffin pulled me closer and spoke through clenched teeth, "Where is that imbecile?"

Turning away from the prying gazes of Booth and Pavon. I spoke to the detective as much under my breath as possible. "He's on a cabin cruiser that just left Pier 15 but I'm not exactly sure where it went."

Griffin was glowering. "And I should give a shit about that because . . . ?"

"Holmes jumped onto it because we'd seen Luis Ortega being strong-armed away on it and—"

"What?" Griffin suddenly took me seriously. "Where was it headed?"

"Out into the bay."

Lieutenant Griffin sharply looked away, scanning the vast bay on which numerous boats and ships were heading in various directions. I caught Pavon and Booth trading a private glance, showing concern, then letting their own eyes drift over oh so casually to scan the harbor.

Had they high-powered binoculars, they might have been able to see some of the drama transpiring just then about a mile offshore, between Angel and Treasure Islands.

⚲

On the flying bridge, Captain Ponytail had just cut the power and was bringing the large cruiser to a stop in the middle of the bay.

Curly brought Ortega up from below, his hands still tied behind him. Curly had a firm grip on the lieutenant's left arm, guiding him to stand in the middle of the deck. "Hold it here, pal. Pavon's guys are real excited to swap boats with us and take you for the ride of your life."

Ponytail had come down from the bridge as a dark blue forty-four-foot Chris-Craft Commander with a powerful inboard engine was rumbling up alongside. One of the Colombian bodyguards who'd accompanied Pavon at police headquarters stood on the bow of the muscular craft and smiled at the sight of the abducted Ortega. A second minion stood amidships with a coiled rope secured to the Chris-Craft. He tossed the coil to

Ponytail, who pulled the two boats closer together, then both of Pavon's men jumped over onto the yacht carrying Ortega.

That was the moment the tarp hiding the tiger's cage flew up in the air, swept away and aside like a toreador's cape by Holmes, who'd returned to his hidden spot by the tiger cage. He shouted "*Voilà!*" as he pulled open the door of the big cat's prison.

The roaring tiger bolted from its hated confines, generating instant pandemonium. The tough guys shrieked as the huge tiger plowed over Ponytail and bashed Pavon's bow guy down with its meaty claw. The other terrified Colombian skittered backward and fell over the gunnel and into the saltwater churning between the boats.

Ortega, having already cut his bonds, simultaneously sprung around and surprised Curly with a powerful roundhouse right. The heavy took it full on and crumpled—down and out.

Meanwhile, the angry tiger easily leapt across the water dividing the boats, creating panic on Pavon's Chris-Craft. That boat's driver jumped overboard and the remaining crewman on deck became the fierce tiger's target. The beast pounced, clawing the screaming man down to the deck.

Seeing that Ortega was in control on the yacht's deck, Holmes dashed up onto the flying bridge, quickly deducing how to operate the controls. He slammed it into gear and gunned the yacht away from Pavon's boat.

On Pier 27, Booth was calmly instructing Lieutenant Griffin. "You might wish to take this young woman in for a mental health check, Detective. She seems unbalanced."

Griffin, more concerned about Luis Ortega, was telling two cops what I'd said, when he was interrupted by Zapper, cockily holding out a cell phone to Griffin, saying, "Like, it's for you, man."

Griffin frowned at the smiling street kid, snatched the phone, and barked tersely, "Griffin."

On the flying bridge of the yacht he was driving, with a brisk, invigorating sea wind blowing his loose hair, Holmes said cheerfully into his cellular, "Greetings, Detective Griffin. This is Holmes."

"I am gonna panfry your limey ass, you stupid son of a—"

"If you'll please look over your right shoulder, Detective," Holmes coolly interrupted, "you will see the approach of a cabin cruiser, and there's someone here aboard that very boat who wants to say hello."

Holmes handed the phone to Ortega, who smiled at the odd Britisher with respect and comradeship.

"Thanks for the penknife," Luis said, handing it back to the detective as he grabbed the phone. "Hey, Griff? It's Luis."

On the pier, phone held to his ear, Griffin listened, blinked with amazement, and then turned to his men. "Listen up! Get our chopper, the Coast Guard, and Animal Services out to that big blue Chris-Craft. There's a tiger loose on it. And there's also a ton of cocaine on board."

Griffin turned to face Pavon and Booth, saying, "Ortega finally did it. He nailed your asses. For now, you're both under arrest for suspicion of kidnapping. We'll add up all the various charges later. And that's your spiffy boat carrying the coke, Pavon?" Getting only a fierce look in response, Griffin said, "Sorry if you're feeling *harassed* by the police again. But from now on you'll have to call your slimy lawyers from a cell."

Griffin waved in a uniformed cop who snapped cuffs onto the silent but furious Pavon.

Booth, however, appeared totally calm as the yacht pulled alongside Pier 27 and Holmes jauntily hopped off and strode over to stand beside me.

"Detective, don't embarrass yourself," Booth said, smiling astutely at Griffin. "You'll never prove that I have any connection to those men out there. After all these years, you should know better."

Griffin shot a blistering *I told you so, you jerk* glare at Holmes. I leaned closely to Holmes' ear and whispered, "He's right. With no hard evidence, Booth might squirm out of this too."

Holmes merely smiled with supreme confidence, "Detective, did you impound Mr. Booth's limousine as I instructed in that anonymous message I left?"

"Yeah," Griffin said. "So what?"

"Perhaps you will find something incriminating within it."

"Oh, I'm afraid not, Mr.—" Booth caught himself then said, "Mr. Whoever-you-are." He smiled privately at Holmes, mindful of how thoroughly he'd destroyed Holmes' credentials.

Holmes was unruffled. "I would nonetheless encourage you, Detective, to make a personal examination of said vehicle."

Griffin glared and muttered at Holmes, "This better be good."

We all walked down to the charcoal-gray limo, and Holmes

nodded toward the back, asking curiously, "What's that I see on the rear seat?"

Griffin stepped closer to look. "A case of wine?"

I recognized that dusty old wooden box. It held the bottles of Holmes' rare wine. I shot a confused look his way, but his stern raised eyebrow prompted my silence. I glanced at Zapper, who was hanging with Slick and his other pals off to one side, all of them trying to suppress knowing grins.

Booth and his bodyguards all seemed surprised, but Booth shrugged it off. "I don't know how that got there, but it's no big deal."

"*Au contraire*, Mr. Booth. I believe it will prove to be quite a large deal," Holmes said knowingly. "That looks to be a case of extremely rare wine, but a chemical analysis will show that those bottles do not contain 1879 Imperial Tokay, but an eighty-seven percent solution of the highest quality cocaine."

A dozen jaws dropped, including mine.

I glanced sharply at Holmes and saw that he greatly enjoyed our mass reaction as he continued. "I should estimate the street value to be in excess of one point seven million American dollars."

Though everyone else on the pier was astonished, Booth remained nonplussed. He even chuckled with amusement. "Whatever the hell it is, I know absolutely nothing about it. I never saw those bottles before."

Holmes' self-assurance remained undaunted. "I believe that a careful search for Mr. Booth's *fingerprints* may prove otherwise."

I glanced at Booth and thought I detected the slightest tightening of his scalp. Was it a tiny crack in his icy composure?

Holmes raised a knowing eyebrow at Griffin who was still not sold. But Holmes' air of supreme confidence gave the detective pause. He grumbled, "Alright, alright, we'll check it out."

"There's also this." Holmes lifted his right hand, palm up, over his own shoulder without even looking, and Zapper placed in his hand a silver thumb drive. "The audiovisual file contained on this flashy drive will also prove helpful in convicting both of these criminals of conspiracy to commit murder."

Holmes tipped the back of his head toward Zapper, "My colleague Mr. Julius Castenada and I witnessed and recorded a rather damning conversation of Mr. Booth's. In it, he details his engineering of the Tiger Murders, as well as planning this exchange of Leftenant Ortega—along with that tiger which was going to eat him alive." I heard horrified gasps from two nearby cops. Holmes continued. "In return for that gift, Booth would receive that blue boatload of cocaine worth some twenty-six million dollars, but *also*"—Holmes paused to be sure everyone was attentive—"it would solidify a new agreement between Booth and Pavon for a massive criminal partnership."

At last, Booth's glacial self-possession began to thaw. A bit of moisture appeared on his temple signaling the realization that he might finally be trapped.

"Working together," Holmes continued, "Booth and Pavon planned to bring San Francisco to its knees." He held out the flash drive to Griffin. "My gift to you, Detective: America's First Holmes Video."

Griffin stared at the Englishman a long moment, then turned his eyes to the crime bosses and said quietly, but with all the power vested in him, "Booth, Pavon, all of you, you have the right to remain silent. You have—" Griffin interrupted himself and called over one of the uniformed cops. "Read all these scumbags their goddamn rights."

Zapper leaned around and held up his hand to Holmes for a high-five, saying. "Holmesy, that was totally *cold*!" Holmes appraised Zapper's raised hand and imitated it, assuming it to be some manner of approbation or salute. "No, no, man—like this," Zapper instructed, slapping Holmes' upraised hand and initiating the Victorian into the ritual.

Then Holmes grasped Zapper's hand with gentlemanly appreciation. "Thank you again, old boy. When it comes to evidence, I'd say we gave them rather a shitload, eh?"

"Bet your ass we did!" Zapper laughed.

I saw Holmes and Ortega share a long look and a warm smile of mutual respect and camaraderie.

Meanwhile, Booth was being cuffed while Griffin watched with deep satisfaction for these arrests he had long sought.

But it made my skin crawl to see Booth's expression of concentrated feral malevolence and his pinpoint-pupil eyes boring into Holmes. The archcriminal's face was flushed, his brows drawn into two hard black lines, while his eyes shone out from beneath them with a cruel, steely glitter. He hissed like a viper at Holmes, "I'm the worst enemy you could ever hope to make, mister. The blood of the Moriartys still runs in my veins. We will meet again—you can count on that."

Holmes cocked an eyebrow, his nostrils flared slightly. I saw that he actually seemed to get a little rush from that possibility.

Right after that I called Karen Ortega, who answered while

crying with happiness, having already heard directly from her Luis. Then Holmes and I walked past all the police officers and back across the pier toward my bike. I was trying to add it all up. "So, when you were 'defending my car' from the street gang, you were really just protecting your stash of cocaine."

"I would've endeavored to check their burglarizing in any event."

"Oh right. But it's interesting that you didn't jump to the protection of property until your own was being threatened."

"Your lack of faith is disappointing, Winslow. Besides, look what we've just accomplished. Your skill at driving us down Telegraph Hill—from where I could clearly observe Booth leaving that lovely restaurant—was critical to the timing of my plan. I had requested your motor-bicycle specifically because, while pursuing Julius when I first spotted him at the library, I also observed how such bikes can maneuver through traffic with more agility and speed than an automobile."

I chuckled. "But wouldn't it have been a hell of a lot easier for us to just wait on the street closer to where Booth was?"

"Ah, but the vista from atop Telegraph is so much more pleasing. And the chase added a touch of drama and excitement, which I thought the adventure-seeking, romantic Miss—" He caught himself. "I beg your pardon—romantic *Doc*-tor Winslow would enjoy." His cagy eyes met mine.

I was adding it all up. "You had alerted Griffin ahead of time."

"Anonymously, as I said."

"And arranged for Zapper's pals to stage that little row to distract Booth's and Pavon's drivers long enough for Zapper to plant the wine bottles."

"Brava yet again, Winslow. Flawlessly analyzed."

"And you asked me to drive right into the middle of it because . . . ?" Suddenly I realized. "Oh, of course . . . because you wanted me to be 'present for the denouement.'"

"Discovered!" He laughed. "And you certainly deserved to see the fruits of your labors."

We were passing a uniformed cop, prompting me to lean closer to Holmes as I whispered, "But planting that case of wine was not exactly *legal*, Holmes."

He wagged his right index finger at me. "But *moral*, Winslow. The ultimate justification: it was highly moral."

We had reached the bike and picked up our helmets, when I suddenly wondered, "But how in the world could Booth's fingerprints be on the bottles?"

"You've been doing very well, *Doc*-tor, but you must keep honing those powers of observation," he said, instructing patiently. "While you were at the restaurant, did you not see Mr. Booth handle a bottle of wine offered to him by a blond French waiter wearing white gloves?"

I nodded, then smiled as I surmised, "And that bottle quickly found its way back into your wine case."

"Exactly."

As I fastened my helmet strap, I realized one question remained. "But how did you know Booth would be in that restaurant today?"

"During my first encounter with him at his home," he said with a sniff, "whilst I was being searched, with my hands leaning on that desktop where I saw the file with Ortega's badge number, I also observed Mr. Booth's appointment calendar, which noted today's luncheon."

We had climbed onto my bike and I kickstarted it as I laughed. "Amazing. And you paid the waiter to offer him the bottle." I put the bike into gear and started to drive off the pier.

Holmes snickered at my naiveté.

"Oh Winslow, Winslow. You look but sometimes you do not see—I *was* the waiter."

19

The California sun was shining brightly the next day as Holmes and I walked out onto the porch of my house on Baker Street. Beside us were Luis and Karen Ortega, just leaving after paying us their respects. Luis was saying, "And of course I'll keep you posted on the case. But it was already airtight even before Pavon and Booth's cronies indicated they'd flip for plea deals."

"What made us happiest though," I said, "was that you survived."

Karen Ortega had happy tears in her eyes as she said, "I'll never be able to thank you both enough for saving my Luis." She suddenly gave Holmes a huge hug, which he was startled to receive but accepted graciously, if stiffly.

"He is a gentleman most worthy of being saved, madam," Holmes said, with a formal nod in the lieutenant's direction, "and he has many more battles to fight."

"Hopefully with you as an ally, sir," Ortega said.

"Whenever I can be of any modest assistance, Leftenant, I

shall, of course, be at your service." The two men shared a firm handshake.

A short time later I was inside, finally unwrapping that morning's *Chronicle,* revealing the banner headline: BOOTH AND PAVON ARRESTED—with the subhead *Has There Been a Holmes-Coming?*

"Hey, look at this!" I walked over to show it to Holmes, who stood beside my TV in an ornery mood, fuming as he tried to decipher instructions from my iPad.

"Mmmm," he grumbled. I wasn't sure if he meant yes or no.

"It tells how Booth's prints were found on the bottle and he's being held without bail. And listen," I read from the article, "Police Lieutenant Luis Ortega, who had been held hostage by the criminals, said that Dr. Amy Winslow, a pediatric surgeon at Saint Francis Hospital"—I felt a lovely rush of pride—"and a civilian consulting detective named Holmes had been of invaluable assistance in bringing the long-suspected underworld chieftains Booth and Pavon within reach of the law."

Holmes flared angrily, "I don't understand!"

"What?" I glanced down at the newspaper. "It's great. Perfectly clear."

"Not the newspaper, Winslow," he replied with extreme frustration. "This digital video recording device." He was kneeling beside my DVR and in a fury over it. "I distinctly thought I'd arranged it to make a transcription of *The All-New America's Most Wanted,* but instead I got a peculiar family drama called *Schitt's Creek.*" He slapped the iPad down onto the nearby couch.

"One of my faves!" I chuckled as I plopped down in my

cushy chair opposite. "Will you tell me a couple of things honestly, Holmes?"

He responded tersely as he stood up, "Why ever would I be other than honest?"

"Well, your answers can sometimes be . . . circuitous." I picked up the book of Doyle's stories. "You say that James Moriarty was your archenemy, your prime adversary, responsible for most of the evil in London."

"Quite so. And also on the Continent. The fiend was the criminal mastermind of the century." A thought struck him. "Of *that* century, anyway."

I riffled the book's pages. "And yet, out of all these many stories, Moriarty actually appears in only two."

He glanced away, uninterested or feigning it, as he took a few restless steps around my living room, reminding me a bit of a caged tiger. "That would have been Doyle's literary choice, I suppose."

"Is it possible there were a number of other cases where you didn't come out on top, but to preserve your sterling reputation, Watson or Doyle chose to omit them?"

Noticing a bit of lint on his sleeve, he brushed it off. "I was not party to the editorial decisions. Nor was I keeping score." He took a French book from my shelf and examined it idly.

"Circuitous answer," I noted, smiling. "Well, you triumphed over the Moriartys this time. And I congratulate you." I set aside Doyle's book about Holmes and gazed at the man himself. There was something else of greater importance I'd been struck by. "I also have to say how truly admirable it was that in order to get Booth arrested you would sacrifice all of your 'special wine.'" His eyes flicked to mine as I continued sincerely, "I know that must have been an extremely difficult decision for you, giving up all of your cocaine."

He lowered his eyes with unexpected modesty. "But nonetheless quite necessary in order to serve Mr. Booth his just deserts." Then, using the book in his hand as a reference, he added, "As Gustav Flaubert wrote to George Sand, '*L'homme n'est rien, l'œuvre est tout.*'"

I smiled slightly. "'The man is nothing . . . the work everything'?"

"Exactly. My actions must never be about me personally, Winslow, but always about serving the greater good, serving the work." He had gripped the book with both hands to emphasize, "My *work* is paramount, and its success must always come first."

"Well, I applaud your decision and appreciate the sacrifice you made."

He brushed it off as inconsequential as he replaced the book on its shelf while grousing cynically, "Besides, who needs cocaine, Winslow? I'm high on life, which I believe is an au courant expression?"

"Well," I chuckled, "it was a while back."

He glanced again at the damnably enigmatic DVR and sighed. "I suppose I must look upon all this as a challenge, as the start of my explorations of an entirely new world. It is just that," he paused, looking away, then said almost in a whisper, "It is just that I am unaccustomed to ever feeling even the slightest bit unsure of myself."

I was surprised that he was being so open with me. "You're certainly not the only one, okay?" I decided to be equally vulnerable. "Listen, in my dealings with you I often feel . . ." I searched for the right words. ". . . oppressed with a sense of my own stupidity. Even though I know I am not. I can feel pretty insecure around you because you're so damned brilliant."

"Mmmm." His nostrils flared infinitesimally as though to inhale the word *brilliant.* Then another thought seemed to strike him, and as he sat down on my couch, his eyes grew slightly distant, murmuring, "Watson . . ."

I frowned, curious. "Watson what?"

"Watson frequently confided he felt the same way." He looked directly at me, which was always unusual. In the entire six days we had known each other his eyes had rarely rested on mine for more than a fleeting moment, particularly since that night he'd saved me from the tiger snake. Then he looked away, as though worried that if he gazed at me for too long, he might discover something about himself that he was not ready to admit.

"I can't apologize for my intelligence," Holmes continued. "I don't rank modesty among the virtues. To underestimate oneself is as wrong as to exaggerate one's powers." He looked toward my feet as he tended to do when he was going to drop a crumb of compliment. "Still, I really must acknowledge my appreciation to you as a helpmate, Winslow. And also as a close . . ." His eyes flitted around while he struggled to find a word he could be comfortable speaking, finally settling on. ". . . confidante."

Okay, I smiled inwardly, that's acceptable.

Still looking down, he continued. "I confess my dear . . . *Doc*-tor, that I am very much in your debt."

Then he met my eyes directly again. Twice in a row? Was it trending?

"You are a conductor of light, Winslow. Some people, without possessing genius themselves, have a remarkable power of stimulating it."

"Wow, Holmes." I smiled wryly. "That is probably the single most backhanded compliment I have ever received." I wasn't sure whether I wanted to thank him or hit him with a pie. But knowing how difficult it was for Holmes to confide in anyone, I tried to remain gracious.

Then I drew a breath. "So. What's your plan now?" I asked quietly, surprised that I was feeling some trepidation about what his answer might be. "A return to England?"

He looked at me and—was that a flicker of actual emotion, faintly similar to when I was lying on top of him at Civita's house?

"In time, perhaps." He looked away again. "But I would be just as much of a stranger there. Presently I am quite content to further explore the possibilities of being a consulting detective here in San Francisco."

I heard a knock at the front door and went to answer, feeling warmed by the idea of Holmes remaining nearby. I glanced back at him over my shoulder, saying, "Good."

As aggravating as he could be, this man brought fascinating possibilities of adventure into my fairly conservative existence. He also brought, as I discovered when I opened my front door, Mrs. Hudson.

"Oh, good morning, Dr. Winslow! Soooo good to see you, lass!" She gave me a loving hug, then blew right on in with a Scottish flourish, wearing a bright blue Berkeley sweatshirt, which gave her a spunky look. She set her large carry bag to one side. Holmes stood up, smiling, and nodded a greeting to her.

I stood there, blinking. "Uh, yes, Mrs. Hudson. Good to see you too." I was trying to get some clue as to why she had suddenly landed in my living room. "What a . . . nice surprise."

"It was for me too, lass." She hugged me and kissed my cheek. Then, grasping my shoulders, she looked with her bright hazel eyes deeply into mine. "Bless your heart. Thank you so much for inviting me to move in here with you." She headed back toward the front door.

Had I heard right? "Inviting you to . . . ?"

Mrs. Hudson called to someone outside, "Right up this way, boys."

I looked out the front window and saw a moving van unloading furnishings that I recognized from Captain Basil's house in Marin County.

I turned to stare daggers at Holmes, who whispered to me, "Well, the estate is being sold out from under the old dear, and you do have that unused artist's garage."

"Well, yes, I do, but—"

"Really, Winslow, where else were she and my belongings to go?" He casually strolled over to peer out the front window. "I mean, you did invite me to remain in residence temporarily, did you not?"

I realized that my face was frozen in a wide-eyed mad-clown grin as I struggled—for the sake of Mrs. Hudson, who was likely in earshot—to keep from exploding all over him. I spoke with a combination of poison and sweetness, "Why yes, Mr. Holmes, I did." By then I was smiling through gritted teeth, speaking sotto voce, "With the emphasis on *temporarily*. But it never occurred to me that you would invite—" A moving man nearly knocked me over while carrying in the 1899 Edison cylinder phonograph.

Holmes shrugged as though it were all so obvious. "The police told me it would take a fortnight or more for the reward money from the seizure of that boatload of cocaine to make its way from Sacramento. And really, we couldn't very well turn kindly old Mrs. Hudson out to sleep on a bench with Lefty, could we?"

"Lefty?" I blurted. "Who is—" Before I could get it out, another voice was heard. An angry one.

"Yo, Holmes-boy! We gotta talk some serious shit, mofo."

Zapper and Slick had burst into the living room, adding to the festivities. I almost expected to see Groucho Marx show up next from *A Night at the Opera* and order two more hard-boiled eggs. Zapper and Slick were not happy. "Hey, man," Zapper growled, "bustin' those guys was like totally *cold* and all, but why didn't you tell us we had our hands on a gazillion bucks in coke?"

"Oh, didn't I?" Holmes said, with feigned innocence.

"Don't you be dissin' us!"

"Julius!" Holmes looked astonished, as though his manhood had been challenged with a filthy epithet. "I would never dream of 'dissing' you. Or anything of the kind!"

"Then how you plannin' to get us our vig?" Zapper demanded as I sank onto the arm of a chair to watch the drama play out.

"'Vig' from the Russian *vyigrysh*," Holmes deduced, "being payment, portion, percentage, I presume?"

"Goddamn right, percentage! We put our asses on the line for you, man, and—"

"So you did. Very effectively, with clear heads, wonderful panache, and—"

"Cut the bullshit, man!" Zapper was practically jumping up and down.

"Calm yourself, Julius." Holmes remained unruffled. "I promise that you, Slick, and all your chums will share in the reward money, and so you shall. I'm told it will be quite a handsome amount, and I have no intention of rubbing you off or—"

"Ripping," Zapper corrected.

"Right!" Holmes said snappily. "But more importantly, I plan to offer you gentlemen gainful employment as my new Baker Street Irregulars."

Slick's beefy face scrunched up curiously. "Say what?"

Holmes gazed with delight toward the days ahead. "Ah, I foresee many future investigations in which your combined street sense and skills could prove invaluable."

"And perhaps on the *right* side of the law," I prompted with a stern edge.

"At least the moral side," Holmes acquiesced. "Investigations for which you and your comrades will always be amply rewarded."

The two boys were mulling it over as Holmes continued. "Additionally, I've arranged for you, Julius, to have an apprenticeship with a security firm. I expect they'll find your particular skills eye-opening and very useful."

Zapper was impressed, possibly even intrigued by the idea. Then Mrs. Hudson pushed in past him. "Excuse me, Mr. Holmes, but someone has come calling."

Oh great, I thought. *Maybe it's Lefty! Or the whole San Francisco Chamber of Commerce welcoming committee!*

Holmes seemed to know better. He turned and casually took a seat in the chair opposite me, turning away to pour himself a cup of tea as he postulated, "Doubtless it is a distressed, attractive young blond female prostitute who has read today's newspaper story and come seeking our aid." Without looking up from preparing his tea, he said. "You are staring, *Doc*-tor. Are you Big Willy?"

Indeed I was. "How would you know that about her?"

"*How*—as you of all people should know by now, Winslow—is one of the most consistent FAQs I hear. The answer, as always, is elementary: because looking out the window, I just ob-*served* the young woman eyeing our house from across the street." He sipped his tea. "She was frowning, troubled, and clutching the newspaper that carried the article about us. Her brassy attire presents her availability as a 'lady of the evening': white ankle boots and an extremely short white dress with red fringe and piping that reveals so much leg and bosomy cleavage as to leave no doubt of her profession being the world's oldest."

Zapper and Slick exchanged a lascivious glance. "Let's check her out, bruh!"

They nearly knocked me off my perch on the arm of the chair in their eagerness to scamper outside. Regaining my balance, I saw that Holmes was smiling arrogantly and authoritatively about his latest deduction. Despite my vexation I laughed at him.

"She's no hooker, Holmes. You just described a cheerleader for the 49ers." I glanced at Mrs. Hudson who was smiling and eagerly nodding confirmation of my own deduction.

"What?" he blinked. "I never read that the men who came to dig gold in 1849 had women to cheer them on." He considered it a moment, "And if they were all dressed like she, it's no wonder there was a gold rush."

"No, no, no," I said, stifling a laugh in order to regain my annoyance. "You are unquestionably a master of many things, but you still have quite a bit to learn about the twenty-first century." Then I needled, "And the proper etiquette for a *temporary* house guest."

Holmes exhaled a belligerent, imperious puff. I smiled

inwardly. God, it was wonderful to have the upper hand on him, if only for a fleeting moment.

With a tight-lipped and decidedly pissy expression, he placed his teacup *precisely* back on its saucer, then stood fully upright, clasping his hands behind his back. He looked into the air above my head, speaking with acidic formality, "I realize that I'm a difficult fellow to share rooms with, but"—he could barely force himself to say it—"might I have your 'permission,' *Doc*-tor, to continue partaking of your hospitality whilst pursuing my contemporary education and ascertaining the cause of the young woman's distress?"

I did enjoy making him dangle uncomfortably but admitted to myself that meeting and working with this irascible character was the most fun I'd had in years. As I later heard Zapper sum up so eloquently, "The dude might be more humble, but there's no police like Holmes."

I had to agree, and I was proud of the success we'd already achieved and wondering what other intriguing, exhilarating, or even perilous experiences might lay ahead.

As I studied the remarkable Englishman standing at attention before me, I also felt deeper issues stirring. I still puzzled over that night after he'd returned from Pier 7, when we gazed at each other for such a long, uniquely connective moment. And also that rush of surprisingly intimate feelings that had sparked a physical reaction—seemingly in both of us—during our breathless face-to-face close encounter on Lieutenant Civita's floor.

It all inspired a deep curiosity within me about how our relationship might evolve.

After pondering all of that, I slowly stood up to fully face him, determined to address his request with a formality equal to his own. I took a regal breath, endeavoring to channel Queen Victoria, and spoke quite firmly.

"Mister Holmes . . ." My uncharacteristically severe posture and bearing caused his eyes to flick to mine, revealing the slightest wisp of insecurity. Exactly what I'd hoped for. Then, emphasizing my commanding role as mistress of the manor, I said with a polite but cautionary tone, emphasizing that he should take my pronouncement very seriously, "For the time being"—I paused, making him wait for it—"I will allow you . . . to be my guest."

Holmes squared his shoulders and lowered his eyes while courteously inclining his head as though accepting a knighthood. He said, almost respectfully, "*Doc*-tor."

Two movers had just brought in his favorite high-backed Victorian chair and set it down behind him. Without even looking back, he eased himself down upon it as if it were his throne. From his frock coat pocket, he drew his cherrywood pipe and deigned to give an audience. "Mrs. Hudson, show the young lady up, if you please."

Mrs. Hudson gave a delighted curtsy, turned to scurry out, but remembered something and looked back, smiling. "Oh, also, Mr. Holmes, I did just as you asked: I personally brought, in my own car, those other three cases of your special wine."

My jaw dropped. I stared, gobsmacked.

Holmes ignored me, saying exuberantly to her, "Excellent, my dear lady!"

As I stood there flustered, Holmes placed the pipestem between his haughty lips, then struck a match with such utter, irreverent cockiness that I saw red. Instantly regaining my full queenly bearing, I inhaled to bellow—then remembered that a monarch need not exercise her lungs. So in a low voice, with deadly, quiet power, I decreed, "*No.*"

He glanced up at me, lit match in hand, so startled that I was barely able to keep from laughing. And I met his gaze with my own imperial authority, declaring, "Only. On. The porch." Then, summoning my most charming Mona Lisa smile, I enjoyed the ultimate pleasure of having the steely-eyed, emphatic, final word: "*De-tec-tive.*"

He registered the turnabout import of the moment. He slowly lowered the burning match, looked away while arching his left eyebrow with annoyance, and sucked in a long breath through his unlit pipe.

Sooner than expected, we received the reward, which was a startlingly handsome amount. Zapper and friends were bedazzled by their shares, which are now reshaping their lives for the better. We were also easily able to purchase the wonderful old Marin County estate. We moved all of its furnishings back there, where they belonged. Mrs. Hudson continues to live there and takes pleasure in tending her beloved gardens. To my extreme personal delight, I am writing this as I enjoy a cup of English breakfast tea, while curled up in a comfy chair by the fireplace in our beautiful Victorian sitting room in Marin.

We still use my house on Baker Street, but the estate is both a retreat and an alternative venue for Holmes to meet more privately with prospective clients who have particularly sensitive issues to resolve. He has a long and growing waiting list.

The prodigious reward also allowed us to establish the

Arthur Conan Doyle & Elizabeth Appling-Winslow Foundation, which provides scholarships to medical students in need—in return for their pledges to keep "paying it forward," following the ethics that my mother passed down to me. The foundation also supports Doctors Without Borders, plus the good work that Charley Moriarty and others do to help San Francisco's underserved communities.

I divide my time between the foundation, my duties as a pediatric surgeon, and assisting Holmes on many investigations, such as our second escapade, which quickly had us off and running: the bizarre and now notorious *Case of the Evaporating Quarterback*—who mysteriously disappeared from the fifty-yard line of Levi's Stadium during the Pro Bowl before sixty-eight thousand witnesses.

Thus continued the most intriguing, dangerous, and invigorating set of incidents, which I've now begun to chronicle: my adventures and misadventures with this singular, extraordinary, and often totally exasperating genius.

The astonishing Mr. Holmes.

*A portion of the author's proceeds
from this work goes to benefit
Doctors Without Borders (Médecins Sans Frontières).*

ACKNOWLEDGMENTS

You would not be reading this book were it not for these people, to whom I am very indebted. They are . . .

Italia Gandolfo and Renee Fountain at Gandolfo Helin & Fountain Literary Management for immediately jumping onboard with my story and so quickly finding the ideal home for it at Blackstone.

Valerie Nemeth, my splendid counselor, for astutely handling the legal aspects.

Josie Woodbridge and Ananda Finwall, my key contacts at Blackstone, for their truly extraordinary collaboration—not just on the novel itself but also for their receptivity to my suggestions throughout the entire publishing process. They could not have been more welcoming or nurturing.

Dana Isaacson not only brought skills that one would expect from such a seasoned editor, but also posed sharp and probing questions that inspired me to dig even deeper. Michael Krohn as copyeditor carried on that inspiration, nudging me to take fresh looks from different angles at many passages, paragraphs, and individual words as we fine-tuned the manuscript.

Alenka Linaschke thoroughly captured the concept I had in mind for the book's artwork and internal design. I'm particularly fond of the figure Alenka created of the Victorian genius standing stalwart on San Francisco's Pier 7 and looking challengingly right at us from the book cover, with the glorious city in the background and mysterious wisps of fog creeping in.

And as always, I am thankful to my wife, Susie, not only for her unswerving support, generosity, and unparalleled humor, but also for her literate taste. From the decades we've spent together, I generally know instinctively as I write a sentence whether it would pass muster with Susie. And if it would, I know I've succeeded.

Finally, we all—including readers everywhere—are indebted to Sir Arthur Conan Doyle. He received his knighthood partly in appreciation for his creation of the many wonderful stories featuring characters that have become—and will always be—iconic and beloved.

It is with humble thanks that we all bow to you, Sir Arthur.